NIGHTWATCHER

By Wendy Corsi Staub

NIGHTWATCHER
HELL TO PAY
SCARED TO DEATH
LIVE TO TELL

Coming Soon
SLEEPWALKER

WENDY CORSI STAUB

NIGHTWATCHER

HARPER·

An Imprint of HarperCollins*Publishers*

This is a work of fiction. Names, characters, places, and incidents are products of the author's imagination or are used fictitiously and are not to be construed as real. Any resemblance to actual events, locales, organizations, or persons, living or dead, is entirely coincidental.

HARPER

An Imprint of HarperCollins*Publishers*
10 East 53rd Street
New York, New York 10022-5299

Copyright © 2012 by Wendy Corsi Staub
Excerpt from *Sleepwalker* copyright © 2012 by Wendy Corsi Staub
ISBN 978-1-62090-329-2
K.I.S.S. and Teal is a trademark of the Ovarian Cancer National Alliance

Printed in the United States of America

*In memory of the thousands of innocent souls
lost on September 11, 2001,
and in honor of my beloved New York,
the greatest city in the world.*

*And again, always, always, for Mark, Morgan,
and Brody, with love.*

*Special thanks to Barbara Mayes Boustead,
Judy McCormick, John McNamara, Karen Sirignano,
and Dave Turkheimer; and especially to my agent,
Laura Blake Peterson & the gang at Curtis Brown,
and my editor, Lucia Macro & the gang at
Avon Books/HarperCollins.*

PART I

*I fear that all we have done
is awaken a sleeping giant
and fill him with a terrible resolve.*
**Admiral Yamamoto after the Pearl Harbor attack,
December 7, 1941**

Prologue

September 10, 2001
Quantico, Virginia
6:35 P.M.

Case closed.

Vic Shattuck clicks the mouse, and the South-side Strangler file—the one that forced him to spend the better part of August in the rainy Midwest, tracking a serial killer—disappears from the screen.

If only it were that easy to make it all go away in real life.

"If you let it, this stuff will eat you up inside like cancer," Vic's FBI colleague Dave Gudlaug told him early in his career, and he was right.

Now Dave, who a few years ago reached the bureau's mandatory retirement age, spends his time traveling with his wife. He claims he doesn't miss the work.

"Believe me, you'll be ready to put it all behind you, too, when the time comes," he promised Vic.

Maybe, but with his own retirement seven years away, Vic is in no hurry to move on. Sure, it might be nice to spend uninterrupted days and nights with Kitty, but somehow, he suspects that he'll never be truly free of the cases he's handled—not even those that are solved.

For now, as a profiler with the Behavioral Science Unit, he can at least do his part to rid the world of violent offenders.

"You're still here, Shattuck?"

He looks up to see Special Agent Annabelle Wyatt. With her long legs, almond-shaped dark eyes, and flawless ebony skin, she looks like a supermodel—and acts like one of the guys.

Not in a let's-hang-out-and-have-a-few-laughs way; in a let's-cut-the-bullshit-and-get-down-to-business way.

She briskly hands Vic a folder. "Take a look at this and let me know what you think."

"Now?"

She clears her throat. "It's not urgent, but . . ."

Yeah, right. With Annabelle, everything is urgent.

"Unless you were leaving . . ." She pauses, obviously waiting for him to tell her that he'll take care of it before he goes.

"I was."

Without even glancing at the file, Vic puts it on top of his in-box. The day's been long enough and he's more than ready to head home.

Kitty is out at her book club tonight, but that's okay with him. She called earlier to say she was leaving a macaroni and cheese casserole in the oven. The homemade kind, with melted cheddar and buttery breadcrumb topping.

Better yet, both his favorite hometown teams—the New York Yankees and the New York Giants—are playing tonight. Vic can hardly wait to hit the couch with a fork in one hand and the TV remote control in the other.

"All right, then." Annabelle turns to leave, then

turns back. "Oh, I heard about Chicago. Nice work. You got him."

"You mean *her*."

Annabelle shrugs. "How about *it*?"

"*It*. Yeah, that works."

Over the course of Vic's career, he hasn't seen many true cases of MPD—multiple personality disorder— but this was one of them.

The elusive Southside Strangler turned out to be a woman named Edie . . . who happened to live inside a suburban single dad named Calvin Granger.

Last June, Granger had helplessly watched his young daughter drown in a fierce Lake Michigan undertow. Unable to swim, he was incapable of saving her.

Weeks later, mired in frustration and anguish and the brunt of his grieving ex-wife's fury, he picked up a hooker. That was not unusual behavior for him. What happened after that *was*.

The woman's nude, mutilated body was found just after dawn in Washington Park, electrical cable wrapped around her neck. A few days later, another corpse turned up in the park. And then a third.

Streetwalking and violent crime go hand in hand; the Southside's slain hookers were, sadly, business as usual for the jaded cops assigned to that particular case.

For urban reporters, as well. Chicago was in the midst of a series of flash floods this summer; the historic weather eclipsed the coverage of the Southside Strangler in the local press. That, in retrospect, was probably a very good thing. The media spotlight tends to feed a killer's ego—and his bloodlust.

Only when the Strangler claimed a fourth victim—an upper-middle-class mother of three living a respectable lifestyle—did the case become front-page news. That was when the cops called in the FBI.

For Vic, every lost life carries equal weight. His heart went out to the distraught parents he met in Chicago, parents who lost their daughters twice: first to drugs and the streets, and ultimately to the monster who murdered them.

The monster, like most killers, had once been a victim himself.

It was a textbook case: Granger had been severely abused—essentially tortured—as a child. The MPD was, in essence, a coping mechanism. As an adult, he suffered occasional, inexplicable episodes of amnesia, particularly during times of overwhelming stress.

He genuinely seemed to have no memory of anything "he" had said or done while Edie or one of the other, nonviolent alters—alternative personalities—were in control of him.

"By the way," Annabelle cuts into Vic's thoughts, "I hear birthday wishes are in order."

Surprised, he tells her, "Actually, it was last month—while I was in Chicago."

"Ah, so your party was belated, then."

His party. This past Saturday night, Kitty surprised him by assembling over two dozen guests—family, friends, colleagues—at his favorite restaurant near Dupont Circle.

Feeling a little guilty that Annabelle wasn't invited, he informs her, "I wouldn't call it a *party*. It was more like . . . it was just dinner, really. My wife planned it."

But then, even if Vic himself had been in charge of the guest list, Supervisory Special Agent Wyatt would not have been on it.

Some of his colleagues are also personal friends. She isn't one of them.

It's not that he has anything against no-nonsense women. Hell, he married one.

And he respects Annabelle just as much as—or maybe even more than—just about anyone else here. He just doesn't necessarily *like* her much—and he suspects the feeling is mutual.

"I hear that it was an enjoyable evening," she tells him with a crisp nod, and he wonders if she's wistful. She doesn't sound it—or look it. But for the first time, it occurs to Vic that her apparent social isolation might not always be by choice.

He shifts his weight in his chair. "It's my wife's thing, really. Kitty's big on celebrations. She'll go all out for any occasion. Years ago, she threw a party when she potty trained the twins."

As soon as the words are out of his mouth, he wants to take them back and not just because mere sec onds ago he was insisting that Saturday night was *not* a party. Annabelle isn't the kind of person with whom you discuss children, much less potty training them. She doesn't have a family, but if she did, Vic is certain she'd keep the details—particularly the bathroom details—to herself.

Well, too bad. I'm a family man.

After Annabelle bids him a stiff good night and disappears down the corridor, Vic shifts his gaze to the framed photos on his desk. One is of him and Kitty on their twenty-fifth wedding anniversary last year; the other, more recent, shows Vic with all four of the kids at the high school graduation last June of his twin daughters.

The girls left for college a few weeks ago. He and Kitty are empty-nesters now—well, Kitty pretty much rules the roost, as she likes to say, since Vic is gone so often.

"So which is it—a nest or a roost?" he asked her the other day, to which she dryly replied, "Neither. It's a coop, and you've been trying to fly it for years, but you just keep right on finding your way back, don't you."

She was teasing, of course. No one supports Vic's career as wholeheartedly as Kitty does, no matter how many nights it's taken him away from home over the years. It was her idea in the first place that he put aside his planned career as a psychiatrist in favor of the FBI.

All because of a series of murders that terrorized New York thirty years ago, and captivated a young local college psych major.

"Back when I first met him, Vic was obsessed with unsolved murders," Kitty announced on Saturday night when she stood up to toast him at his birthday dinner, "and since then, he's done an incredible job solving hundreds of them."

True—with one notable exception.

Years ago, the New York killings stopped abruptly. Vic would like to think it's because the person who committed them is no longer on this earth.

If by chance he is, then he's almost certainly been sidelined by illness or incarceration for some unrelated crime.

After all, while there are exceptions to every rule, most serial killers don't just stop. Everything Vic has learned over the years about their habits indicates that once something triggers a person to cross the fine line that divides disturbed human beings from cunning predators, he's compelled to keep feeding his dark fantasies until, God willing, something—or someone—stops him.

In a perfect world, Vic is that someone.

But then, a perfect world wouldn't be full of disturbed people who are, at any given moment, teetering on the brink of reality.

Typically, all it takes is a single life stressor to push one over the edge. It can be any devastating event, really—a car accident, job loss, bankruptcy, a terminal diagnosis, a child's drowning . . .

Stressors like those can create considerable challenges for a mentally healthy person. But when fate inflicts that kind of pressure on someone who's already dangerously unbalanced . . . well, that's how killers are born.

Though Vic has encountered more than one homicidal maniac whose spree began with a wife's infidelity, the triggering crisis doesn't necessarily have to hit close to home. Even a natural disaster can be prime breeding ground.

A few years ago in Los Angeles, a seemingly ordinary man—a fine, upstanding Boy Scout leader—went off the deep end after the Northridge earthquake leveled his apartment building. Voices in his head told him to kill three strangers in the aftermath, telling him they each, in turn, were responsible for the destruction of his home.

Seemingly ordinary. Ah, you just never know. That's what makes murderers—particularly serial murderers—so hard to catch. They aren't always troubled loners; sometimes they're hiding in plain sight: regular people, married with children, holding steady jobs . . .

And sometimes, they're suffering from a mental

disorder that plenty of people—including some in the mental health profession—don't believe actually exists.

Before Vic left Chicago, as he was conducting a jailhouse interview with Calvin Granger, Edie took over Calvin's body.

The transition occurred without warning, right before Vic's incredulous eyes. Everything about the man changed—not just his demeanor, but his physical appearance and his voice. A doctor was called in, and attested that even biological characteristics like heart rate and vision had been altered. Calvin could see twenty-twenty. Edie was terribly nearsighted. Stunning.

It wasn't that Calvin *believed* he was an entirely different person, a woman named Edie—he *was* Edie. Calvin had disappeared into some netherworld, and when he returned, he had no inkling of what had just happened, or even that time had gone by.

The experience would have convinced even a die-hard skeptic, and it chilled Vic to the bone.

Case closed, yes—but this one is going to give him nightmares for a long time to come.

Vic tidies his desk and finds himself thinking fondly of the old days at the bureau—and a colleague who was Annabelle Wyatt's polar opposite.

John O'Neill became an agent around the same time Vic did. Their career paths, however, took them in different directions: Vic settled in with the BSU, while O'Neill went from Quantico to Chicago and back, then on to New York, where he eventually became chief of the counterterrorism unit. Unfortunately, his career with the bureau ended abruptly a few weeks ago amid a cloud of controversy following the theft—on his watch—of a briefcase containing sensitive documents.

When it happened, Vic was away. Feeling the sudden urge to reconnect, he searches through his desk for his friend's new phone number, finds it, dials it. A secretary and then an assistant field the call, and finally, John comes on the line.

"Hey, O'Neill," Vic says, "I just got back from Chicago and I've been thinking about you."

"Shattuck! How the hell are you? Happy birthday. Sorry I couldn't make it Saturday night."

"Yeah, well . . . I'm sure you have a good excuse."

"Valerie dragged me to another wedding. You know how that goes."

"Yeah, yeah . . . how's the new job?"

"Cushy," quips O'Neill, now chief of security at the World Trade Center in New York City. "How's the big 5–0?"

"Not cushy. You'll find out soon enough, won't you?"

"February. Don't remind me."

Vic shakes his head, well aware that turning fifty, after everything O'Neill has dealt with in recent months, will be a mere blip.

They chat for a few minutes, catching up, before O'Neill says, "Listen, I've got to get going. Someone's waiting for me."

"Business or pleasure?"

"My business is always a pleasure, Vic. Don't you know that by now?"

"Where are you off to tonight?"

"I'm having drinks with Bob Tucker at Windows on the World to talk about security for this place, and it's a Monday night, so . . ."

"Elaine's." Vic is well aware of his friend's long-standing tradition.

"Right. How about you?"

"It's a Monday night, so—"

"Football."

"Yeah. I've got a date with the couch and remote. Giants are opening their season—and the Yankees are playing the Red Sox, too. Clemens is pitching. Looks like I'll be channel surfing."

"I wouldn't get too excited about that baseball game if I were you, Vic. It's like a monsoon here."

A rained out Yankees-Red Sox game on one of Vic's rare nights at home in front of the TV would be a damned shame. Especially since he made a friendly little wager with Rocky Manzillo, his lifelong friend, who had made the trip down from New York this weekend for Vic's birthday dinner.

Always a guy who liked to rock the boat, Rocky is also a lifelong Red Sox fan, despite having grown up in Yankees territory. He still lives there, too—he's a detective with the NYPD.

In the grand scheme of Vic Shattuck's life, old pals and baseball rivalries and homemade macaroni casseroles probably matter more than they should. He's rarely around to enjoy simple pleasures. When he is, they help him forget that somewhere out there, a looming stressor is going to catapult yet another predator from the shadows to wreak violent havoc on innocent lives.

September 10, 2001
New York City
6:40 P.M.

"Hey, watch where you're going!"

Unfazed by the disgruntled young punk, Jamie continues shoving through the sea of pedestrians, baby carriages, and umbrellas, trying to make it to the corner before the light changes.

Around the slow-moving elderly couple, the dog on a leash, a couple of puddle-splashing kids in bright yellow slickers and rubber boots . . .

Failing to make the light, Jamie silently curses them all. Or maybe not silently, because a prim-looking woman flashes a disapproving look. Hand coiled into a fist, Jamie stands waiting in the rain, watching endless traffic zip past.

The subway would have been the best way to go, but there were track delays. And God knows you can't get a stinking cab in Manhattan in weather like this.

Why does everything have to be such a struggle here? Everything, every day.

A few feet away, a passing SUV blasts its deafening horn.

Noise . . .

Traffic . . .

People . . .

How much more can I take?

Jamie rakes a hand through drenched hair and fights the reckless urge to cross against the light.

That's what it's been about lately. Reckless urges. Day in, day out.

For so long, I've been restrained by others; now that I'm free, I have to constantly restrain myself? It's so unfair.

Why can't I just cross the damned street and go where I need to go?

Why can't I just do whatever the hell I feel like doing? I've earned it, haven't I?

Jamie steps off the curb and hears someone call,

"Hey, look out!" just before a monstrous double city bus blows past, within arm's reach.

"Geez, close call."

Jamie doesn't acknowledge the bystander's voice; doesn't move, just stands staring into the streaming gutter.

It would be running red with blood if you got hit.

Or if someone else did.

It would be so easy to turn around, pick out some random stranger, and with a quick, hard shove, end that person's life. Jamie could do that. It would happen so unexpectedly no one would be able to stop it.

Jamie can feel all those strangers standing there, close enough to touch.

Which of them would you choose?

The prune-faced, disapproving biddy?

One of the splashing kids?

The elderly woman, or her husband?

Just imagine the victim, the chosen one, crying out in surprise, helplessly falling, getting slammed by several tons of speeding steel and dying right there in the gutter.

Yes, blood in the gutter.

Eyes closed, Jamie can see it clearly—so much blood at first, thick and red right here where the accident will happen. But then the gutter water will sweep it along, thin it out as it merges with wide, deep puddles and with falling rain, spread it in rivulets that will reach like fingers down alleys and streets . . .

Imagine all the horror-struck onlookers, the traumatized driver of the death car, the useless medics who will rush to the scene and find that there's nothing they can do . . .

Nothing anyone can do.

And somewhere, later, phones will ring as family members and friends get the dreaded call.

Just think of all the people who will be touched—tainted—by the blood in the street, by that one simple act.

I can do that.

I can choose someone to die.

I've done it before—twice.

Ah, but not really. Technically, Jamie didn't do the choosing. Both victims—the first ten years ago, the second, maybe ten days ago—had done the choosing; they'd chosen to commit the heinous acts that had sealed their own fates. Jamie merely saw that they got what they deserved.

This time, though, it would have to be different. It would have to be a stranger.

Would it be as satisfying to snuff out a life that has no real meaning in your own?

Would it be even better?

Would it—

Someone jostles Jamie from behind.

The throng is pressing forward. The traffic has stopped moving past; the light has changed.

Jamie crosses the street, hand still clenched into an angry fist.

Chapter One

September 10, 2001
New York City
7:19 P.M.

Allison Taylor has lived in Manhattan for three years now.

That's long enough to know that the odds are stacked against finding a taxi at the rainy tail end of rush hour—especially here, a stone's throw from the Bryant Park tents in the midst of Fashion Week.

Yet she perches beneath a soggy umbrella on the curb at the corner of Forty-second and Fifth, searching the sea of oncoming yellow cabs, hoping to find an on-duty/unoccupied dome light.

Unlikely, yes.

But *impossible*? The word is overused, in her opinion. If she weren't the kind of woman who stubbornly challenges anything others might deem impossible, then she wouldn't be here in New York in the first place.

How many people back in her tiny Midwestern hometown told her it would be impossible for a girl like her to merely survive the big, cruel city, let alone succeed in the glamorous, cutthroat fashion publishing industry?

A girl like her . . .

Impoverished, from a broken home with a suicidal drug addict for a mother. A girl who never had a chance—but took one anyway.

And just look at me now.

After putting herself through the Art Institute of Pittsburgh and working her way from an unpaid post-college internship at Condé Nast on up through the editorial ranks at *7th Avenue* magazine, Allison finally loves her life—cab shortages, rainy days, and all.

Sometimes, she allows herself to fantasize about going back to Centerfield to show them all how wrong they were. The neighbors, the teachers, the pursed-lipped church ladies, the mean girls at school and their meaner mothers—everyone who ever looked at her with scorn or even pity; everyone who ever whispered behind her back.

They didn't understand about Mom—about how much she loved Allison, how hard she tried, when she wasn't high, to be a good mother. Only the one girl Allison considered a true friend, her next-door neighbor Tammy Connolly, seemed to understand. She, too, had a single mom for whom the townspeople had disdain. Tammy's mother was a brassy blonde whose skirts were too short, whose perfume was too strong, whose voice was too loud.

Tammy had her own cross to bear, as the church ladies would say. Everyone did. Mom was Allison's—hers alone—and she dealt with it pretty much single-handedly until the day it ceased to exist.

But going back to Centerfield—even to have the last laugh—would mean facing memories. And who needs those?

"Memories are good for nothin'," Mom used to say,

after Allison's father left them. "It's better to just forget about all the things you can't change."

True—but Mom couldn't seem to change what was happening to them in the present—or what the future might hold.

"Weakness is my weakness," Brenda once told a drug counselor. Allison overheard, and those pathetic words made her furious, even then.

Now Mom, too, is in the past.

Yes. Always better to forget.

Anyway, even if Allison wanted to revisit Centerfield, the town is truly the middle of nowhere: a good thirty miles from the nearest dive motel and at least three or four times as far from any semi-decent hotel.

Sometimes, though, she pictures herself doing it: flying to Omaha, renting a car, driving out across miles of nothing to . . .

More nothing.

Her one friend, Tammy, moved away long before Mom died seven years ago, and of course, Dad had left years before that, when she was nine.

Allison remembers the morning she woke up and went running to the kitchen to tell her mother that she'd dreamed she had a sister. She was certain it meant that her mom was going to have another baby.

But that couldn't have been farther from the truth. In the kitchen, she found the note her father had left.

Can't do this anymore. I'm sorry. Good-bye.

God only knows where he wound up. Allison's only sibling, her half brother, Brett, wanted to find him for her sake after Mom died.

"Well, if you do, I don't want to hear about it. I never want to hear his name again," she said when her brother brought it up at the funeral.

It was the same thing her mother had told her after her father left. Mom considered Allison's deadbeat dad good for nothin'—just like memories. True as that might have been, Allison couldn't stand the way the townspeople whispered about her father running off.

The best thing about living in New York is the live-and-let-live attitude. Everyone is free to do his or her own thing; no one judges or even pays much attention to anyone else. For Allison, after eighteen years of small-town living and a couple more in college housing, anonymity is a beautiful thing. Certainly well worth every moment of urban inconvenience.

She surveys the traffic-clogged avenue through a veil of drenching rain, thinking she should probably just take the subway down to the Marc Jacobs show at the Pier. It's cheaper, arguably faster, and more reliable than finding a cab.

But she's wearing a brand-new pair of Gallianos, and her feet—after four straight days of runway shows and parties—are killing her. No, she doesn't feel up to walking to Grand Central and then through the tunnels at Union Square to transfer to the crosstown line, much less negotiating all those station stairs on both ends.

Not that she much likes standing here in the deluge, vainly waiting for a cab, but . . .

Lesser of the evils, right?

Maybe not. She jumps back as a passing panel truck sends a wave of gray-brown gutter water over the curb.

"Dammit!" Allison looks down at her soaked shoes—and then up again, just in time to see a yellow cab pulling over for the trench-coated, briefcase-carrying man who just strode past her, taxi-hailing arm in the air.

"Hey!" she calls, and he glances back over his shoulder. "I've been standing here for twenty minutes!"

More like five, but that's beside the point. She was here first. That's her cab.

Okay, in the grand scheme of Manhattan life, maybe that's not quite how it works.

Maybe it's more . . . *if you snooze, you lose.*

And I snoozed.

Still . . .

She's in a fighting mood. The Jacobs show is huge. Everyone who's anyone in the industry will be there. This is her first year as—well, maybe not a Somebody, but no longer a Nobody.

There's a seat for her alongside the runway—well, maybe not *right* alongside it, but somewhere—and she has to get to the Pier. *Now.*

She fully expects the businessman to ignore her. But his eyes flick up and down, taking in her long, blond-streaked hair, long legs, and short pink skirt. Yeah—he's totally checking her out.

She's used to that reaction from men on the street.

Men anywhere, really. Even back home in Center-field, when she was scarcely more than a kid—and still a brunette—Allison attracted her share of male attention, most of it unwanted.

But as a grown woman in the big city, she's learned to use it to her advantage on certain occasions.

Oh hell . . . the truth is, she made the most of it even back in Nebraska. But she doesn't let herself think about that.

Memories are good for nothin', Allison. Don't you ever forget it.

No, Mom. I won't. I'll never forget it.

"Where are you headed?" The man reaches back to open the car door, his gaze still fixed on her.

"Pier 54. It's on the river at—"

"I know where it is. Go ahead. Get in."

She hesitates only a split second before hurrying over to the cab, quickly folding her umbrella, and slipping past the man—a total stranger, she reminds herself— into the backseat.

A stranger. So? The city is full of strangers. That's why she moved here, leaving behind a town populated by know-it-all busybodies.

Anyway, it's not the middle of the night, and the driver is here, and what's going to happen?

You're going to make it to the Marc Jacobs show, something you've been waiting for all summer.

After the show there's an after-party to launch Jacobs's new signature fragrance. It's the hottest ticket in town tonight, and Allison Taylor is invited.

No way is she going to miss this—or arrive looking like a drowned rat.

She puts her dripping umbrella on the floor as the stranger climbs in after her and closes the door.

"I'm going to Brooklyn—take the Williamsburg Bridge," he tells the driver, "but first she needs to get off at Thirteenth and West."

"Wait—that's *way* out of your way," Allison protests.

"It's okay. You're obviously in a hurry."

"No, I know, but . . ." Jacobs is notorious for starting late. She can wait for another cab.

"It's fine."

"Never mind," she says, unsettled by this stranger's willingness to accommodate her. What, she wonders uneasily, does he expect in return? "Listen, I'll just—"

"No, I mean it. It's *fine.*" He motions at the cabbie, who shrugs, starts the meter, and inches them out into the downtown traffic.

Alrighty then. Allison faces forward, crossing her arms across her midsection.

She tried to let this guy off the hook. It's going to take him forever to get to Brooklyn with a West Side detour, but . . .

That's his problem.

And mine is solved.

Allison leans back, inhaling the fruity cardboard air freshener dangling from the rearview mirror and the faint cigarette scent wafting from her backseat companion. Unlike some reformed smokers, she doesn't mind it. In fact, she finds the tobacco smell pleasantly nostalgic, sending her back to college bars and rainy, lazy, coffee-drinking afternoons in Pittsburgh.

Sometimes—wrong as it is, weak as it is—she finds herself craving a cigarette, even now.

When she first got to New York three years ago, she quickly went from mooching happy hour butts to a two-pack-a-day habit. Smoking helped mitigate job stress, city stress, love life stress—and kept her thin. In her industry, that's crucial.

Then her old college roommate Becky came to New York for a job interview and they got together—Becky's idea, of course. Though they'd been friends in college, Allison had closed that chapter of her life and wasn't anxious to revisit the past. Nothing against Becky, but for Allison, moving on meant leaving people behind. It was an old trick she'd learned from her childhood friend Tammy, who certainly had the right idea. Life was just easier that way.

As they caught up over drinks, Becky watched Allison light a fresh cigarette from the stub of another, and said, "Wow, I always thought you were too much of a control freak for that."

"What do you mean?"

"I mean chain-smoking. Cigarettes can kill you, you know."

Allison shrugged. "We're all going to die someday."

"Maybe, but—"

"*Maybe?* Not *maybe*, Becky! Everyone dies. It's a fact of life."

Becky gave her a long look, then shrugged. "Whatever. All I know is that you're an addict if you smoke like that, Al. And addicts aren't in control."

She was right, of course. Jesus. The moment she heard the word *addict*, Allison made up her mind to quit.

But she waited until after Becky had flown home to Pennsylvania. Waited because she hates I-told-you-so's, and waited because, yes, she likes to be in control. Likes, wants, needs . . . she *needs* to be in control.

Who'd blame her? After all she's been through in her life . . .

"So . . . I'm Bill."

She turns to look at the man who commandeered her cab—or vice versa, depending on how one chooses to look at it.

"Allison."

"Nice to meet you, Allison. What do you do?"

"I'm a style editor at *7th Avenue* magazine. How about you?" she asks, noting that he has green eyes. Nebraska-field green eyes.

"Finance," he tells her. "I'm an investment banker."

Ah—forget the field. Those are money green eyes.

This guy couldn't be more not *your type.*

Allison has nothing against money, of course—but she's completely clueless about finance. Then again, she also knows nothing about science, yet she was head-over-heels in love with a biologist for almost a year.

And look how that turned out.

Justin was the one person in New York who got to know the real Allison—at least, as much of herself as she's ever shared with anyone. She'd dated here and there in college, but those relationships were superficial and physical.

With Justin, she eventually learned to let her guard down a bit. She shared things with him she'd never shared with anyone. Yes, and as soon as she was comfortable with the idea of someone having access to her past, her apartment, her innermost thoughts—*bam.* It was over.

Their June breakup was abysmal. Cheating, lies, accusations . . .

Thank God she's finally over it. Over it, and moving on.

Just yesterday, while folding dryer-hot clothes in her building's laundry room, she mentioned to her chatterbox neighbor Kristina that she's ready to meet someone new.

"Yeah? Good luck with that." Kristina, an aspiring Broadway actress, shook her mop of dark curly hair. "Do you know that it's been almost six months since Ray and I broke up? Half a year. I figured I'd have replaced him by now—not to mention all the stuff he took when he moved out. But I'm not having any luck getting a new boyfriend, or a new espresso maker or CD player or—"

"Um," Allison cut in, "it can't be *that* hard to get a new CD player, can it?"

"It's impossible when you're flat broke. I can't even afford a new Walkman. I haven't had music in my apartment for months now, and it's killing me. Meanwhile," she went on, clearly following her own unique brand of logic, "I've figured out that the only available guys in this city are married."

"Doesn't that mean they're *unavailable*?"

Kristina leveled a look at Allison. "Not necessarily."

Allison didn't know what to say to that. For all her eagerly embraced big-city sophistication, the Midwestern farm girl in her occasionally stirs with disapproval.

Anyway, Kristina certainly had a point about the scarcity of eligible men in New York. The fashion industry isn't exactly crawling with straight guys, and where else—*when*—is Allison supposed to meet someone? She works too hard and late to have much of a weeknight social life, and on summer weekends, the city becomes a ghost town. Pretty much everyone who's anyone leaves for the Hamptons—which she definitely can't afford.

Probably because you know nothing about finance and investments, right?

Maybe it's time to learn. People seem to keep talking about the flat economy, and here she is with no nest egg and very little to show for the fairly decent salary she's finally making—other than the overflowing contents of the closet in her one-bedroom apartment, which, incidentally, is decorated with a lot of really great furniture.

Then again, is that so wrong? What else in this life—including a beach house share—can possibly guarantee the immediate gratification of an Alexander McQueen dress or Dolce & Gabbana bags?

Not even just *immediate* gratification. Unlike summer, or relationships, a good purse can last forever.

"So you're coming from work?" Bill asks, and she steals a glance at his left hand. Aha! Ring finger bare. A good sign.

Marital status might not matter to Kristina. It might not matter to a lot of women.

Memories are good for nothin'. . .

Well, it matters to Allison. Single is essential.

"Actually, I was at the BCBG show." At his blank look, she adds, "Max Azria." Still blank. "The designer. It's Fashion Week."

"Oh."

He might as well have said, *Whatever.*

"How about you?" she asks, to keep the conversation going. "Coming from work?"

He shakes his head. "My office is downtown. I had a client meeting up here after the market closed."

"Oh." *Whatever.*

So much for scintillating small talk.

Whatever . . .

Story of my life.

Allison leans her head back wearily, gazing through the rain-spattered windshield at lower Manhattan's distant skyline, the twin towers shrouded in misty twilight gloom.

Stepping off the elevator on the fifth floor after a long, hard day of secretarial temp work, Kristina Haines immediately spots the large box sitting in front of her door.

What on earth . . . ?

Someone left her a gift. Wow.

A gift wrapped in white paper stamped with red hearts, topped by a big red bow.

Hearts. Kristina breaks into a smile. Her downstairs

neighbor Mack finally made his move. It's about time.

She unlocks the door, then holds it open with her foot as she contorts herself to lift the box. It's heavy—but not too heavy.

The wrapping is clumsily assembled, to say the least. Uneven seams, and too much tape—almost as though a child wrapped it. Or a guy. Most guys probably aren't very good at wrapping presents.

She wouldn't know. The only thing her lousy ex-boyfriend ever gave her was an occasional bouquet of flowers from the Korean deli on the corner. Usually only when he guiltily came home late—from God-knows-where—and the flowers were half price and wilted.

Giddy, Kristina puts the gift-wrapped box on the table and tilts it around, checking all six sides for a card, but finds nothing. It must be inside.

She tears off the paper . . .

A CD player?

That's what the box says.

She smiles. It's so sweet. She's mentioned a few times to Mack how much she misses having music in the house.

There's a shrink-wrapped CD stuck to the top with Scotch tape: *Songs in A Minor* by that new R&B singer Alicia Keys.

Hmm. R&B is not really her style. She's kind of surprised Mack didn't give her a collection of show tunes or something—he knows, after all, about her musical theater aspirations.

Maybe he figures she has all the Broadway cast albums—which she pretty much does— and wants to introduce her to something new. He's really into music—not that he's ever mentioned this particular artist.

Oh well—maybe she'll like it. Maybe the songs will have special meaning to her.

To us. *Me and Mack.*

Her heart is pounding. This is the turning point. This means there actually is going to be a *me and Mack.*

She pulls the CD off the package and sets it aside. Still no card, she notes—and the flaps are sealed with thick manufacturing tape, meaning it's not inside the box, either.

Okay—so he obviously wants to be her secret admirer for the time being. She'll play along.

Smiling, she opens the silverware drawer and searches for a blade. A butter knife won't cut it— literally—and of course Kristina, being a vegetarian, doesn't have steak knives.

She jerks open another drawer. Ah, there—it figures Ray didn't take the paring knives when he left; he never did any cooking. Not that Kristina does, either.

She grabs a nice big sharp knife from the drawer, idly wondering what Mack's favorite meal is, whether it involves meat, and whether she can learn to prepare it if it does—or even if it doesn't. Who knows? Maybe she'll become a gourmet chef.

Oh, come on. Really? You?

She glances at the whiteboard attached to the kitchenette's lone patch of wall space. Ray used it to keep himself organized. It was, ironically, one of the few things he left behind when he moved to his new apartment down on Warren Street.

The whiteboard was covered with his usual lists, reminders, and appointments.

Kristina took smug satisfaction in erasing it all. Then she wrote, in its place, *Anything is possible.*

Her neighbor Allison, who lives in the apartment

below, once said that, on a gloomy day when Kristina really needed to hear it.

"Anything is possible—that's my philosophy," Allison told her, and Kristina decided to make it her own as well.

She looks at the words every day, and reminds herself that she believes them.

Especially now.

After hurriedly slitting the seams on the box, she tosses the knife aside, a little too carelessly. Oops—a momentary inspection reveals that she just nicked the countertop. Oh well. She's not going to live here forever, and anyway, it's cheap, crappy laminate.

She turns her attention back to the box, opening it and pulling out her Styrofoam-encased prize.

"Wow, Mack," she whispers, thrilled. This is definitely the most romantic gift she's ever received.

As the cab slows in front of Pier 54, Allison glances at the meter and fumbles in her bag for her wallet.

"Here's my card."

She looks up to see her backseat partner—was his name Bob? Bill?—holding out a business card. Surprised, she takes it, looks at it.

Bill.

William, to be exact. William A. Kenyon, of Keefe, Bruyette, & Woods, Inc.

"Why don't you give me a call and we'll go out sometime," he suggests, and she's even more surprised, considering he hasn't said two words to her since midtown.

"I . . . I have one, too, somewhere in here." She goes back to digging in her purse, feeling around for the small leather case.

"One?"

"A business card."

"That's okay," he says with a wave of his hand. "Just call me."

The cab pulls up alongside the curb. She probably should give Bill back his card with a *thanks, but no thanks.*

Instead, because it's easier—and because she's lonely, and it might be nice to go on a date some night, even with a Mr. Wrong who expects *her* to do the calling— she tucks the card into her bag. "Sure."

Maybe she'll call. Probably not, though.

She pulls out some cash, offers him a twenty. "Here— for the cab. I really appreciate it."

"Not a problem. Keep it."

"But—"

"Just call me," he says again. "Maybe I'll let you buy me a drink."

Oh, ick. She opens the door and gets out with a wave. "Thanks again."

"See you later."

I highly doubt that, Bill.

Putting him out of her head, she moves on.

It's taken Kristina quite some time to remove the packaging and set up the CD player. It's a lot more complicated than her old one; it plays multiple CDs, and there are a number of different settings: shuffle, song repeat . . .

She figures she'll learn how to work it all when she reads the instruction leaflet—which will have to wait.

Right now, she just wants to hear some more music.

Not Alicia Keys, though.

Sorry, Mack.

She did put on the CD he gave her, but wound up fast-forwarding her way through the album. It's not really her cup of tea, and anyway, she's anxious to hear all her old favorites. It's been much too long.

Now she's listening to Barbara Cook singing Sondheim—ah, that's much more like it—and keeping a close eye on her watch.

Every weeknight at around seven forty-five, Mack gets off the subway over at the Canal Street station, then walks the couple of blocks to his apartment building.

Our *apartment building.*

Kristina prefers to think of it that way because she and Mack do, after all, live under one roof. Just not behind the same door.

But maybe someday . . . especially now that he's made his first move, after all these weeks of flirting . . .

Anything is possible.

When the weather is nice enough for Kristina to perch on the fifth floor fire escape, she's able to spot Mack in the distance, heading home. She discovered that by accident one evening about two months ago, when she was sitting out there to escape the heat.

This is an old building; no central air. Kristina used to have a small window unit, but of course Ray took it when he left her like the Grinch leaving Whoville.

The breakup was the first in a series of events that left Kristina wondering if she should just give up and move away, make a fresh start.

That was before she fell for Mack, of course.

Anything can happen.

That's why you love New York. A girl like you can be waitressing one day, starring on Broadway the next.

That's how it was supposed to work, anyway. But right after Ray moved out, Kristina lost her waitressing job because the health department closed down the restaurant. Then she tore a ligament during a dance workout—which wound up requiring surgery she couldn't afford, particularly without health insurance. And of course, the injury has put her Broadway show auditions on hold for God only knows how long.

As a result, she's been isolated not just from the friends she and Ray shared as a couple, but now also from all her dancer friends and all her restaurant friends—pretty much her entire social circle. She doesn't even have family now, other than her mother's sister in England and her father's cousins somewhere out West, who didn't even show up for his funeral.

It's been a long, hot, lonely summer, and Kristina has spent it falling madly in love with the guy who moved into the apartment below her on June first . . . *with his wife*.

Yeah. Mack is married.

Carrie. That's her name. Mack's wife.

Kristina rarely sees her. She has some kind of Wall Street job, and she leaves the building really early in the morning, way before Kristina gets up.

But now that Kristina is doing office temp work at an accounting firm in the Chrysler building, Mack is pretty much on the same morning schedule.

She used to hate riding in the building's ancient elevator, which takes forever even without stopping at other floors. She used to particularly hate when it stopped on the fourth floor and Mrs. Ogden, who smelled of old fish, would get on. Kristina was secretly almost relieved when her granddaughter found her dead on the floor of her apartment one day, having fallen, the way elderly people do, and hit her head.

Now that Mrs. Ogden is gone and Mack has moved

into her apartment, whenever Kristina presses the down button and the doors close after her, she's disappointed when it descends all the way to the lobby. On good days, it creaks to a stop on the fourth floor and Mack steps in.

He's not the best-looking guy she's ever known. He's nice and tall, but somewhat lanky for her taste. His black hair is razor-trimmed above his ears, and he's usually freshly shaven and wearing a suit. A little too put together, as far as she's concerned. She's always been a fan of shaggy-haired guys, the kind who go around in ragged jeans with five o'clock shadow; guys who might be hiding a tattoo or . . . something. Guys with an edge.

That's *so* not Mack.

But somehow, it doesn't seem to matter. For some reason, she's drawn to him anyway.

Wife and all.

"I didn't go looking for it. It just happened."

How often did she hear those words from her mother, a British war bride? Mum liked to tell the story of how she fell for Kristina's father, a young American soldier who'd married his high school sweetheart the evening before he shipped out.

Their love story was a romantic and thrilling happily-ever-after tale. Daddy divorced his hometown wife right after the war, married Mum, and they stayed madly in love until the end. Mum died a few years ago with Daddy holding her hand, and he went less than six months later—a heart attack, officially, but Kristina is certain it was a broken heart. He simply didn't want to live without the woman he loved.

Anyway—Kristina didn't go looking for this, either. It just happened. On that hot July night when she happened to be hanging out on her fire escape and spotted Mack below, something about him just clicked with her.

Maybe it was the way he was walking—the way his feet expertly navigated the crowded city sidewalks while his head seemed to be somewhere else, a million miles away. Somehow she sensed, even from a distance, an aura of unsettledness about him.

Until that night she'd assumed—when briefly she'd seen him in passing, and even more briefly given him a passing thought—that he was one of those boring, happily married, hopelessly domesticated guys.

That night on the fire escape, though, it occurred to her that that might not be the case.

Now she knows for sure that it isn't.

Poor Mack.

And poor me, Kristina thinks, pacing her apartment, wondering how she'll manage to accidentally-on-purpose run into Mack tonight. The fire escape is out of the question in this weather.

Too bad, because it's the perfect setup. Whenever Kristina spots Mack in the distance, coming down the block, she dashes down the four flights of stairs to the lobby. Then she takes her time checking her mailbox in the small vestibule by the door, waiting for him to come in from the street.

He always seems pleasantly surprised to see her. If he thinks it's unusual that she's often getting her mail at the precise moment he walks in, he hasn't mentioned it.

They ride up in the elevator together, and she's grateful that it takes so long, even though there's never enough time alone with him. Sometimes she wishes the elevator would just get stuck between floors. She fantasizes about what might happen between them then, trapped in that small space together for hours, even days.

She wonders who would make the first move. Usually she imagines that it would be he because that's sexier, but in reality, she probably wants it to be she. Yes, because part of what she loves about him is that he's a decent guy. A guy who's willing to make a commitment. A guy who wouldn't make a pass at another woman.

Maybe that's a crazy way to think about it, but Kristina can't help it.

Crazy.

She's crazy about him.

Maybe just plain old crazy, Kristina thinks as, aptly, Barbara Cook croons Sondheim's "Losing My Mind."

Kristina lives for those elevator rides with Mack. She's pretty sure that one of these days, they're going to wind up in each other's arms regardless of whether they're stuck between floors.

After all, he's not happy with his wife. He hasn't come right out and said that, but she can read between the lines; can see the flicker of discontentment in his green eyes whenever he mentions Carrie.

Is it any wonder? His wife doesn't exactly have a sparkling personality. Not that she's unpleasant, but . . . she's just kind of quiet. Keeps to herself.

Plus, Carrie used to be in relatively good shape and pretty, but Kristina has noticed an obvious weight gain lately. Even her face looks bloated. In fact, she actually asked Mack—maybe a week or so ago—if Carrie was pregnant.

She was dreading the answer, because she knew that Mack having kids would change everything. It's one thing to be in love with a married man. It's another to be in love with a married man with a child.

She was secretly elated when he told her that Carrie

wasn't pregnant, and she could swear Mack actually winced when he said it.

Obviously, his wife is simply letting herself go, and when that happens, the marriage is in trouble.

Barbara Cook has stopped singing.

Kristina wants to hear the song again. She should probably figure out how to use the replay setting, but she's too wrapped up in Mack to figure out anything more complicated than pressing the play button.

"The sun comes up, I think about you . . ."

Yeah, tell me about it, Barbara.

Kristina hasn't even seen Mack since Friday night, but it's hardly out of sight, out of mind.

She spent the better part of Saturday and Sunday afternoons in the building's basement laundry room, because sometimes she runs into him there over the weekend. This time, all she got for the effort was the knowledge that every stitch of clothing, bedding, and bath linens she owns is clean.

And now, because she can't wait outside in the rain and she can't quite see down the street from the window, she may have to go another whole day without seeing him.

That can't happen.

Maybe she should plant herself downstairs in the vestibule and wait till he shows up.

There's really no logical reason for a tenant to linger there, though—and there's one pretty solid reason not to.

Jerry.

You never know when you're going to run into the building's part-time maintenance man, who seems to lurk around the hallways even when he's not fixing something. He works at several other buildings in the neighborhood—Kristina knows that because he once told her, in one of his awkward, stilted, non-sequitur attempts at conversation. But lately, he's been around here a lot more than usual.

Or maybe it's just that Kristina herself has been around here a lot more than usual, and she keeps running into him.

"Doesn't he give you the creeps?" Kristina asked her neighbor Allison, when they were chatting in the laundry room yesterday afternoon. Jerry had come in and out several times, ostensibly to fix a washing machine that seemed to be working just fine.

"I don't know—he's just kind of simple-minded, I think."

"What about the stuff that's been stolen around the building lately?" Kristina pointed out. A few tenants have reported thefts over the past couple of months. Not major heists—just loose cash, some jewelry, and—oddly—women's clothing.

"Including their underwear," Kristina added with a shudder.

"How do you know that?"

"They told me—you know, the people who got robbed. Whoever did it is a pervert, and it seems like he must have had keys, too. I mean, it's not like the doors were broken down."

"Yeah, but the windows were open. Someone could have easily crawled in from the fire escapes. Look, I really doubt it was Jerry. He's really just a kid—"

"He's twenty-four."

"That's how old I am, exactly. He seems younger. How do you know his age?"

"He told me once. Like I care."

"Well, in any case . . ." Allison shrugged. "I can't imagine him hurting a fly. He seems harmless."

"Okay, maybe he's not a thief. But harmless? The way he was looking at us . . ." Kristina shuddered again.

"Not us—*you*."

True. For some reason, Jerry didn't appear to be the least bit interested in Allison, who happens to be a drop-dead-gorgeous blue-eyed blonde.

No, he seemed fixated on Kristina—continually sneaking glances at her as he crouched in front of the washing machine, then falling all over himself to retrieve a rolling quarter she dropped.

Yes, he always acts utterly smitten when she sees him around the building—which is much more often than she'd like. It's almost as if he's lying in wait for her . . .

The way you lie in wait for Mack?

She weighs the risk of running into Jerry if she goes downstairs right now against the risk of not seeing Mack for another twenty-four hours.

Easy decision.

Kristina hurries over to the full-length mirror.

Checking her reflection, she tosses aside the tweed suit jacket she wore to her temp job and unbuttons the second button of the white blouse beneath. After a moment's hesitation, she also daringly unbuttons the third, for optimum cleavage.

Hmm—still a little frumpy. She makes a mental note to take her knee-length skirt to a tailor to be shortened after this wearing. The suit is a couple of seasons old, but it's still decent, and Allison mentioned yesterday that miniskirts are back in style. Kristina has great legs, a dancer's legs. Why not show them off?

She does a quick makeup touch-up and dabs perfume

behind each ear. Then she spreads her fingers and rakes them from her scalp to the ends of her curly, shoulder-length dark hair, tousling it just enough to look bedroom sexy, but not bed-head messy.

There. Good to go.

She slips her feet into a pair of pumps and hurries for the door, glancing at her watch. Perfect timing.

She hurriedly descends four flights of steps to the first floor, opens the door from the stairwell . . .

And literally crashes into the bulky, imposing figure of Jerry.

Kristina wobbles on her feet. Jerry puts his hands on her upper arms to steady her. Her nostrils twitch at the ripe scent of his sweat.

"Sorry!" he says.

"It's okay."

She's no longer wobbling, but he doesn't move his hands. She looks pointedly down at them. His fingernails are dirty. His grip is unpleasantly strong.

She flinches.

He gets the hint.

Removing his hands, he shoves them into the pockets of his jeans. A lot of young guys are wearing their pants baggy, ragged, and low lately—a trendy nod to gangsta rap—but Kristina knows Jerry isn't making a fashion statement.

No, with him, it's classic, clueless-handyman butt crack.

Between that and his breath—which is bad, no surprise there—it's all she can do to hold back a shudder. Especially when she sees him take in her deliberately displayed décolletage.

That's not for you! That's for Mack!

Beneath his blond crew cut, Jerry's plump face is flushed. "Kristina . . ."

He knows her first name?

Maybe that shouldn't be surprising, but somehow, it is. Or at least, the sound of it on his lips. Surprising, and repulsive.

"Are you busy?"

"Busy?"

"Yeah. I thought . . ." His hands push deeper into his pockets, his shoulders hunching toward his jowls. He licks his lips and a strand of saliva stretches between them until he speaks again. "I thought—I mean if you aren't busy—then maybe I thought—I mean, I did think—that you could . . . that maybe we . . ."

Dear God, no. No, no, no.

She's shaking her head, but he doesn't seem to get it; he keeps right on fumbling his way through an invitation of some sort.

"If you like cake, I thought . . . Do you like cake? I do. I love it. And we could . . . I could—"

"I'm sorry, I can't," she blurts. "Sorry."

He stares at her, eyes wide, jaw hanging.

"Look." She tries to brush past him. "I'm really busy and—"

"If you're busy," he blurts, stepping into her path, "we can—"

We? This time, she doesn't even try to hold back the shudder.

"Thanks, but I can't. No. No."

She waits for him to retreat, perhaps hanging his head in defeat.

But he stands there in front of her, looking at her, his gray eyes shadowed.

Kristina shrugs and starts to step around him.

Jerry holds his ground.

Unsure whether to be infuriated or frightened, she casts her gaze at the ceiling and says, "Excuse me. I need to get my mail."

Still, he doesn't move.

How dare he? He's just standing here, blocking her way.

"If you don't move," she says levelly, "I'm going to call the cops and have you arrested."

Without another word, Jerry steps aside.

Shaken, Kristina walks down the corridor toward the vestibule, eyes focused straight ahead.

But she can feel him standing there staring after her, and it's giving her the creeps.

Just before she enters the vestibule, she impulsively lifts her right arm and raises her middle finger.

"Jerk," she mutters, flipping him off without looking back to see if he's still watching.

Something tells her that he is.

Chapter Two

You're late, Mack."

"I know. Sorry." He tosses his keys on the table just inside the apartment door.

Flicking on the light, he spots Carrie across the room on the couch, her arms wrapped around her knees. She's wearing a black suit and sheer pantyhose; no shoes. Her long brown hair looks stringy, as though it got soaked in the rain.

It isn't unusual to find her just sitting there, brooding. She does that a lot; always has.

But tonight, her black leather pumps are lying right here by the door, as though she kicked them off on her way in. Her red trench coat is draped over a chair at the dining table.

The old Carrie would never dream of putting damp fabric on polished wood; before she sat down, she would have hung it up, and placed her shoes neatly on the shelf in her half of the closet. She would have towel-dried her wet hair and brushed it.

"Did you go someplace after work?" asks the new Carrie, with a hint of suspicion.

"I stopped off for a beer with Ben," Mack lies, and turns on another lamp to dispel the rainy evening gloom. "Why are you sitting here in the dark?"

"It wasn't dark when I sat down."

"Well, it is now."

"Well, I guess I didn't notice."

Mack digests that as he sits on a chair to untie his black dress shoes.

"Are you okay?" he asks reluctantly, knowing she wants him to, knowing he has to, knowing the answer.

"Not really. Are you?"

He shrugs and stands up again, shoes in hand. His socks are damp from wading through gutter rivers.

"Maybe it'll happen next month," he tells Carrie, starting toward her, thinking that if he can just touch her—hug her—it'll be better between them.

"That's so easy for you to say," she snaps, stopping him in his tracks. "You're not the one who had to give up coffee and wine and sushi and cigarettes—"

"Yes, I did! I quit smoking with you!"

"But you didn't have to. You chose to."

Right. Because they were a team, and he was showing her support, and anyway, it was a nasty habit he never should have started. But back in his advertising agency days, pretty much everyone in the bullpen smoked—at work, and in the bars where they went to decompress after long days and nights on the job.

"You don't have to give up coffee and wine and sushi forever," he reminds Carrie, but she talks over him.

"—and you're not the one who has to shoot yourself full of hormones, or have raging headaches because of them, or go to the doctor's office once a month to be injected with test tube sperm, or sit around waiting to see if you'll start bleeding fourteen days later or not."

"No," he says quietly. "I'm not the one who has to do any of that."

He's just the one who has to supply the test tube

sperm at the doctor's office—an experience he can't help but find humiliating.

"Can't I just, uh, do it at home and then bring it into the office?" he asked Dr. Hammond early on.

"Theoretically, Mr. MacKenna, that's possible," she told him, "but there's a very small window of time when the semen is viable. How long does it take you to get here from home?"

"By subway? About an hour, give or take . . . and by car, depending on traffic . . ."

Too long, as it turned out.

When you live in lower Manhattan and the clinic is up in Washington Heights, there's only one way to produce a semen sample: walk past the knowing medical staff into the little room stocked with outdated dirty magazines and porn videos and—thank God—a sturdy lock on the door.

Medical mission or not, the former Irish Catholic altar boy in him can't help but feel vaguely guilty and embarrassed.

Yes, Mack knows it pales, in the grand scheme of things, next to everything his wife has endured as a precursor to—God willing—nine months of pregnancy and childbirth. He knows because Carrie minced no words in telling him, the one time he dared to complain to her.

"Are you freaking *kidding* me? You're actually complaining to *me* about jacking off into a cup?"

Clearly, he wasn't allowed to voice his distaste for the process; his feelings didn't matter. To Carrie, he was, apparently, an insignificant participant.

"Anyway," she ranted on, "I know you resent me for the move downtown, but you went along with it, so—"

"I don't resent you. I wanted to make your commute shorter."

"You're thinking that if we had stayed where we were, the clinic would have been right around the corner."

Maybe he was thinking that. But it was beside the point.

He'd embraced the idea of moving downtown—anything to make Carrie happy—and she was the one who'd done all the legwork, choosing the neighborhood, the old brick building, the apartment itself. She said it really did make her life easier—the convenience factor, anyway.

And what about my life?

By far, the most difficult part of this whole process—from where he sits—is putting up with Carrie's mercurial moods, one of the many unpleasant side effects the doctor had warned them about. Apparently, the fertility drugs can cause everything from nausea to psychosis—with a whole range of symptoms in between.

"You might find yourself touchier than usual," Dr. Hammond warned Carrie on that long-ago day in the office.

Touchy? Touchy would be a pleasure. *Touchy* would be the old Carrie on an ordinary good day.

Lately, it's hard to remember that he was ever drawn to his wife's strong-willed assertiveness. Hard to remember, for that matter, that she ever smiled, or laughed, or showed affection, or told him how much she loves and needs him . . .

She used to do those things, though. Not often, by any means—but she did. There was always a vulnerable side to her, carefully shielded from the rest of the world by a steely veneer. She's been through a lot in her life. She doesn't choose to let many people in.

Back when he first fell in love with her, Mack was touched—and honored, on some level—that he was the one she chose. The only one who got to know the real Carrie. The old Carrie. As well as anyone would ever know her, anyway.

But lately, she's gone missing. Lately, Mack finds himself wanting to scream at the fire-breathing creature that shares his apartment, *Who are you and what have you done with my wife?*

"Look, it's all temporary," he reminds her—and himself—now. "It's all going to be worth it. I promise."

There was a time when she'd have nodded her agreement, or at least greeted his words with silent acceptance.

Carrie glares at him. "How can you make a promise like that? It's not working, and you know it."

"Give it time."

"How much more time do I have to give?"

"As much as it—"

"I can't take it," she cuts in. "I just can't. I can't take it."

Trust me—neither can I.

"Don't you want to be a mother?"

Mack's question—the one she once would have answered readily, affirmatively—is greeted with ominous silence.

Don't you dare change your mind, Carrie.

Don't you dare forget how badly we want children.

If only she were willing to go a different route—a surrogate, or adoption . . .

But she vetoed both those options months ago. She would prefer to conceive and carry a baby, and the doctor told her it's physically possible, so she refuses to consider other options. That's Carrie. Present a challenge, and she'll see it through to the death.

Meanwhile, all this tension is killing Mack.

Killing *them*.

There was a time last year, after they'd eloped, when—as much as he wants children—he might have considered himself and Carrie a family of two.

Now she's been pulling away—and okay, he'll admit it: so has he, his nerves are dangerously frayed by her moods and the uncertainty of their future. The bond between them seems to be growing more taut with every passing day. Something has to give, or it's going to snap.

What's going to snap, Mack? Carrie demanded when he warned her just the other day. *The bond? Or you?*

He didn't reply. He didn't know.

"Carrie," he says, looking directly at her, "do you want a baby, or not?"

This time, she answers the question. "No," she says flatly, "I don't. Not at this price."

So there it is. That's it. It's not going to happen.

Hadn't he realized, deep down inside, that this was coming? Hadn't he been preparing for this moment in the back of his mind? Hadn't he thought of all the things he was going to say to convince her to change her mind?

Maybe. But somehow, now that the moment is here, he knows that nothing he says can make a difference.

He turns abruptly.

"Where are you going?" Carrie calls after him as he strides away.

"To bed."

"At this hour?"

"I didn't sleep last night."

"So what else is new?"

Insomnia—he's suffered from it, on and off, all his life. Lately, it's come back with a vengeance.

Mack doesn't reply, just closes the bedroom door behind him.

Rather, he means to close it.

But frustrated anger gets the best of him; he slams it shut. Then, for good measure, he hurtles his shoes against the wall, one after the other.

"What the hell are you doing?" shouts the stranger in the next room.

I don't know. I don't know what the hell I'm doing.

Mack sinks onto the edge of the bed and buries his head in his trembling hands, wondering how it came to this.

"No," Jerry mutters, pacing down the street, heedless of the people around him. He has another one of his blinding headaches. It hurts so badly . . . *he* hurts so badly.

"No. No, no, no . . ."

That's what she said. Kristina. Just like that: *No.*

She didn't even consider what he was trying to ask her, or how much courage it took for him to do it. She didn't even care that his feelings would be hurt.

No.

And then—to add the ultimate insult to injury—she gave him the finger.

How could she?

He's angry, so angry, and it's all her fault.

No—all *Jamie's* fault.

Jamie is the one who told Jerry that he could have a girlfriend now. Mama always said no to that—no to girlfriends, no to friends, no to everything. But Mama's not around anymore, and Jamie is, and Jamie says Jerry can have a girlfriend if he wants.

He *does* want to.

He wants to love a girl and have her love him back— just like in that song he likes so much, the one by Alicia

Keys. The one where she sings about how she never loved someone the way that she loves you.

Jerry likes to play that song over and over and over and think about Kristina.

Sometimes Jamie puts up with it; other times, Jerry has to turn off the music because, as Jamie says, it can drive a person crazy, playing over and over and over like that.

The other day, Jamie said, "Enough already! If you're so in love with this girl, then do something about it."

"What?"

"Let her know you like her. Maybe . . . send her a gift, to start. Like a secret admirer. That will get her interested. Send her something she likes."

"Cake?"

"No, not cake."

"Everyone likes cake."

"Something more . . . personal. Special. What does she like?"

"Music." Jerry thought about that. "I like music, too. I like Alicia Keys. But I can't send her music because she doesn't have a CD player anymore."

"Then that's what you'll send her. I'll help you. You'll get her interested, make her curious, and then you'll tell her it was from you, and you'll ask her out."

"I . . . I don't know what I'd say."

"I'll help you," Jamie said again.

What would Jerry do without Jamie?

"We'll practice, okay?"

"Practice?"

"You get one chance, Jerry. You gotta get it right. I'll tell you what to say."

Somehow, the words sounded a lot smoother when Jamie said them. Jerry couldn't manage to make them sound good even to himself, in the mirror, practicing. He heard the quaking in his voice and saw how his hands were twitching, and he knew he wasn't ready.

Jamie didn't listen, just said to go for it. Jamie made me do it. I knew I needed another day, maybe two, to get ready for this.

But then, out of nowhere . . .

"There she is!" Jamie whispered, and sure enough, there she was, Kristina, right there on the closed-circuit TV screen.

Not long after she'd carried the CD player into her apartment, Jerry saw her coming back out.

Last week, Mr. Reiss, the building's owner, had cameras installed in the building's public areas, hoping to catch a burglar who had broken into a few apartments. He showed Jerry where they are and how they work, and he told him to keep an eye on things.

Jerry did.

He especially kept an eye on Kristina.

"She's probably coming to thank you for the gift," Jamie said.

Confused, Jerry protested, "But she doesn't know it was from me yet."

"Sure she does. Go!"

So Jerry was waiting there in the hall when she burst through the stairwell door right in front of him, so close that he could smell her, and see down inside her shirt, and . . .

And he got to actually touch her at last, and her skin was so soft and warm, just like he'd always imagined . . .

And he heard Jamie's voice echoing in his head, and he heard Alicia Keys singing about falling in love, and he heard his own voice, out loud, talking to Kristina, saying her name, asking her to go out with him . . .

No.

That's what she said, and it was over, just like that.

"Whatever you do, don't blow it, Jerry," Jamie had said, at the end of that pep talk about Kristina—and what did Jerry go and do?

He blew it. She said no.

Jerry stops walking and tilts his throbbing head back. His face is wet. Rain. Tears.

He screams into the New York City night, *"Noooooooooooo!"*

Stepping out of the cab in front of her five-story brick apartment building, Allison wobbles a little on her four-inch heels. The pinot grigio she drank at the Marc Jacobs after-party went straight to her head after a long day and very little food.

Did she even have *any* food?

She honestly can't remember. There must have been some at the party, but hardly anyone in the industry ever eats in public. Hell, hardly anyone in the industry ever eats, period.

Sometimes, Allison amuses herself by imagining her glamorous colleagues finding themselves plopped down in the middle of her hometown.

Back in Centerfield, parties—not that Allison was invited to many—were invariably casual, jeans-and-flannel, chow-down affairs, with everyone bringing a dish-to-pass. Hellmann's-laced appetizers, creamy Campbell's soup casseroles, Velveeta in any number of forms . . .

If there was food at the Jacobs party, she's pretty sure

none of it contained a single ingredient you'd find in the packaged goods aisle at ShopRite.

She'll never forget what it felt like to be out there on the riverfront tonight with the world's most famous, glittering skyline as a backdrop; rubbing shoulders with the beautiful people; making small talk with Sarah Jessica Parker and Hilary Swank in the glow of what seemed like thousands of candles . . .

It was magical, that's what it was. The kind of night she dreamed about when she was a food stamps kid back in Centerfield.

Still walking, Allison fumbles in the bottom of her purse for her keys, and her heel wedges in a sidewalk crack. She stumbles, staggers, but somehow manages not to fall.

"Nice save!"

Startled by the voice, Allison looks toward it and sees that someone is sitting in the shadows on her building's concrete steps.

Her first thought is for her safety. It's late, and the street is deserted, and someone's been breaking into apartments lately . . .

But a burglar wouldn't linger.

She steps closer and it takes her a moment to place the man's familiar face: Mack, who moved in across the hall from her a few months ago after Mrs. Ogden died.

"You okay there?" he asks.

"Oh, I totally planned that. It's part of my new work-out routine."

He laughs. "Seriously—are you all right?"

"I'm fine, thanks." Embarrassed, and hoping he doesn't think she's drunk—*is* she drunk?—she tilts her open handbag toward a streetlight's glow, still fumbling for her keys.

On the steps, Mack flicks a lighter, and she looks over to see him with a cigarette between his lips. It surprises her, for some reason—and so does the fact that he's wearing a pair of threadbare faded jeans with flip-flops and an ancient-looking Bon Jovi concert T-shirt.

He's always struck her as a clean-cut, button-down type the kind of guy who, if he even drinks, prefers Bud to bourbon. And probably in a nice glass mug, too, as opposed to straight from the bottle.

Noticing her taking it all in, he holds up a pack of cigarettes.

Well, well, well—a Marlboro man.

"Want one?" he asks.

Desperately.

But she shakes her head. "I quit a few years ago."

"Yeah. Me too. Not that long ago, but . . ."

She contemplates that—along with his clothing and the reckless note in his voice. "Um, are you okay?"

He doesn't answer her at first, just exhales a cloud of smoke. Then he says, "Sure."

"Really?"

Ignoring that, he says, "Kind of late to be coming from work, don't you think?"

"I was at a party."

"Did you have a good time?"

"Definitely."

"What kind of party was it?"

Surprised that he'd even care, she tells him about it as he sits and smokes and nods, with apparent interest in his green eyes. Too light to be Nebraska-field green, but not money green, either. So different from Bill, the seemingly self-absorbed guy whose cab she shared earlier tonight. His business card is somewhere in the bottom of her purse—hopefully along with her keys.

Too bad Mack is married, she finds herself thinking.

But that doesn't mean he can't become a friend. A nice, normal friend, as opposed to the over-the-top, self-absorbed fashionistas she's met through her job.

That's what's missing in her life in New York. Normal friends, the kind of people she can really talk to. Few people here even know about her troubled small-town past—not because she's unwilling to tell, but because she hasn't come across many people who'd think to ask. Not even Kristina. She talks a lot, but doesn't ask questions.

Maybe I don't ask enough, either, Allison thinks.

Funny how she assumed, until tonight, that she knew everything about this guy, and it turns out she doesn't know anything at all, really. Not even his first name—assuming Mack is an abbreviation for his last—or where he works.

Now who's self-absorbed?

To be fair, she's never had much opportunity to find out, since she's only ever spoken to him in passing. Same with his wife—although she knows that Carrie is an executive assistant at a global financial firm called Cantor-something. Allison always remembers the first part of the name, because it makes her think about horses and, by association, Nebraska.

"It's spelled differently," Carrie said when Allison mentioned the horse connection to her one day not long ago, and Carrie shook her head. "It's Cantor—with an O. Not canter, with an E."

"No, I know, but they sound the same."

"But they're *not*," Carrie snapped.

Wow—someone has major PMS today, Allison remembers thinking.

Carrie always struck her as one of those hyperefficient women who is perpetually preoccupied and ready to move on to the next thing. Not unfriendly, just . . . busy. Lately, though, she seems to have developed a hint of malcontent.

Maybe that's why her husband is out here in the middle of the night, alone, smoking.

"Mack, can I ask—what's your name?" Allison blurts out.

He raises an eyebrow at her. "Uh—it's Mack. Are you *sure* you're okay?"

"No, I mean—that's short for MacKenna, right?" At his nod, she goes on, "I just wondered what your first name is."

"James. My father was in the music industry—he worked for a record label—and my mother thought it would be cute to name me Jimmy Mack—you know, after the song. It was really popular the year I was born."

"Which was . . . ?"

He grins. "I'm not telling. Look it up. Martha and the Vandellas."

"I will." She pauses. "So everyone called you Jimmy Mack?"

"No one did, thank God. Not even my mother. My family called me Jimmy until I started school, and then there were four other kids with that name in my kinder garten class."

"Guess it was popular."

"Still is. How many Jimmys, Jims, and Jameses do you know?"

She thinks about it. "A bunch."

"Exactly. That's why everyone's called me Mack all these years." He takes a drag on his cigarette.

After a moment of silence, Allison asks, "So . . . what do you do? For a living, I mean."

"What is this, an interview?"

She shrugs, not sure what this is, exactly. She just knows that she's curious about him—and anyway, he doesn't seem to mind. He's smiling.

"I told you about my job," she points out.

"True." He taps the cigarette with his forefinger, dropping an ash. "I sell advertising for a television network."

"Really?"

"You sound shocked."

"Shocked is . . . I mean, that's a strong word. But I am surprised."

"Why?"

The wine is making her unusually candid. "I don't know—that just sounds kind of . . . I don't know, more laid back than . . . uh . . ."

"Than I am?"

"I didn't mean—"

"Don't worry." He breaks off to yawn deeply, then adds, "Trust me, a lot of people say that. Usually people who haven't known me for very long."

"Why? Have you changed?"

"Doesn't everyone?"

Not me.

Allison always knew what she wanted out of life, and that it would mean putting Centerfield behind her. She prides herself in having set goals and stuck to her plan for achieving them.

"But," Mack says, "it's too bad people have to go and change, because if they didn't, relationships would be a hell of a lot easier, don't you think?"

"I don't know about that." Relationships—is he talking about his wife?

"C'mon—you know it's true. Think about it . . ."

She doesn't want to think about it. She's tired, and she might be drunk, and he might be drunk, too—and this conversation has gone on too long.

Allison pokes around inside her bag, looking for her keys. "Uh-oh."

"What's wrong?"

"My keys . . ." Suddenly remembering where she put them, she unzips the lining pocket. "Oh, thank goodness. I thought I lost them."

"That would not be good."

"No, but Kristina—do you know Kristina Haines? She lives upstairs?"

"Yeah, I know Kristina."

The bit of edge in his voice causes something to click in Allison's brain, and she remembers what Kristina said the other day about married men.

Is it possible that Kristina and Mack . . . ?

"What about her?" Mack is asking.

As Kristina herself said, anything's possible. Even carrying on a sordid affair right under Allison's nose—not to mention Carrie's.

For some reason, she'd really like to believe that Mr. Nice Guy here is happily married. Somebody has to be, right? Somebody other than her brother in Nebraska, anyway.

Brett got married right out of high school. His wife is from Hayes Township and her name is Cynthia Louise. Naturally, everyone calls her Cindy-Lou—except Brett, who calls her Cindy Lou-Who.

And Allison, who insists on calling her just plain Cindy.

Her brother lives with his wife and their kids on Cindy's parents' cattle farm—a fate worse than death, Allison thinks, but she'd never say it to Brett.

No, because if she did, she's pretty sure he'd say the same thing about her living here, and she really doesn't want to hear it.

"Kristina . . ." Mack prods.

"No, Allison."

"No—I mean, you were saying something about Kristina?"

"Oh! Right." Allison clears her throat. "Just—we gave each other spare sets of keys a while back, but I wouldn't want to wake her up at this hour to get mine. Anyway . . . now that I have them . . ." She jangles the keychain and checks her watch. "Wow—it's really late. I'd better go in. Big day tomorrow."

"Yeah? What's going on?"

She smiles. "You really want to know? This maternity clothes designer, Liz Lange, is doing the first Fashion Week maternity show ever and she's actually using pregnant models."

"That's . . . great." Mack isn't smiling, and he suddenly seems very interested in tapping a nonexistent ash from the end of his cigarette.

Did I say something wrong? Allison wonders.

She hesitates for a moment. "Well, good night. I'd better go get some sleep."

"Wish I could do the same thing."

"Why can't you?"

"Insomnia."

"Oh." She eyes his drink and cigarette, wondering whether she should inform him that alcohol and nicotine aren't exactly sleep aids.

Probably not. He probably already knows that, and if he doesn't, why should she be the bearer of bad news?

"Maybe you should try warm milk or something," she suggests.

"That would be like trying to put down an elephant with a Tylenol PM."

"Well then maybe you should try a tranquilizer dart."

Her quip is rewarded with an actual laugh.

"Believe me, I've tried just about everything. I've been dealing with this for as long as I can remember."

"That stinks."

"Yeah . . . but that's how I'm wired. I'm used to it. Like Zevon says, I'll sleep when I'm dead, right?"

"Zevon?"

"Warren. Warren Zevon."

She shrugs.

"Are you too young to know that song?"

"I'm twenty-four."

"Yeah . . . too young." He grins and shakes his head.

"How old are you?"

"I told you—look it up. But here's a hint: I'm old enough to have listened to Zevon's first album as a kid. He was a friend of my dad's. Anyway, it's a good song. 'I'll sleep when I'm dead.' And that's my motto."

She smiles, though for some reason, what he's saying doesn't sit well with her.

Ten minutes later, as she crawls into her own bed and closes her eyes, those words are still echoing in her head.

I'll sleep when I'm dead . . .

PART II

Hell is empty and all the devils are here.
William Shakespeare, *The Tempest*

Chapter Three

September 12, 2001
New York City
3:07 A.M.

The police officer, wearing his NYPD uniform and a bright orange reflective vest, materializes in front of Jerry the moment he rounds the corner onto West Broadway.

"Sorry, buddy. You can't go down there."

"Look! Look what they did!" Jerry points with a trembling hand to where flames still burn in the night, down at the far end of a dust-coated thoroughfare lined with shattered storefronts and burned-out cars, the ground littered with paper and debris. "Look at that."

The cop says nothing, just stands there, a sentry at the fiery gates of Hades.

"I was already down there," Jerry tells him, "earlier today. There were a lot of firemen. But I'm not a fireman."

"Oh, no?"

"No. I always wanted to be one, but a lot of firemen died so I'm glad I'm not one, because I don't want to die."

"No one does, kid."

The cop's eyes look red and swollen, Jerry notices.

Maybe it's the smoke in the air, or maybe he's been crying.

On television, they said that it wasn't just the firemen who died when the towers fell. A lot of policemen did, too. And all those people on the planes, and the people who worked in the World Trade Center . . .

"Listen, kid, you can't go down there, so—"

"But why not?"

"Restricted zone. Go on, turn around."

Jerry turns around and walks away. A few yards from the cop, he turns to take one last look at the massive destruction down the street, and rage builds within him.

Look what they did.

Look what they did.

Lying in bed five blocks north of the smoldering tomb, Kristina can hear the usual wee-hour sirens . . . but not the usual intermittent sirens. These are constant.

Conspicuously absent tonight is the occasional drone of planes that have just taken off from LaGuardia or JFK or Newark. Every airport in the metropolitan area—every airport in the entire country—is closed.

But every so often—just often enough to keep Kristina's nerves on high alert—comes the shattering roar of an aircraft flying low enough to rattle the tall loft windows.

Fighter jets.

Fighter jets over New York City.

Surreal.

Please make it stop. Please make it all go away.

She lies flat on her back with the quilt pulled taut beneath her wide-open eyes, as if to protect her from any-

thing that might drop out of the sky. Planes . . . bombs
. . . debris . . .

People.

She saw them this morning—scores of human torches
falling or jumping from the burning towers; grotesque,
limb-flailing freefalls branded into her brain.

Like so many of them, Kristina greeted the day with
an early alarm clock, coffee, the *New York Post*, a
crowded subway ride, a short, sunny stroll to her job
in an iconic Manhattan skyscraper. The city, scrubbed
clean in last night's rain, was spectacular. Now, part of
it lies buried beneath a heap of debris and toxic dust.

What if the Chrysler building had been hit instead of
the World Trade Center?

But it wasn't. You're alive.

When the second plane hit the second tower, she
fled her office on the fifty-fourth floor of the Chrysler
Building, not waiting for evacuation orders.

"Hey, where are you going?" one of the secretaries
asked as Kristina raced past on her way to the elevators.

"Home."

"You can't just leave!"

She didn't bother to respond. As far as she was concerned, she was running for her life.

She took the subway downtown and emerged to find
her neighborhood blanketed in smoke. She doesn't
really remember making a conscious decision to walk
all those blocks south to see what was going on; she
simply fell in with other gawkers swimming against
the sea of frightened tower refugees.

But after a few minutes of watching it unfold in front
of her—a few minutes of seeing those desperate jumpers, hearing bystanders' screams as they came down

and the staccato death explosions when they hit the ground—Kristina was overcome. She turned abruptly and ran home, arriving right before the first tower fell, most likely engulfing the very spot where she'd stood watching.

She was one of the lucky ones. She'll live to greet another day in a world that will never be the same. The city feels foreign to her now, *her* city—the city she loves because, as she so often says, *anything* at all can happen here.

I'll never say that again. Never. Never!

She keeps thinking of Mack. He works in midtown. She hasn't seen him all day or night. She went down and knocked on his door a few times, but no one was home.

Still, he must be okay; he *has* to be okay, but . . .

Carrie. Mack's wife.

Kristina knows she worked someplace down in the financial district. Carrie might have been hurt today, or killed.

Kristina can't bear to let her mind go there. Every time it starts to, shame sweeps over her and she shoves aside the notion of Mack, widowed and suddenly, truly, available.

She didn't want Carrie to *die*. Jesus. She didn't conjure today's nightmare like some crazy voodoo curse.

Of course she didn't.

And this isn't about her. This is a global catastrophe. This was, as President Bush said in his televised speech earlier, an act of war.

War. Here. In New York.

Kristina keeps thinking of her mother, in London during the blitz sixty years ago. Mum used to talk about lying terrified in the dark basement shelter as planes buzzed the skyline; about pulling her blanket over her mouth and nose to help blot the smell of burning rubble.

Did it work for you, Mum? Because it isn't working for me. The windows are closed, and so are the vents; the fire is a mile away and the wind is blowing south, but I can still smell it.

Kristina's mother died of lung cancer. Never smoked a cigarette in her life.

But all those nights in London during the air raids, lying awake, breathing toxic fumes . . . maybe, in the end, the enemy bombs got her after all.

Will the same thing happen to me?

Another fighter plane roars over Manhattan.

Please make it stop.

Please let me fall asleep.

Sleep, she knows, is the only way to escape this nightmarish world.

But sleep won't claim her, not when her thoughts won't stop and her mind's eye keeps replaying unbearable images and her entire body is clenched: her jaw, her fists, the muscles of her legs . . .

A spasm seizes her right calf and she squeezes her eyes shut, flexing her toes.

Please make it go away.

When at last it subsides, she opens her eyes to a sight more horrific than anything she's seen in the last eighteen hours.

Jarring as a plume of toxic smoke in a clear blue September sky, a long human shadow has fallen on the wall beside her bed.

She's home alone; she lives alone, and yet . . .

She's *not* alone.

And she was wrong. Sleep isn't the only way to

escape this world. Before she can escape it, though, the worst moments of her young life are yet to come.

The water runs red with blood, spiraling into the drain.
Blood in water.
Blood . . . everywhere.
Blood on Jamie's hands, and the white sheets of Kristina's bed, and the wall beside it.
Blood in the streets of Manhattan . . .
Blood everywhere. So much blood.
I still can't believe it.
Right before Jamie's eyes, on a beautiful September morning, the very images that had been pure fantasy for so long blazed to life—although "life" seems to be the wrong term. The polar opposite, really—it was *death* that was all around.
Disembodied limbs, a head whose eyes were fixed in horror, a stranger's severed torso spilling entrails . . .
Or was that Kristina Haines?
Jamie can't remember, exactly, what happened outside during the day and what happened later, much later, in the middle of the night in Kristina's apartment.
Bloody guts on the streets . . . or bloody guts on the sheets?
Grinning broadly, Jamie repeats the thought aloud, in a singsong whisper, like a recitation from a Seuss-gone-wrong children's picture book.
"Bloody guts on the streets . . . bloody guts on the sheets . . . I do not like them, Sam I am." Grinning, Jamie looks up into the mirror above the sink. "Oh, but I do. I do like them, Sam . . . I . . . am . . . *not.*"
Funny how you manage to forget; how you can look in the mirror and be caught off guard by your own reflection.

But this is me. Jamie turns off the tap and reaches for a towel. *This is me, for the time being.*

The sink has to be wiped down. When it's dry and clean, not a trace of blood, Jamie checks to make sure that nice little souvenir is still safely wrapped in a plastic bag. Yes. Good. No one would ever know it was there: no visible back pocket bumps, no telltale stains oozing through the fabric.

It's time to leave the bathroom; time to rest. It's been such a long day that it's hard to remember what it was like before everything went crazy . . .

Before fantasy melded with reality; before the grisly chaos so long pent up inside Jamie's head exploded in the real world, before the exhilarating realization that it was okay to finally act on another long-forbidden urge.

It was okay, though. Punishing Kristina was the right thing to do.

But it's not just that. Maybe it started out that way—teaching her a lesson because she was mean to Jerry—but it was more than that.

On this particular day . . . night . . . morning . . . the old rules don't matter anymore.

Nothing matters anymore.

I want to do it again.

I want to make the choice again.

I want to watch someone else die.

I want to feel someone die.

I want to make someone die.

Yes. It can happen again.

It can happen—it *will* happen—whenever, wherever, to whomever Jamie chooses.

But right now, it's time to rest.

* * *

With a deep sigh, Jerry sinks his aching head back against the pillow.

There have been many long, terrible days in his life, but this was by far the longest, and the most terrible.

He's lived in New York City all his life. This is his home. And now . . .

Look what they did.

He closes his eyes, squeezing hard, but he can't shut out the terrible scenes he encountered today. Smoke, and fire, and firemen dying, and all those people jumping out the windows, falling through the sky . . .

Fallin'.

The song, his song, still echoes through his head.

It was playing in the background just a little while ago when at last, *at last*, Kristina said the words he's been waiting so long to hear.

Not the part about being sorry for saying no when he asked her out. That was nice to know, of course—that she hadn't meant to hurt him.

But it was the rest of what she said that resonated with him.

He could hear the heartfelt passion in her voice; passion that made her words quaver and her pitch much higher than usual.

"Jerry, I love you!" she told him. "I've always loved you, and . . . and . . . and I always will. I just wanted you to know that. Okay? Okay? Oh God . . ."

She was crying, he realized. Was it because she was upset that she had hurt him when she'd turned down their date? Or because of all that had gone on today in the city, their city, the city where they'd fallen in love?

Or was she simply so overwhelmed by her feelings for him that she was sobbing with joy?

He doesn't know. It doesn't matter.

"I love you, too," he told Kristina, over and over, until Jamie said it was time to say good-bye.

But maybe that wasn't a good idea. Maybe he shouldn't have listened to Jamie.

Maybe he should go see if Kristina's okay. Because the more he thinks about it, the more certain he is that she's not.

Allison was at the Liz Lange fashion show when it all began to unfold this morning. Someone said that a plane had just crashed into the World Trade Center, and a buzz of confusion rippled through the Bryant Park tent, but the show went on as planned.

As gorgeous pregnant models strutted the catwalk in designer outfits, Allison put the plane crash out of her head and focused on the task at hand.

Afterward, alarmed by the smoke rising in the blue sky over lower Manhattan, she tried to call the office from her cell and couldn't get through.

"Don't bother," a scurrying stylist called to her. "The phones are down!"

Unsettled by the growing sense of panic on the street around her, she made her way back to her office as fast as she could walk in a pair of pointy Christian Louboutin stilettos.

The lobby security post, usually manned by a joyful Rastafarian named Henry, was eerily deserted.

Upstairs, she found everyone in her department glued to a conference room television, where the alarming truth was made clear at last.

"How many people were in there?" she asked Luis, a production editor and her closest friend at work.

"Tens of thousands."

"How many died?"

Luis shook his head. She saw that he was holding an orange plastic prescription bottle, tapping it like a maraca against the open palm of his other hand.

Seeing her looking at it, he passed it to her, a silent offering.

"What is it?" She was already twisting off the white safety cap, noticing—and not caring—that the label bore an unfamiliar name.

"Xanax. My sister's shrink prescribes it for her but she doesn't take it that often so she gives it to me."

"You carry it around with you every day?"

"I keep it in my desk drawer. I thought this job was stressful but—" Luis's brown eyes flicked to the television screen, with its doomsday images. He murmured something in Spanish, then said, "Go ahead—take it, Allison. It'll calm you down."

She knew, only too well, what Xanax does. She knew because it was one of the many drugs her mother used to take back in the grim old days in Centerfield.

Centerfield—if she were there right now, she wondered, would she feel safe?

Was there anyplace in the world where she would ever be able to feel safe again?

Allison—who grew up seeing what drugs, even prescription drugs, can do to a person, and swore she'd never touch them—swallowed two Xanax.

That made it better, but she still wasn't insulated from the horror—not by any means.

Trapped in her midtown office building—well aware that any one of the landmarks around her could be a target—she could only watch the ruins burn, on TV and out the window. The subways weren't running, the bridges and tunnels were closed. Manhattan island was truly cut off from the rest of the world.

Someone told Allison that Helene, the magazine's formidable art director, had earlier received a hysterical phone call from her sister, trapped on a high floor of one of the towers. Allison couldn't wrap her fuzzy head around the fact that sophisticated, intimidating Helene had reportedly lost her composure when the tower collapsed, sobbing openly before her husband showed up to escort her off to wherever the families of the victims were gathering.

It seemed everyone in the company was connected, by varying degrees, to someone who worked in the twin towers or for the FDNY or NYPD. Everyone but Allison.

She wasn't from this area; she didn't have a firefighter uncle or a cousin in food service at Windows on the World or a high school boyfriend who worked at a trading desk.

While she had lived in the city long enough to have made a network of friends, those relationships weren't close enough—or meaningful enough—or maybe it was just the Xanax—for her to be frantic over their whereabouts today. Operating under the assumption that none of them would have reason, in the course of a Tuesday morning, to have been down at the World Trade Center, she was pretty sure they were all safe.

And if she was wrong about that . . .

I don't want to know was her initial reaction. *Not yet. Not today.*

The phones were down, but e-mail was working, and she found several worried inquiries in her in-box. There were repeated e-mails from her brother, a few from friends, and even one from Justin, her ex. As she typed out reassuring replies, she thought about all the people whose queries to loved ones in New York would remain forever unanswered.

When, mid-afternoon, word came that the commuter trains were running again out of Grand Central and Penn Station, some of Allison's suburban colleagues left the office. Presumably, they made it home to their leafy bedroom communities in Westchester and Long Island, Connecticut and New Jersey, away from the death and the danger.

Allison stayed on, huddled in the conference room with Luis and a couple of others who lived in lower Manhattan and beyond.

No one spoke of trying to get home until well after the sun had gone down, and even then, it took a long time for anyone to actually venture out there.

"Are you leaving?" people would ask Allison, who at some point that evening had swallowed a couple more Xanax tablets to maintain the numbness.

"I'm going to wait a little longer," she told her co-workers as, one by one, they slipped away into the strange, terrible night.

She was going to wait . . . for what? She had no idea. For another attack? For some kind of all-clear? For daybreak?

Only when everyone else had gone did Allison realize that she had no desire to spend the night alone in a strange place. The news was reporting that there were pockets of downtown neighborhoods where the power had been restored. Hers was reportedly one of them. She forced herself to go.

Out on the street, she immediately spotted a cluster of camouflage-clad, machine gun–carrying National Guard soldiers. That was when it hit her: no matter where she spent this dreadful night—in her office or in her apartment—she would be alone in a strange place.

She took a cab as far south as she could—to a road-block at Union Square. She got out of the cab, tossed the driver a twenty-dollar bill without asking for change, and watched him speed away.

Feeling like she'd wandered onto the set of a World War II movie, she approached the soldiers and police manning the barricade.

"I live down there," she said.

"Do you have ID?"

She handed over her New York driver's license, grateful she'd even bothered to get one. No one drives in New York City; it's been years since she got behind a steering wheel. But she was eager, when she first moved here, to sever her connection to Nebraska and become an official New Yorker. Thank goodness she'd endured the endless wait at the DMV on that long-ago day.

"Okay—you're clear," the national guardsman told her, after checking her address on the license. He waved her past the barricade.

She faltered. "But . . . what do I do?"

"You're clear," he repeated. "You can go home."

"How?"

He looked down at her feet, and she got the point. There was no other way.

She started walking. Breathing smoke and dust and jet fuel fumes, she searched for the comfort of famil-iarity, but found nothing. Life as she knew it was over.

After the first block, she stopped to lean against a pole and take off her shoes. She removed one, set down her foot to balance on it while she took off the other, and found herself stepping on a shard of glass.

It was most likely a piece of a beer bottle. But as she picked the glass out of her flesh, a cavalry of refrigerated trucks rattled past her on their way downtown. In that moment, the horrible reality hit her all over again and she immediately put the shoe back on.

God only knew how far the wreckage of buildings and airplanes—and human remains—had scattered.

As she limped all those blocks, her skin rubbed raw against the unforgiving leather straps.

Now she's home, her heels and toes blistered and bleeding.

In some perverse way, she welcomes the pain. Physical suffering—she can deal with that. Physical pain—that can heal.

But the other pain, the pain inflicted by catastrophic loss—that pain is seared deeply into her soul. The Xanax may be a balm, but it's only temporary. She'll make sure of that. She can't—she won't let herself—go down that self-destructive road. Not after what drugs did to her mother.

Memories are good for nothin'. . .

Right.

Just over twenty-four hours ago, she stood in this very spot on the street in front of her building, doing exactly what she's doing right now: hunting through her purse for the keys to her apartment.

Her neighbor Mack was here. She told him about the glorious Marc Jacobs party—the last hurrah, it now seems, in a city that believed itself immune to the afflictions of the great unwashed.

God only knows if Mack is even alive tonight—rather, this morning, because it's well past midnight now. And his wife, what about her? Carrie worked down there.

Cantor Fitzgerald. That's the name of her company. Allison recognized it as soon as she heard it on the news earlier. A reporter said the firm occupied the top floors of the north tower.

Was Carrie there?

Did she make it out alive?

Numb with exhaustion, Allison pushes the troubling question from her mind.

She robotically unlocks the front door, crosses the threshold into the vestibule, closes the door behind her. Pausing at the row of mailboxes, she can't imagine there might be anything in her box that hasn't been rendered obsolete.

Magazines, sales fliers, department store credit card bills . . . it's all so meaningless. The things that mattered most to Allison when she left this morning for the Liz Lange fashion show seem utterly insignificant now.

As she moves past the mailboxes toward the elevator, Allison hears a sound at the far end of the hall.

A door opens.

Someone comes out of the stairwell.

In the murky light, she can just make out a human shadow. Who would be lurking around the halls at this hour, on this night?

Jerry? The burglar? Insomnia-stricken Mack?

Her first guess was correct.

She watches Jerry step briefly into the splash of light from a hallway bulb before disappearing into an alcove where the door to the back alley is located. A moment later, she hears the door open quietly, and then close.

Allison presses the up button.

Several stories above, the elevator grinds into motion. She rests her forehead against the wall, waiting for it to come and carry her home.

Chapter Four

Standing in the dimly lit corridor outside his office, Mack watches the copy machine rhythmically spit one flier after another into the mounting stack in the tray. Carrie's face stares up at him from the pile, frozen in an unnatural smile. Mack snapped the picture last spring, at his family's annual Saint Patrick's Day party, not long after they started infertility treatments.

Large gatherings are always somewhat uncomfortable for Carrie, who told him early on in their relationship that she wasn't used to big families.

"That's too bad," Mack said easily, "because I have one."

"That's too bad," she returned, and he remembers thinking that she was teasing.

She wasn't.

She married him anyway, just a few months after they met. He proposed on a whim. They eloped—the only way she'd do it. She didn't want a big family wedding like his sister and cousins, or even a small church wedding in Jersey, at his hometown parish. Anyway, his mother was dying; a big wedding, even if Mack wanted one, would have to wait until after she was gone. And after she was gone . . . what would be the point?

So it was just the two of them, Mack and Carrie, spur

of the moment in a far-off town with a justice of the peace.

Later, he realized that his judgment had been clouded by grief over his mother's illness, both when he proposed to Carrie, and when he agreed to elope.

He should have known it would break his mother's heart to learn, after the fact, that her only son—yes, a grown son, but still—had run off and married a girl she barely knew. Hell, a girl Mack himself barely knew.

As a result, in the scant time she had left, Maggie MacKenna never warmed up to her new daughter-in-law. She wasn't unkind to Carrie, but she didn't embrace her the way she had various friends—or even stray cats—Mack and his sister, Lynn, had brought home over the years. Nor did she immediately consider Carrie one of the family as she had Lynn's ex-husband, Dan. Even after his sister separated from her ex—headed for an amicable divorce, as she likes to say, and she and Dan are living proof that such a thing exists—Dan remained more a part of Maggie MacKenna's family than Carrie ever would be.

Mack always thought it was mostly the elopement that upset his mother, but after Maggie died last fall, Lynn revealed that their mother didn't think Carrie was right for him.

"Mom called her a cold fish," his sister said matter-of-factly one day as they sorted through mementos in their childhood home back in Hoboken, preparing to move their father into an assisted-living facility. "She said she would have talked you out of marrying her if you'd let her know in advance."

Those words made him cringe—though he probably always knew on some level how his mother felt about his wife. But hearing the truth especially bothered him because it was too late to change his mother's mind—or to share with her some of the things about Carrie she didn't know. Things Carrie had made him swear never to tell anyone. Things that, if he'd dared break that promise to Carrie, might have made his mother feel differently about her.

But Mom is dead, and Dad—who always deferred to his wife anyway—is in his own little world now, slowly losing his mind to Alzheimer's.

To her credit, easygoing, talkative Lynn doesn't need reasons to like anyone. On the few occasions Carrie visited her home, Lynn tried to make her feel welcome.

Still, Mack remembers the March day the photo was taken as being particularly uncomfortable, because it was spent surrounded by his sister's kids, all their cousins, and various relatives amid the easy, happy chaos of effortlessly established families.

Okay, maybe that's not quite accurate; maybe parenthood is never achieved effortlessly. Particularly when the future holds amicable divorce.

But at the party, Lynn, a teacher, laughed about how she and Dan timed all three of her pregnancies so that she could deliver in March or April for optimum maternity leave. And their cousin Belinda wryly referred to her own youngest children—newborn twins—as "oops" babies. And all Mack could think was that it wasn't fair, and he knew Carrie was thinking the same thing.

His wife's melancholy state is clearly evident in the photograph taken that day. Carrie's mouth is dutifully bent into a smile but her blue eyes are grim. Her brown hair falls limply past the green carnation Great-Aunt Nita had pinned to her lapel without asking. Carrie's face looks pasty, wearing too much makeup in an effort to conceal her dark circles and blemishes—hormonal effects on her ordinarily clear complexion.

The infertility drugs have since caused considerable bloating to her face and a considerable weight gain. She's been complaining about it, but until now, Mack hadn't realized just how drastic the change has been.

Would anyone even recognize his missing wife from this photo?

Possibly. But he chose it only because it's the one shot of her that fits the bill.

"You need to use a good close-up on your missing persons flier," he was told by someone—a cop? an orderly? a FEMA volunteer?—over at NYU Medical Center. That was where Mack—along with hundreds of other distraught New Yorkers—converged this afternoon upon hearing that the hospital had received hundreds of injured victims, many without ID or even the clothes on their backs, burned beyond recognition. "For all you know," a kindly Red Cross worker told Mack, "your wife could be among them. She could be unconscious. Unidentified."

All day, rumors were flying among the frantic families of the missing. Everyone talked about dazed, dust-covered Trade Center employees wandering the streets in shock, some suffering from amnesia. Carrie could be one of them, people kept telling Mack. Or she could be buried alive in the wreckage. The rescuers were digging feverishly, trying to get to the trapped survivors— surely there were trapped survivors.

Realizing the paper tray is about to overflow, Mack removes the stack of fliers to make room for more. The paper is hot to the touch.

Hot.

Fire.

He puts the fliers aside and thinks of the flames that engulfed the building where his wife works.

Worked. The building is gone.

Carrie is gone.

Gone . . . gone . . . gone . . . gone . . .

The mantra runs through Mack's brain in perfect rhythm with the copy machine.

Allison half expected to find her one-bedroom apartment buried beneath a layer of dust and debris, the windows blown out and smoke billowing in from the night.

Somehow, though, other than the blinking display on the microwave's digital clock, everything was just as she left it this morning.

This morning, less than twenty-four hours ago—in another lifetime.

She wandered through the rooms, checking, though, just to be sure.

She gazed at the coffee cup sitting in the kitchen sink, its milky beige dregs dried in the bottom.

She drifted into the bathroom and saw the hairspray, brushes, and makeup cluttering the bathroom sink.

In the bedroom, shoes were strewn across the floor in front of her closet, having been hurriedly tugged on in her frenzied, last-minute effort to find the perfect designer heels to wear to the fashion shows. She'd model them before the mirror and then kick them off in frustration, grabbing another pair.

The woman who left here wearing designer stilettos with a four-and-a-half-inch heel never dreamed she'd be hobbling home through a war zone.

On an end table in the catalog-perfect living room, the answering machine light was flashing. There were several new messages. Three were from her brother; he left them before Allison sent him an e-mail from the office telling him she was safe.

Brett's voice sounded increasingly worried, and in the final message Allison could hear Cindy Lou-Who in the background, shouting something about one of the towers collapsing.

The other messages were from a scant handful of friends. College friends, and New York friends, but none from Centerfield. No one back there would have her number, or care enough to track it down and check on her. Tammy Connolly, the one hometown friend who might have cared, left town long before Allison ever set her sights on New York City, and would have no idea she's living here.

All of the messages had come in during the first hours after the attacks, before the power went out. As Allison reset the machine, she found herself idly wondering if anyone tried to call while it was out of commission and then worried when they couldn't get through.

It would have been nice to think that there are lots of people out there who care about her.

Now, as Allison heads wearily back into her bedroom to change her clothes, she thinks about the walls she began constructing back in her childhood; walls she hasn't been overly anxious to dismantle as an adult.

Maybe it's time to start taking them down, start letting people in.

She sinks wearily onto the edge of the big mahogany sleigh bed, takes off the shoes at last, and hesitates, eyeing the wastebasket beneath the bedside table, wondering if she should just . . .

Uh-uh. No way.

For one thing, that would be wasteful. You don't throw away a perfectly good, extremely expensive pair of shoes.

For another, throwing them away would be like giving up. It would mean she can't imagine a scenario where she'd ever wear those beautiful shoes again.

Anything is possible. That's your philosophy, remember?

She carries the shoes to her closet, pulls out the box they came in, tucks them inside wrapped in layers of tissue, and returns it to the shelf. Then she does the same with the pairs she picks up from the floor, all frivolous sandals with impossibly high stiletto heels.

She can't imagine setting foot outside her apartment in anything but running shoes—or maybe combat boots—but life might get back to normal someday.

It always has, right? No matter how bad things have been. Every time she's hit rock bottom, she's told herself that there's no place to go but up.

This is different, though, whispers the little voice in her head, piping up like the frightened child she never wanted to be—never allowed herself to be.

This is different from waking up one morning to learn that her father had abandoned his family, different from coming home from school to find her mother unconscious, having OD'd—again.

As far as Allison was concerned, whatever happened back in Centerfield was never anybody's business but her own.

But this—what happened today—this happened to millions of people. It happened to everyone, really.

We're all in it together, Allison thinks, and somehow, somewhere deep down inside, she finds comfort in the idea of camaraderie.

She thinks about her coworkers, her friends, her neighbors . . .

Kristina. Is Kristina okay?

And Mack, and his wife . . .

But it's too late—too early—to call anyone.

Allison wearily slips out of her dress.

She's about to toss it over the footboard of her bed. Instead, she finds a hanger, drapes the dress over it, and returns it to the closet, where it can wait until the day when fashion matters again.

"Mack?"

Startled, he whirls around to see Ben Weber, the director of advertising sales. He's Mack's boss—and one of his closest friends.

"Sorry, didn't mean to scare you," Ben says. "Any news?"

"No. Where have you been?" Mack absently notes that Ben is no longer wearing the dark suit he had on earlier. He's changed into jeans, a Yankees cap, and a hooded Cornell sweatshirt.

"I went home to see Randi and Lexi, remember?"

Mack doesn't remember—but he nods anyway.

He thinks back to everything that led up to this surreal act—his being here, at his deserted workplace in the middle of the night, printing out a missing persons flier for Carrie—and it's like waking up and trying to remember the details of a nightmare.

He forces his mind back, back, all the way back to the Tuesday morning alarm clock after a restless couple of hours' sleep. He remembers hitting the snooze button, then pretending to go back to sleep as Carrie moved around the bedroom getting ready for work, slamming things moodily.

He was going to be late, but he knew that if he got up while she was still there, he'd have to acknowledge what she'd said last night—that she was finished. That she didn't want a baby after all.

He couldn't deal with that—with *her*—that morning.

Something clicked in Mack's brain as he lay there, avoiding his wife. It was as though he'd been looking at his life through a blurry binocular lens for months, and then all at once, things became clear.

He finally knew what he had to do.

And he did it. He did it quickly, impulsively, before he could lose his nerve.

And he didn't regret it when it was over.

He got dressed, got to work, and just as he was getting ready to go out on his first sales call of the day, Ben burst into his office and told him about the plane hitting Carrie's building. It was as if someone had abruptly jerked the focus dial in his brain, and everything was fuzzy again.

Still is.

Now, trying to piece together the rest of his day, Mack is dimly aware that Ben was by his side for the duration. Ben walked with him from NYU Medical to Saint Vincent's Hospital to Bellevue. Ben helped him negotiate chaotic seas of frantic people searching fruitlessly for loved ones at the hospitals and triage centers set up at Chelsea Piers, the Staten Island Ferry terminal, Stuyvesant High School. Ben asked all the right questions, the questions Mack couldn't seem to articulate, and he gave out information to all the right people.

Through it all, Mack vaguely recalls Ben making furtive, sporadic phone calls to his wife, whenever cell service would allow. And yes, he remembers that at one point, Ben asked Mack if he'd be okay for a little while alone while he went home to check in on his family.

How long ago was that?

Where was I when Ben left?

How did he know to find me here?

Mack rubs his palms against his burning eyes, wondering if he's suffering from mere exhaustion, or post-traumatic amnesia.

"Did you stop back at your apartment?" Ben is asking.

Mack nods, vaguely remembering going into the apartment, looking around, and leaving again. "She wasn't there."

Such a stupid, stupid thing to say. Ben knows she wasn't there. If she had been *there*, Mack wouldn't be *here*, printing out hundreds of missing persons fliers.

"Was the power back on yet?"

Was it? Was it?

He puts both hands behind his aching neck and laces his fingers together, pulling, stretching . . . stalling.

"Remember," Ben prods, "when we stopped there this afternoon, the power was off."

Everything is a blur, and he's so tired, but it's starting to come back to him . . .

"Mack?"

"The power was back on this time—and the phone was working. There was a dial tone . . ."

"Did you check the messages?"

He nods. There were a bunch of calls from his family, his friends, people he's met in all phases of his life. An old fraternity brother, his high school prom date, a former neighbor, several distant cousins . . .

Everyone wanted to know if he was okay.

A few—those who know Carrie, and know where she works—were concerned about her. Mack's sister, Lynn; her ex-husband, Dan; and Ben's wife, Randi, who met her only once or twice—he's pretty sure those were the only people asking about Carrie.

That, then, is the extent to which he's cut himself off from all those people who were part of his old life. But what else is he supposed to do? His wife and her needs come before everything else.

"I'm not a social butterfly, like you," Carrie often says, with a smile that doesn't reach her blue eyes. She has no close friends or family. After all she's been through in her life, she's uneasy in large groups of people, preferring to be alone with Mack. Just the two of them.

And the two were supposed to become three.

We were going to have a baby.

What about our baby?

Mack's throat aches.

You know it was never going to happen anyway. She told you that. It wasn't meant to be.

But still . . .

"Randi sent this for you." Ben is handing him something wrapped in tinfoil.

He takes it. It's warm. "What is it?"

"Roast chicken. She made it for dinner earlier."

Mack closes his eyes briefly, imagining Ben's wife in their kitchen, cooking chicken for dinner.

Such a simple thing.

Chicken. Dinner. A wife.

The regret Mack couldn't muster this morning engulfs him at last. What he wouldn't give, right now, for an ordinary night at home. *With* Carrie.

What he did this morning felt right at the time, but maybe he'd been too impulsive, too drastic.

Maybe?

Jesus, Mack. You don't get more drastic than that.

"And—here," Ben says, and Mack opens his eyes to see his friend holding out a sheet of paper—the thin, manila kind little kids use for coloring. "Randi said Lexi made this for you before she went to bed."

Lexi—Mack hasn't even seen her in a few years. "How does she know . . . me?"

"I mention you sometimes, or talk to you on the phone. So . . . she knows who you are. And I guess she heard me and Randi talking about . . . what happened."

Mack takes it from him and sees that it's a crayon depiction of a pair of stick figures holding hands. Both are smiling and one is clearly female, wearing a triangle of a skirt. The sky above them is scribbled blue and decorated with a big yellow sun that's the same shade as the long hair on the female stick figure.

That's all. Just sky and sun, not a hint of black smoke.

"That's you and Carrie," Ben tells him.

Mack swallows hard over the ache in his throat and folds the sheet of paper into quarters, then shoves it into his back pocket. He tries to speak, but he can't find his voice—and anyway, what is there to say?

"If anyone could have gotten out of that tower, Mack, it was Carrie. She was a strong person, right? I mean—*is*. She *is* strong."

Mack nods, ignoring Ben's slip. Ben knows that Carrie works—*worked*—at Cantor Fitzgerald, on the 104th floor of the north tower, ten or twenty floors above where the plane hit. As far as Mack knows, no one who was up there at the time has been accounted for.

At one of the hospitals, he ran into the weeping wife of one of Carrie's colleagues. She said her husband had called her to say they were trapped and there was no way out.

She sobbed hysterically when she described to Mack how she'd hung on until the phone went dead. Mack hugged her and murmured words of hollow comfort.

"At least you have that," he told her. "At least you had a phone call."

"You didn't?"

No, Mack said, Carrie didn't call from the burning tower, and she didn't pick up her desk phone or her cell phone when he tried to reach her. That was before the telephone system buckled under the strain of all those people trying to reach loved ones in New York City; before the steel support beams buckled in the intense heat and the towers of terror came tumbling down . . .

"You've got to have hope, Mack."

Feeling a hand on his arm, he looks up to see Ben watching him. Ben, with his wife at home cooking dinner, and his child tucked safely into her bed. Ben, who barely knows Carrie because she had no interest in getting to know him, or letting "outsiders" into their lives.

"She could be alive. She could be out there some-where, just waiting for you to find her."

"I know," Mack tells Ben. "I have hope."

It isn't the first lie he's told lately, and somehow, he's certain it won't be the last.

Numb with exhaustion, Allison turns off the television and walks into her bedroom, yawning.

She's just spent the last hour watching the news, lis-tening to F–16s flying overhead, and wondering how she's ever going to sleep tonight.

But it's now or never. The sun will be coming up soon.

As she climbs into bed and reaches over to turn off the lamp, something on the bedside table catches her eye: the business card from the man she met Monday night—the one who shared his cab with her.

William A. Kenyon, who works at an investment bank.

She looks at the card.

The firm is Keefe, Bruyette, & Woods, Inc.—and the address jumps out at her: *Two World Trade Center.*

Allison stares at it for a long time, then carefully sets the card back on the bedside table.

She'll call him tomorrow. Just to make sure he's all right. Maybe they'll go out on a date. Maybe he's Mr. Right, after all.

Or *was.*

Maybe she'll never know.

She turns off the lamp.

Pulling the covers up to her neck, she listens to the eerie sounds beyond the open window. After a while, amid the wailing sirens, occasional passing trucks, and the buzz of fighter planes, she realizes she can hear faint strains of music.

It's that song by Alicia Keys—"Fallin'"—and it seems to be coming from somewhere above.

Kristina's apartment? Allison hasn't heard music playing up there in months. Kristina said she can't even afford a CD player, and she's often mentioned that she doesn't like pop music. An aspiring Broadway dancer, the girl is obsessed with musical theater—she hums show tunes when she's doing laundry—when she's not talking, that is.

The music seems to be playing directly above Allison's apartment, but maybe not. Maybe it's coming from someplace else, and it's audible tonight because the city is so quiet, or because Allison's hearing is particularly honed.

In any case, she can hear it clearly enough to make out the soulful piano melody and hear the lyrics: *"How can you give me so much pleasure . . . and cause me so much pain . . ."*

When the song ends, it starts right up again—and then again, and again, finally lulling an uneasy but exhausted Allison to sleep.

"What do you mean you went over there, Jerry? Why would you do that?" Jamie paces, trying to absorb what Jerry is saying; what Jerry has done.

"She said she loved me. I just wanted to see her, and . . . and . . ." Jerry sobs. "I saw what you did. Why did you have to do that, Jamie?"

"You knew she had to be punished for what she did to you. I told you it was time to say good-bye."

"But I didn't know you meant . . . Jamie, she's *dead*."

"How did you get in and out of the apartment, Jerry?"

"She's dead . . . I didn't want her to die."

"Stop your blubbering."

"I can't. I'm sad."

"You're going to be a lot more than sad if you don't listen to me carefully. Tell me how you got in and out of the apartment when you went over there."

"With my key."

"Jesus, Jerry . . . You shouldn't have done that."

"Why not?"

"Did you forget about the surveillance cameras?"

"Yes! I forgot! Did you forget, too? What if there's a picture of you?"

"I went in and out through the fire escape window. There's not a picture of me . . . but there's going to be a picture of *you*. Dammit, Jerry."

"I'm sorry," Jerry sobbed. "Why are you so mad?"

"Because when they find Kristina, they're going to look at that tape to find the killer, and they're going to see a picture of you."

"But that's okay, because I didn't do it."

"They're going to think that you did."

"I'll tell them that I didn't. And don't worry, Jamie . . . I won't tell them that you did. I can keep a secret. Mama taught me how."

I'll just bet she did.

But right now, Jamie has other things to think about. That video footage needs to be removed from the building.

Looks like there will be no rest tonight for the weary after all.

Chapter Five

Kristina?" Allison calls through the closed door and knocks, yet again.

Still no reply.

Inside the apartment, Alicia Keys is singing "Fallin'"—*again*. So the music was—is—definitely coming from here.

Something is wrong.

That was her first thought when she woke up a little while ago—after sleeping for a solid seven hours—to find the sun streaming in the windows.

Something is wrong.

Her gaze happened to fall on the business card on her nightstand . . . the card that reads *Two World Trade Center* . . . and the horror of yesterday's attack immediately washed over her.

Even as it all came back, she realized she could still hear the music coming from upstairs.

The same song—that's what has her feeling so uneasy. If it were just a radio playing, she probably wouldn't think twice. No one, however, plays the same damned song over and over again if everything is okay.

But everything is *not* okay—not here in New York City.

Allison knocks again, calls her friend's name again.

Is Kristina in there? Is she pushing replay every time the song ends?

That doesn't seem very likely—yet is it any more far-fetched than anything else that's happened in the last twenty-four hours?

"Kristina! Come on, if you're there, just tell me you're okay!"

As she waits in vain for a reply, she goes over the last conversation she had with Kristina in the laundry room the other day, trying to figure out if there's any chance she might have been in the towers yesterday, or on a plane.

Kristina mentioned she'd just started a long-term temp job. It's in midtown, though—not downtown. Allison is certain of it, because Kristina commented on how crowded the uptown trains had been during rush hour all last week.

"I just hope it gets better," she said, "because I can't stand and hold on to a pole all the way to midtown and back every day. If I could at least get a seat . . ."

Allison, who takes the same subway line, shook her head. "I wouldn't count on that."

"Well, hopefully I'll get back to waitressing soon. Or dancing—as soon as my leg heals and I can get back to auditioning. Because let me tell you, this rush hour subway schedule really bites."

"You don't have to tell *me*," Allison said with a grim smile.

At this particular moment, though, she would give anything to be on the subway, wedged shoulder to shoulder with hordes of fellow New Yorkers, riding to the office to begin a normal workday.

Instead, the city lies in smoldering ruins around her, thousands of its citizens murdered.

Is it possible Kristina Haines was among them?

She works in midtown, Allison reminds herself yet again. There's no reason she'd have been in the World Trade Center. Still . . .

Allison tried calling her friend before she came up here, and she actually managed to get through. The line rang, anyway. But only once, and then the answering machine picked up.

"Kristina, it's Allison," she said. "I'm just calling to check in. You know, after . . . yesterday. Call me as soon as you get this and let me know that you're safe."

She hung up, wondering if Kristina had a cell phone, and how she could find the number.

She went through the motions of an ordinary day, taking a shower, blow-drying her hair and pulling it back into a rubber band. She dressed in her softest, most threadbare jeans and an old T-shirt, finding a measure of solace in pure physical comfort—the only kind to be found on this grim day.

In the kitchen, she made coffee, poured a cup—and then let it grow cold on the counter as she paced in bare, still-sore feet. She concluded that she wouldn't be able to breathe easily until she knew that everything was okay upstairs.

Obviously, it isn't okay.

Staring at Kristina's closed door, she presses fisted fingers to her mouth, resting her chin on her palm, wondering what to do next.

Maybe she should go back down and get her key to Kristina's apartment. But it would be wrong, wouldn't it, to go barging in there?

Allison glances at the other closed doors in the hallway.

There are three apartments on every floor in the building. The tenants in apartment 5B moved out at the end of August and it's still vacant. But maybe the elderly woman who lives in 5C will at least know whether Kristina was home yesterday afternoon or evening.

Allison goes down the hall and knocks on that door.

No one answers.

She knocks again, waits another minute, and gives up. The woman's grown daughter visits every afternoon; she probably came yesterday and got her mother out of here. Especially if there was no power in the building.

A lot of people who live in the building probably stayed someplace else last night, put off by the barricades and the soldiers and the dust and debris and smoke.

So then what am I doing here? Allison wonders as she turns away from Kristina's door.

The answer is simple. She has no place else to go.

Clearly, Kristina did. Maybe she left the music on before she left for work yesterday morning, and accidentally pressed the auto-replay button.

No—the power went out for a while after the attacks.

Well, maybe that triggered some kind of electronic problem with the CD player.

The CD player she said she didn't even have.

For some reason, the thought keeps nagging at Allison, and she's not sure why.

Aiming the remote at the television set, Jamie channel-surfs with one frustrated thumb click after another.

Wall-to-wall coverage of yesterday's attack, and not just on the local stations. But none of the networks—

not even the cable news—have been airing any of the graphic images anymore.

Yesterday, they showed it all. Yesterday, you saw raw footage of people dying right there in front of you, in real time, in real life—and then again, later, in endless recaps.

Today, though every channel is still playing and replaying the same scenes—the planes hitting the towers, the towers falling, the dust cloud chasing down and enveloping hundreds of people running for their lives—the blood and gore have been edited away, like a movie made suitable for a PG–13 audience.

Lame. That's what it is.

Jamie wants to see it all again—the jumpers falling through the air, the bloody pulverization on the sidewalks, the body parts . . . death. How glorious it would be to see death again, right up close.

But not just on television.

I want to touch death again. I want to make it happen again.

Jamie's hands itch with the urge to squeeze a knife handle, hard; fingers ache to dip into warm, sticky blood.

Jamie smeared it on the walls, the windows, even the ceiling. It was necessary to climb onto the bureau to accomplish that. From there, it was possible to see that tiny red droplets spattered all over the ceiling.

Her wounds had spurted blood that far. Impressive.

Even as a child, Jamie had wondered what it would be like to take a life. Practicing on Dumpster rats, and then stray cats—even a neighbor's pet dog—that was satisfying, at the time. But it was nothing like this.

Even that first human kill a decade ago—that wasn't

nearly as satisfying as this had been. That happened so quickly; it wasn't planned. And the second kill, a few weeks ago—it was planned, yes, but not like this.

Practice makes perfect.

Jamie smiles.

Making Kristina do things, and say things, and feel things . . . watching Kristina suffer . . . it was better, far better, than anything Jamie had ever imagined.

How long, with the city in chaos, will it be before anyone misses her?

That reminds me . . .

Jamie opens a drawer, pulls out a videotape, and puts it into the VCR.

It was pretty risky to backtrack to the scene of the crime last night to retrieve the surveillance camera footage, but it would have been even riskier not to. Thank goodness Jerry confessed what he'd done, or there would have been trouble. Huge trouble.

Now we're safe.

Jamie begins fast-forwarding through the footage, zipping past hours' worth of empty hallways, and then . . .

Movement.

Bingo. There's Jerry, walking into the building, his key ring in hand . . .

There's Jerry on the fifth floor, unlocking the door to Kristina's apartment . . .

There's Jerry, moments later, bolting from the apartment looking stricken. He races past the elevator to the stairwell . . .

There he is exiting on the first floor, and—

Wait a minute.

There's something else.

Someone else.

Jamie's eyes narrow on the figure waiting by the elevator. That's Allison Taylor.

It's obvious from the footage that Jerry doesn't notice her.

But she definitely notices Jerry.

Back on her own floor, Allison glances at the MacKennas' door.

Should she . . . ?

Yes. She should. It's the right thing to do.

She forces herself to walk over to the door, hesitates again.

What if the news is bad?

But what if it's not? At least she'll have some peace of mind about something on this awful day.

And if it *is* bad news . . . she'll have to hear it eventually. Might as well be now. Maybe there's something she can do to help.

As she knocks, though, she finds herself hoping no one is home. That way, she'll have done the right thing, but can avoid dealing with this right now.

She immediately hears a stirring of footsteps inside, though, and the door is thrown open.

Mack stands there, looking as though he's aged a year since she saw him smoking on the stoop.

He's wearing suit pants and a rumpled white dress shirt with the tie loosened around his neck—yesterday's clothes, Allison guesses, and knows that's not a good sign.

His face is drawn and pale. His green eyes are underscored with purple-black shadows, his cheeks and mouth with black stubble. His short dark hair is sticking up on top of his head in tufts. As if to demonstrate how it got that way, Mack shoves his splayed fingers into his hair and leaves them there for a moment, just standing there looking at her with his palm resting at the top of his forehead in a gesture of distracted dismay.

"I thought you might be . . . someone else," he tells Allison.

Carrie. That's what he thought. That's what he *hoped*.

Okay. Now she knows. The news is not good.

She clears her throat, trying to figure out what to say.

All that comes to mind is *I'm sorry*, but that has a sense of finality that feels wrong—unless he's heard for sure that his wife is among the casualties. If that were the case, he wouldn't have opened the door with such expectancy, or looked so despondent when he saw who was—rather, who *wasn't*—there.

"Do you want to come in?" he asks.

"Do you want . . . should I?"

He nods. "Sure. Please."

The last word strikes a chord, and her heart goes out to him. She'd assumed he was just being polite when he asked her in, but maybe not. Maybe he doesn't want to be here alone.

She crosses the threshold. He closes the door after her.

All this time living across the hall, and she's never been inside this apartment. Mrs. Ogden kept to herself, and so far, so have the MacKennas.

The layout is the mirror image of Allison's own place: a small entry area widens into a rectangular living room with a small kitchen alcove on one side and doors leading to a bedroom and bath on the other.

The furniture is IKEA bland—blond wood and beige upholstery, boxy lines. Allison's eye goes right to the lone splash of color: a red belted trench coat draped over the back of one of the chairs at the small dining table. She's seen Carrie wearing it on rainy days. She probably had it on Monday, the day before . . .

"I haven't heard from her," Mack says, and she turns her focus back to his weary face. "I keep wondering why. Some people she works with—she was on the 104th floor, I don't know if you knew that—some of them called their husbands and wives. She didn't call me."

"Maybe she tried and couldn't get through." Allison speaks in a rush, wanting—*needing*—to give him hope.

Even false hope?

She ignores the disapproving voice in her head. "The local lines were all jammed up. Is there someone else who might have heard from her? Someone outside the city, maybe?"

He's shaking his head before she finishes speaking. "She doesn't have anyone else."

That strikes her as an odd thing to say. Maybe he just means that Carrie is from New York City, and others she might have tried to reach would be here, with snarled phone lines.

But the phrasing—*she doesn't have anyone else*—it just seems so definitive, almost as though Carrie has no one in the world but him.

Almost like me, Allison finds herself thinking. *If I were in a life-or-death situation and needed to connect with someone, who would I call?*

I wouldn't call anyone—because I'm self-sufficient.

She's been taking care of herself for years—even when her mother was alive. She never had anyone to lean on, or depend on.

"I keep wondering what it means that I didn't hear

from her," Mack goes on. "Because she's always been a caller, you know? She'll call ten or twelve times a day. She likes to stay in touch."

He's thinking Carrie didn't survive the initial blast long enough to make a call.

Maybe that was a blessing, Allison thinks, remembering what she witnessed yesterday on television—all those people trapped in a towering torture chamber, people who concluded that jumping to certain death was the most merciful way out.

Allison thinks of her mother—of the choice Brenda Taylor made, seven years ago.

For the first time, she experiences a glimmer of an emotion other than the anger and disgust and pity that always accompany the memory of her mother's suicide.

Allison always thought of her as a coward, taking the easy way out. But maybe she was wrong. Maybe there is no easy way out.

"I made these . . ." Mack picks up a sheaf of paper and hands it to her.

She finds herself looking at a child's drawing of a stick figure man and woman. Puzzled, she looks up at Mack, not sure what to make of it.

"Oh, that—Not *that*." He snatches it away. "That's—my friend's daughter . . . she felt sorry for me, so . . . it's, you know, supposed to be me and Carrie . . ." He trails off, swallows hard.

Her heart goes out to him.

She looks down at the paper now on top of the stack. It's a photo of a woman beneath the bold black word "MISSING."

"Do you think it looks enough like her?" Mack asks.

She knows the image is of Carrie, of course—her

name, "CARRIE ROBINSON MACKENNA," is right beneath it—but it obviously wasn't taken recently. It doesn't look much more like her than the little girl's crayoned drawing, with its smiling mouth and lemon yellow hair.

But Allison assures Mack that the photo is fine, wondering if it even matters anyway.

If Carrie was at work on the 104th floor of the first tower that was hit, and the plane struck the building a few floors beneath her, then how would she have gotten out? The stairways must have been blocked by that massive fire. All those people jumping, falling . . . they wouldn't have been doing that if there was any other way out.

"I have to go put up these fliers," Mack says. "I already did a bunch last night—this morning, really—but then I thought I should come back home to see if she was here."

"Maybe she was here earlier, and then she left and went looking for you."

"No. She wasn't home. If she had been, she would have changed her clothes, or . . ."

"Maybe she didn't want to—"

"No," Mack cuts in sharply, "if she'd been here while I was gone, I'd know it."

"Maybe—" Seeing the look on his face, Allison clamps her mouth shut. She hates herself for needing to deny out loud what he must already know, and has maybe even accepted.

But, having stepped into the middle of a virtual stranger's tragedy, she can't seem to help herself. For some reason, she's compelled to keep dangling useless lifelines before Mack—like tossing a length of sewing thread to a drowning man-overboard.

He takes a deep breath and says flatly, "Carrie left for work yesterday morning, and she never came home. Period."

He's trying to convince himself of that, Allison finds herself thinking, *as much as he's trying to convince me.*

God knows it's probably true, and yet . . .

It's almost as though he's trying to make this harder on himself, even, than it has to be.

She remembers yet again how he was sitting alone outside the other night, seemingly troubled. Maybe he'd had a fight with his wife. Maybe he's feeling guilty now, on top of everything else.

Whatever the case, he's on the verge of falling apart, poor man.

She feels oddly tempted to reach out and put her arms around him.

You can't do that. You barely know the guy.

Does it even matter, though, at a time like this?

In a crisis of this magnitude, the usual boundaries come down—it's like she and Mack are shipwrecked, with nowhere else to go and no one else to count on.

Allison reaches toward him, yet can't quite bring herself to touch him. Instead, she holds out her hand, palm up. "Listen . . . why don't you give me some of those fliers? I can take them out and put them up in the neighborhood."

"You don't have to do that."

"I want to." For all she knows, he's completely cut off from his usual support system. "Do you have anyone else . . . helping you? Friends? Family?"

"My friend Ben was with me all yesterday and last night, but he had to go home and get some sleep. My sister called a few times, but she lives out in Jersey. She said she'd come into the city, but . . ."

"You should let her. I'm sure she wants to be with you."

Mack shakes his head. "She's a single mom, and her kids are scared—so is she, I think. She's better off at home."

"Is she your only family?"

"She's the only one I'm really close to anymore." He yawns deeply, covering his mouth with his hand. "Sorry."

"Did you sleep at all last night?" Even as she asks the question, Allison remembers what he said about having insomnia.

If he couldn't sleep before all this, how is he ever going to sleep again?

"No, but I'm fine. I just made coffee." Mack gestures toward the kitchen.

From here, Allison can see the clean, empty glass carafe sitting on the coffeemaker's burner. A can of grounds is out on the counter, a silver measuring scoop and stack of white paper filters beside it.

"I don't think you did," she tells Mack.

"What?"

"I don't think you made the coffee."

He distractedly follows her gaze. Again, his fingers rake through his hair, and his palm comes to rest on his forehead. "I could have sworn . . . I'm losing my mind. I keep forgetting things."

"That's understandable. You're exhausted."

"Story of my life."

"Maybe, but . . ."

"I know. This is different. I can't believe this is happening."

For a moment, they're both silent.

"Listen, I'm pretty sure I actually *did* make coffee a little while ago . . ." Allison offers Mack a tight smile, and is gratified when he returns it. "Why don't you come across the hall and have some? Then you can come back here and rest and I'll go hang up fliers for you."

"But what about . . . don't you have someplace else to be? Work, or something else you have to do?"

She shakes her head. "Not today. Today is . . . the city is at a standstill."

"But you don't have to—"

"Look, it's fine. Please just let me help you. And you know, I heard yesterday . . . there are people in hospitals all over the city, and in Jersey . . . maybe Carrie—"

"I know. I've been checking. I'll keep checking. Maybe."

He picks up his keys and cell phone and follows her across the hall.

"Are you limping?" he asks.

"It's just blisters on my feet. I'm fine."

As Allison unlocks her door, she remembers why she left her apartment in the first place. Turning to Mack, she asks, "You haven't heard from Kristina, have you? From upstairs?"

"No. Why?"

Remembering her suspicion that there might have been something going on between Mack and Kristina, she chooses her words carefully. "She's not . . . around."

If he'd been involved with Kristina, surely he'd already have checked in on her, but clearly, this is news to him.

Allison watches him digest the information. He looks troubled—but not distressed.

"She works in midtown, though," she quickly adds. "I'm sure she's fine."

She isn't sure of anything, but Mack's wife is missing and that's all he needs to worry about.

* * *

Mr. Reiss usually calls in the mornings to tell Jerry which buildings he needs to visit that day and what to do when he gets there.

Today, he didn't call.

Jerry waited a long time, wondering what to do. He kept thinking about this burned-out bulb in the third floor hallway of the four-story building on Greenwich Street. He decided he should just come and fix it.

Now, standing on a stepladder, he feels a sense of accomplishment. He untwists the broken bulb, stashes it in his tool belt pouch.

At least there are some things in this world that can be fixed right now.

When he thinks of the mess they made downtown . . .

Who's going to clean it all up?

How is it ever going to be the same?

It's not. It's not going to be the same.

When he got on the subway at Times Square to come down here, the train took a long time to arrive and when it did, it was almost empty. It made a couple of stops, then came to a complete halt, and there was an announcement Jerry couldn't understand. That's how it always is on the subway. You can't hear what they're saying.

Some people left the car, but Jerry stayed there until a policeman came and told him to get off.

"But I have to go to work."

"You'll have to walk from here," the policeman said. "This is the last stop today."

You always have to do what the police tell you to do. That's the law. Mama taught Jerry that years ago.

So Jerry got out, and he walked.

At Fourteenth Street, there were more policemen,

and soldiers, too, with guns. They wouldn't let him go past at first.

"We need your ID," they kept saying, but Jerry didn't know what that was. They kept asking questions he didn't know how to answer, and he got confused and scared.

Finally, he started crying. "I'm going to be late for work, and I'm going to be in trouble."

"Just let him go through. Can't you see he's a retard?" one of the soldiers said. "He's not going to hurt anything."

Retard—Jerry's heard that word before. The kids used to call him that in school, and they hurt him almost as badly as Mama did. With their words, though, not their hands.

"I'm not a retard," Jerry muttered as he walked all those blocks down to Greenwich Street. "I'm *not* a retard."

He's smart. He knows how to get around the city and how to find his way to work and back. He learned a long time ago to always look for the twin towers to get his bearings when he comes out of the subway. Wherever they are, that's downtown. South.

When the subway is up and running again, how is he ever going to figure out which way to go when he comes out onto the street?

Now he'll never know which way to turn. He's going to get lost.

But he shouldn't think about that now. He shouldn't think about anything that makes him feel sad or bad.

Maybe he should turn off the music. He's wearing his Walkman, playing the CD that has his favorite song, the one that reminds him of Kristina.

Now that she's gone, it makes him a little sad. He still

likes hearing it, though, especially now that he knows she loved him back. She said so.

That's why it's such a shame that Kristina had to die.

But she was so mean to him—she'd made him cry, and Jamie said she had to be punished for that.

Jamie was right.

Mama always said the same thing. She would say that if you do something wrong—especially something that causes someone else to suffer—then you have to pay the price.

Jerry sighs. It's always been that way. It was like that long before Jamie came—which was the same day Mama left.

One morning, he woke up and she was gone, and Jamie was there. He hasn't seen Mama since.

Jamie reminded Jerry that Mama had decided to move away.

"Remember, Jerry? She told you she wanted to go live far, far away from here. Across the ocean. Remember?"

Jerry didn't remember, at first. But Jamie kept reminding him of it, until finally he remembered. Mama had moved away, and she had arranged for Jamie to come take care of him. Yes. That's right. That's how it happened. He just forgot.

As he looks down to grab the new light bulb he carefully balanced on the nearest rung, he's startled to see someone standing at the foot of the ladder.

Grabbing the light bulb just before it falls, he manages to steady himself and the ladder. He rips off his headphones and looks down again.

The person is a woman, and she says, "I'm so sorry!"

In the shadowy hall, she looks like Kristina.

Well, maybe not her face. But she does have curly hair, kind of like Kristina, though hers is a reddish color. She's a bit heavier-set, and she has large breasts. He can see the curve of them from here—can see right down inside her V-necked T-shirt.

"Are you the maintenance man?" she asks, then mutters, "Of course you're the maintenance man. Why else would you be standing on a ladder fixing a light?"

Is she talking to Jerry? "I don't know," he says, just in case.

"You don't *know* if you're the maintenance man?"

"No, I am. But you asked why else I would be—"

"Oh, right." She nods her head really fast, and Jerry, with interest, watches her breasts jiggle. "Never mind. What's your name?"

"Jerry."

"Jerry. I'm Marianne. I just moved into the back apartment on the second floor. When you're done with that, can you please come down? I have a couple of things I need help with."

"What things?"

"One of the windows is stuck, and I need to get it open because they just redid the floors and the fumes are pretty bad. And there's something wrong with my stove. I think the pilot light is out, and I'm afraid I'm going to blow up the whole building—"

She catches herself. Clapping a hand over her mouth, she blocks Jerry's view inside her shirt.

"I keep forgetting," she says, after a few seconds, uncovering her mouth, opening up the view again. "About . . . you know. What happened yesterday."

"It's terrible. It's a mess. It's sad."

"Did you . . . know anyone?"

"Anyone . . . ?"

She hesitates, rephrases the question. "Is everyone you know okay?"

"No," Jerry tells her desolately, thinking about Kristina.

"I'm sorry."

He nods. He's sorry, too. So sorry. He feels bad it has to be this way.

And that's strange because *Jamie's* the one who did the punishing. Not Jerry. And Jamie doesn't feel bad at all.

"No one talks to you that way," Jamie told Jerry this morning. "No one treats you that way, giving you the finger. No one makes you cry. She got what she deserved, after the way she treated you."

Jamie is right, Jerry thinks as he threads the new light bulb into the socket.

Kristina got what she deserved. But Jerry is going to miss her.

He gives the bulb a final twist and suddenly, the hallway is illuminated.

He looks down to see Marianne still standing there. Wow—she's pretty. Even prettier than he thought.

"So can you come down to my place after this?" Marianne asks, smiling up at him. She has a nice smile.

"Sure I can," Jerry tells her, and pushes Kristina from his mind like a visitor who's overstayed her welcome.

"Kitty?" Vic calls, stepping into the house. "Kitty, I'm home."

He hears her running footsteps overhead. "Up here, Vic!"

She appears at the top of the stairs—beautiful, familiar Kitty. She's wearing a navy sweat suit that bags on her slender frame, and glasses instead of contact lenses. Her short, dark hair could stand to be combed, and she's makeup-free—unusual for the middle of a weekday afternoon.

It isn't like his wife to look so thrown together. The last thirty hours have taken their toll.

She flies down the steps and into his arms.

Given everything he's done and seen over the years, it takes a lot to break him down. But right now, as he holds his wife tightly against him, Vic is on the verge of tears. There's a cannonball of an ache in his throat, and swallowing only makes it worse. He doesn't dare try to speak just yet.

Kitty pulls back to look up at his face—damage assessment.

But of course he's fine, physically. He was in his office at FBI headquarters nearly forty miles southwest of Washington—and the Pentagon in Arlington—when yesterday's events unfolded.

"Have you eaten? Are you hungry?"

"No."

"No, you haven't eaten, or no, you aren't hungry?"

"No to both." He's just spent a grueling twenty-four hours poring over flight manifests and working to create profiles of the hijackers. Food is the furthest thing from his mind—along with sleep. He has a feeling it's going to be a while before he has time for either.

"I only have a minute," he tells Kitty. "I just have to grab a couple of things, and I wanted to see you before I go."

She nods. Though they've only spoken sporadically since yesterday—basically just long enough for her to assure him that she and all four of the kids are safely accounted for—she's been an FBI spouse long enough to know that he won't be hanging around Quantico—

much less their townhouse—any time in the near future.

"Florida?" she asks, obviously having kept tabs on the investigation. They've tracked several of the hijackers to flight schools down south.

"New York."

"New York." She takes a deep breath, exhales through puffed cheeks. "Any word on John or Rocky?"

Vic shakes his head, tries to swallow past the cannonball in his throat. Rocky's wife answered Vic's e-mail yesterday afternoon saying that he was safe. But O'Neill was reportedly at his post in the World Trade Center when the building came crashing down.

"Rocky wasn't down there, but John's missing," Vic tells Kitty thickly. "I talked to him on the phone Monday night. Did I tell you that?"

"No. What did he say?"

Vic thinks back to that last conversation; remembering how they talked about Vic having just turned fifty, and John facing the same milestone in just a few months.

He didn't make it.

O'Neill's death hasn't been confirmed, and his body might never be found, but a telltale emptiness swept through Vic yesterday morning when he watched the towers fall. He knew in that moment that his friend was gone—and in the next, as the room full of FBI agents exploded into a fresh frenzy, that he couldn't afford the luxury of grieving the loss.

The work has to come first right now. Hell, the work always comes first.

What if, God forbid, it had been his wife or his kids in those buildings or on those planes? Would he be expected to compartmentalize his feelings and carry on?

Probably.

And I'd do it.

Annabelle did.

No one had even been aware until yesterday that she had a fiancé. An army major who worked at the Pentagon, he's now gravely injured at the Burn Center at Washington Hospital Center.

Annabelle has been stoic and efficient as always.

"Vic?" Kitty touches his sleeve, and he looks at her, caught off guard, again, by her uncharacteristic washed-out appearance.

They've been together for thirty years. Most of the time, he's convinced she knows what he's thinking. Sometimes, he hopes that she doesn't.

"I have to go," he tells her gruffly.

"I know you do. Please be careful."

She says it every time he leaves.

"Don't worry," he always replies.

Not this time. This time, the cannonball is clogging Vic's throat so he just nods, and goes upstairs to get his things.

Despite two cups of black coffee—Allison brews it good and strong, just the way he likes it—Mack is starting to fade quickly. Sitting on her couch in front of the endless breaking news reports, holding the sandwich she insisted on making for him, he tries to restrain another deep yawn.

"You should sleep."

He looks up to see her watching him, again sitting in the chair opposite the couch. Like a butterfly, she tends to alight for a minute or two, then flutters off again to accomplish some other task: making the sandwich, refilling his cup, watering her lone plant, washing out the coffee carafe . . .

Maybe she's uncomfortable having him here. Or maybe she just likes to stay busy—one of those people with a lot of nervous energy to burn.

She's so different from Carrie, who always spent so much of her time at home sitting, very still, lost in thought.

When they first met, that made Mack uncomfortable. He'd struggle to think of things to say, trying to draw her out. Sometimes he was rewarded; most of the time, he was not.

Eventually, he learned to just let her be, but he never stopped wishing there was a way to make his wife more . . . less . . .

Hell, he doesn't even know *what* he ever wanted from Carrie.

But yesterday morning, when he was lying there pretending to be asleep, and she was getting ready to leave for work, he realized what he *didn't* want.

He didn't want to talk her into becoming the mother of his child. Even if he could get her to change her mind about what she'd said . . .

It wouldn't be right.

She was not equipped—not at this stage in her life, anyway—to devote herself wholly to another human being. Not Mack himself, and not a baby.

Every child deserves a mother who will provide unconditional love and nurturing. He won't provide his own child with anything less.

"Why don't you just put your feet up and lean back for a while?"

Allison's voice drags Mack's thoughts away from Carrie.

He's grateful for that. He doesn't want to keep remembering what happened with his wife yesterday morning.

Allison turns off the television. "I'm sorry, but . . . I can't watch any more of this. They're not saying anything new right now, and they keep showing . . ."

"I know." He shrugs. "I feel immune to it now."

They both fall silent.

"Do you hear that?" Allison asks after a moment.

"Hear what?"

"The music coming from upstairs. I forgot about it, but now that the TV is off, I can hear it again."

He listens and nods, hearing faint strains of an Alicia Keys ballad.

Allison frowns. "I hope she's okay—Kristina, I mean."

"I hope so t— Wait a minute. She told me about a million times that she doesn't even have a CD player."

"She told me the same thing."

"Why would she say that if it wasn't true?"

"Who knows? Maybe she's a compulsive liar."

"Or maybe the music is coming from the television."

"Same song over and over?"

"Okay, maybe she went out and bought herself a CD player," Mack says reasonably, and sets the sandwich plate on the coffee table between a stack of fashion magazines and a stack of flyers.

He can't bear to look at Carrie's face staring up at him from beneath the word "MISSING." He turns his head to avoid it and finds himself locking gazes with Allison.

"I'll go put those up," she tells him. "You can go lie

down, or just stay here if you don't want to be . . . you know, there."

"You don't have to put them up," he says, "and I don't mind being . . . there."

But the truth is, he does. He doesn't want to be home, alone, thinking about what happened to Carrie.

It's strange to be here though, too, isn't it? Just sitting here in unfamiliar surroundings on a weekday afternoon with this barefoot blonde who popped up out of nowhere, offering to help . . .

He'd chatted with Allison in passing around the building. She was hard to miss, with her striking looks and lanky build made taller by the high-heeled shoes she was always wearing.

Only the other night, though, when he was sitting outside and she stepped out of that cab, did they have a real conversation. He can't even remember much of what they talked about, but he knows he connected with her on some level.

Oh hell. Maybe he was flirting. He'd had a drink—two—and he was pissed at his wife, and—

And let's face it, Allison is beautiful.

But of course he wasn't going to do anything about that.

He still isn't. He's just here because . . .

"Any port in a storm."

He looks at Allison in surprise, wondering if she somehow read his mind. "What?"

"Haven't you ever heard that saying? Any port in a storm," she repeats. "It means when you're in real trouble, you accept the help you're given, even if it's not what you'd have chosen."

He finds himself smiling faintly. "So are you the port? Or is your couch the port?"

"The couch is the port for you right now. Go ahead, lie down and rest for a while."

Carrie wouldn't have liked this, he finds himself thinking. She always felt threatened by other women, though he'd never given her reason to think he might stray.

He wouldn't. Of course not. But sometimes, when he looks at other women, talks to other women, he wonders what his life might be like had he made a different choice.

Kristina Haines—with her dark curls and brash personality—reminds him of his college girlfriend, Sheryl. Whenever he's talking to Kristina—which is quite often, because he's always running into her around the building and she's quite the sparkling conversationalist—he thinks about Sheryl, wondering about the road not taken.

Now, with Allison, Mack finds himself doing the same thing, God help him. *Carrie's* the one he should be focused on right now. After what happened . . .

What kind of man am I? How am I ever going to live with myself?

Allison picks up the sheaf of flyers from the table. "I'm going to go put some bandages on my blisters, find some comfortable shoes, and go out and take care of these." If Carrie were here, she'd be sizing up Allison, wondering why she's being so nice.

But if Carrie were here . . .

Then I wouldn't be.

No, Mack wouldn't be here with Allison, letting her feed him and help him.

He keeps protesting, but the truth is, he needs her. Well, he needs someone—and right now, she's the only one around. It's that simple.

* * *

Out on the street, carrying the flyers and a roll of masking tape, Allison takes a deep breath.

Her lungs fill with putrid air; air that reeks of smoke and metallic industrial fumes laced with the stench of burning rubber—like a spatula that's melted against the dishwasher's heating coil—and, perhaps, with burning flesh.

She doesn't know what that smells like. But all those people who died yesterday disappeared into thin air . . . this air. The air Allison is breathing.

Trying to shut out macabre thoughts about microscopic particles that might be invading her lungs, she begins walking down the deserted block. There are parked cars along the curb, but there's no traffic; there are no pedestrians; there is no distant rumbling of a subway train passing underground.

In the distance, she can hear sirens, and it occurs to her that they might have nothing to do with what happened yesterday. It's too late for that. But the world is still turning; people are out there living and dying the way they always have been.

But maybe Allison was wrong yesterday. Maybe the optimistic young woman who had just spent a magical evening at an opulent fashion designer party is gone forever. She didn't burn alive in the jet fuel fireball or disintegrate in the mountain of debris when the towers collapsed, but like all the other lost souls—*hundreds? thousands?*—Allison Taylor, the Allison she used to be, did not survive the attacks.

Nor did New York itself—*her* New York, a glittering playground for beautiful people. It's as if the city— *her* city—has been transformed into the dust-layered, debris-strewn landscape of a distant planet, populated by wide-eyed, shell-shocked mortals.

She sees more and more of them as she walks a couple of blocks over to Broadway and turns north. People are out on the streets, but they aren't in a perpetual hurry, as New Yorkers tend to be. They're wandering, loitering, standing, staring.

Staring at the smoke still rising from lower Manhattan; staring into the pages of the *New York Post*, with its black headline that reads *ACT OF WAR*; staring at the faces that gaze out from a litter of missing flyers like the one Allison is holding.

They're everywhere, the fliers. Hanging on buildings and poles and the blue plywood walls that shield construction sites. Hanging, some laminated and some not, around the necks of people themselves, like miniature sandwich boards.

Allison walks over to a shuttered deli whose fluted gray metal security gate is papered in flyers. She tapes Carrie's among them, then steps back to look at the tragic patchwork of names and faces.

Hearing a sob beside her, she turns to see a middle-aged Hispanic woman struggling to reach an empty spot high on the gate. In her hand is a homemade poster with a grainy photo of a smiling young man. It's written entirely in Spanish, but Allison took enough Spanish in school to recognize a couple of the words.

Mi hijo querido.

My dear son.

"Here," Allison says gently, "let me help you."

The woman looks up, her face etched in sorrow and bewilderment.

Allison gestures, and the woman, registering grateful comprehension, hands over the poster.

Standing on her tiptoes, Allison tapes it high on the gate, between a photo of a tanned, smiling twenty-odd-year-old woman grinning and brandishing a margarita, and a close-up of a proud new daddy gazing down at a swaddled newborn.

So many lives shattered, so many people gone forever.

"*Gracias*," the crying woman tells Allison.

"*Lo siento.*"

I'm sorry.

With a heavy heart, she starts to turn away from the wall—then turns back, having just caught a jarring glimpse of a familiar face in one of the posters.

It takes her a few moments to locate it again—a wedding portrait: glowing bride, grinning groom. He's the one Allison vaguely recognizes, but she doesn't place him until she reads the print below the photo:

William A. Kenyon, employed by Keefe, Bruyette, & Woods, last seen on 88th floor of South Tower. If you have any information at all please call wife Stephanie at 718–555–2171.

Wife Stephanie.

Nausea churns Allison's stomach.

Why don't you give me a call and we'll go out sometime? he'd asked that night in the cab.

She'd been pretty sure he wasn't her own Mr. Right—but it didn't occur to her that he might already be someone else's.

She looks again at the wedding photo, rereads the text below it. *If you have any information at all . . .*

For a brief, crazy moment, Allison considers calling Stephanie. She wouldn't tell her the whole truth . . .

No, she'd just say that Stephanie's husband had done a good deed and given her a ride downtown on what will most likely turn out to have been his last night on earth. She'd paint him as a Good Samaritan who took pity on a perfect stranger . . .

But maybe Stephanie wouldn't see it that way. Maybe she'd see it for what it really was—a married man bending over backward for a blonde in a short skirt.

Call me . . . Maybe I'll let you buy me a drink.

Rest in peace, Bill, she thinks, turning away from the poster and Stephanie's phone number. *Your wife has enough pain to deal with. I hope she never finds out what kind of man she really married.*

She rounds the corner and is startled to see that the people who are out on the sidewalks are all standing still, facing south toward the World Trade Center wreckage. Turning to look in that direction, she sees the red flashing lights of a police motorcycle escort coming up the avenue. It's moving slowly, in somber silence, leading a large truck—a refrigerated sixteen-wheeler.

"Bodies," she hears a bystander murmur, as others sob audibly and someone speculates that the truck is heading to the morgue.

Shaken, Allison watches it pass.

Then she goes back to traveling the bleak streets of this war-torn foreign city, putting up posters on every available surface, fitting them in like puzzle pieces among the others.

MISSING . . . HUSBAND . . . WIFE . . . FATHER . . . MOTHER . . . SON . . . DAUGHTER . . . BROTHER . . . SISTER . . .

So many lives shattered, Allison thinks again, so many people gone forever.

Yesterday, she was so sure she didn't know any of them personally.

Today, she found out that she did—to varying degrees.

William Kenyon.

Carrie Robinson MacKenna.

What about Kristina Haines? Where is she?

If she still isn't answering the phone or the door by the time I get back home, Allison decides, *I'm going to use her key and let myself in.*

Chapter Six

A re you *sure* you don't want me to come?" Lynn asks, and Mack clenches the cell phone hard against his ear, frustrated.

Lynn doesn't really want to be here, in the city. He knows it, and so does she. But her guilt—big sister guilt, Catholic guilt—forces her to keep telling him she'll be glad to get into her Volvo wagon and drive into the city to be with him in his time of need.

"I'm positive," he tells his sister yet again as he gets off the couch—Allison's couch.

He'd taken his shoes off and put his feet up, as she'd suggested before she left, but he hadn't planned on actually falling asleep here. The next thing he knew, his ringing cell phone woke him.

"You shouldn't be alone, Mack."

"I'm fine. Listen, you've got the kids to take care of. You don't need—"

"Dan would come over and stay with them," she cuts in. "He's not working today. All of his patients canceled their appointments. "

"*All* of them?"

"Do you know how many people are missing from there, Mack?"

There, of course, is Middletown, New Jersey, where Mack's former brother-in-law is a dentist.

And no, he doesn't know how many people are missing from that particular place, but before he can reply, his sister murmurs, "I'm sorry."

"For what?"

"For even bringing that up. Right now, I know, the only missing person who counts is Carrie."

Carrie. Jaw clenched, Mack paces across the living room in his socks. As Lynn talks on, doing her best to find hope where they both know there is none, he finds himself craving a cigarette.

Yes, he quit for Carrie's—and their future child's—sake, but when the pressure is on at work—or at home—he indulges in a pack of Marlboros.

The truth, though, is that there's not much pleasure in it anymore. Psychologically, he might still crave the experience, but physically, he's lost his taste for tar and nicotine. It's kind of sad, really. On some level he always thought of smoking as an old girlfriend waiting in the wings—something he could go back to, if he got really desperate.

Well, you don't get much more desperate than this, pal.

Mack busies his thoughts with random details—anything so that he doesn't have to think about cigarettes, or about his wife, about what happened to her.

He notes the view of the street from Allison's window, notes the significant amount of natural light in this apartment as opposed to his own apartment across the hall, notes the cozy, stylish decor straight out of a Pottery Barn catalog. He admires the richly textured fabrics in warm colors and the expertly distressed wooden furniture with contemporary Mission lines.

There are distinct decorative touches, too—baskets, candles, a vase of fresh flowers, albeit a bit wilted. On an end table, several oversized hardcover art books are held upright between a pair of granite bookends. The nearby bookshelf is crowded with an eclectic mix of titles from recent best-sellers to the familiar vintage butter-colored spines of the Little House on the Prairie books he remembers Lynn reading when she was a girl.

As she drones on in his ear, he looks around for framed photographs. You'd expect to find them scattered in a room like this, but there are none.

Well, the same is true in his own place. Naturally, Carrie has no snapshots of family or old friends, and she doesn't want Mack's on display, either. When they were first married, he stuck a snapshot of Marcus, the boy he'd once mentored through the Big Brother program, under a magnet on the fridge.

Marcus was in the army now, stationed in Europe, and he'd sent a smiling picture of himself wearing army fatigues. One day, Mack noticed that it had disappeared from the fridge. When he asked Carrie about it, she said she'd put it away.

"It's my kitchen, too," she said. "I don't want a total stranger looking at me every time I walk in there."

Last year, after Mom died, when he and his sister cleaned out their parents' house to put it on the market, Lynn took pretty much everything that had value— sentimental, or otherwise. She offered Mack every treasure they unearthed, but he kept shaking his head, saying there was no room in his tiny Manhattan apartment for any of it.

Not the cherry armoire made by Great-Uncle Paddy, or the lace curtains his parents had brought back from their first trip to Ireland, or his mother's antique bone china.

Certainly not the cherished, aging family dogs, Champ and Bruiser—the tail end, as it were, in a series of strays and rescues soft-hearted Mack brought home over the years.

Carrie didn't like dogs.

Well, she claimed she was allergic, but Mack never saw evidence of that. He noticed that on the rare occasions they visited Lynn, whose canine menagerie now includes Champ and Bruiser, Carrie didn't sneeze or wheeze. She just recoiled.

"Are you sure you don't want anything?" Lynn kept asking him that last day in Hoboken, and in the end he impulsively salvaged a stack of vintage ancestral photos from the wallpapered dining room wall.

"What are you going to do with those?" Carrie asked when he brought them home.

"Put them up?" Seeing her expression, he said, "No? Not put them up?"

"Not put them up."

"Why not?"

"I don't know—I don't want them around."

"But why not?" It was a typical discussion for them— her stubbornly ruling something out, him trying to make sense of her reasoning.

"I don't know . . . They're strangers. I'd feel like they were watching me."

"That's ridiculous."

"Maybe. But I can't help it."

"Is it that you don't have any pictures of your own?"

"No! Maybe it just seems too . . . you know, personal, to put all that stuff out there for anyone to see."

She was talking about the pictures, he knew—but Mack didn't miss the metaphor.

"Carrie was so strong, Mack," Lynn is saying, and he's jolted back into the conversation. "If there was a way out of there, she would have found it."

"You're the second person who's said that to me today."

"Said what?"

"How strong Carrie is." He clears his throat. "But some of that is just a front, you know, to hide her weaknesses."

There's a moment of silence on the other end of the line. "What weaknesses?"

Mack stops pacing. Maybe it's time to come clean—with Lynn, anyway—about Carrie Robinson's troubled past.

But before he can say another word, he hears a jingling of keys at the door. Allison must be back.

"I have to go," he tells Lynn as he hurriedly returns to the couch and sits. The furtive reaction is instinctive; he's not sure where it comes from. Maybe he doesn't want her to think he was snooping around her apartment.

"Wait," Lynn protests. "Just tell me what you mean about—"

"Later."

"But—"

"I'll call you back in a little while." He hangs up just as Allison opens the door.

Seeing him with the phone in his hand, she asks expectantly, "Any news?"

"No. That was my sister. Everything is status quo."

She doesn't look surprised. She isn't expecting him

to get any news, he realizes—not good news, maybe not even bad news. Nothing definitive. Not for a long time.

He thinks about the jet fuel that incinerated the top of Carrie's building and everything—everyone—it encountered. He thinks of the massive destruction downtown. It's going to take weeks for them to dig through it. Months, more likely. Maybe even years.

The families with missing loved ones are going to have a long wait before anyone confirms anything . . . but surely the truth is painfully clear.

"I checked the hospitals while I was out there," Allison tells him. Her mood is noticeably more subdued; he wonders how bad it was, out on the streets today. He doesn't want to know. Not yet.

"Which hospitals?" he asks.

"Saint Vincent's, NYU Medical, Bellevue . . ."

"She's not in any of them. I checked yesterday and I called earlier. I know they've identified most of the survivors who were admitted, and . . . the ones who didn't pull through, too. None of the ones who haven't been identified match Carrie's description, so . . ."

"That doesn't mean—"

"I know." He closes his eyes. "I know."

"At Saint Vincent's, they told me that they just opened a crisis center for Cantor Fitzgerald employees."

Mack nods. A company representative called his cell phone to tell him about it a few hours ago, right after Allison left. The woman said that Howard Lutnik, the head of the company, was expected to speak to the families there sometime this afternoon. He was out of the building yesterday morning, and so he survived.

How, Mack wonders, is he going to face all those people whose loved ones didn't?

"It's at the Pierre Hotel," Allison says, and then pauses.

Sitting there with his eyes closed, he can feel her watching him. He can't bring himself to meet her gaze.

"Maybe you should go," she says.

"I will. Just not . . . yet."

Feeling Allison's movement, Mack opens his eyes and sees her across the room, opening a desk drawer. After a moment of hunting through the contents, she closes it and opens the next one down.

"Oh—there it is." She pulls something out.

"What is it?"

"The key to Kristina's apartment. I'm going to go up and check on her."

When Marianne Apostolos asked the maintenance man to come into her apartment, she figured it would be a quick, straightforward process. He'd come in, he'd get the window unstuck, he'd fix the stove, he'd get out.

Nope. It took this guy forever to open the living room window, which had apparently been painted shut just before she moved in. He's been tinkering in the kitchen for a couple of hours now, and she's beginning to think either he's stalling, or he has no idea what the hell he's doing with the stove. He *did* seem a little slow— mentally slow, that is—when she spoke to him.

Or maybe he's just upset. Earlier, when she asked him if everyone he knew was okay in the aftermath of the attacks, he said no. He's probably distracted by his loss. Who wouldn't be?

She's got to give him credit for at least showing up for work on a day when most people—Marianne herself included—didn't bother. As an administrative assistant for a market research firm, she's not exactly essential personnel.

She's spent the day in her new, unfamiliar surroundings, trying to keep busy unpacking moving boxes, keeping an anxious eye on the clock as the afternoon wore on. She promised her mother she'd come over for dinner, because of course Ma doesn't want to be alone one minute longer than is necessary. She never does, but especially not tonight. She's freaking out about what happened yesterday.

Yeah—who isn't?

Marianne is doing her best to keep her mind off things, but it's not easy. Especially when the fighter jets buzz overhead and the faint smell of smoke is drifting in through the open windows.

She can't even close them, because the super had the hardwood floors refinished over the weekend before she moved in, and the place still reeks of varnish. It's better to risk breathing in a hint of smoke from the burning ruins downtown than to asphyxiate on polyurethane fumes, right? Even if it is a constant reminder of what's going on in this city.

At least she doesn't have cable installed yet, so she isn't tempted to park herself in front of the television news. Which is exactly what her mother is doing.

Ma keeps calling to cry about what happened, and to wonder what the world is coming to, and to tell Marianne to be careful.

"I'm always careful, Ma," Marianne tells her. "I've been on my own since I was eighteen, and I know how to take care of myself."

Funny—for years, she thought her mother did, too. After all, the woman had raised five kids, worked full-time as a seamstress at Bond's, and always kept things running smoothly in the same three-bedroom Broome

Street apartment where she's lived for more than half a century now.

But after Pop died last year, Marianne discovered that her mother is virtually helpless on her own. That's why she gave up her own apartment on the Upper West Side, to be closer—but not *too* close—to Ma, who expects her to come running for every little thing, as well as three check-in phone calls a day.

"Why do I have to call you so much, Ma?" Marianne asks—often.

The answer is always the same. "You need to make sure I didn't fall and kill myself. If I ever don't answer, you come right over here and let yourself in with your key."

"What if you're just in the bathroom?" Marianne couldn't resist asking.

"Better safe than sorry. That's why you have my key, and now I have yours."

Why, Marianne wonders, *did I let her talk me into giving her the spare to this new place?*

All she needs is for her mother to come over and let herself in without warning.

Ma doesn't know about Rae, of course. She's always asking when Marianne is going to find a nice husband and settle down.

Marianne used to toy with the idea of coming out to her family, but the older she gets, the more she wonders why she'd put herself—and them—through the heartache. They wouldn't accept her lifestyle, and that would hurt a lot more than it hurts her to keep certain things to herself.

"Listen, if you're so afraid of falling and killing yourself, Ma, you should stay off the stepladder," Marianne advised her. "No one your age needs to worry about dusting the ceiling."

She was wasting her breath, of course. Cobwebs are her mother's worst enemy.

"Why don't you just move back in with her?" George, the youngest of Marianne's four older brothers, asked, clueless about Marianne's lifestyle—certain aspects of it, anyway, that she might not want to share with their religious mother, anyway.

"Why don't *you* move back in with her?" Marianne shot back.

But of course, Ma would never let that happen, even if George were willing. She's always talking about how busy Marianne's older brothers are with their jobs, their wives, their kids. George and Marianne are both single, but as the only daughter, Marianne is the one who's expected to look out for her mother.

So, on September first, she moved out of her old place, dumped all her belongings in this new one, and then left with her girlfriend, Rae, on the weeklong cruise they'd planned for months. Early Sunday morning, as they sailed back into New York Harbor, a fellow passenger snapped a photo of the two of them on deck with the twin towers against a pink-streaked dawn sky in the background.

The next morning, Marianne brought the film to the one-hour development place near her office as Rae flew off to Denver on a business trip. She's there now, stranded indefinitely—but at least she's safe.

Marianne keeps looking at the photograph of her and Rae at sunrise just four days ago, the twin towers standing in the background like proud sentinels guarding the home port.

What if Rae's flight had been for Tuesday morning instead of Monday? What if she'd been going from

Newark to California instead of to Denver? What if, when she flies home, her flight is hijacked?

"Don't worry," Rae said when they spoke on the phone this morning. "I'll be fine. Nothing's going on here. I'm just worried about you in New York. Be safe. If anything ever happened to you . . ."

"Nothing is going to happen to me," Marianne promised her.

She sighs, using a box cutter to slit the packing tape on the bottom of the carton she just emptied. This one was full of books she's never had the time to read and will most certainly never have the time to read now that she's doubled her commute to her uptown office, but she carted them all to the new apartment anyway.

After flattening the box, she adds it to the growing stack on the living room floor, then sticks her head into the kitchen.

The large-boned hulk of a maintenance guy is kneeling in front of the open oven door. He's not tinkering, not even moving a muscle, just seems to be staring off into space.

Maybe he's thinking about whoever it is that he lost yesterday.

She clears her throat, and still, he doesn't move. She steps closer and realizes he's wearing headphones. They're attached to a Walkman clipped to his belt, and she can hear music coming from them.

She reaches out and touches his shoulder. He jumps, then sees her and pulls off the headphones.

"Sorry," she says. "Didn't mean to scare you again. I keep doing that to you, don't I."

"It's okay, Marianne."

Marianne?

Maybe she *did* introduce herself earlier, but it seems a little jarring that not only does he remember her name—she doesn't remember his—but he actually used it. That just feels . . . overly familiar.

Or maybe you're just overly touchy because he's a man. And you're not into men, and sometimes it bugs you when they're into you. Right?

Whatever. "Um," she says, "I have to be someplace by five, so . . ."

"I'm almost done."

"Are you sure?"

He nods vigorously.

She checks the clock on the stove above him. Oh, crap. "Listen, I have to go get ready right now, or I'm never going to get out of here on time, and then my mother will think something horrible happened to me."

"What? Why would she think *that*?"

Taken aback by his wide-eyed dismay, Marianne shrugs. "She always thinks that."

"But *why*?"

He's like a child, she realizes, suddenly feeling sorry for him. The world must be a hard place for a guy like this. A boy in a man's body.

"Never mind. It's just my mother. It's how she is. Aren't they all?"

He greets her forced smile with a troubled expression, and she wonders why the heck she's bothering to do all this talking.

Because even though you feel sorry for him, there's something about him that makes you nervous, that's why.

"I'm going to go get ready. Just finish up and let yourself out, okay?" She doesn't wait for a reply.

In the bedroom, Marianne closes the door, then, as

an afterthought, presses the lock button in the middle of the knob.

It pops right out again.

Dammit—she never noticed the lock didn't work when the Realtor took her through the apartment.

Maybe she should mention it to the maintenance guy while he's here . . .

But then, he's the *reason* she's locking the door.

Forget it. She lives alone; she'll never have any reason to use the lock after this. The sooner that guy gets out of here, the better.

She quickly sheds her T-shirt and jeans, changing into another T-shirt and a fresh pair of jeans. After running a brush through her hair and shoving her feet into a pair of sneakers, she grabs her shoulder bag and hurries over to the bedroom door. Throwing it open, she finds herself face-to-face with the maintenance man.

Marianne lets out a little scream. "What are you *doing*?"

"I'm sorry, Marianne."

"What are you *doing*?" she repeats.

"I'm finished. I fixed it for you."

"Good. Great. I told you to go ahead and let yourself out when you were done."

"Oh."

He doesn't move. Obviously, he wants something.

Her heart is racing. What if . . . ?

Oh! A tip. That must be it. For a second there, she almost thought he was going to make a pass at her.

She reaches into her bag, fishes a couple of dollars from her wallet, holds them out to him. "Here," she says. "Thank you."

"What is that?"

"It's a tip." *Isn't that what you were waiting for?*

He looks at it, then at her, bewildered.

What the . . . ?

"Thank you," he says after a moment, taking the money and putting it into his pocket. But he continues to stand there.

"Look, I really have to go."

"Do you like music?"

"Excuse me?"

"Do you like music?" He's fumbling with his Walkman. He pops the cover, ejects the CD, and holds it out to her. "Here."

"What is it?"

"Music. Here."

She starts to shake her head, but he's thrust the CD into her hand. "You'll like it. It's good."

"You don't have to—"

"I want you to have it. Okay?"

"But—"

"It's a present. From me."

She forces a smile. "That's very sweet . . ." His name . . . what's his name?

He knows yours.

Yes, and that troubles her.

"Cake," he blurts. "Do you like cake?"

"I don't know what you mean . . ."

"I want to have cake with you."

It's not a sly euphemism—not with this guy—but he is making a pass. Clumsily, and she doesn't want to hurt him.

"That's sweet, but . . ." She gives a little shake of her head. Ordinarily, she would just hint that she's not interested in men, but she's not sure he'd even grasp that concept.

"Or something else," he goes on in a rush. "It doesn't have to be cake. What do you like? I like hot chocolate. Do you?"

"I . . . I don't . . ."

"What do you like?" he asks again. Demands, really, and not only is she running out of patience, but he's setting her nerves on edge.

She glances instinctively at the apartment beyond his massive shoulders. Still not entirely familiar with the layout and traffic pattern, she wonders if she could make a break for it if she had to get away from him.

"I'm sorry," she tells him, "I really have to go now. My mother is waiting, and worrying . . ."

"Why?"

Oh geez. "I told you—she worries. I have to go."

"Wait . . ."

Please let me go. Maybe her trepidation is off-base, but she can't help feeling vaguely threatened.

"Do you want to go out on a date, Marianne? Please?"

She takes a deep breath. As gently as possible, she tells him, "No. I . . . can't."

He just looks at her, and the pain in his gray eyes makes her more sad than anxious.

"Please . . . ?" he asks in a small, pitiful voice.

"I'm sorry," she says. "It's just—"

He turns abruptly and bolts before she can attempt the explanation he wouldn't have understood anyway. She watches him open the door and disappear into the hall. She can hear his footsteps fading away.

Shaken, she goes over to close the door, and the footsteps stop abruptly. Realizing he's somewhere down the hall, she closes the door and dead-bolts it.

She's not going anywhere right now. No way. Not with *him* lurking out there.

* * *

Conscious of Mack's eyes on her as he sticks his feet into his shoes, Allison dials Kristina's number again. This time—having spent the afternoon breathing the stench of death in the midst of all those grieving New Yorkers—she doesn't really expect an answer.

Hearing a click on the other end of the line, though, she has a moment of false hope—then realizes it's a recorded voice.

"Hi, you've reached Kristina. Leave a message and I'll get right back to you."

"Hey, are you there? It's Allison, from downstairs. Call me when you get this." She hangs up the phone.

"Maybe she's screening," Mack suggests.

"I don't think so. I left a message yesterday. If she's there, then she would have at least called me back after she got it, to tell me she's okay."

"Are you sure about that?"

Allison shrugs. It's not as though she and Kristina are close friends—certainly not close enough for her to predict Kristina's reaction in these circumstances. But when things like this happen, you check in on your neighbors, right? Like she did with Mack.

"Well, I haven't heard footsteps up there," she tells him, "so I don't think she's home, but if she is . . ." She toys with Kristina's key. "I just want to know she's okay."

"If you let yourself into her apartment and she's not there, you still won't have an answer."

"No, but I might be able to tell if she came back yesterday afternoon before she left. Then I'll know she's all right."

"Yeah, well, what if she didn't come back? That doesn't mean something happened to her."

"I know. But she must have been back, because the power was out most of the day, and someone turned the music on."

It's the music that's bothering her, really. It's just out of the ordinary. She can't help but picture Kristina, all alone up there, playing the same song over and over in a catatonic stupor brought on by yesterday's horrific events.

That's better than thinking she might actually be a victim, of course. But still—

"Maybe there was an electrical surge," Mack says, tying his sneakers, "and the CD player went into some crazy looping cycle on its own."

Right. The CD player Kristina suddenly acquired since Sunday afternoon.

"I thought of that," Allison tells him. "At least I can turn it off so that I can sleep tonight."

Not that she didn't manage to sleep last night in spite of the music—and the day's drama.

But she'd had all that Xanax in her system. It probably knocked her out. Tonight, that won't be the case.

She shouldn't be talking about sleep, though—or the lack thereof—with Mack.

Heading for the door, she tells him, "I'm going to go up. You can hang out here for as long as you want."

"Thanks, but I need to get back home."

He follows her out. It probably should be an awkward moment, as they linger for a moment in the hallway between the doors to their respective apartments. Somehow, it isn't. They might have been virtual strangers less than forty-eight hours ago, but now they're friends. Friends who have been through hell together—and have yet to come back.

"Thanks for everything."

"You're welcome."

Mack unlocks the door, and Allison starts away, then turns back to call, "Let me know if you need anything later."

"I won't."

"You won't let me know? Or you won't need anything?"

Maybe he didn't hear the question; maybe he did and chooses to ignore it. Without answering, he disappears into his apartment and closes the door behind him.

She takes the stairs up to the fifth floor and knocks on Kristina's door.

Nothing but music from the other side.

"Kristina?"

No answer.

Allison puts the key into the lock.

"Kristina, I'm coming in," she calls. "I have your keys, remember? If you're there, and you don't want me to come in, just tell me."

Silence.

Allison turns the key, turns the knob, pushes the door open.

"Kristina? Are you in there? Kristina?"

She forces herself to cross the threshold. A few steps in, she can see that the bedroom door is open.

"Kristina?" she calls, walking toward it. "It's Allison."

She stops short.

And screams.

Chapter Seven

Yesterday, while dozens of his fellow NYPD officers were dying, Rocky Manzillo was in a Bronx hospital, sitting naked in a gown that tied in the back, waiting for someone to come shove a scope up his ass.

His wife, Ange, sat in a chair beside him, leafing through *Good Housekeeping* and occasionally complaining that there was no TV in the room. She never misses *The Today Show*.

"Can't you sacrifice Matt and Katie just once for the man you love?" Rocky asked her. "Look what I'm doing for you."

"You're not doing this for me. You're doing it for *you*," Ange said without looking up from the article she was reading. "You want to die, Rocco?"

"What kind of question is that? Who wants to die?"

"Colonoscopies save lives."

"Maybe," Rocky told her, "but as far as I'm concerned, colonoscopies are a real pain in the—"

"Give it a rest. It was funny the first time you said it, but enough is enough."

He fell silent, increasingly irritated by the way Ange licked her finger every time she turned a page, and brooding about the upcoming procedure. No, this sure as hell wasn't his idea.

There he was, sailing along, living life, feeling good, all three of his kids grown up and out on their own. Then he turned fifty, and suddenly everyone he knew was up his ass about his weight, his cholesterol, his colon—everyone was up his ass about getting something shoved up his ass. Everyone: Ange, Rocky's doctor, even his oldest pal, Vic Shattuck.

"Did you have that colonoscopy yet?" Vic asked Saturday night when they were having a whiskey nightcap after Vic's fiftieth birthday dinner down in D.C.

"Did *you*?"

"I just turned fifty. *Your* birthday was last spring, and Ange said—"

"Yeah, yeah, I know what Ange said. Ever since Katie Couric did that damned colonoscopy on the air last year, she's been after me."

"Who's been after you? Katie Couric?" Vic asked, deadpan.

"Yeah, me and Katie, we got a thing."

"She's cute—but can she make a decent meatball? Because Ange's meatballs . . ." Vic shook his head. "No one makes them better. Not even your mother."

"Don't ever say that to my mother."

"You think I'm nuts? I won't. I know your mother."

He sure does, and has for forty-five years. Rocky, Ange, and Vic started kindergarten at P.S. 77 in the Bronx together in 1955, and graduated James Monroe High School together in 1967. By then, Rocky and Ange had been going steady for two years. They were engaged in '68, but their plans were put on hold when Rocky was drafted. He got back from Vietnam in '72, and Vic was best man at their wedding the following year.

Now look. Fifty years old, all three of them. Graying hair, weathered faces, grown kids . . . stupid medical tests.

"Look, the colonoscopy is scheduled, okay?" Rocky told Vic. "For this Tuesday. So Monday, I don't get to eat anything at all, I get to drink down some stuff that'll make me shit my brains out, and then Tuesday I get to go to the hospital and someone's going to—"

"I know how it works, Rocky." Vic made a face.

"Yeah? You schedule yours yet?"

"Not yet. Tell me how it goes, and I'll consider it."

"It'll go fine. They're not going to find anything because there's nothing wrong with me and this whole thing is a waste of time!"

But when Rocky came to after the colonoscopy late that morning, he was sure he was going to eat those words. He could tell Dr. Lee was disconcerted when he came into the recovery room to talk to him and Ange, who'd been reading magazines in the television-less waiting room for the last two hours, her cell phone turned off in compliance with hospital regulations.

"Great news," the doctor said.

"I was out for a month and the Sox won the World Series?"

Dr. Lee didn't even crack a smile; it was as if he hadn't even heard Rocky's quip.

"Your colon is clear," he said simply, and briskly went over the report and showed them some pictures that made Rocky squirm. Then he said Rocky could get dressed, shook his hand and Ange's, and left.

"I really thought he was going to say he'd found something," Rocky told Ange as she handed him his gold wedding band, which she'd worn for safekeeping while he was under anesthesia.

"I thought so, too," Ange said. "He wasn't his jolly self. And even the nurse was acting funny when she came out to the waiting room to get me."

As soon as they got into the car and turned on the radio, they knew why.

Rocky's impulse was to get the hell downtown, but Ange, who was at the wheel, insisted he was in no condition—after all that anesthesia and two days without food—to go anywhere just yet.

She was right, of course.

She had been right, too, when she discouraged their three sons from following in their father's footsteps, as Rocky had.

That's how it works in this city, or at least in the blue-collar Bronx neighborhood where Rocky grew up and still lives. Sons follow their fathers into the NYPD or FDNY, whichever is the so-called family business.

Rocky's father and grandfather had been cops; he expected his own boys to join the force. But Ange insisted on sending them all to college first. The boys balked at that as much as Rocky did, but Ange was boss. They went away to school, even Donny, their youngest, who'd worn a toy police badge and gun belt for about as long as he'd been walking and talking.

One by one, to Ange's relief and Rocky's disappointment, their sons had broken with tradition and settled into lives that didn't revolve around law enforcement in New York.

Donny, the one who'd had his heart set on being a cop, grew his hair down to his ass, started a band, and plays the bar scene in Austin. That wasn't okay with Rocky until today. No one is flying planes into bars in Texas.

Unlike several of their childhood friends, especially

those who had followed their fathers into the FDNY, the Manzillo boys were all safe in distant states when the World Trade Center collapsed.

When Rocky got out of the car back at home after the colonoscopy, he was so light-headed he nearly passed out. By the time he'd finally pulled himself together and was feeling strong enough to head downtown, it was mid-afternoon. Before leaving the Bronx, he stopped off at his church, Our Lady of Mount Carmel, to light a couple of candles.

Over one votive, he prayed for all those lost souls, sensing—though he didn't yet know for sure—that some of his friends and their sons were among them.

Over the other, he offered a prayer of thanks. He might have been lost, too, had he not been at the hospital when the buildings collapsed.

That damned colonoscopy had saved his life—but not in the way it was intended.

At the precinct, he found a couple of cops holding down the fort. Everyone else, they told Rocky, was down at ground zero.

"What? Ground zero?"

"That's what they're calling it now."

"They, who? The press?" Rocky asked.

"Everyone."

"Not New Yorkers."

"*Everyone.*"

For some reason, that irked Rocky. Somehow, it felt like an admission that the terrorists had forever claimed a piece of New York. He vowed not to call it ground zero; he refused to think of it as anything but the World Trade Center.

"Anyone heard from Murph yet?" Rocky asked, wondering about his longtime partner T.J. Murphy, whose kid brother Luke is with the FDNY. The two forces—NYPD and FDNY—have had a longtime rivalry, but it's a friendly one where the Murphy brothers are concerned.

Rocky had been trying to call Murph, but his phone kept ringing into voice mail.

"Talked to him earlier. Luke's missing" was the chilling—and perhaps inevitable—answer to Rocky's question.

Murph had to be distraught. Luke was a good fifteen years younger. Murph was more father than brother to him, their father having died on duty before Luke was even born.

Rocky was a few blocks above the site, making his way south through a dust-shrouded ghost town littered with burned-out cars and abandoned ladder trucks, when sirens and unintelligible bullhorns erupted. A panicky wave of humanity surged toward him.

"What's going on?" he asked a couple of rescue workers who scurried past, wearing white facemasks and hard hats.

"Secondary collapse. They're evacuating. C'mon, you gotta get outa here."

Rocky turned and went north again. *Ran* north, remembering the billowing tsunami that engulfed this spot yesterday as each tower came down.

But this collapse, thank God, was nowhere near as devastating. This time, the office tower was half the size of the Trade Center towers, and there were no people in it.

Rocky waited for the all-clear with a group of fellow NYPD officers who had been down at the scene. They briefed him on procedures at "the pile," and told him what he could expect to find when he finally got there.

They also added scores of names to his running mental list of personal friends and acquaintances, all of them first responders, who were missing.

By the time the rescue operations resumed, Rocky had absorbed the barrage of new information. He steeled himself for what lay ahead, certain he was prepared.

After all, he's a homicide detective. On any given day, he anticipates coming face-to-face with the worst horrors imaginable.

But this . . . this was unimaginable; you're never prepared for something like this. It was as if Rocky's worst murder scene had collided with his experience in Saigon; civilians don't die by the thousands here in America on an ordinary Tuesday morning. Rocky had been drafted and plunged, without basic training, directly into the front lines of a vicious war.

This, like war, was hell.

This . . .

This was ground zero.

Two hundred and twenty floors of steel and glass, walls, doors, carpets, desks, computers, couches, files, paper . . . all of it had vaporized into dust and smoke drifting like mist in glaring searchlights.

Hundreds of volunteer medics were poised to tend to the survivors, undaunted by the lineup of refrigerated trucks that had dispatched soldiers carrying body bags. Those soldiers emerged in somber twos and threes carrying the bags between them, loading them onto the trucks for the long trip uptown to the morgue as the medics stood by, idle and helpless.

Flames burned undeterred by blasting fire hoses. Bulldozers and plows pushed at the mound and cranes lifted mangled chunks of building out of the way.

Power saws and blow torches cut at the mangled beams in an effort to gain access to the survivors who had been buried alive.

Barking rescue dogs nosed through the ruins; robots and cameras were lowered into dangerous crevices; firefighters and cops descended via ropes into the yawning pit to find only torn, burned, and dismembered bodies, emerging soot-covered and sobbing. Hundreds of firemen alone were among the missing. *Hundreds*. Thousands of civilians. *Thousands*. The numbers were staggering.

Someone handed Rocky a mask and he joined the bucket brigade. Tears ran down his face as he passed along heavy containers bearing chunks of concrete and insulation and tangled wire and twisted metal. Every bucketful of debris that was dug away from the pile increased the chances of finding someone . . .

Or so Rocky thought at first.

But as time wore on, he realized he was wrong; every bucketful seemed to drive home the futility of their efforts to save a life, even just one.

There were fragments of lives—shoes and desk photographs and computer disks and papers—and there were fragments of people. But not a single living soul emerged.

Everyone kept saying they just had to find the pockets where the survivors are buried alive, just had to get the fire under control, just had to stabilize the wreckage, just had to dig down deep enough . . .

Rocky talked the talk and walked the walk. But as the eerie, surreal night gave way to harsh daylight, and the dreadful day marched on toward darkness again, he gave up hope that anyone was going to come out of that smoldering tomb alive. The search, he realized, was fruitless, and yet it went on, because it was the only thing anyone could do. Search, and hope.

He looked everywhere for Murph, but didn't spot him. A few guys said they had seen him earlier, and he was, predictably, distraught. For all Rocky knew, Murph was still there on the pile somewhere, but the scene was just too chaotic to find him.

Then, out of nowhere, as the sun set over the dusty, smoky city, came the call that catapulted Rocky back to the real world; an equally grim, but infinitely more familiar, world.

There had been a homicide in his district.

A homicide? What the . . . ?

All in a day's work, but Jesus, this was no ordinary day.

In the wake of the mass murder of thousands of New Yorkers, crime was down, way down, all over the city. Hordes of Good Samaritans filled the streets; looters were nonexistent.

Yet someone had come into Kristina Haines's apartment and hacked her to death with a knife that might have come from her own kitchen, judging by the ransacked drawers.

It had happened sometime Tuesday night or early this morning—*after* the attack on the city.

It takes one sick bastard to steal yet another life— and in such a gruesome way—in the aftermath of a terrorist attack that killed thousands.

But hunting down sick bastards—this is Rocky Manzillo's specialty. This, he can handle. This murderer will not slip through his fingers. Few have, over the course of his career.

In fact, only one major case in recent history comes to mind—a perp Rocky privately dubbed the Leprechaun Killer. A young woman was killed in her apartment in the wee hours after Saint Patrick's Day by a man who followed her inside and was captured on the building's security cameras. The apartment was ransacked and it looked like a robbery, but the body was so hacked up that Rocky suspected there might be more to it. Either the guy hated this woman, or he was projecting his hatred for someone else. Rocky was even more troubled by an ominous clue that was found at the scene and never released to the press or the public: a green boutonnière. He suspected it was a serial killer's calling card and braced himself for another murder, but it hadn't happened.

Yet, anyway.

Eighteen months later, the Leprechaun Killer is still at large. The fingerprints that were lifted from the flower were run through the database and came back without a match.

But this new search, Rocky vows, will *not* be fruitless.

On a regular night, after working at the building on Greenwich Street, Jerry would take the subway back up to his apartment in the West Thirties. But this isn't a regular night, and when he gets to his usual station, the gates are closed and the globe light is red instead of green.

He stops, confused, wondering what to do.

"Station's closed," a police officer tells him. "Trains aren't running from here. Walk up to Union Square and get on there."

"I . . . I don't know how to go from Union Square," Jerry tells him.

The officer looks closely at his face. "Just ask someone when you get up there. They'll help you."

Jerry walks uptown. But when he gets to Union Square, he sees the barricades and the soldiers and the police officers, and he keeps going. They called him a retard.

"I'm not a retard," he mutters. "I'm not a retard."

He walks all the way home through streets that are mostly deserted and much too quiet. The quiet bothers him, but he can't listen to music on his Walkman the way he usually does, because he gave his CD to Marianne.

He wishes he hadn't done that, because she was mean to him.

And because music—like cake—helps to calm his thoughts, keeping his mind off things he doesn't want to think about.

Today, there are lots of things he doesn't want to think about. Like Marianne. And Kristina. And the airplanes crashing into the towers and making them fall, and the big mess that made. And Mama.

No, he doesn't like to think about her at all—even now that she's gone. When he thinks about Mama, he gets a scared feeling inside, like something is going to happen to him. Something bad.

It's dark by the time he reaches the big apartment building. The neighborhood is called Hell's Kitchen, but Jerry doesn't know why. The streets are lined with regular buildings and nothing reminds him of a kitchen or hell—not outside, anyway.

It's nice here. A lot nicer than where he and Mama used to live, up until a few years ago. That was in New York, too, but not Manhattan.

That was where Jerry met Mr. Reiss's wife, Emily—back in the old neighborhood. She was a nice lady with long brown hair and big brown eyes that reminded

Jerry of a doll he'd seen somewhere once, a long time ago; a doll in a frilly pink dress. Emily never wore a pink dress, though. She just wore regular clothes, and an apron, because she volunteered at the soup kitchen, handing out hot meals.

You didn't even have to pay for the food, and that was good, because back then, Jerry didn't have a job or any money.

He mentioned that to Emily one day, and she asked him if he would like a job.

"I might be able to help you out," she said, "if you're willing to work hard."

Jerry was excited. "I am! I want to be a fireman!" he told her, and she laughed.

"I don't know about that—but maybe my husband can give you some work. He owns some apartment buildings, and he always needs help. He'd probably pay you under the table, if that's all right."

"That's all right," Jerry said, though when he pictured himself and Mr. Reiss crouched under a table, he wondered why he would want to do that.

He was disappointed that he couldn't be a fireman, but he soon got over it. He felt important, going to work almost every day and getting paid.

It was funny, though—Mr. Reiss never paid him under a table, the way Emily said. He paid Jerry wherever he happened to see him, like in the hall, or out in front of the building, or in the boiler room. He would just reach into his pocket and he would count out some bills into Jerry's hand.

"You don't need money," Mama told him when he started working. "You don't even know how to buy things."

She was right, so every time Mr. Reiss gave him his

pay, Jerry gave the cash right to her. She saved it all up, and that's how they moved into this building.

Now, he puts the cash into a drawer so that Jamie can use it.

Jerry takes out his key ring. It's heavy. On it are keys to the building where he lives, and to all the buildings where he works, and to some of the apartments, too, in those buildings.

Mr. Reiss said he doesn't have to carry all those keys around with him all the time, but he likes to. It makes him feel good, knowing that he can unlock things whenever he wants to.

He just wishes he could use it to unlock the front door of his building sometime. It's supposed to be locked, but it never is. Jamie says the lock is broken. Jerry would fix it if he worked here, but he doesn't.

He walks through the unlocked door and is glad, as always, that he gets to use a key to open the metal box for the mail.

There are bills with Mama's name on them. Jamie takes care of the bills now that she's gone. Jamie takes care of everything.

Jerry walks to the elevator bank and presses the button, anxious to get inside and take off his shoes. His feet hurt from all the walking, and his head is starting to hurt again, too.

On his floor, Jerry unlocks the door and starts to tiptoe inside. Then he remembers. She's gone. He doesn't have to sneak in anymore, hoping she won't hear him and yell at him—or worse—for something he did or didn't do.

This apartment has two bedrooms—tiny, but Jerry has his own private space.

In the old apartment, there was only one bedroom,

and it was Mama's. There was nowhere for Jerry to go to get away from her, nowhere to hide.

In that apartment, he slept in the living room, on a pullout couch with big hard lumps in it and a bar that hurt his back. There were bugs, too, a lot more bugs than there are here. Sometimes he felt them crawl over his skin in the dark.

That terrified him. He hates bugs, all kinds of bugs—bugs that fly and bugs that crawl and even bugs that Jamie says aren't really bugs, like worms and spiders.

Some nights, when Jerry was young and living in the old apartment, he was too uncomfortable to sleep at all, and so he lay awake, afraid, until the morning light chased away the shadows and the bugs.

"I was there with you—don't you remember?" Jamie asks sometimes, but Jerry doesn't remember that.

Jamie tells him about things that happened to him in the old apartment. Usually, the things Jamie tells him aren't nice at all, and Jerry is glad he doesn't remember.

He likes to remember nice things—like Mama making cake. Mama made the best cake. Most of the time, she didn't let Jerry have a piece, but once in a while, she did. Sometimes, when she was sleeping, he even snuck some out of the kitchen. Just a little bit, so that she wouldn't know it was missing. He was careful not to drop any crumbs, not just because Mama would know, but because he knows now that bugs and rats like the smell of rotting food.

Mr. Reiss taught him that. He taught Jerry a lot of things, but not as much as Jamie taught him.

"Do you miss Mama?" Jamie asks sometimes, and Jerry wonders what would happen if he said yes. Would she come back?

He doesn't miss Mama. Mostly, he was afraid of her.

"I was, too," Jamie said. "I was always afraid of her."

"Did she hurt you, too?"

"Yes, but mostly, it was you."

"She still does. She hurts me a lot."

"No, Jerry. That's over. That's not going to happen anymore. She went away, remember? And now I'm here, and nothing will ever hurt you again."

"How do you know?"

"Because I won't let it. Just like when you were a kid, Jerry, and I would try to make sure Mama didn't hurt you. Don't you remember that at all?"

Jerry didn't. So Jamie told him all about it, about protecting Jerry when things got bad, and how one night, Mama hurt Jerry so badly that his head was smashed open, and Jerry started to remember.

"Is that why it always hurts me now?" Jerry asked, and Jamie told him that it might be.

"I went away after she did that," Jamie said, "because I was afraid she would do the same thing to me if she ever found me."

"Did she?"

"No. Never. But I found her," Jamie said darkly.

"And me."

"And you."

"Don't ever leave me again, Jamie."

"I won't. I promise."

"And if Mama ever comes back, you can make sure she doesn't hurt me."

"She won't be coming back, Jerry. I promise you that, too."

"But what if she—"

"Trust me. She won't."

Jerry hopes not. He really does.

Now, as is his new habit upon coming home, he walks over to her bedroom door.

Mama always spent a lot of time in her room with the door locked. Sometimes, Jerry would hear her talking in there, but he never saw anyone go in or out.

"Mama?" he calls, and knocks.

No reply from behind the door.

He tries the handle, just to be sure.

Yup, it's still locked, just the way she left it when she moved away.

Sometimes, Jerry thinks about trying to get it open, but Jamie told him not to.

"Why would you want to go in there?"

"It's probably dirty. I should clean it."

"It's not dirty. Don't worry about it, Jerry."

But Jerry worries, because there's a bad stink coming from Mama's bedroom, and he's afraid it will attract bugs and rats.

"Ms. Taylor . . . ?"

Seated in a small room at the local police precinct, Allison looks up to see a rumpled-looking, middle-aged man in the doorway.

He's wearing a dark tie whose point rides a good inch above his belt, and a dark shirt under a dark sport coat that, should he ever attempt to button it, would most certainly strain over his potbelly. There's about as much salt-and-pepper hair in his bushy eyebrows and mustache as there is on his shiny head. He has sharp, shrewd eyes, but they're not unkind.

"Detective Rocco Manzillo." He strides over, shows her a badge, shakes her hand.

A strong smell wafts in the air between them. The smell of smoke, and burning rubber, and . . .

And she doesn't want to think about what else.

"Were you down there?" Allison asks him, and he looks taken aback.

Maybe she was wrong.

But he nods.

Of course. The smell is distinctive, burned into her lungs and her memory.

"I'm sorry," she says, wondering how many cops were killed and whether he knew any of them. Every officer she's encountered today, both here at the station and back at the building, and even earlier, on the street, has been professional and efficient, but they all seem to have a vaguely preoccupied demeanor.

Detective Manzillo gives a weighty nod. "And I'm sorry about your friend."

Her friend. Allison swallows and clasps both hands, hard, around the paper water cup someone gave her earlier.

Kristina is dead.

Not just dead. Murdered.

Allison saw her there, on her bed, covered in blood . . .

She shudders, remembering.

"Ms. Taylor, I need to ask you some questions, okay?" Detective Manzillo is sitting across the table from her now, taking out a pad and pencil. With the thick accent of a native New Yorker, he launches into a series of questions, most of them routine—her full name, age, occupation, etc.

She already went through all this information with the other investigators, back at the scene. It's necessary, she knows, but exhausting to relay it all again; she's been answering questions from the moment she screamed and Mack came running.

He was the one who called 911.

Even now, she can't stop picturing the grisly scene as she numbly answers Detective Manzillo's questions, relieved he isn't asking anything that requires considerable thought.

Until: "When was the last time you saw Kristina Haines?"

She already discussed this with the cops at the scene. Ordinarily, she might have recalled it with ease days later, but too much has happened since that lazy weekend afternoon. Now, the details of her last encounter with Kristina lie almost out of reach beyond a yawning chasm, all but buried in the rubble of a seemingly distant past.

She clears her throat. "I saw her on Sunday afternoon."

"Tell me about it."

"There's not much to tell. I mean, she was in the laundry room, and I came in, and we chatted while we washed our clothes."

"About . . . ?"

"Oh God, I've been trying to remember everything she said. It was just small talk, really. We talked about her new temp job, and her commute . . ."

Detective Manzillo scribbles on his pad. "What else?"

"Um, we talked about how hard it is to find someone to date in this city, and—I already told the other police officers this—she mentioned that her ex-boyfriend had taken her CD player when he moved out, and she said she missed having music around. Did the other officers tell you that?"

"Yes. Tell me exactly what she said about it if you can."

She searches her memory and does her best to quote Kristina word-for-word, then asks Detective Manzillo, "Is there a CD player in her apartment now? I mean,

obviously, there must have been, because I heard the
music, but I didn't see one . . ."

I only saw her.

Covered in blood.

Dead.

"Yeah, there's a CD player. The song that kept playing in her apartment," Detective Manzillo says, "did
you recognize it?"

"It was 'Fallin'' by Alicia Keys. I know the song,
but—I mean, I'd never heard Kristina play it."

"Do you know if the song might have had any signifi-
cance to her?"

"I don't know. It's popular. I hear it all the time on
the radio."

He nods, scribbling on his pad. She notices that his
pencil point is worn down to a nub. That bothers her.
Some people can't tolerate fingernails on a chalkboard or
squeaking Styrofoam. Allison has always gotten chills
when the wood of a dull pencil scrapes against paper.

"Tell me about Kristina's ex-boyfriend."

She drags her attention away from the pencil. "His
name was Ray. I don't know his last name, but—"

"We've got it. We're already checking him out. Did
she have any contact with him lately?"

"Not that I know of. But I mean, it's not like I talk
to her all the time. We're just neighbors, really."

"Not friends, then?"

"Kristina is the kind of person who talks to everyone
about anything and everything, so . . . it's kind of hard
not to be friends with her."

She watches Detective Manzillo write something on
his pad. The damned pencil lead is almost flat. Fixated
on it, she shudders.

"How long have you known Mr. MacKenna?"

Startled by the shift in topics, she looks up. "A few months—ever since he moved into the building—I think that was May or June. But I didn't know him well at all until the last day or two." She explains about Mack's wife; about how she's been trying to give him support.

The detective writes it all down as if he's hearing it for the first time, but she doubts that's the case. The first officers to arrive at the scene separated Allison and Mack. They called for backup, then ushered Allison into her apartment to be questioned and Mack into his.

She has no idea where he is now. If they brought him down to the precinct, too, she hasn't seen him.

"How would you describe Mr. MacKenna's behavior today?"

"What do you mean?"

"You spent time with him this afternoon. How did he behave?"

Her temper flares at the absurdity of the question—unless no one told him about Carrie, which seems unlikely.

"You know his wife is missing, don't you?"

"I know. How did he behave when you were with him?"

"How do you *think* he behaved?"

The detective is silent, watching her, waiting.

"He was upset," she tells him, not bothering to hide her irritation. "That's how he behaved."

"Upset."

"Yes."

More silence. Clearly, he's waiting for her to elaborate.

"You know—upset—distracted, and worried about his wife."

"Did he mention Kristina at all?"

Grasping where he's going with this—*disturbed* and *perturbed* by where he's going with this—Allison shakes her head. "Mack never brought her up. I did. I was worried because I hadn't heard from her and I asked if he had."

"Why would you think he might have?"

"You mean why would he have heard from her? Because they're neighbors. We're all neighbors. You check in on your neighbors when something like this happens."

Something like this . . .

Nothing like *this* has ever happened before. Who's to say how people can be expected to behave in the aftermath of a terrorist attack of this magnitude? This is uncharted territory.

Which means you probably shouldn't assume anything, Allison tells herself. *About anyone.*

Earlier she had speculated that there might be something going on between Mack and Kristina. Now she wonders what Mack told the cops about their relationship and whether there was, indeed, anything to tell?

But of course, no matter what happened between them, he had nothing to do with her murder. Allison is a hundred percent certain about that.

A hundred percent? Really? Why? Because he seems like a great guy? Because you feel sorry for him?

What if her instincts about him are completely off?

For all she knows, he's a cold-blooded murderer in disguise.

A murderer whose wife happened to fall victim to a terrorist attack just yesterday? And then, what? He just snapped and killed his mistress?

Anyway, Kristina *wasn't* his mistress. Allison had

dismissed that theory when she got to know Mack today.

Yes, you know him so well. You got to know him in . . . what? A couple of hours in the middle of a crisis?

Assume nothing, Allison. If you've learned anything in the past few days, it's that nothing in this world is ever one hundred percent certain, ever.

"What did Mr. MacKenna tell you when you asked if he'd heard from Ms. Haines?" Detective Manzillo asks.

"That he hadn't. That was pretty much it."

"Pretty much?"

This guy is relentless.

Well, of course he is. That's his job. Allison wants him to do his job and find Kristina's murderer, doesn't she?

"That was it," she clarifies. "That was all he said about Kristina."

Although . . . was it? She thinks back, wishing she'd been paying more attention to the details. But her concern about Kristina wasn't exactly the primary topic of her conversations with Mack today.

"Was she seeing anyone now, do you know?"

"Seeing? You mean dating? I have no idea." Allison hesitates. "If she was, she didn't say."

"Then you never talked about your love lives?"

"No, we did. But there wasn't really anything to say."

He rests his chin on his fist and stares hard at her. "What is it that you're not telling me?"

Allison bites down hard on her lower lip to keep it steady and forces herself to look him in the eye as she shakes her head.

"Ms. Taylor, this is a murder investigation. You're a key witness."

Key witness to a murder, on top of everything else.

How much stress can she possibly handle before she breaks?

Come on, now, Allison. You've been through worse. Get a grip.

Worse. Yes. She's definitely been through worse. This wasn't like before, with her mother.

But then, she'd been prepared for her mother's death. And though it was hardly from natural causes, it wasn't at the hands of a homicidal maniac.

"You have an obligation," Detective Manzillo is saying, "to tell me everything you possibly can about what happened the last time you saw the victim, whether or not you think it's relevant."

"I know, I'm just . . . I'm trying to remember what she told me about her love life and how she said it, exactly."

"Do your best." His blunt pencil is poised over his notepad.

Looking away so that she won't have to watch him write with it, she recounts what Kristina said about married men being the only available guys in this city.

He nods, making lengthy notes.

Did she just incriminate Mack? In an extramarital affair, if not a murder? If something like that were exposed now . . .

She thinks about Bill Kenyon's wife, Stephanie; about how she was hoping, just a little while ago, that Stephanie will never find out about her late husband's roving eye.

She thinks about Carrie MacKenna. If it turns out Mack really was sleeping with Kristina Haines, and it all comes out in the aftermath of her murder, then it's a blessing that his wife will have died without knowing the truth.

You don't know that, though. You don't know that

there was an affair, you don't know that Carrie wasn't aware of it if there was one, you don't even know that she's dead . . .

You don't know anything, do you?

Detective Manzillo thinks she does, though. She can't even come right out and tell him that she honestly doesn't believe anything was going on between Mack and Kristina, because that will only confirm that she's considered the possibility. And then he'll think she's hiding something.

"Was anyone else in the laundry room while you and Kristina were there?" he asks.

"No. I was surprised about that, because sometimes all the machines are full and you have to wait, but it was nice out that day so people were probably out doing— Wait!" Suddenly, she remembers. "Yes, someone else was in the room."

Detective Manzillo regards her with interest, as though he senses she's about to reveal something important.

"The building maintenance man—he was there."

"In the laundry room?"

"Yes, and—oh my God, I can't believe I didn't think about this until now." Her pulse quickens. "He was in the first floor hallway, too, when I got home late on Tuesday night—or Wednesday morning, actually."

"You saw him there?" the detective asks sharply. "You're sure?"

"Positive. It was kind of dark, and I was a little bit out of it, but . . ."

"Out of it?"

Should she tell him about the Xanax?

No. He might discredit what she's saying, and she knows what she saw.

"I had just walked all the way home, and I was exhausted," she says, "and—you know, shell-shocked. Like everyone else."

"What time was it?"

She shakes her head. "I don't know. I'm sorry. Late. I didn't look at my watch that I remember, and when I got home, all my clocks were flashing because the power had gone out."

"Okay. What was he doing when you saw him?"

"He was on the first floor, coming out of the stairwell, and he went right out into the alley."

"Did he see you?"

"I don't think so."

The detective nods, writing everything down. "What's his name?"

"It's Jerry."

"What's his last name?"

"I don't know."

"Where does he live?"

"I have no idea. I'm sorry. He's just always kind of hanging around the building, fixing things. On Sunday, when we were in the laundry room, he was working on a washing machine but Kristina said she didn't even think it was broken."

"Do you think she was right?"

"I don't know—I wasn't really paying much attention to him, I guess. But Kristina mentioned that he gave her the creeps, and I did see the way he looked at her . . ."

"How?"

"You know—like he was interested."

"Leering?"

She considers that. "I wouldn't say leering. It was kind of more . . . I don't know, innocent. There's something wrong with him, mentally—he's kind of slow or something. More like a boy than a man, is how I would describe it."

"Is there anything else you can tell me about him? Anything at all?"

She searches her memory. "I can't think of anything— other than that Kristina thought he might have been responsible for the burglaries that happened over the last couple of weeks. Did you know about that?"

"Yes. Why did Kristina think he was responsible?"

"She just didn't trust him, I guess. I told her I thought he was harmless." Allison swallows hard. "Do you think he killed her?"

Detective Manzillo looks her in the eye. "What do *you* think?"

"I honestly don't know."

She's just glad she's back to being certain—well, ninety-nine-point-nine percent certain, anyway—that it wasn't Mack.

Chapter Eight

Allison closes the door behind her, shutting out the squawk of a police radio coming down from the fifth floor.

Before they parted ways in the elevator just now, Detective Manzillo told her they'd have cops around all night, working on the case.

Maybe that should make her feel safe.

It doesn't.

It means the monster who killed Kristina is still out there somewhere.

She locks the dead bolt . . . the same precaution Kristina might have taken before someone got in anyway and killed her.

Or was he already inside her apartment, waiting for her?

Did he climb in from the fire escape after she was sleeping?

Heart pounding, Allison goes straight to the living room, to her own window that overlooks the fire escape. It's locked. So are all the others.

And there's no one hiding under the bed, in the closet, behind the shower curtain . . .

Okay. *Okay.*

Breathing a little easier, she takes off her sneakers and jacket, finds a bottle of Poland Spring and an apple in the fridge, and carries both to the living room. She's not really thirsty or hungry, but she has to do something.

Years ago, she learned that going through the motions of ordinary activity—eating, drinking, sleeping, working—can work wonders in the midst of a catastrophe.

Everyone keeps talking about how important it is to move on, to go about business as usual. Anything less, people say, would be letting terror win.

Allison has never let terror win—not even when she was a child who feared the worst every day, and then saw the worst come to pass.

For years before her mother's suicide, Allison was aware of Brenda Taylor's desire to take her own life, knowledge that came courtesy of several harrowing, deliberate overdoses.

She would come home from school or her part-time job at the Convenient Mart to find her mother unconscious, having swallowed a handful of sleeping pills. Sometimes Allison was able to rouse her, or force her to vomit.

Once, she actually had to call 911, but that was a last resort. After that, her mother was sent away to a treatment facility, and Allison had to live in foster care for months. When her mother was "cured," the two of them were allowed to go back home together.

But Mom had fooled the authorities, fooled the staff at her rehab center—fooled everyone but Allison.

She was still using; she was still going to die. It was inevitable.

That Allison would be left alone didn't matter to Brenda, or perhaps didn't even occur to her. She wanted to escape so badly that she was willing to abandon the child she loved to the cold, cruel world she despised. Weakness was her weakness. She wasn't strong enough to fight for Allison, or for her own life.

So, yes, Allison lived with terror, but she didn't let it get the best of her. She got herself out of bed every day, and went to school, and came home and did her homework and ate and slept . . .

She forced herself to keep on going, and in the end, terror did not win.

Tonight, she'll set the alarm clock, and tomorrow, she'll go to work. If the office is open, that is.

Please, let the office be open.

She sits on the couch and sips some water, listening to the hum of the refrigerator and distant sirens in the night, and thinking about the past.

She can't help it.

Memories are good for nothin', her mother's voice echoes back to her, but Allison shakes her head.

Memories are good for something, *Mom. When you lose yourself in them, you don't have to think about what's happening in the here and now, or what might happen tomorrow.*

But then, you had your own way of ignoring all that, didn't you, Mom? You had your own way of making sure you wouldn't have to deal with the future.

Allison puts aside the water bottle and the untouched apple and wonders if she should have checked in on Mack when she got back. His door was closed; she doesn't know if he's in there or not.

Still unsettled by the questions Detective Manzillo asked about him, Allison forces herself to put aside emotion and think about it with pure logic.

Could Mack have been romantically involved with Kristina and covered it up when Allison asked him about her?

Yes.

Could he have killed Kristina?

It's such a preposterous assumption, that a man who had just gone through what he'd gone through, a man who seems so normal, would be capable of—

Logic, Allison.

All right.

Yes.

Yes, he could have killed Kristina.

Allison doesn't want to believe that he did—really, she has no reason to believe that he did—but he *could* have.

That's the question she asked herself.

And that's the honest answer.

Back when they were newlyweds, Ange used to worry about Rocky spending long hours on the case with female detectives.

"You might be tempted," she would say.

"Trust me, Ange, these are no Charlie's Angels."

These days, Ange is much more secure, and Rocky usually works his cases with Murph. But if his wife could see Detective Lisha Brandewyne, who's working the Haines murder case in Murph's absence, she'd certainly have instant peace of mind.

In her mid-thirties, with close-cropped dark hair, a stocky build, and nicotine-stained teeth and fingers, Brandewyne is no Charlie's Angel. She's not even a Cagney or Lacey.

But Rocky's not that shallow. His main problem with

her—aside from the fact that she's a chain-smoker—is that she isn't Murph.

He misses Murph, and he's worried about him, and about Luke.

For the time being, though, he's got to focus on the case, with Brandewyne's help. She's not inept, but she was only recently promoted to detective, and she's still got a lot to learn, as far as Rocky is concerned.

Back at the scene of the homicide, they find Timmy Green stretching yellow crime scene tape across the doorway of Kristina Haines's apartment. His last name suits him. He's younger than Brandewyne, even younger than Rocky's youngest son; he's been on the job for less than a year.

After greeting him, Rocky ducks under the yellow tape. Brandewyne starts to follow suit, but her head grazes it. Green lets out a monster curse as the spool flies out of his hand, rolling down the hall, unfurling tape as it goes.

"Oops—sorry," Brandewyne says.

Green growls something as he goes to retrieve the spool.

It's not like him. Ordinarily, he's a mild-mannered kid.

For a moment, Rocky and Brandewyne watch him attempt to rewind the tape. It keeps twisting. Green curses again.

"Give it here." Rocky holds out his hand.

Wordlessly, Green puts the tape into it.

Brandewyne disappears into the apartment.

"Any word from the medical examiner's office?" Rocky asks Green as he winds the tape.

"They're still trying to get someone over here. They're pretty overwhelmed, though—I don't know when it'll be."

"Pretty overwhelmed," Rocky echoes, shaking his head. "That's one hell of an understatement, Green."

"Yeah? Here's another one for you, Rock: this has not been a good day for anyone."

"Yesterday was worse," Rocky returns. "For all of us."

"Yeah, well . . . definitely for her." Green gestures with his head toward the bedroom, where the victim awaits transport to the morgue.

Ordinarily, the M.E. would have been here already—and ordinarily, you'd have an army of detectives working the scene, the witnesses, the computers and labs . . .

The NYPD always taps into its significant supply of manpower to quickly solve an ugly murder like Kristina Haines's.

But today, every available guy is down on the pile, or working to secure and protect the city, or to catch the mass murderers who brought down the towers.

Today, Rocky is juggling multiple duties and reminding himself that he owes it to Kristina and her family—if he ever manages to find any family—to give this case his full attention.

He hands the crime scene tape back to Green. "Here you go. Hang in there, kid. Things will get better."

"You think? Really?"

"They always do, don't they?" Rocky walks into the apartment, thinking about his own three boys, praying they'll never have to see the things their father has seen today, thankful that he hasn't had to endure what other fathers have today.

There are guys down there on the pile digging frantically for their own kids. Murph, with his brother who's like a son to him, is one of them.

How do you survive something like that? How do you go on?

He pushes the thought from his mind. He has a job to do.

In the bedroom, he finds Brandewyne scribbling notes, and Andy Blake and Jorge Perez, the CSU guys, packing away their equipment. Kristina Haines lies dead on the bed between them.

Dead. Slaughtered.

Brown, dried blood is spattered and smeared everywhere—on the walls, the ceiling, the bed—all over Kristina herself.

She's curled up on her side as if she's asleep in the middle of a blood-soaked floral comforter, wearing silky black lingerie.

When Rocky first got to the scene, the song was still playing and the room was lit only by candlelight. There were candles all around the room, on every surface. Some had melted away and gone out; others still flickered around the bed, like fire surrounding a sacrificial altar.

Brandewyne looks up from her notes. "That sick son of a bitch really did a job on her."

Another understatement. Beyond the savage knife wounds, Kristina's right middle finger is missing. Missing—as in hacked right off her hand.

"Did the finger turn up yet?" Rocky asks the CSU guys.

"Nope. Guess he took it with him." Perez shakes his head. "Something to remind him of the romantic evening."

At first glance—judging by the victim's clothes, the music, the candles—this looked like a late night date gone horribly wrong. Rocky guessed that the killer had come in through the door, invited by Kristina, and then, after he snapped and killed her, went out through the window and down the fire escape, as indicated by the traces of blood that were found there.

But when you get into stuff like this—the seemingly symbolic mutilation, the killer taking a grisly trophy— you tend to lean away from crime of passion, and more toward something more . . . ritualistic.

Maybe he came in *and* out through the window.

Or maybe he let himself in with a key.

"Okay, we're out of here," Perez announces, as he finishes buttoning up his gear. "You guys gonna wait around for the M.E.?"

"Don't have much choice, do we?"

"You could be here waiting all night," Blake warns.

"What do you want me to do," Rocky snaps, "go downtown and drag them away from the goddamned pile?"

The CSU guys fall silent. Shifting her weight, Brandewyne goes back to her notes. Rocky rubs his pounding temples with his fingertips.

Yeah. Everyone's nerves are frayed; everyone's exhausted.

Rocky passed four different delis on the way here— places where he ordinarily stops to get some caffeine to see him through a rough overnight—and they were all closed. He wishes he'd thought to grab a go-cup full of the battery acid that passes for coffee down at the station house.

"Hang in there, Rocky," Perez tells him, heading toward the door.

"You too, Jorge."

As Blake follows Perez past Rocky, Rocky pats his

upper arm, a typical parting gesture. But his hand rests there a little longer than usual, offering an added measure of support.

He and Ange went to Blake's wedding last spring down in Breezy Point, Brooklyn. Two of the groomsmen—including the bride's brother—were with the FDNY. Rocky's afraid to ask about them. Having glimpsed the gaunt expression in Blake's eyes, he doesn't have to.

"You take care of yourself, Andy," Rocky tells him.

"You too."

They disappear into the hall. He can hear them out there, talking to Green.

Left alone in the apartment with Brandewyne and the dead girl, Rocky walks over to the bed and surveys the body.

"You want to notify the next of kin?" Brandewyne asks. "Or do you want me to do it?"

"You can do it."

"Why did I know you were going to say that?"

Rocky shrugs and hands her a folded slip of paper. "It's not the parents—they're both dead. She was an only child. She has an aunt and uncle who live in England."

"It's late there. Should I wait till morning?"

"Sooner the better."

"Right. They'll have to make travel arrangements."

"They're going to have to swim over if they want to get here anytime soon," Rocky says darkly, before Brandewyne goes into the next room to make her call.

He looks at Kristina. "Who did this to you?"

Jerry the maintenance man is certainly a likely suspect, considering the fact that he'd likely have the keys to Kristina Haines's apartment *and* was lurking in the hallway in the wee hours of Wednesday morning, right around the time she was killed. Was he a secret admirer? A stalker? It's possible.

Anything is possible.

Those very words are scrawled on a whiteboard in Kristina's kitchen.

Who wrote them? Kristina herself, alone in the big city, reminding herself to hope and dream?

Or was it her killer, sending an ominous message?

Point taken, Rocky thinks. Anything *is* possible.

He keeps reminding Brandewyne that this case might not be nearly as cut-and-dried as it seems. Seasoned detectives know that when it comes to homicide, things are not always as they appear to be. You have to look beyond the obvious.

Rocky ponders the series of burglaries reported in the building over the last month or so. Several tenants had reported that someone had entered their apartments while they were out during the day and stolen personal items—mainly costume jewelry and women's clothing. Among the missing belongings listed on the police reports Rocky scrutinized: a black negligee that exactly matches the description of the one Kristina Haines was wearing when she died.

There were no signs of forced entry in any of the burglaries, according to the reports, indicating that the thief had either come in and out through an unlocked outside window, or through the door—with a key.

Were the burglaries a prelude to murder?

Had Kristina interrupted a burglary in progress in her own apartment?

Nothing about the elaborately staged crime scene would seem to indicate that, but Rocky isn't ruling anything out.

Kristina Haines wasn't even the first person to die in that building in the past few months. Elvira Ogden, the old lady who lived in an apartment on the floor below, had fallen and hit her head back in May. Rocky will take a closer look, but that death really looks like an accident. Anyway, very little about that death—aside from the location—had anything in common with this one.

Kristina was an attractive woman; chances are, Jerry isn't the only guy who'd noticed. There must have been others. Rocky just has to find and question them.

Easier said than done. Right now, it seems no one in this city is where he or she is supposed to be.

Earlier, Brandewyne found contact information for Ray, Kristina's ex-boyfriend, in her desk. But he lives down on Warren Street, near ground zero. The whole area has been evacuated.

Brandewyne couldn't reach the building's owner, Dale Reiss, either. A recently retired corporate accountant, he lives with his wife, Emily, in Battery Park City, and that's also been evacuated. God only knows where he is tonight.

The tiny basement office—which houses the surveillance camera footage of the building's public areas—can't be searched without a warrant. Rocky requested one from the assistant district attorney, but he has a feeling it's going to be a long wait with the office in chaos. The *city* in chaos.

Kristina's neighbors—people who might have known something, seen something, heard something—weren't evacuated. But like thousands of lower Manhattan residents, they fled anyway.

Only Allison Taylor and James MacKenna seem to have stayed in the building overnight. But when it comes to tracking down Jerry the maintenance man, neither of them even knows the guy's last name.

"He kind of comes and goes," MacKenna said. "As far as I know, he doesn't have regular hours—but I've never paid much attention to him, and I'm hardly ever home on weekdays."

MacKenna was cooperative when Rocky talked to him, but he seemed edgy and distracted—understandably so. The guy's wife worked in an investment firm close to the top floor of one of the towers, just beneath Windows on the World. As far as anyone knows, no one made it out alive from that part of the building. The escape routes were cut off; that's where most of the jumpers came from.

Rocky's questioning was thorough, of course, but he found himself wanting to go easy on MacKenna, who didn't have much to say anyway. He didn't seem to know Kristina Haines well enough to shed any new light on the investigation.

Or so Rocky believed—until he saw the way Allison started squirming around when he asked her about men Kristina might have been seeing.

Allison Taylor had told him that Kristina didn't have a boyfriend and, as of Sunday, wasn't even seeing anyone. Not as far as she knew, anyway.

But there was something about the way she behaved when Rocky started down that line of questioning that made him wonder if she was telling him the whole truth. She was visibly squirming in her chair at one point.

Does she know more than she's telling about Kristina's love life?

Maybe he misread her, and she doesn't.

Maybe there's nothing more to know, and Jerry the maintenance man is Rocky's guy.

But when Rocky thinks about the way Allison fidgeted and shifted her weight when he spoke to her . . .

It'll be necessary to keep close tabs on both her and MacKenna right now. And with the decreased manpower and disrupted communications systems, that's going to be yet another challenge.

"But don't you worry," Rocky tells the dead girl. "I'm going to find out who did this to you, and I'm going to make sure he gets what's coming to him."

Him . . . or her.

When Mack gets home after being questioned, the building is crawling with cops.

Two uniformed officers are posted outside on the street, another is stationed on the ground floor by the elevators, and judging by the squad cars and vans parked at the curb, there must still be a couple of guys upstairs, too, in Kristina's apartment.

He slides the dead bolt, and leans against the door for a minute. His heart is pounding hard, as though he's just run all the way home chased by the devil, rather than catching a ride back from the precinct with a police officer.

Get a grip, Mack. Get a grip.

With an icy hand, he flips a couple of light switches, making sure everything looks . . . right.

It does. How can it, when everything is wrong?

The way Detective Manzillo looked at him, and questioned him . . .

He was just doing his job. But Mack has watched enough television crime shows to know that the person who discovers the body is always a potential suspect.

Technically, Mack didn't discover the body. But he's the one who reported it.

A chill slips down his spine. He doesn't need this right now. He really doesn't.

His gaze falls on a few stray missing fliers lying on the table.

It's crazy, like one of those movies where the action keeps escalating until it goes too far and you don't buy into it anymore, because it could never really happen. Not like that.

Yeah, well, truth, as they say, is stranger than fiction. This is really happening.

Mack goes to the kitchen, fills the teakettle, sets it on the burner, and turns on the flame.

Then his eye catches the bottle of Jack Daniel's still sitting on the counter from the other night. He turns off the flame and pours himself a stiff bourbon.

Standing there, he downs most of it in a few gulps. It burns his throat and weakens his knees, but it warms him from the inside out, banishing the chill better than tea ever could.

He tops off the glass and carries it into the living room, turns on a lamp, and sits on the couch.

Now what?

What do you do when life as you knew it has ceased to exist?

You search for something, someone familiar, that's what you do. You reach out to someone who knows you well and will stick by you no matter what happens.

No matter what.

As a haze of bourbon settles over him like a heated blanket, Mack dials the phone.

Rounding the corner onto Sixth Avenue, Jamie sees that the bodega, run by an affable dark-skinned man named Mo, is open. Good. Most of the other shops and restaurants along the four-block walk over here were closed, and have been since Tuesday afternoon.

But at Mo's, the lights are on and the door is propped open. He prides himself on being open round the clock; he reminds his customers of that whenever he hands back their change and their bagged purchases.

"You come back anytime," he always says in his thick Middle Eastern accent. "I am here twenty-four-seven, all the time, weekends, holidays . . . all the time."

He means it literally. Unless he has an identical twin, Mo himself is perpetually at the cash register, ringing up cigarettes, newspapers, and lottery tickets; soda cans, coffee, toilet paper . . . like all good New York bodegas, Mo sells a little of everything.

"Don't you ever go home to sleep?" Jamie sometimes wants to ask Mo, but never does.

Tonight, Mo utters the usual "Hello, hello," but he glances up only briefly from the open *New York Post* on the counter in front of him.

The two small aisles of grocery are picked over— the canned goods and bottled water shelves completely bare. People must be stockpiling supplies, fearing the end of the world.

Funny—everyone thought that would happen last year, when the millennium dawned. There was a collective sigh of relief when it passed uneventfully. No one ever imagined the Armageddon that lay ahead.

Jamie plucks an Entenmann's box from the shelf, taking it as a good omen that there's one kind of cake left—and it happens to be Jerry's favorite—chocolate, with chocolate frosting.

Back at the counter, Mo's newspaper is open to a bold headline stretching across the top of both pages: *BIN LADEN'S SICK BOAST NOW REALITY.*

"That is it?" Mo asks, glancing down at the Entenmann's cake.

"That's it."

Mo rings it up, takes the bills, hands back coins, puts the cake box into a slippery white plastic bag, and hands it over. "Thank you." Tonight, that's all Mo says before he goes back to reading his paper, his round black eyes fretful behind his wire-rimmed glasses.

Out on the street, Jamie backtracks to the apartment in Hell's Kitchen.

Funny how some parts of the city are teeming with security, and others are completely deserted. Even where there is security, the soldiers and cops don't always bother to ask for ID. If you don't look like their idea of a Muslim terrorist, you can pretty much skirt the barricades.

Don't they know you should never judge a book by a cover?

Stupid. They're so stupid. They think they know everything, and they don't know anything at all.

Jamie walks past Ladder 21, the neighborhood firehouse, with its growing shrine of flickering candles and flowers in memory of its many missing men. Jamie used to see them, laughing and joking around beyond the wide open doors, or clinging to the sides of the big red trucks as they raced off to fight a fire somewhere. A fire that could be conquered, unlike the still raging inferno that swallowed the men of Ladder 21 and hundreds of others who were sent to battle it.

Sirens wail in the night even now, and a military jet roars through the sky, tracing a path along the Hudson River just a few blocks west of here.

Jamie doesn't like it. Any of it. This day—this night—hasn't unfolded the way it was supposed to.

Allison Taylor was supposed to be taken care of, before she could go blabbing to the police about seeing Jerry in the hall the night Kristina was murdered.

But it's too late. Before Jamie could get to Allison, she found Kristina. There's a certain pleasure in imagining Allison's reaction to the meticulous, bloody handiwork left behind in Kristina's apartment. But that pleasure doesn't come without a price.

With a sinking heart, Jamie watched from the shadows as the police took a pale, shaken Allison away for questioning. Of course she was going to tell them she'd seen Jerry at the scene of the crime.

By now, they must know.

By now, they'll be looking for him.

He shouldn't be easy to find, but still . . .

"You have to stay home for a while, Jerry," Jamie told him earlier. "You can't go anywhere without asking me first."

"But I have to go to work."

"No, you don't. Mr. Reiss called and told you not to come in for a few days, remember?"

Jerry shook his head.

"Sure, he did. He called, and you talked to him."

"I don't remember," Jerry protested.

"Think about it. He told you not to come to work for a while, and then I told you I'd get you some chocolate cake. Remember?"

Jerry thought hard, then shrugged and nodded. "I guess so. Sometimes I forget things."

"We all do, Jerry. It's okay."

Sometimes, it's frightfully easy to plant "memories" in Jerry's poor, damaged brain.

But it's for his own good. It always is.

Poor Jerry.

Apparently, he met a woman today, made a move, and the woman turned him down. "All I did was ask her to have cake," Jerry blubbered, "and she said no."

Surprise, surprise.

But it's Jamie's job to take care of Jerry now.

You never should have left him alone ten years ago. Why did you go? What were you thinking?

I thought it was all over for Jerry. How could I know he'd survived?

And as soon as I found my way back to him, I did what I could to make it right.

Jerry has suffered enough in his life. And now he's hurting again.

I have to make this right, too.

"Maybe this girl is married," Jamie told Jerry, "or—"

"She's not married. She lives by herself. She just doesn't like me." Jerry let out a moan. "I don't want to be alone anymore. No one wants to be with me. Mama's gone and now . . ."

"But you're not alone. You have me."

"No—not that. I want a girlfriend. I want love."

Who doesn't?

We all want love.

Some people find it over and over again. Some people never find it at all.

"It's not fair," Jerry wails.

"No. It isn't."

"It hurts so much. Make it stop hurting. Make someone love me."

"I can't do that, Jerry. You know that."

"Yes, you can. You said when you came that you'd make things better."

Yes. Better for Jerry.

And better for me.

"Are you sure this woman lives by herself?"

"Yes."

"What's her name?"

"Marianne."

"Last name?"

"I . . . I don't know. I just know where she lives."

"That's great, Jerry. That's perfect. Don't you worry about a thing. You know what I'm going to do? I'm going to go out and get you that cake I promised you. I'll take care of you, just like I promised."

And I'll take care of Marianne.

And then I'll take care of Allison.

It might be too late to keep her from telling the police about Jerry . . . but it's not too late to punish her for what she did. No, it's never too late for that.

Jamie's mouth curves into a smile.

"Ma—it's me," Marianne says into the phone.

"Who?" her mother asks, as she always does. As if any other female voice would call her Ma. As if anyone else in the world calls her every single night, at ten on the dot.

"Me! Marianne!"

"Oh—Mare-Mare."

Oh, for the love of . . .

Marianne hates the childhood nickname, but her mother clings to it as fiercely as she clings to Marianne herself.

"I'm just making sure you're okay, Ma. Are you getting ready for bed?"

"Not yet. I'm watching the news."

"Still? I told you earlier, you have to turn that off. It's only making you more nervous."

"I like to know what's going on."

"Nothing is going on. It's over. You're safe."

Her mother doesn't believe that. She frets, for a few minutes, about the terrorists and what they did and what they might do next. Then she asks Marianne what she ate for dinner.

"Soup," she lies.

"From a can?"

"It was fine, Ma."

"If you had come here, you could have had kakavia. Homemade."

After all these years, her mother still thinks she enjoys fisherman's stew. Rather than point out—yet again—that it's her brothers who like it, not her, Marianne says simply, "I couldn't come. I'm sorry. I told you, I had the repairman here, and I couldn't leave."

"I know. I'll see you tomorrow. I still have leftover lamb from when you were here Monday night."

Of course you do.

Her mother still hasn't learned how to cook for just one person, or two. Everything she makes would easily serve a dozen people. That's never going to change, Marianne thinks with weary affection.

"Don't forget to call me in the morning," her mother says.

"Do I ever?"

"All last week—"

"Ma, I was on a ship. Out at sea. Remember? I couldn't call."

"But now you're home."

"And your phone will ring at seven-thirty. Same as always. Okay?"

"Okay. I love you, Mare-Mare. You sound tired. Get some sleep."

"I will," she tells her mother glumly, and hangs up the phone.

No, she won't. She'll be lucky if she sleeps at all, with everything that's gone on. The terror attack . . .

The move . . .

The nut job handyman who spooked her into barricading herself into the apartment—even closing and locking all the windows despite the polyurethane fumes . . .

Rae stuck halfway across the country . . .

And God only knows when—or *if*—she's coming back.

Marianne looks at the sunrise photo they had taken on the cruise ship just days ago—arms around each other, laughing, in love. They spent their whole vacation talking about moving in together. How could things have changed so drastically since then?

The twin towers in the background are now, more than ever, a harbinger of disaster. The whole world has changed since Sunday morning. Everything about it. Everyone in it. Even Rae.

"I really do think you should move in with me when you get back," Marianne told her earlier on the phone, before she called her mother.

"I don't know, Marianne," Rae said. "I've been thinking . . . I'm not sure I want to come back to New York."

"What? What do you mean? You love it here. You *moved* here! You said you've been dreaming of living here since you were a little girl!"

"I know, but things are going to be different now. The city is a target. It's not safe. I'm thinking maybe I should move back home."

"To Ashtabula?" Dumbfounded, Marianne reminded

her, "You left there for a reason. You said it was too conservative, there was never anything exciting to do, your neighbors were homophobic—"

"But there aren't any suicide bombers in Ohio, Marianne."

"That's ridiculous! You can't—"

"Listen, right now, I don't know what I want to do, okay? Except go to bed and forget about all this horribleness. And you should do the same."

Marianne spent a futile couple more minutes trying to convince her girlfriend that New York is where she belongs; that if Rae could just come back here, she'd feel at home again.

But in her heart, she doesn't believe that. Even she herself doesn't feel at home here now. Life in New York is never going to be the same. But will life anywhere else in this country ever be the same?

"We're all targets, Rae," she pointed out. "It's not just New York. They hate Americans. Ohio is in America, too."

"Well, I'd feel a hell of a lot safer there than I would in New York—and so would you. Admit it."

"No way." Marianne isn't giving up on New York, no matter what's happened—or what *might* happen. Her family and friends and memories are here, she was born here, and she's going to die here—of old age, God willing, and not at the hands of terrorists.

She climbs into bed, furious at Rae. How can she be such a coward?

Then she turns off the light, sinks back onto the pillow, and wonders . . .

How can you*?*

Just this evening, she canceled her dinner at her mother's, afraid to leave the apartment because the handyman gave her the creeps. Not only did she upset her mother, but she now hasn't eaten all day—there's not a crumb of food in the apartment—and the combination of low blood sugar and varnish fumes has given her a ferocious headache.

This is crazy.

I'm *crazy.*

Marianne sits up, climbs out of bed, and marches over to the bedroom window. She hesitates only a moment before unlocking the latch and raising it.

Immediately, a cool night breeze gusts into the apartment and she sucks it into her lungs gratefully. Maybe the wind has changed direction since this morning, because the air doesn't even smell smoky anymore. Or maybe it does, but she just can't tell because it's still fresher than the stale, varnish-laced air she's been breathing for the last six hours or so.

The ever-present sirens are louder now, but that's okay. She already feels better.

She opens the windows in the living room, too, and notices that the one that had been painted shut earlier now rises easily, courtesy of the creepy handyman.

Just beyond its screen is the fire escape.

For a moment, Marianne considers climbing through the window and sitting outside for a little while, to clear her lungs *and* her thoughts.

But she dismisses the idea. It's late, she's tired . . .

And sad.

Is Rae really going to leave New York?

For a moment, she toys with the idea of going with her.

Ashtabula . . .

No.

It isn't just about leaving her hometown and her

mother—her family, her roots—behind. It's about fear.

Rae is leaving New York because she's afraid.

If Marianne follows her, it would be for the same reason. Not that she's afraid to live in New York, because she isn't. Bad things happen everywhere.

But it would mean she's afraid to let go, afraid to go back to being alone, afraid to start over . . . again.

Fear is what took hold of her mother after her father died. She had let herself become so dependent on him that she had no idea how to live without him.

Marianne never wants to find herself in that position, ever.

She loves Rae . . . but she can live without her.

She goes into the bathroom, opens the small vented window there, then hunts through the medicine cabinet supplies she unpacked just this afternoon.

She's out of Advil, but there's a sample packet of Tylenol PM. Perfect—it'll take care of her headache *and* her nerves. She swallows the two capsules with tap water from her cupped palm and goes straight back to bed.

She takes one last glance at the cruise photograph of her and Rae before she turns out the light.

Things will look brighter in the morning, she promises herself, closing her eyes and waiting for the sedative to do its thing as sirens wail on in the night.

In a midtown hotel room lit only by the blue light from the muted television, Vic dials a familiar phone number. He's exhausted, and he only has a few hours before he has to head back out again, but his need to make this connection is as important as his need for sleep.

Ange Manzillo answers on the first ring with a breathless, "Hello?"

"Hey, it's just me."

"Vic?"

"Yeah. Sorry to call so late. I hope I didn't wake you up."

"Are you kidding? Who can sleep? We've got fighter planes buzzing over the house."

"I know—I'm here." He keeps an eye on the television, where a split screen shows footage of the burning towers from yesterday and a FEMA agent being interviewed live, plus several bullet point announcements and a news crawl along the bottom.

"You made it to New York, then?" Ange asks. "How did you get here?"

"I flew," he says simply.

"But I thought the FAA—oh. Right."

Right. She gets it. When you're with the FBI and you're investigating a terror attack, chances are, you're not grounded with everyone else.

Ange lets out a heavy breath. "It's really bad down there, Vic."

"I know."

"Did you see . . . ?"

"Yes."

He saw.

He saw the gaping hole in the skyline from his window seat on the government plane, and wondered about all those doomed passengers yesterday—what they were thinking, feeling, fearing.

He saw the smoking wreckage up close, from the ground, and he thought about his friend O'Neill, who last spring might very well have been on the trail of the men who ultimately took aim with an airplane missile and murdered him.

He saw the ravaged faces of the rescue workers and

the frightened faces of the people who live here. None was familiar and now, after two of the longest and loneliest days of his life, that's what he craves more than sleep or food or a hot shower. He craves a familiar face.

"Is Rocco back?" he asks Ange hopefully.

"No. I haven't seen him at all since yesterday afternoon. He was down on the pile all night and most of today—and then he had to go work a homicide. Can you believe that?"

"Believe what?" he murmurs, leaning closer to the screen to read the newly posted death toll estimate.

"Even now, people are killing each other in this city. You'd think that would be the last thing on anyone's mind after what happened."

You'd think . . .

Ah, but Vic knows better.

Vic knows that what happened on September 11 was the tipping point for a few unbalanced people who were already teetering on the brink of madness and violence.

He just hopes Rocky hunts down whoever committed this particular homicide before he can strike again.

With a gasp, Allison sits straight up in bed, her heart pounding.

Not from a nightmare, though. She wasn't asleep.

She's been lying here for hours, trying to relax her mind and body enough to drift off. But just now, just as she finally felt herself beginning to doze, a thought barged into her head out of nowhere.

Just as she had the key to Kristina Haines's apartment . . .

Kristina had the key to Allison's.

How could she not have thought about that until now?

Now, in the middle of the night, when she'd convinced herself at last that she's safe here, behind her locked door.

Allison gets out of bed and walks through the dark rooms to the door. She stares at it for a long time, long enough to imagine that she's seeing the knob turning slowly, ever so slowly, from the other side.

That's enough.

Tomorrow, she'll have the locks changed.

Tonight . . . she won't let fear rob her of any more sleep, but she won't take any chances, either.

She wedges the back of a wooden dining chair under the doorknob.

Will that really work?

She has no idea. But in case it doesn't, she goes into the kitchen, opens a drawer, and takes out a chef's knife with a long blade.

This works.

She carries it back into the bedroom and climbs into bed. When at last she falls asleep, her fist is clenched around the handle of the knife.

Delirious with pain, bleeding from a vicious stab wound in her side, Marianne struggles for breath.

"Say it," the guttural voice is insisting, somewhere above her. "Say it!"

"P . . . p . . . p . . ."

"Say it or you'll die!"

Die . . . she's going to die anyway. No matter what she says, no matter what she does . . . she knows she's going to die. Here, on the floor beside her bed, wearing scanty lingerie she was forced to put on, part of a sick, twisted game.

She thought that if she just did what she was told, she would survive. Put on these clothes, light these candles; play this music, the CD Jerry had given her earlier . . .

"Do exactly what I tell you to do, and you'll live."

She believed that, at first. Now, frantic with fear and pain, she realizes there's no way out of this alive.

"Pl-please . . ." She gasps, drowning in her own blood. "Noooo . . ."

Fear . . . Marianne went to bed thinking that she wouldn't let it get the best of her. She would never be afraid to live alone, as her mother is.

Fear . . .

She thought she knew what that was.

Now she knows she had no idea.

"Say it!"

She can feel something cold and hard pushing against her cheek. Oh God. Is it the blade of the knife? Or is it a gun?

"I . . . I . . ." She struggles. Somehow, she's got to get it out.

It's the only chance she has.

She drags in a wet, shallow, agonizing breath, manages to choke out, "I'm . . . sorry . . ."

"Say the rest. Go on."

I'm dying. I can't . . .

"Say it! Now!" The cold, hard thing presses against her cheek.

"I . . . love . . . you . . . Jerry."

Those words, ending on a gurgle of blood in her throat, are Marianne Apostolos's last.

Chapter Nine

When the alarm goes off on Thursday morning, Allison rolls over and hits the snooze button, same as she does every weekday at seven A.M. She's about to doze off again for a few minutes, as usual, when she remembers.

Her eyes snap open.

The terror attack.

Kristina.

The knife.

Is this what it's going to be like from now on? Will she spend the first few seconds of every morning in blissful oblivion before harsh reality hits her all over again?

It was like this after her mother died. But only for the first few days, when her brother came to stay with her in the house in Centerfield.

She would wake up in her own bed and she would think everything was normal—a relative description, in her world, anyway.

Then it would hit her, and she'd force herself to get up to face another long day of packing up her mother's things and dealing with strangers who were obligated—professionally, morally, guiltily obligated—to help her. They only made things harder, all of them, regardless of their motives. She didn't want anyone's pity—not even her brother's.

"You want to come back and live with me and Cindy-Lou?" Brett offered—reluctantly, she could tell. "I can ask her folks if it's okay . . ."

"No, thanks. I want to finish school here," Allison told him.

And the second she had her diploma, she wanted to get the hell out of there—not just Centerfield, but Nebraska, the Midwest.

So Brett signed some papers, and she went to live with a foster family on a farm just outside of town. Every morning before dawn, a rooster's crow would jar her from a sound sleep, reverberating instant awareness about where she was—rather, where she *wasn't*—and what she had lost.

That was hard.

Is this harder?

Maybe they're a blessing—those first few misty moments of morning, when you're allowed to forget what your life is really like today.

But then you remember and you suck it up and deal, the way you always have.

Allison sits up and pulls back the covers. The knife is there, on the mattress.

Great. She could have rolled over on it and cut herself in her sleep.

She leaves it there, gets out of bed, and goes over to the window. Looking down at the street, she notes that there are no longer police cars parked in front of the building.

What does that mean?

Is it over?

Did they arrest Kristina's killer sometime in the night?

Was it Jerry?

The way he behaved in the laundry room . . .

And the way he furtively ducked out into the alley that night . . .

It had to be Jerry.

Not Mack . . .

No way.

Allison goes into the living room and takes the chair out from beneath the doorknob. For all she knows, Kristina's killer *could* have tried to get in here with the key sometime in the night, and *could* have been stopped by the chair.

Somehow, though, Allison doubts it.

She starts a pot of coffee, then starts the computer, thinking she can find the names of a couple of locksmiths and call one this morning. As the brewing and the booting get under way, she showers and throws on a T-shirt and the same jeans she wore yesterday, the one pair of functional old Levi's she keeps around for cleaning days and sick days.

Farm girl clothes, she used to call them, back in Nebraska. She used to wear black spandex and suede stilettos to school when everyone else was in jeans and boots—the kind of boots you wear to muck out stalls. Even the girls.

Allison vowed she would never go out in public looking like that.

Yesterday, she left the building in these tattered jeans, and she had on sneakers, no less, on the streets of Manhattan.

Yesterday, it didn't seem to matter. Today, though . . .

today will be different. Today, she needs to look like herself again, feel like herself again. That's important.

People like to say that what's on the outside doesn't count, but they're wrong, as far as Allison is concerned. It's always best to look like you've got it together even when the world is falling apart around you and you're falling apart inside. That way, at least you can pretend you're okay, and people give you some space. If you feel like hell and you *look* like hell, people hover, trying to help.

Before her mother's funeral seven years ago, one of the church ladies insisted on taking Allison shopping in Omaha for something "suitable" to wear to the service. The drive was interminable—the lady kept talking about how Allison had nothing to worry about, because God was going to save her.

Really? Is God going to give me my mom back— not my mom the way she was, but healthy and strong, wanting to live, wanting to take care of me . . . And, while he's at it, is he going to give me a dad, too? Not my dad. A decent one. One who will stick around.

She didn't say any of that to the church lady, of course. Her mother had taught her to be polite to her elders. Her manners always seemed to catch people off guard, though. Given the way she and Mom lived, they probably assumed she was a rude, rough-around-the-edges brat.

When the church lady walked Allison into Von Maur, the fancy department store, she loudly informed the saleswoman that "this little lady's mama has just killed herself, isn't it awful? She was on *drugs.*" That last word was stage-whispered, and delivered with a knowing, disgusted nod. "Poor little thing needs something respectable to wear to the funeral."

The saleswoman, a glasses-on-a-chain, grandmotherly type whose name tag read Eileen, looked at Allison not with pity, but with sympathy. That was the first time she ever realized there was a tremendous difference between the two.

"Come with me," Eileen said, and led her toward the dressing room.

The church lady started to follow, but Eileen told her the dressing room area was much too small.

When they got there, Allison saw that it wasn't, and she wanted to hug Eileen. Especially when she starting bringing in clothes—armloads of clothes, beautiful clothes, far nicer than anything Allison had ever owned.

She picked out a black crepe Ralph Lauren dress.

Her mother would have loved to see her in it. She used to tell Allison about the beautiful clothes she'd had when she was growing up, before she got mixed up in trouble, got pregnant with Brett—not even sure who the father was—and her wealthy family disowned her.

The black dress was expensive. When the saleswoman rang it up, the church lady paled a bit beneath her rouge, but she handed over her credit card with a forced smile.

The dress is still hanging in the back of Allison's closet, draped in dry cleaner's plastic. It's a classic style. She could wear it again, really—if she wanted to. She doesn't. But she won't get rid of it, either. It's a reminder—oddly, not a sad one.

When Allison pulled that luxurious dress over her head that morning in the dressing room, she felt a glimmer of hope.

It's only a dress, she reminded herself, looking in the mirror, twirling back and forth and admiring the way the fabric swished around her legs.

And yet . . . that dress helped her to cope during that terrible time in her life. It helped more than anything else: more than the church lady's chatter and the minister's eulogy about a woman he'd never met, more than Brett's gruff attempts to comfort her or the foster care system's attempts to pick up the pieces of her life.

That dress changed her on the outside. Quite miraculously, she no longer looked the part of a forlorn orphan. She looked like a young woman who was quite capable of taking care of herself.

And that was what she did.

It's only a dress . . .

It's only fashion . . .

Was it just yesterday that she'd thought it would never matter again?

Somewhere outside, she can hear sirens wailing.

There have always been sirens, there always will be. They just sound louder now because there is no other street noise.

Allison goes over to her closet, pulls out a Badgley Mischka dress with the tags still on, and hangs it on the hook on the back of the door. She'll wear this today.

Back in the kitchen, she pours a cup of coffee, then takes it into the living room and sits down at the computer. She finds several e-mails—including one from her supervisor, sent late last night, and addressed to the entire department.

Office will be open Thursday. Please report in if possible.

Good.

She switches over to a local news Web site, wondering if there will be anything about Kristina's murder— and, perhaps, an arrest.

But of course, there's nothing at all. Thousands of

New Yorkers were murdered on Tuesday; Kristina is lost amid the mass hysteria and grief.

Detective Manzillo gave Allison his card last night. "Call me if you think of anything else that might help," he said. "Or if you need anything," he added, an obvious afterthought.

She takes it out, toys with it, looks at the phone.

She doesn't need anything, really, and she can't think of anything else that might help.

She puts the card into her wallet, goes back to the kitchen, pours another cup of coffee, and carries it over to the door. Then she stops and looks at the locks.

Who knows what's going on out there this morning? For all she knows, Jerry the handyman could be lurking in the hallway, waiting to pounce.

No—if he killed Kristina, he'd be as far away from here right now as he could get, wouldn't he?

Anyway, she's already concluded that she can't stay barricaded in her apartment from now on. That would be letting terror win.

She sets down the coffee while she unfastens the chain and all the locks.

Again, she hesitates, remembering how vulnerable she felt last night—how uncertain she was about everything. Including Mack.

Is this a bad idea?

Maybe.

But she's doing it anyway.

She picks up the mug, opens the door, and sticks her head out just to be sure there's no one lurking.

The hallway looks empty; it *feels* empty.

Allison takes a deep breath to steady her nerves and carries the coffee across the hall to Mack's door.

* * *

The morning sun streams in the east-facing, fortieth floor windows just off Times Square. It's a comfortable apartment in a doorman building, with high ceilings, a terrace, and large rooms—by Manhattan standards, anyway. The kind of apartment most twenty-three-year-olds barely earning twenty thousand dollars a year would be hard-pressed to afford.

But, as Nora Fellows informs Vic, she shares the apartment with thirteen other women.

"Thirteen?" Vic echoes, not sure he heard her correctly.

"Yup. We're all flight attendants, based out of JFK. It's basically, like, a crash pad, you know?"

A pretty, blue-eyed redhead, Nora is just a few years older than Vic's daughter Melody, and she reminds him of her. She has the same pert attractiveness and slight build, uses the same slang and speaks with the same inflections.

Yet unlike Vic's daughter—as far as he knows, anyway, which is a chilling thought—Nora Fellows very likely had a run-in with one of the suicide bombers who brought down the World Trade Center.

Yesterday, she called the police to report an incident she'd witnessed on a flight last month. The locals passed along the information to the FBI.

Now, operating on a few hours' sleep and at least four cups of coffee, Vic sits in a folding chair across from Nora. Beside him is Detective Al Lozen from the NYPD.

When they were introduced this morning, Vic asked Lozen if he knows Rocky.

"Name sounds familiar," Lozen said. "Is he . . . okay?"

That was a loaded question. Ever since Vic arrived in

New York yesterday, he's heard people asking it of each other. *Is he okay? Are they okay? Is everyone okay?*

Translation: *Did you lose someone on Tuesday?*

"He's okay," Vic told Lozen. "How about you? Everyone okay?"

Lozen shook his head grimly, and Vic regretted asking.

The guy's NYPD, lives in Brooklyn. Every New Yorker, especially every cop, knows someone who died on Tuesday. Everyone's lost someone—for most, it was more than one. Some people have lost not just family members and friends, but dozens of colleagues and acquaintances.

Besides O'Neill, Vic's own list includes a couple of childhood pals from the old block back in the Bronx, and several men and women with whom he's crossed paths over the course of his career.

"You know, I have two daughters," Lozen is telling Nora, "and they share a bedroom and bathroom, and you should hear how they fight. I can't imagine how all of you girls don't go crazy and kill each other."

"We're never all here at the same time," Nora assures him, "so it works out. A lot of flight attendants live this way. It doesn't make sense to have your own place when you're hardly ever home, right?"

Lozen agrees, and Vic glances at his notes. Time to get down to business.

At the moment, Nora has the apartment entirely to herself. Her roommates have been stranded since Tuesday at airports all over the world. None, thank God, were aboard American Flights 11 or 77 but Nora knew several of the flight attendants and both pilots who were killed when they crashed.

"I would have been flying myself on Tuesday." She

plays with the hem of her sweatshirt, which is a couple of sizes too big. "Not on the planes that went down—I always fly out of JFK—but still . . ."

"Why weren't you flying that day?" Vic asks.

"I ate at this new Thai place and got food poisoning on Monday night. I should have known not to eat there, because that place was such a hole in the wall, you know? It was so bad . . . I mean, it seems crazy to even worry about something like that *now*. After everything that's happened to all these people . . . people I know . . . like, nothing else even seems to matter, you know?"

"It's okay," Lozen tells her. "So you were sick . . ."

"Yes, and I couldn't fly. So I was here, and I've been watching TV, and when they started saying that the planes were hijacked by Middle Eastern men—I totally remembered that guy from last month. And I thought I should call."

Vic nods. "Tell me exactly what happened on August twenty-fourth."

She takes a deep breath. "Okay. I was working a flight from Miami to JFK, first flight of the morning. I noticed a passenger acting suspicious. He was sitting the bulkhead, you know . . . at the front of coach, and just sort of . . . paying really close attention to what we were doing as we boarded the passengers and got ready to take off. Then I saw that he was talking into a little tape recorder. He was speaking in a foreign language. But he spoke English, too, you know—pretty well."

She went on to describe how she'd reported his actions to the lead flight attendant, who told her to go into the cockpit and bring it to the captain's attention. She did, and was told to keep a close eye on the passenger.

"I tried," she tells Vic, "but, I mean, I was busy, especially after we took off, and . . . to be honest, he wasn't really doing anything. He was just watching. And recording himself. At the time, it bothered me, but I had no idea . . . I mean, if I had known what could happen . . ."

"You did the right thing, reporting him. Tell me about the rest of the flight."

She does. It was uneventful, the passenger disembarked, and she never saw him again.

"Would you recognize him if you did?" Vic asks as his personal cell phone vibrates in his suit coat pocket.

"I don't know. Maybe."

"Excuse me for a minute, please." Vic steps into the hall and pulls out the phone. "Vic Shattuck."

"Vic. Jesus, it's good to hear your voice."

"Rocky. Yours, too."

"Yeah? Even though I'm talking with my mouth full? I thought you said that was a bad habit."

A faint smile crosses Vic's face. Amazing what connecting with an old friend can do for a person, even in the midst of a crisis. "We were five when I said it," he points out, "and it is a bad habit."

"Yeah, well, there are worse," he says, chewing. "Ange made me a frittata and I don't want it to get cold."

Vic imagines Rocky sitting at the worn oval table in the kitchen of his duplex in the Bronx, a stone's throw from the block where they grew up—and really, just ten miles or so from here.

If only Vic could drop everything and go up to the Bronx and eat some of Ange's home cooking and shoot the shit with Rocky, and make the world go away.

Too bad it doesn't work like that. Not today, and not for him. Never.

"Listen," he says hurriedly, "I've got to call you back, Rock. Sorry. I'm in the middle of something."

"Aren't we all. Call me when you can."

"I will." Vic quickly hangs up and for a few seconds, stands there imagining what his life would be like if he hadn't followed this path. If he were, say, a psychiatrist, the way he'd intended to be when he'd first gone to college.

For one thing, he'd be better rested, and closer to home . . . and there sure as hell wouldn't be a gun in his pocket.

But this is the life he chose for himself; he's doing what he always wanted to do.

No—what he always *had* to do.

Jaw set, Vic returns to the living room and hands Nora Fellows a sheet of head shots. "Do you recognize any of these men, Nora?"

Nora looks it over, then gasps and points. "That's him. That's the guy on my flight."

Vic nods with grim satisfaction, his momentary desire to flee all but forgotten.

One step closer.

Something pokes at Mack's cheek, startling him awake.

He opens his eyes to see a child standing over him. What the . . . ?

He blinks and she's still there and he has no idea who she is, or where he is and his head is pounding so badly it's no wonder he can't think straight.

The child opens her mouth and, without turning her head or moving her gaze away from Mack, shrieks, *"DADDY, HE WOKE UP!"*

The shrill blast splinters Mack's skull like a sledgehammer.

He closes his eyes and swallows back a tide of nausea. When he opens them again, the little girl has been replaced with Ben. He's holding a steaming mug in one hand, a green plastic soda bottle in the other.

"Black coffee?" he asks. "Or ginger ale?"

Mack swallows hard. "Neither."

"If you puke on that carpet, my friend, Randi will kill me. And then I'll kill you. So— bathroom's that way." Ben points over his shoulder.

"I don't need—" Mack gulps, sits up, and finds that he's entangled in a puffy purple quilt. He manages to extract himself, runs past Ben, and makes it to the bathroom just in time.

As he kneels miserably on the tile in front of the toilet, he tries to piece together how he wound up here, at Ben's apartment.

He remembers calling Ben from home and asking if they could get together for a little while. The last thing he remembers, he'd found his way to the midtown pub where Ben had promised to meet him for a beer. Or was it a drink?

Judging by how wretched he feels, it was both, and many of each. He smells strongly of stale cigarette smoke, too, and he recalls buying a pack somewhere along the way to the pub.

He rinses his mouth with water and spots a tube of toothpaste that has a picture of Barbie on it. He squeezes some of the sparkly pink goo onto his finger and rubs it over his teeth. He hasn't finger-brushed since his sleeping-around days, before he met Carrie.

Carrie.

He spits out the disgusting toothpaste, which tastes of fruit and flowers, and it's all he can do not to throw up in the sink. After splashing cold water over his stubbly face, he dries off with a towel.

Today's newspaper is sitting on top of a closed wicker hamper, the sections in disarray, as if someone had been reading it and put it aside hastily. Mack finds the front page, scans the headlines, then leafs through the section, skimming the news.

Five minutes later, he folds the paper open to a page, tucks it under his arm, and makes his way back to the living room.

Ben is there, waiting. Wordlessly, he holds out the mug and the bottle.

Mack takes the bottle, but he's not convinced he can stomach even ginger ale right now.

"Drink," Ben tells him.

Mack opens it and takes a cautious sip. It goes down, stays down.

"Sit." Ben gestures at the couch. The purple quilt is now neatly folded at one end, a pillow on top of it.

"Ben, I'm sorry . . ."

"Sit," Ben says again, taking his arm and steering him over to the couch. "It's okay."

"Thank you." Mack sinks onto the couch, the newspaper on his lap, and sips some more ginger ale. It's not helping, but it's not hurting, either.

Ben is in a chair opposite the couch, watching him warily.

Is he worried I'm going to throw up on the rug? Or worse?

What the hell happened last night?

What did I do?

Why am I here?

Mack vaguely remembers that he called Ben because he needed a shoulder and an ear.

What did I say?

"Feeling better?" Ben asks. He's wearing a suit, Mack notices.

"A little better. Are you . . . are we . . . is the office open today?"

"It is, but no one expects you to be there. I'm just going for a little while, to get a few things squared away. You can stay here if you don't want to go home. Randi and Lexi will be around."

Mack's eyes widen—ow, that hurts, everything hurts—and he tells Ben, "Lexi—that was Lexi just now, waking me up."

Ben's daughter. He hasn't seen her in months. Maybe a year. Years? And yet she drew a picture of him and Carrie holding hands on a sunny day.

"Yup—that was Lexi. Only I told her not to wake you up, just see if you were awake. I know you have a hard time falling asleep, and staying asleep—although I guess if last night didn't knock you out, nothing could."

Last night . . .

Mack hasn't a clue. Even this morning, right here and now, is hazy.

"I was so out of it, I didn't even realize that was Lexi," he tells Ben. "She used to be . . ."

"A baby?" Ben smiles faintly. "Yeah. I guess they grow up."

Inevitably, Mack's thoughts shift to Carrie, and the baby they were trying to conceive.

That's never going to happen now.

Oh, hell, that was never going to happen anyway. Tuesday morning . . .

"Listen, Mack?"

He looks up to find Ben watching him, still looking worried, as if he knows . . . something.

But how much?

Ben clears his throat. "I'm glad you told me about Carrie, and if you don't mind—I want to tell Randi about it."

"Wh-why?"

"You know—she's always felt kind of bad about things. That we never saw much of you anymore once you got married, or . . . I mean, we both thought it was us, that we rubbed her the wrong way or something."

"No. It wasn't you. It was Carrie. She just had a hard time with . . ."

"People," Ben supplies, as Mack simultaneously concludes his sentence with "Everyone."

Ben nods. "Well, now that I know the truth—it changes the way I see her. I wish I could go back, knowing what I know now. Maybe it's too late to change things, with everything that's going on—but it helps that I know."

"How?"

"I don't know . . . it just does. That's why I want to tell Randi. She'll feel better about it, too."

"What . . . what are you going to tell her, exactly?" Mack's heart is racing.

"You know—what you told me. About her past. It explains why she was the way she was. I mean why she *is* the way she *is*," he amends hastily.

"You don't have to do that," Mack tells him.

"Do what? Tell Randi?"

"No—talk about Carrie like she's still alive."

"She could be."

Mack shakes his head. No more lies. "She isn't, Ben. She's never coming home."

"You don't know that."

Wordlessly, Mack hands over the newspaper, folded

open to the article about Cantor Fitzgerald. He watches Ben read about how yesterday afternoon, at the Pierre Hotel, the chairman informed the families that not a single Cantor employee out of the thousand or so who had been at work on Tuesday morning had made it out alive. Not one.

When Ben finishes reading the article, he puts the paper aside and looks at Mack.

He knew, Mack realizes. *He already knew.*

"I'm sorry, Mack."

He nods.

"What are you going to do?" Ben asks after a few moments of somber silence.

"Go on," Mack says simply. "What else is there to do?"

Stepping from the bright morning sunshine into her office building, Allison is greeted with a prompt "Good morning, *mon*!"

As her eyes adjust to the dim lighting in the lobby, she spots the dreadlocked security guard back at his post. "Henry! It's so good to see you."

Ah, there it is again—that inexplicable urge to make physical contact with someone she really doesn't know all that well; someone who—like Mack—she has seen in passing as she goes about her daily business and never really thought much about until now.

It's all she can do not to race over and throw her arms around Henry, but she merely smiles.

"Good to see you too, *mon*. Everything is okay?" he asks in his lilting Jamaican inflection.

How to answer that?

With a simple nod and another question is probably the easiest way. "How about with you?"

Henry shakes his head. "I knew a few people."

The words are spoken so softly she can barely hear them, but the sorrow in his big black eyes speaks volumes.

"I'm so sorry."

"Yeah, *mon*. Me too."

For a moment, they're both silent.

Then Henry slides a clipboard across the counter to her. "Here . . . I need you to sign in."

"Sign in?"

"New world—new security procedure. I need to check your bag, too . . . sorry."

"It's okay." She opens her shoulder bag and he pokes around inside quickly.

"I never saw you wear shoes like this." The twinkle returns to Henry's eyes as he gestures at the sneakers tucked into her bag. She wore them to walk up to Union Square, then put on her heels before taking the subway to midtown.

"Shh—don't tell anyone."

"I won't. I wouldn't want you to get fired, would I?"

It feels good to share a little laugh with Henry, after all the grim faces on the streets and in the subway, dozens of black SUVs with government plates parked all over midtown . . . and now this: new security measures at the office.

Allison can't help but think that it's going to take a lot more than having visitors sign in and checking their bags to make this building secure. For one thing, Henry is often zoned out in a ganja-induced haze. For another, there's a basement entrance that opens out to an alleyway where the smokers hang out. They keep the door propped open all day so they can come and go freely.

I guess that's going to have to change now, Allison

thinks as she waits for the elevator. *A lot of things in this city are going to have to change if anyone is ever going to feel safe again.*

She takes the elevator alone up to the tenth floor—unusual at this time of morning—and finds that all is dark behind the glass doors that lead to the *7th Avenue* offices.

As she pushes through the doors, she realizes how useless they are. They aren't even locked. Anyone could walk right through them.

Allison looks around for a light switch. Not finding one, she shrugs and makes her way down the darkened corridors to her own office.

She turns on the desk lamp, sits at her desk, and wonders if anyone else is going to show up. Everything is so still without the hum of office machines, voices, ringing telephones. It's unsettling.

Maybe she should just go home.

To what, though?

More emptiness?

Even Mack appears to have abandoned the apartment building now. He didn't answer her knock earlier, or the phone call she placed when she got back to her apartment. She left him a message, telling him she was going to be at work today, then dumped the coffee she'd poured for him down the sink.

Maybe he just didn't want to see or talk to her. Or anyone.

Maybe Carrie turned up—or her remains were found, and he went off to make funeral arrangements.

Maybe something happened to him, just like something happened to Kristina.

Maybe he was arrested for what happened to Kristina.

Allison doesn't want to consider either of the last two

possibilities, but they're perhaps just as likely as the others.

She thrums her fingernails on the desk and looks at the phone.

Should she call a locksmith first, or try calling Mack again?

She picks up the receiver, dials Mack's number.

It rings and goes right to the answering machine, just like before. "Hi . . . it's Allison Taylor again. I just wanted to let you know that I'm at work, and you can call me here if you want, or try my cell phone. I hope . . . I hope you're okay." After leaving her numbers, she hangs up.

Remembering what she saw yesterday in Kristina's apartment, she swallows hard.

What if something happened to Mack?

The thought is too horrible to push aside. She takes a card from her wallet and quickly dials the number, before she can change her mind.

This time, there's an answer—a gruff, hurried one—on the first ring.

"Yeah, Manzillo here."

"Detective Manzillo, this is Allison Taylor. I'm—"

"I know who you are," he cuts in. "What can I do for you? I'm in my car on the Bruckner and I always lose the signal right near here, so talk fast."

"I was just wondering what's going on with . . . the case. Did you get him yet?"

"Get who?"

"You know . . . whoever killed Kristina."

She holds her breath, praying that they got him, whoever he is—praying that it's not Mack, praying he didn't get to Mack.

"Not yet," Detective Manzillo tells her. "Is there anything else you can think of that might help with the case?"

"No. Nothing, except . . . well, there are two things. One is that Kristina had the key to my apartment, and I'm worried that . . . um, do you know if it was still there?"

There's a pause. "Do you know where she kept it? Because I know that the only keys on her key ring were to the front door of the building, her own apartment, and the mailbox. We checked them out."

"I don't know where she kept it, but she definitely has—*had* it. Could I, do you think, have a look around her apartment just to make sure it's still there?"

"I'll have to do that myself," the detective tells her. "I'll get back to you as soon as I can. What's the other thing you wanted to mention?"

Oh. *That.*

"I just wondered if you knew where Mack—I mean, Mr. MacKenna—is, because I don't think he's home and I can't reach him."

As soon as she blurts it out, she regrets it.

Especially when she's greeted with silence on the other end of the line.

"I'm just worried something might have happened to him," she adds hastily. "It's not that I, you know, think he's . . ."

Guilty.

She can't say the word; that would mean admitting she's considered that he might, indeed, be guilty.

Still, Detective Manzillo says nothing.

"Sir?"

Silence.

After a moment, she realizes the connection was lost. Hanging up the phone, she wonders how much he heard.

About a minute later, her phone rings. She hesitates, wondering what would happen if she ignored it.

It could be a work-related call—though she doubts it.

It could be Mack, getting back to her.

Or it could be Detective Manzillo again, freshly suspicious of Mack, thanks to her.

Reluctantly, she picks up the phone. "Allison Taylor."

"Sorry, we got cut off before," Manzillo says briskly. "I was asking if you can think of anything else that might help us with the case."

And I was putting my foot into my mouth, but you apparently didn't hear any of that.

Relieved, Allison tells him, "No, there's nothing else. But I'll call you if anything comes up."

"Do that. And please be careful."

"I will."

She hangs up and spins her desk chair to the window, gazing absently at the skyline and thinking about Mack. He's a stranger and a married man—a *widowed* man. Newly widowed. Why does he matter so much to her?

Maybe it's because she recognizes in him a kindred spirit. Like her, he seems alone in the world, whether he really is or not. She sensed it even on Monday night, before his wife went missing—which is odd, when you think about it.

She's sick of thinking about it.

So think about something else. Anything else.

Realizing she's gazing out at the Chrysler building spire, she's glad her office window faces north and not south. At least she won't have a daily view of lower Manhattan's scarred skyline.

It's hard to imagine that just forty-eight hours ago, on a beautiful morning like this one, the clear September sky exploded in flames.

A faint sound reaches Allison's ears.

Instantly on high alert, she spins abruptly in her chair, looking expectantly toward the doorway.

Beyond lies the bullpen—a large, open space filled with desks, work cubicles, file cabinets, and office machines.

"Hello?" she calls, and waits for a response from a coworker who probably didn't realize someone else is here on the floor.

But there's no reply.

Heart pounding, Allison stands.

She's as certain she's not alone as she is that terrible things can happen out of nowhere, out of the clear blue September sky.

She sees nothing, hears nothing, but there are countless nooks where an intruder might be hiding, waiting to pounce, waiting to do to her what he did to Kristina Haines.

"Did Mack leave?"

Ben nods, closing the bedroom door behind him and watching Randi pull a sweater over her head.

"Where did he go?" she asks when her head pops out the neck hole.

"Home, he said."

"I was going to see if he wanted some breakfast."

"I gave him coffee, and ginger ale," Ben says, sitting on the bed, "and he barely got that down."

"Poor guy." His wife sits beside him. He can smell the lotion she always uses before bed at night and when she gets out of the shower in the morning. The scent comforts him; it always does, especially when he comes home after a hard day at work.

He thinks about Mack, going home to an empty house, and he wonders what he would do if something happened to Randi.

I would die, he thinks, and on the heels of that thought, *No, I would go on.*

What else is there to do?

Mack . . .

He'll go on, just like thousands of other people in this city who lost their spouses.

"Ben?" Randi's shoulder-length dark red hair is mussed from the sweater; he pats a couple of strands into place, then presses a kiss to her shoulder. "What's that for?"

"I love you." He rests his cheek against her shoulder, breathing her lotion scent.

"I love you, too, Benjy . . ."

She calls him that when she's in a good mood or feeling playful and affectionate.

"But I hope you're not getting any ideas," she goes on, "because Lexi might walk in any second now."

"I wasn't getting ideas, but now that you mention it—she's watching *Blue's Clues*, and we can lock the door . . ."

Randi laughs, giving his head a gentle push off her shoulder.

"Sorry, but you have to go to work, and I have things to do." She reaches over to the nightstand for her watch. Strapping it on her left wrist, she says, "Tell me about Mack."

"Thanks for not giving me a hard time about meeting him." Ben shakes his head. "He was shit-faced by the time I got to him."

"What's going on? Besides Carrie, I mean . . . as if that's not enough. But you said his neighbor . . . ?"

"Was killed." He nods. When he climbed into bed beside Randi in the wee hours, after wrestling Mack home from the pub and onto the couch, he briefly told her what was going on.

"But not at the World Trade Center on Tuesday," Randi clarifies.

"No. It happened in her apartment—she lives in his building. I guess someone broke in and killed her."

"Oh my God. Did he know her?"

"He said he did, but not very well."

"I'm sure it's upsetting—I mean, any other time, it would probably be devastating. But with his own wife missing—"

"That's what I wanted to talk to you about. He told me something about Carrie—you know, why she is the way she is."

"How *is* she?"

Ben raises an eyebrow at Randi. " 'Standoffish' is the nicest word I can think of. How about you?"

"Same." She sighs. "The other one rhymes with 'witch' and starts with a B, and now I feel really horrible about ever having said that about her."

"Want to feel worse about it?"

"Oh yes, please," she says dryly. "I'd *love* to feel worse."

"When she was a little girl, her family had mob ties. I'm not clear on the details, but I guess there was a murder and she and her parents were put into the witness protection program."

Randi just looks at him.

"What?" he says.

"I don't know . . . the *witness protection* program?"

"Why are you saying it like that?"

"Like what?"

"Like you don't believe it."

"Because I'm not sure that I do."

"You think Mack is *lying* about it?" he asks incredulously.

"I didn't say that."

It's Ben's turn to just look at her.

Unlike him, Randi has always been incredibly intuitive. Where Ben pretty much likes everyone he meets and tends to give strangers the benefit of the doubt— and has been burned for it, many a time—Randi is far more wary, far less trusting.

What she likes to say is that she has a highly functioning bullshit detector. Ben wouldn't argue with that.

He's come to rely on her judgment whenever they cross paths with new people—though back when they first met Carrie Robinson, he didn't need his wife to tell him that they weren't going to become a cozy foursome with the MacKennas. Even easygoing Ben found his best friend's new girlfriend to be disappointingly stiff and reserved. Carrie was the kind of woman who, at a group dinner, would turn and talk to her date as if no one else were even present—when she talked at all.

Had Mack ever asked him, afterward, what he thought of Carrie, he was prepared to be truthful. Well, as truthful as he could be. Randi had coached him on what to say: *I'm sure she's a nice person, and if you're happy with her then I'm happy for you, but just make sure you take it slow.*

Mack never asked.

Mack, who had been best man at Ben's wedding seven years ago, eloped without ever having told Ben he was engaged.

On Randi's advice, he swallowed the hurt and invited

Mack and his new bride out to dinner to celebrate their wedding. Mack made excuses every time they tried to set a date. Ben got the hint.

His friendship with Mack eventually got back on solid footing, but he saw Carrie only a couple more times—once at the office Christmas party, and once when Mack was presented with a sales award.

They never discussed Carrie, other than in passing.

But last night, when Mack drunkenly confided in him about Carrie's past, Ben immediately forgave her. Now, thanks to Randi, he has misgivings about her all over again.

"Tell me what you're thinking," he tells his wife.

She shrugs. "It sounds far-fetched. That's all."

"There is such a thing as the witness protection program, you know. It's—"

"I know what it is, Ben."

Ben. Not Benjy.

"It's been around for a long time," he tells Randi, "and real people are in it—families with kids. Why couldn't Carrie have been one of them?"

"I'm not saying she wasn't."

"Then what *are* you saying?"

"Just—"

"Mommy?"

They look up to see Lexi standing in the doorway.

"Can I have some Goldfish crackers?" she asks, and then, without missing a beat, "I thought you went to work, Daddy."

"And I thought you were watching *Blue's Clues*."

"It's in a commercial. I hate commercials."

"We don't say *hate*," Randi automatically corrects her.

"Especially about television commercials," Ben puts in.

"Why not?"

"Because," he tells his daughter, "they're how Daddy makes a living."

"Shouldn't you get to work, Daddy?" Randi asks, looking at her watch. "The sooner you get there, the sooner you'll be able to get out and come home."

"You're right." He plants a kiss on her cheek, and one on the top of Lexi's dark head.

"Bye, Daddy. I love you."

"Love you, too. And you—and we'll talk later," he tells Randi meaningfully as he heads for the door, wondering again about the mysterious Carrie Robinson MacKenna.

"Is someone there?" Allison calls again, standing poised in the doorway of her office, her eyes scanning the bullpen.

She skims right past the shadowy corner behind the copy machine. Crouched there, Jamie can clearly see the exquisite fear in her blue eyes.

This is going to be good.

Allison reaches back and plucks a small pair of scissors from the pencil cup. She holds them like a dagger, her elbow bent, her trembling fist wrapped around the finger holes, the closed blades poised before her, ready to make contact.

Nice try, but those are no match for this.

Jamie glances down at the eight-inch chef's knife that had once belonged to Kristina Haines. The blade is clean now, but her blood—and Marianne's—still stains the wooden handle.

Now Allison's will join the mix.

It's just a pity this time won't be like the last two . . . setting the scene with lingerie, candles, music . . .

You can't have everything.

No, but still . . .

Maybe it would have been better not to track her down here at the office. It was so easy—too easy—to slip in through the basement door, propped open with a plastic bucket, cigarette butts littering the concrete around it.

Jamie rode the elevator up from there. Had it stopped on the lobby floor, there might have been trouble—though even if the security guard had noticed someone inside, he might have assumed it was just an employee who had gone out for a smoke.

But the elevator didn't stop.

And here I am . . . and here she is.

Finding Allison alone was incredibly fortuitous. Jamie had expected it to be quiet here—quiet enough to do what has to be done and beat a hasty retreat.

This is perfect, though. She's alone, just as the others were.

Does she sense that she's about to die?

Kristina Haines knew it.

So did Marianne.

Jamie made sure of that.

Telling them they were about to die made it more satisfying, somehow. Their terror—Jamie's power.

This is different. Allison is tense, watchful, but she doesn't really know what's about to happen. Tempting as it is to prolong the inevitable, it will have to be quick.

Does that really matter? The knife plunging into flesh will yield the same result, won't it? There will be blood, hot and sticky. There will be death.

Trembling with anticipation, Jamie straightens and inches a cautious step forward.

Allison, looking in the opposite direction, is oblivious.

Jamie takes another step.

The glorious moment is so close, so tantalizingly close . . .

And then it happens.

Voices reach Jamie's ears; Allison's, too. She jerks her head in the direction of the reception area, again skimming her gaze right past Jamie's hiding place.

"Hello?" she calls, and her face is etched in relief when the voices call back to her.

Moments later, a pair of coworkers appear in the bullpen.

Jamie watches Allison greet them, the scissors discreetly held at her side now that the threat has evaporated . . . or so she seems to think.

That's all right, Allison.

I'll see you later.

And next time, it's going to be on your turf . . . on my terms.

Being able to fall asleep anywhere, at any time of day—it's a good quality in a detective. Or so Rocky likes to remind Ange, when she scolds him for never staying awake through a movie when they sit down to watch one on cable.

Today, she's the one who told him to go lie down for a while as soon as he finished eating the hot frittata she had waiting when he walked in the door.

"Breakfast, and *then* bed . . . yeah, why not?" He gave her a weary kiss on the cheek.

"Go forget about everything for a while," Ange told him, briefly stroking his temple with her fingertips.

Rocky went off to the bedroom thinking that despite everything, he was a lucky man. His last thought before drifting off was that he probably should have gone back down to the crime scene to make sure Kristina's killer hadn't stolen Allison's key from the scene.

But by the time she'd mentioned it, he'd already been on his way home. And in his heart, he honestly doesn't believe that if the killer set his sights on Allison, he'd need that key to get in. Either he already has one, or he has another method of getting in and out.

Now, awakened by the ringing telephone, Rocky opens his eyes and gets his bearings.

The milky light filtering through the sheer drapes indicates that it's still daytime—good. That's good.

The phone that's ringing is his cell—not so good.

Unless it's Vic, calling back.

He snaps open the phone and says, "Yeah, Manzillo here."

"Rock . . . we got another one."

It's not Vic. It's Tommy, the station house desk sergeant.

"You got another what?" Rocky sits up fast, his thoughts racing. Another terrorist attack, another building down, another ground zero . . .

The answer catches him off guard.

"Another 10–55, Rock."

10–55—police code for Coroner Case.

"Same MO," Tommy continues. "Looks like some one crawled through her fire escape window at night. Same signature—sexy nightie, candles, music. Same sick bastard. I'd say we got some kind of serial killer on our hands."

Chapter Ten

Allison?"

She jumps, and looks up to see the executive editor, Erik, standing in the doorway of her office. A tall, sandy-haired man with elegant Nordic good looks, he captured her attention on her first day here. She thought he was flirting with her and developed a crush on him. Turns out, he's just super-friendly—and gay. Just another of the ineligible bachelors in her life.

Reminded of her laundry room conversation with Kristina, she shudders.

"Sorry," Erik says, "I didn't mean to scare you."

"It's okay, I'm just . . ."

She trails off, not wanting to tell him that she stumbled across a murder yesterday, and has spent the last three hours jumping at every little sound. Some people share every detail of their personal lives at the office. She's never been one of them.

"Don't worry, everyone's a little nuts today," Erik tells her.

She smiles faintly. "Did I say I was nuts?"

He smiles back. "Hey, at least you came into work. Hardly anyone else bothered—not that I blame anyone for being afraid to leave home after . . . everything."

Yeah, well, some of us are afraid to stay home after . . . everything.

Afraid?

She despises the word, has been fighting it—fighting fear—all morning.

After all, nothing actually even *happened*—other than her imagination playing tricks on her, making her think someone was hiding in the bullpen.

Yes, and her coworkers almost caught her wielding a pair of scissors like one of those hapless, helpless horror movie heroines who try to fend off the bad guy with some ridiculous nonweapon.

I couldn't help it, though. In that moment, when I grabbed those scissors, I was scared.

So? She's been scared plenty of times in her life, but she's always stayed strong.

That's not about to change. She won't let it. She won't curl up and die like her mother did.

Strength is my strength.

Then again—so is her active imagination. It's always been an effective coping mechanism. On the very day she woke up to find that her father had left, her imaginary sister came to stay.

Winona, Allison called her.

She'd dreamed about her the night before, and she seemed so real that somewhere in the back of her mind, she almost believed that she was.

A child psychiatrist could have had a field day with that, she supposes. But of course, her mother was too busy going crazy herself to worry about whether her daughter had.

"I just wanted to tell you," Erik is saying, "that you might as well go on home. There's nothing to do here."

He's right, of course. She's been trying to stay busy all morning, but routine paperwork was all she could find to occupy her jittery hands. The phones are quiet, and there's been no e-mail—not work-related, anyway.

The handful of employees who showed up have mainly been congregating in the corridors and the small office kitchen, talking in hushed tones about what's going on in the city, trading information, rumors, horror stories, and the good news that several people had been pulled alive from the rubble at ground zero.

Allison pretty much kept to herself in her office, waiting for one of the locksmiths to call her back. She'd left messages for several.

She kept thinking about Kristina. And Mack.

Maybe Carrie had been one of the people who had been rescued. Maybe she's coming home after all.

Allison fervently hopes that's the case.

"So," Erik says, rocking back on the heels of his alligator shoes, "if you want to clear out of here, go ahead. I'm going to."

"I guess I might as well, too, then. What about tomorrow?"

"Take the day off." Seeing her disappointed expression, he amends, "Or come in if you want. But I honestly don't think business is going to be back to normal until Monday."

Normal . . .

Monday?

Allison is certain it's going to be a long, long time before anything feels normal.

She leaves the office, takes the subway back downtown to Union Square, trades her heels for sneakers, and walks the rest of the way home.

Without traffic, the streets are still eerily quiet down

here in the frozen zone. Missing posters are taped to every available surface. Allison can't bear to look at the faces smiling out from the photographs, suspecting that none of those people are ever coming home now.

Clusters of cops in orange vests and NYPD caps are posted on corners and at closed subway entrances. National guardsmen, armed and wearing camo, patrol the streets. The only civilian pedestrians are neighborhood residents who, like Allison, provided ID and were cleared at the police barricades at the northern boundary of the zone. They gather in somber little groups in front of buildings or scuttle along with their heads bent, as if they're afraid of what they'll see if they look up.

Unaccustomed to the gaping hole in the southern skyline, Allison, too, keeps her head down until she gets back to her building.

She'd been hoping she might find a police car parked in front, but there isn't one.

Wondering if the building is as empty as it looks— and feels, even from here—she unlocks the door and steps inside. It closes hard behind her, and she jumps. Again.

No. Get over it. You're fine. Everything is fine.

But that's not true—not by a long shot. She can try all she wants to convince herself that she's not in danger, but the truth is, her neighbor was murdered in this very building.

Okay, so everything isn't fine.

But what is she supposed to do? Where else is she supposed to go? This is her home. Even if she had someplace else to go—someplace far away from here—how would she even get there? She doesn't have a car, there are no flights, and for all she knows, no trains, either.

She's stuck here, in this building. It is what it is.

Fine. So get moving.
You'll feel better in your own apartment.

Walking across the empty vestibule and down the vacant hall to the elevator may not be the hardest thing Allison has ever had to do in her life, but it's definitely on the list.

Her rapid footsteps seem to beat in time with her pulse, and she looks over her shoulder repeatedly, making sure she's alone. Yes. Alone is good.

Reaching the elevator, she presses the up button. If the building has been empty since she left for the office earlier, then it should still be here, on the first floor, shouldn't it?

But it isn't.

Hearing the elevator begin its creaky, rattling, painstaking descent from the upper floors, she wonders if this means that someone is up there.

She forces herself to stand her ground and wait for it, but she keeps thinking about Jerry, remembering how he popped out of the stairwell the other night.

Had he just come down from Kristina's apartment?

Had he spotted Allison standing there?

What if he knew she'd seen him? What if . . . ?

When at last the elevator arrives, she almost expects him to jump out at her when the doors open.

But it's empty. Of course it is. The building is empty.

Or is it?

She rides up to the fourth floor. Tempted to make a run for her own door, she makes a quick detour and knocks on Mack's. No answer.

She doesn't bother to knock again or call out to him. The sooner she's behind locked doors, the better.

She opens her door, steps inside, and is about to lock herself in when she thinks better of it.

What if someone really did take the key from Kristina's apartment and he's in here? Waiting? Hiding?

What are you going to do, protect yourself with scissors again? Or the chef's knife?

It's still in her unmade bed, she realizes.

Taking her cell phone out of her pocket, she flips it open and dials a 9 and then a 1. Keeping her thumb poised over the 1, ready to press the button again if something happens, she moves quickly from room to room, checking to make sure she's alone.

She sees the knife still lying on her bed. About to pick it up and carry it with her, she thinks better of it and tucks it underneath the pillow. She has other knives in the kitchen. It's probably a good idea to keep one close at hand at night, just in case.

Mission accomplished, she returns to the door, triple locks it, and exhales at last.

Now what?

Get busy. Stay busy.

She checks her answering machine. No messages.

Checks her e-mail. No messages.

She calls several locksmiths back and leaves more messages. Why isn't anyone picking up? She needs more numbers to try. She'll have to look for some on the Internet. She doesn't even have the Manhattan Yellow Pages.

She changes her clothes, boils water for tea, takes out a mug . . .

Busy, busy.

Don't let fear win.

She makes toast with the heel of a loaf of whole grain bread that's verging on stale, and considers going out to get some groceries. It would give her something to do—something constructive.

But she didn't notice any open stores on her walk home from Union Square. And even if she were to come across one nearby, how fresh would the food possibly be? With no traffic in this frozen zone these last few days, restocking neighborhood markets must be impossible.

Chances are, she'd have to walk all the way back up to the supermarket on Fourteenth Street to find an open store, let alone one with decent food. And then she'd only be able to buy as much as she could carry all the way home on foot.

While she really has no desire to stay locked in her apartment all day, she doesn't have the energy to venture far from here, either. Not when errands that were once no-brainers are now fraught with complications.

She paces restlessly through the apartment, and nearly jumps out of her skin at a rattling sound in the kitchen. On its heels, though, is a high-pitched whistling.

The tea kettle.

As she pours hot water over a tea bag in the mug, her hand shakes so badly that water sloshes over the rim.

She really could use some fresh air. Not because she's too frightened to stay in.

No, of course not.

You don't let terror win.

She just wants to find someplace where she can breathe fresh air for a while, that's all . . .

She wants to breathe easily . . .

Just *breathe*.

With Brandewyne at his side clutching an unlit cigarette—no smoking at the crime scene, Rocky was compelled to remind her—he stands in the doorway,

surveying the carnage beyond as Alicia Keys sings
"Fallin'" on a CD player by the bed. It's set to keep
looping the same song over and over, just like the one
in Kristina Haines's apartment.

The victim—Marianne Apostolos, age thirty-three—
lies curled up on her side in her blood-soaked bed.

This, he knows, is what her brother saw when he
came over to check on her. His mother had sent him
over here with Marianne's spare key after Marianne
missed her morning check-in call.

"Thank God Ma didn't go over there herself," the
broken man kept saying when Rocky and Brandewyne
talked to him down at the precinct a short time ago. "It
would have killed her."

Rocky nodded grimly, knowing that George himself
will have to live with this scene branded into his soul
for the rest of his life.

It's one thing to lose someone to natural causes—old
age, illness. But when someone slaughters a defense-
less woman in her own home . . .

And for what? Kicks? Revenge?

Andy Blake is kneeling beside the corpse, gathering
forensic evidence as Jorge Perez snaps photos of the
scene.

"Jesus," Rocky mutters, stepping closer. "This is a
bloodbath."

"I know, brutal, right?" Blake shakes his head. "What
the hell do you think she did to deserve this?"

Rocky knows Andy doesn't actually believe anything
Marianne could have done warranted this violent fe-
rocity. But he's feeling short-fused after too little sleep
and too much stress, and it's all he can do not to make
a harsh response to that inane comment.

Nicotine-deprived Brandewyne's filter is obviously

not working as effectively; she snaps, "If you actually think anyone deserves to die like this, Blake, then you're a real—"

"Take a chill pill, sweetheart, I didn't mean it that way."

"Sweetheart? I'm not your sweetheart."

"You got that right."

Ignoring the two of them, Rocky strides over to the victim and takes a closer look.

Like Kristina Haines, she's wearing lingerie—a white satin nightgown trimmed with lace. Like Kristina, she's been savagely stabbed all over her body. And like Kristina, she's missing a middle finger.

Rocky can't see the evidence of that at the moment— her hands are already bagged to preserve the evidence. But the finger is gone—sawed off while she was still alive, according to the CSU guys.

That detail of the Haines case was never released to the public—not that anyone in the press was paying the slightest bit of attention anyway. Everyone was consumed with the much larger story; Kristina's murder didn't even make the papers.

Still . . . if it had, there would have been no mention of the missing middle finger.

Only the cops working the case—and Kristina's killer—could have known about that.

Now a second body turns up, also missing the middle finger of her right hand?

"She fought pretty hard," Perez comments. "We found some skin scrapings under her nails, and there was some hair tangled in her fingers."

"*Tangled?*" Rocky is taken aback. Both Allison Taylor and James McKenna had described the prime suspect, Jerry, as having a crew cut.

"Yeah, a few strands of it," Perez tells him.

"Strands?" Having traded the cigarette for a pen, Brandewyne scribbles something on her notepad. "So it was long hair?"

"Yeah."

"How long?" Brandewyne asks.

"Pretty long . . . we'll measure, but—"

"Could it be her own hair?" Rocky cuts in impatiently.

"Nope. Hers is shorter and curlier and reddish."

"What color was this?"

"Looks like dark brown."

Before Rocky can ask another question, his cell phone rings. He steps into the next room to answer it, glancing at the window near the couch and noticing the iron grillwork of a fire escape just beyond the screen. Looks like the CSU team dusted the sill and sash for prints.

So this guy—the guy they're calling the Nightwatcher down at the station house—climbs up fire escapes and slithers into his victims' apartments in the dead of night. He must know them well enough to be sure they live alone . . . among other details.

He snaps his phone open. "Yeah, Manzillo here."

"Rocky, it's Tommy. Get this: that building? The one where the Apostolos girl was killed?"

"Yeah . . . that's where I am right now. What about it?"

"Who do you think the owner is? Go ahead, take a wild guess."

"What is this, *Jeopardy*?" he snaps, not in the mood for games. "Who?"

"Dale Reiss," comes the reply, "and guess who works there as a handyman?"

* * *

When Allison first came out to sit on the stoop earlier this afternoon, the sun was shining. Now the sky is overcast and the wind has shifted in this direction, carrying the acrid scent of burning.

Maybe she should go back inside . . .

But there's nothing to do there.

Nothing to do out here, either; no one to talk to, nowhere to go . . .

She's spent the better part of the last hour sitting on the stoop, leafing through an issue of *Vogue* in the warm September sunshine.

But now the sky is growing overcast and the wind has shifted. How can she focus on the magazine's glossy glamour? All she wanted to do when she came out here was sit and read and breathe, but now her every breath is tainted with death fumes from the fire still burning farther downtown.

Maybe she should give up and go back inside. But the thought of being back in her apartment, behind all those locks . . .

Locks that may be useless if Kristina's killer stole her key . . .

Better to sit out here just a little longer, inhaling bad air and brooding, inexplicably feeling as though she's survived something horrific only to face something even worse looming on the horizon.

It's because of what happened to Kristina, she knows.

Or maybe it goes all the way back to her mother.

Every time Mom tried to kill herself and failed, Allison was left with a growing sense of impending doom. She used to mentally rehearse what she would do when it actually happened—when her mother finally succeeded in taking her own life.

She always assumed it would be afternoon or early evening, because that was how the trial runs had unfolded. But she was wrong.

She didn't come home at dusk one day to find that Brenda Taylor had OD'd again. No, she was right in the house when her mother finally killed herself. In the house, but sound asleep. Helpless.

Why, Mom? Why did you do it when I was there, in the next room? Why didn't you at least wait until I was gone, so I wouldn't feel as though there must have been something I could have done if only I'd gotten up sooner?

It was four A.M. when she awakened, got up to go to the bathroom, and found Mom lying on the tile floor there, cold and still and rock-hard. Bloody vomit was caked around her mouth and her eyes were fixed, as they so often were, on something only she could see.

This time, Mom wasn't going to blink and drift reluctantly back to the real world. This time, she was gone for good, and Allison was left alone in Centerfield to face the gossip, and the financial fallout, and the cops and the social workers who said they had only her best interest in mind.

Maybe that was true.

Maybe not.

Maybe everyone had an agenda. Maybe they still do.

But that doesn't matter; they don't matter. You're the only one who does. You just have to take care of yourself; just keep going through the motions of living, every minute of every day, no matter what happens, until one day you realize you're actually living again.

Allison stands up, brushes off her jeans—the same old jeans she keeps picking up from the floor and putting back on—and looks up at the building.

She notices the metal fire escape that zigzags down the brick face. It's meant to save lives; there was no such escape for all those people who burned to death in the World Trade Center, and yet . . .

Did someone climb that network of narrow stairs in the dark and crawl through Kristina's window? Would she be alive if not for that?

As Allison shakes her head at the irony, a human shadow falls across the steps in front of her. Someone is standing behind her.

It's broad daylight and she's outside on an urban street, but it might as well be the middle of the night—and the middle of nowhere—for all the comfort that brings. The skin on the back of her neck prickles with awareness, and she's afraid to turn around, afraid of what—whom—she might find there. Afraid.

Dammit.

Slowly, she turns her head, bracing herself to come face-to-face with Jerry.

But it's Mack.

He looks like hell. Yesterday's five o'clock shadow has turned into full-blown scruff, his hair is wiry, and his blue chambray shirt is wrinkled and untucked from equally wrinkled khakis. His eyes are hidden behind dark glasses, but she can feel the gloom radiating from them.

"Are you okay?" she asks him, though the answer is obvious.

He shakes his head mutely.

"Where have you been?"

"At the Pierre, and . . . I, uh, registered."

"Registered?"

"Carrie. Missing persons."

As if his legs can no longer support his weight, he sinks onto the step at her feet and sits facing the street, hugging himself, shoulders hunched.

"I heard that they pulled some people out alive this morning," she tells him. "Maybe Carrie—"

"No," he says, "that was just a rumor."

"But—"

"People *were* pulled out, but they were firemen who were part of the rescue effort."

"Oh." Deflated, she sits beside him. She sees that his hands are trembling, clasped around his bent knees.

"I have to get some hair from her hairbrush and bring it to the Armory later, for . . . DNA. It's so they can . . . you know. It's a long shot, but maybe they'll find her. I mean . . . her body. Then at least I can bury her."

Allison doesn't know what to say to that. To any of this.

After a long moment, she reaches out and touches his arm.

He looks down at her hand resting on his sleeve, and then up at her face.

She can't see his eyes behind the dark glasses. Maybe that's a good thing, she thinks, and wishes he couldn't see hers, either.

"What are you doing?"

Startled by Jamie's voice, Jerry jumps back, away from Mama's closed bedroom door.

"Nothing!" He shakes his head rapidly.

"I told you not to open that door, remember?"

"I wasn't going to open it," Jerry lies. "I was just looking at it."

"Are you sure about that?"

He bobs his head up and down, feeling nervous and not sure why. "It's just . . . it smells bad. I thought maybe she left food in there or something."

Jamie doesn't say anything about that, only, after a long pause, "Whatever you do, Jerry, don't open that door. *Ever.* Got it?"

"Got it." Jerry hesitates. "Can I have some cake?"

"Jerry, how many times do I have to tell you? You don't have to ask me. Just take it. It's for you."

"Thank you, Jamie. That was so nice of you."

Jerry goes to the kitchen. The Entenmann's box is sitting on the counter. He opens it and sees just one small square of cake is sitting in the crumb-filled pan.

"Jamie? Did you eat my cake?"

"No. I told you, it's for you, all of it. You must have eaten it and forgotten. You do that a lot. Your memory is bad because of your head injury."

Yes. That's right. Jerry's memory is bad. Sometimes, he doesn't even remember the head injury, but that's fine with him. He just wishes he remembers eating the cake, because he loves cake.

He opens the silverware drawer. Something moves inside: a fat cockroach skitters toward the shadows and disappears through a crack.

Jerry recoils and slams the drawer closed. He'll eat with his hands.

He grabs the hunk of cake, swallows a dense, fudgy-sweet bite, and it comes back to him: last night, he ate the rest of the cake himself. He stood right here at the counter, tears rolling down his face and Marianne's words echoing through his head as he shoveled cake into his mouth until he felt sick.

She said she loved him.

That surprised him, because she didn't act like she

loved him when he saw her at her apartment yesterday afternoon. She didn't even seem to like him very much.

I guess I was wrong about that, Jerry thinks, wetting his finger and running it along the bottom of the foil tray so that the crumbs stick to it. He licks his finger and sticks it into the tray over and over again, until every last morsel of cake is gone.

But it isn't enough.

"Jamie? Can I please have more cake?"

"Yeah . . . okay."

"When?"

"Later. I'll go get you some."

Jerry considers that. "Can you go get it now?"

Jamie sighs. "Sure, Jerry. I'll get it now."

"Vic?"

He sets down his plastic glass of Coke and turns to see Rocky Manzillo standing behind him.

"Well, would you look who's here." Vic gets to his feet to greet his friend.

It's been less than a week since they saw each other, but he notices that Rocky's aged in that time. The hair he has left is grayer, the lines around his eyes deeper than they were on Saturday night. These aren't laugh lines, either. Not by a long shot.

Ordinarily, they greet each other with a jovial handshake or a casual clap on the back. Today, though, Vic gives his friend a quick, hard hug, which Rocky returns fervently.

"I didn't expect you to show," Vic tells him.

"I was in the neighborhood, headed up the FDR when I called Ange to check in. She told me you left a message that you were here eating, but I thought I might have missed you."

"You didn't. I ordered dessert." He settles back into the booth and gestures at the padded brown vinyl bench opposite him. "Sit down. Got time?"

"I'll just grab something quick. I'm on a case."

Rocky sits across from him and Vic looks around the crowded coffee shop for the lone waitress. There she is, taking an order from a pair of weathered-looking streetwalkers.

Following his gaze, Rocky comments, "Nice clientele. How'd you pick this place?" He plucks a cold, mealy French fry from the plate Vic pushed aside a few minutes ago.

"It got a top rating in Zagat's," Vic tells him. "Right above Le Cirque."

"Funny guy." Rocky takes another fry and eyes the crusty, congealed remains of Vic's grilled cheese sandwich.

"Actually, this was the first place I saw when I came out of the Midtown Tunnel. First thing I've eaten all day and it's going to be a long night."

"Yeah, no kidding. So you've been over in Queens?"

Vic nods.

"Where, at the airports?"

Vic nods again. He's spent an exhausting afternoon interviewing airline employees.

"Got any leads?" Rocky reaches for the sticky-looking ketchup bottle on the table and unscrews the cap. Seeing that the top of the bottle is gummy with blackish ketchup goo, he makes a face and takes a napkin from the holder on the table.

"Maybe." Vic shrugs. "You know I can't get into details."

"Yeah, yeah. I know. You guys have a lot of rules."

You guys. Their friendship has never been entirely immune to the legendary tension between the FBI and local cops, but Vic learned long ago to let comments roll off his back.

He watches Rocky wipe off the neck of the bottle, pour some ketchup onto the plate, and sprinkle a liberal amount of salt over the pool and the cold fries.

"That's not good for you, Rock . . . you know that, right?"

"What's not good for me? Salt? French fries? Ketchup?"

"All of the above."

"What's wrong with ketchup?"

"*That* ketchup?" Vic shoots the grungy bottle a dubious look. "I thought you were on a diet."

"Who told you that?"

"Ange. On Saturday night. She said the doctor wants you to drop thirty, forty pounds."

"Ketchup isn't fattening, Vic."

"Never mind. How did the colonoscopy go?"

"My ass is clean as a whistle. Okay? That what you want to hear?"

"Congratulations, Rock. That's what everyone wants to hear."

The waitress, a wizened redhead with nicotine stained fingers, materializes with a pot of coffee and a slice of pie with rubbery-looking blueberry filling.

"Here you go," she tells Vic, setting the pie in front of him, turning his cup right-side-up in the saucer, and pouring coffee. She addresses Rocky. "You eating, hon?"

"You bet, hon. What's quick?"

"Everything's quick here."

"Yeah? I'll have the meatloaf."

"Trust me . . . you don't want the meatloaf, hon," she tells him, taking a pen from behind her ear and an order pad from her pocket.

"No? Then give me the chili."

"Onions? Sour cream? Cheese?"

"The works. And coffee."

"You got it." She walks away.

"How's the coffee?" Rock asks Vic, who just took a sip.

"How do you think it is?" Vic shakes his head. "She tells you not to order the meatloaf, so you order the chili?"

"What's wrong with that? She didn't tell me not to order that."

"Forget it. Tell me what you're working on. Unless you can't."

"The hell with can't. I'm old school. I need all the help I can get right now," Rocky tells him. "My partner, Murph—his brother's missing. He's down on the pile. I'm working the case with a female detective I'm not crazy about."

"Why not?"

"She smokes."

"A lot of cops do."

"Yeah. I hate it. So does Murph. Anyway, she's just not seasoned enough. Kinda like these French fries." He dumps more salt on them.

"Tell me about the case, Rocky."

"Down at the station house, they've got a name for this bastard. The Nightwatcher. Bona fide serial killer."

Vic looks up from a forkful of pie. "How many murders?"

"Only two so far." Curtailing what Vic was about to say, Rocky quickly adds, "I know, I know, you need three, right? Technically? For it to be a serial killer?

Never mind—don't answer that. I know you guys got a lot of rules. But from where I sit, this is a serial killer."

"Tell me what's going on."

Vic listens with interest as Rocky describes the case between sips of black coffee, cold French fries, and spoonfuls of chili that actually looks—and smells—pretty good. A lot better, at least, than the wedge of cardboard and blue goo pie Vic opts not to finish.

"So the long hair that was in the second victim's fist—that's got me confused," Rocky tells him. "Because it was looking like we had a male perp on our hands. But now . . ."

"Men do have long hair."

"Yeah, no kidding. Have you seen my son Donny lately?" Rocky shakes his head. "But Vic, listen, there was nothing sexual involved here. With cases like this, when the killer is a man, you've almost always got rape involved, you know?"

"*Almost* always," Vic echoes. "There are other motives—the thrill of the kill, or some mission to rid the world of a certain kind of person . . ."

"What's your take on this one?"

"What's the victimology?"

"Both single women. Both live alone in buildings owned by the same guy, with the same handyman—my prime suspect, if I could track him down."

"You can't?"

"No one I talked to even knows the guy's last name."

"What's his deal?"

"Sounds like he was infatuated with the first victim. The second one, I'm not sure. She just moved in yesterday, and she was a lesbian, so . . ."

"He might not have known that."

"Maybe not. Her family sure as hell didn't . . . but

they do now. She had her girlfriend listed as the emergency contact in her Filofax and there was a picture of the two of them on the bedside table—crazy thing is, the twin towers were in the background. But I don't even think her brother noticed that. He was as upset when he figured out his sister was gay as he was that she was dead." Rocky shakes his head sadly.

"What about the other victim? Any chance she was a lesbian, too?" Vic asks, considering the mission killer theory.

"No. At least, doesn't look that way."

"The missing middle finger makes me think your unsub made a move on these women and they literally or even figuratively flipped him off."

"Yeah, I know, I thought of that. And remember—this *guy* might be a woman."

"Female serial killers are rare," Vic points out.

"Yeah, I know, but—"

"They usually kill people who are close to them—or at least, people with whom they have a relationship. And they do it a lot less violently, less sadistically, than your Nightwatcher does. Their motives tend to be financial gain, or if not, then they're sometimes part of a killing team."

Vic notices that Rocky has set down his spoon and is absorbing everything he's saying, wearing a thoughtful expression.

Before he can ask Rocky what he's thinking, Vic's phone rings.

It's the New York field office, calling with a lead on one of the hijackers.

On his feet immediately, he throws a couple of bills on the table. "I've gotta go. Sorry. Story of my life."

"Mine, too," Rocky tells him wearily, and offers a grim, silent farewell toast with a cup of bad coffee.

Well, this really hasn't been a good day for Jamie.

Not unless you count what happened in the wee hours of the morning, in Marianne's apartment down on Greenwich Street.

That was good. That was great. That was sheer *bliss*.

But it's all been downhill from there.

When Jamie first left Allison at her office building this morning—alive and well, regrettably—there was considerable comfort in the prospect of seeing her again.

Not just seeing her.

Touching her. Killing her.

Maybe even cutting off her finger, taking it along to add to the collection.

Jamie smiles, remembering.

With Kristina, that was a fitting punishment—cutting off the finger she'd used to humiliate Jerry after he'd worked up the courage to ask her out.

When Jamie sawed it off, she was still alive, still conscious—at the beginning, anyway. She passed out before it was completely detached. Jamie woke her up, showed her the bloody stump of bone and tendon between her index and ring fingers.

"Look! See what you made me do? Look at that!" Jamie shoved the severed finger in her face. "How do *you* like it? How does it feel to have someone give *you* the finger?"

She didn't answer, of course. She couldn't. Jamie had gagged her with a dish towel from her kitchen.

But her eyes registered enough horror and pain to

make up for the screaming or moaning Jamie yearned to hear, but couldn't risk letting others hear.

And then there was Marianne.

She might not have actually given Jerry the finger, but Jamie cut hers off anyway, just for the hell of it. Just because it was fun, and funny, and oh so satisfying.

The moment the knife split the skin about an inch below the knuckle, bright red blood appeared, like water filling an irrigation ditch. Just a little added pressure was needed to cut through the thin layer of flesh. And then came the hard part—sawing through the bone. The blade was nice and sharp, though. It didn't take too long.

In fact, it didn't take long enough.

Jamie made Marianne watch. She didn't pass out, but she vomited and, because she was gagged, nearly choked to death.

Jamie couldn't have that. Marianne still had to talk to Jerry. By the time the vomit-soaked gag was removed, she was too weak to scream and alert the neighbors. But she managed to do what she was told. She told Jerry she was sorry, told Jerry she loved him. That made Jerry feel a lot better, after the way she had treated him.

All Jerry needs is love. Such a simple thing, and yet, such a difficult thing for someone like him to find.

It isn't his fault that he is the way he is.

It's his mother's fault.

And finally, she's been punished.

So have Kristina and Marianne. Next, it will be Allison's turn.

Should I cut off her finger, too, when the time comes? How will she react? Will she faint? Struggle? Try to scream?

Jamie can't wait to find out.

Yet as the afternoon dragged on, even the anticipation of Allison's murder has worn thin.

I really thought it was going to happen today. I wanted it to happen today. I so wanted to see blood, feel blood, touch blood . . . today.

Today . . .

Even now, Jamie's hands ache to grab hold of that knife handle again; they've been aching so badly that Jamie couldn't bear to leave the knife behind at the apartment.

No, it's right here, in Jamie's pocket, just like the old days.

There's something deliciously empowering about walking down the street knowing the knife is at the ready, just in case . . .

No. I'm not going to use it.

I could, though, if I felt like it. That's what counts.

But Jamie won't be taking any chances. Not today. Not with the police actively investigating Kristina's murder, and undoubtedly aware—thanks to Allison—that Jerry was in the vicinity that night.

It wouldn't be easy for them to track down Jerry, though. He gets paid off the books, strictly in cash; there's no record of his address in the office files—Jamie checked—and Dale Reiss probably doesn't even know where he lives.

But what if he does?

Or what if his nosy wife, Emily, the good-deed-doer, has Jerry's address written down somewhere for some reason, like to send a Christmas card or something?

For all Jamie knows, the cops are on their way to the apartment right now. And if they get inside, they're going to find a lot more than they bargained on.

Dammit.

This is all Allison Taylor's fault.

She has to be punished. The sooner, the better.

But first . . . Jerry needs cake. It's the only way to keep him quiet and content.

Mo's bodega is open, of course. Today there's an enormous American flag hanging in the window.

Maybe that shouldn't be surprising, given the sudden burst of patriotism all over the city, but something about it seems . . . *off.* Jamie isn't sure why. Maybe the flag is just too big, or too prominently displayed, covering all the sale signs taped to the glass. Just too . . . deliberate.

Inside, Mo is behind the counter, as always. Today, though, he's not lost in a newspaper. He's keeping a wary eye on a young man who's standing over by the refrigerated soda compartment.

Potential shoplifter? Probably.

He's just a kid, really—sixteen, maybe seventeen. Short and skinny. He's wearing low, baggy jeans and a backward Mets cap. Leaning against the open door to the compartment, he's obviously taking his sweet old time looking through the soda cans.

Jamie brushes past him and checks the end cap where the bakery goods are kept. The shelf is bare. *Dammit!*

Ah, that's right—Jamie bought the last box of chocolate cake yesterday, and restocking is obviously an issue with all that's gone on. Still . . .

Jamie's hand twitches, wanting to touch the knife . . . just to make sure it's still there, of course. Not to . . . *do* anything. Because of course, there's nothing to do. Running out of cake—that's not a reason to—

"Excuse me," Mo calls.

Startled, Jamie looks over, and is relieved to see that he's talking to the kid.

"Keep door closed until you figure out what you want! If you let warm air in, fridge doesn't work!"

"Shut up, freakin' towel head," the kid mutters.

Mo didn't hear him.

Jamie did.

The cake shelf is still bare, and the kid is still standing staring at the soda cans, and the store is suddenly feeling hot and close despite the draft from the propped-open door to the street and the propped-open door to the fridge.

"Excuse me, excuse me," Mo calls again. "You need to close door!"

"Yeah? What are you going to do if I don't? Blow me up?"

Mo scowls, but ignores him, turning away. He opens a newspaper, jerking the page so hard the paper tears.

Jamie looks from him to the young punk, and back again.

Poor Mo. He doesn't deserve this . . . this . . . misplaced hatred.

He looks up as Jamie walks toward the door. "Can I help you?"

"No, thanks," Jamie tells him.

But I can help you.

Chapter Eleven

Thursday evening, Allison takes a deep breath and knocks on the door to Mack's apartment.

He's inside—she knows that, because she heard him come in about ten minutes ago.

She'd been waiting for hours for his return from the grim task of delivering his wife's DNA to the midtown Armory, where a registry has been set up for those missing after the attack.

Earlier, Allison watched live televised news footage of the mob scene there. The cameras unabashedly zeroed in on distraught family members pushing their way past satellite trucks and reporters, curious bystanders, religious groups keeping vigil . . .

She looked for Mack, but she didn't see him.

She wishes he hadn't turned down her offer to go with him, or even instead of him. But he was adamant that it was something he needed to do alone.

After he left, she walked to Union Square and found an open supermarket. The shelves and cold compartments were picked over, and one of the clerks, an NYU kid working part-time, said the delivery trucks hadn't been able to get into the city since Monday.

"We're hoping they'll get here tomorrow," he said,

"so if you live in the neighborhood, you might want to wait."

"I don't," Allison told him. "I'd better get stuff now, while I can."

"Where do you live?"

"Hudson Street, off Canal."

"And you're *staying* there?"

"I'm not in the evacuation zone."

"But still. There's asbestos in the air down there."

Allison didn't know what to say to that.

There's probably asbestos in the air up here, too.

Or, *Do you think I'd be breathing asbestos if I had anywhere else to go?*

She didn't say anything. Not then, and not as the kid told her his politics, which basically translated into the United States being filled with crass capitalists and warmongers who asked for it and got what they deserved.

Allison lugged home heavy bags filled with chicken and vegetables and milk and bread, all of which could be fresher. But at least none of it was past the expiration date.

Back at her apartment, safely locked inside, she made soup.

It wasn't something she'd ever attempted to do before—unless you counted mixing a can of Progresso lentil soup with a cup of cooked ditalini.

But it suddenly seemed like a good idea to learn how to cook, a good idea to do something for Mack, a good idea to keep her hands and her thoughts occupied.

Busy, busy, busy . . .

Stay busy, and you won't think about the scary stuff.

After browsing through an Internet recipe database,

Allison put the chicken in a pot with carrots, onions, celery, and salt and filled it with cold water. Eventually, it smelled like chicken soup, and it looked like chicken soup, so . . . it must be chicken soup, right?

Pleased with herself, she deboned the chicken, added noodles to the broth, poured it into a jar, and waited for Mack to come home.

Now that he's here—now that she's knocked—she suddenly wonders if she's overstepping her boundaries. Remembering all those people she saw on the news, gawking at the victims' families, she wonders if he'll think she's just another curious ghoul.

But she's not. She's . . . a friend. A friend he's known just a few days, but perhaps the only friend who's here, in person, right now when he so clearly needs someone.

Or does he?

How do you know what he needs?

Maybe she's the one with needs. Maybe she needs to help him more than he needs—or wants—to be helped. Maybe she's sick of being alone, or . . .

No. She's not afraid to be alone.

It's more the opposite, actually. She's afraid *not* to be alone. When you let people in, you're vulnerable. When you don't, you have nothing to lose.

Mack's door opens, and it's too late for second thoughts.

He stands there, looking even worse for wear than he did earlier. Looking like he needs a friend, or soup, or sleep, or . . . something.

"I'm sorry to bother you," she says. "I just wanted to bring you this."

He looks down at the jar she offers, then up at her face.

"It's chicken soup," she hurriedly goes on. "I don't

know if you have any food in the house, or if you've eaten, or if you're hungry, but . . ."

Shut up, Allison. You're rambling.

She stops talking and looks at him, wishing she knew him well enough to know what he might be thinking behind that opaque gaze.

"Thank you," he says, and takes the jar. "Do you want to come in?"

"I don't want to bother you."

"It's okay. I was just . . ." He rakes a hand through his hair. "Oh, hell, I don't even know *what* I was doing. Come in."

Walking into the apartment, she experiences a flicker of misgiving, remembering what happened to Kristina.

But then, she no longer has any doubts about Mack, does she? He's ensnared in his own tragedy; he doesn't deserve a shred of suspicion.

The apartment looks exactly the same as it did when she was here yesterday, right down to the red coat still hanging over the back of a chair where Carrie presumably left it.

Seeing her glancing at it, Mack says, "I should probably hang that up, shouldn't I? Or . . . figure out what to do with it?"

What is she supposed to say to that?

She watches him pick it up and stare at it for a moment. Then he puts it back on the chair. "I'll do something with this later. God knows what. What do you do?"

She shrugs helplessly.

When her mother died, the church ladies came and bundled up all her clothes and sent them to charity. That's what you do, they said. Give them to someone who needed them.

I needed them, Allison remembers thinking, one day when she was sitting on the floor in her mother's empty closet and crying. It wasn't that her mother had anything she would have worn—not in public, anyway. But she could have slept wrapped in one of her mother's shapeless sweaters, smelling her mother's scent in the yarn embrace.

No one ever gave her the chance. She was seventeen. Everything was handled for her.

Mack is a grown man. He can do this himself, in his own way, whenever he's ready.

"Have a seat," he says, gesturing vaguely toward the living room furniture.

She sits on the couch and tries to think of something to say.

He puts the soup on the kitchen counter and comes into the living room, looking out the window and then perching on the arm of the couch. But only for a moment, and then he is up again, restless.

"Do you want something to eat or drink?" he asks.

"No, I'm fine, but why don't you sit down and eat some soup? It's still hot."

"I will. Just not right now. I'm not really hungry."

"Are you sure? Have you eaten today?"

"I . . . I don't even know. I can't remember. I know that sounds crazy, but . . ." He shakes his head. "Everything is crazy, you know?"

"I know."

If she knew him better, she would make him sit down at the dining room table and she would pour the soup into a bowl and hand him a spoon.

But it's not her place to do that. It's probably not even her place to be here.

"I brought her hairbrush down there, to the Armory, and her toothbrush," he says abruptly.

"I . . . I'm sorry."

"I had to take a number and wait on a folding chair for them to call it. There were so many people there . . . some didn't talk at all, some were crying, hysterical. I was number 1448. I keep looking for meaning in that, you know? But there isn't any. In the number, or . . . any of it."

Oh God. This is tragic.

He goes on, staring into space, almost as if he needs to recap it for himself more than for her, "They were calling ten numbers at a time. When they called mine, they took us downstairs. They read off the names of people who were injured at the hospitals." He shrugs, not bothering to state the obvious: Carrie's name was not among them.

"Then I had to fill out a twelve-page report. I had to write down anything that might help them . . . you know, identify her body. They wanted to know if we have kids, you know, for DNA—or if she has parents, or siblings . . ."

"She doesn't?"

"No. Just me. I mean, we were trying to have kids, but . . ."

"I'm so sorry," Allison repeats, struggling not to blink and let the pooling tears escape her eyes. He isn't crying. How can she start?

"It wasn't so bad, really. I mean, in a way it was horrible, but in another way . . . I was doing something. Something for her. You know?"

She thinks about the day the church lady bought her the Ralph Lauren dress, about how her mother would have loved to have seen her in it.

This is nothing like that, but . . .

Grief.

Yes. She knows grief.

"I know what you mean," she tells him, surreptitiously wiping her cheek. A tear is rolling down it. Dammit.

"You do? Did you lose . . . someone?"

"Not, you know, on Tuesday. A long time ago, though. When I was a kid. My mom."

"I lost mine, too—just last year, not when I was a kid. That had to be hard for you."

"Yeah."

"The thing I keep thinking about—with my mom— is that she didn't like Carrie."

Startled by that admission, Allison notices that the mask has lifted. Now she can read the raw, honest emotion in his expression.

"A lot of people didn't like her," he tells her. "And in the end, I was one of them."

Allison stares, shocked. Maybe she heard him wrong. She must have heard him wrong.

"I'm sorry," she says, "what was that?"

He sighs heavily. "Things weren't working between Carrie and me. And I don't know what to do with that now. I feel sick when I think about how I was feeling, what I said, what I did . . ."

Whatever she was expecting when she came over here, this isn't it.

"I hurt her. I don't know why I'm telling you this, but I feel like I have to tell someone."

Looking at him, seeing the glazed, faraway expression in his eyes, she's suddenly uneasy.

What does he mean, he *hurt* her?

"I keep thinking," he goes on, more to himself than

to her, "if I could go back and relive Tuesday morning, would I do it the same way? You know, if I knew what was going to happen."

She nods. As if she knows.

She doesn't know, though. She doesn't know what he's talking about.

She thinks about Kristina, and she wonders. About Mack. Again.

"The thing that sucks," he says, "is that I know I did what I had to do. Anything else would have been—"

Interrupted by the buzzing of the wall intercom by the door, he looks over at it.

Startled, Allison follows his gaze. "Are you expecting someone?"

"No."

Mack hesitates, then walks slowly over to the intercom.

Her thoughts racing back to Kristina, Allison remembers that there was no sign of a break-in at her apartment. Either her killer got in with a key or through an unlocked window, or she let him in the door.

Mack nods and presses the intercom button. "Who is it?"

Allison's heart sinks at the reply.

"NYPD. We need to talk to you, Mr. MacKenna."

From the window of her sister's spare bedroom in Jersey City, Emily Reiss has a perfect view of lower Manhattan. She knows the vantage was a major selling point when Jacky bought the east-facing condo on a high floor.

Now, some might consider it a drawback to see the sun rise every morning over the permanently altered— and still smoking—skyline.

Emily certainly does.

She closes the blinds and turns away, wondering how long she and Dale are going to have to stay exiled in New Jersey. Jacky says she doesn't mind, and she probably doesn't—she's a neurologist and isn't around much. But her live-in boyfriend, Frank—a writer who works from home—doesn't seem particularly pleased to have given up the room he uses as an office.

"We really need to think about moving into a vacant apartment in one of your buildings," Emily tells Dale, who's lying on the futon.

Either he's so engrossed in the *Times* that he doesn't hear it, or—more likely—he doesn't want to hear it.

"Dale?"

He looks at her over the top of the paper. "Let's just see how things go with our own building first."

"You keep saying that, but how do you *think* things are going to go?" Their idyllic little corner of the world, adjacent to the Trade Center, is now a crime scene, layered in toxic dust and littered with broken airplanes, broken buildings, broken bodies.

They weren't home when the planes hit, thank goodness, and they haven't even been allowed back to collect their property. That's the least of Emily's worries.

She never wants to go back there. *Ever.*

"There are empty apartments in all of your buildings, Dale," she points out. "Pick one—I don't care which one—and let's move in."

"It's not like they're furnished, Emily."

She shrugs. "We'll get furniture."

"You make it sound so simple."

"You make it sound impossible."

But the problem, she knows, is not furniture. It's that

the buildings Dale owns—inherited from his father—
aren't nearly as nice as the building where they live now.
Lived.

"It's all about quality of life," Dale frequently tells
Emily. "Without it, you've got nothing worthwhile."

Their quality of life has certainly never been lacking.

Dale always made a nice salary as a corporate accountant, but was able to retire a few years ago after
unexpectedly inheriting a small fortune from his father.
Unexpected in the sense that Mortimer Reiss was the
kind of robust man who seemed as if he was destined
to live forever. But he was just in his mid-sixties when
a freak traffic accident took his life, making Dale an
overnight multimillionaire—and reluctant landlord.

Mortimer had started flipping real estate years before
it became fashionable. At one point, he owned two
dozen properties in lower Manhattan, but over the last
decade made a killing selling off all but the few buildings Dale still manages. Those, too, will be listed as
soon as the market picks up a little. Unlike his shrewd
father, Dale doesn't want to deal with tenants, rent col-
lecting, and maintenance, and Emily, who usually sees
things eye to eye with her husband, doesn't blame him.

Throughout twenty years of marriage, Dale's affinity
for the finer things in life has meshed fairly well with
Emily's decidedly charitable outlook. They've always
had enough money, and both have been free to spend
it—or give it away—as they've seen fit.

But in the weeks ahead, she realizes, they might not
agree on their priorities. They need a roof over their
heads, and a luxury doorman building might not be an
immediate option.

About to leave the room to make dinner—the least

she can do for Frank, with Jacky working late—she remembers something and turns back to Dale.

"You should call Jerry."

"Jerry? Why?"

"You call him every day to tell him where he's supposed to be working. When was the last time you touched base with him?"

"Tuesday morning. But I'm sure he doesn't expect me to be calling him in to work when all this is going on."

Emily stares at him and shakes her head.

"What?"

"Never mind. I'll call him," she says. "I should have before now, just to make sure he and his mother are okay."

"I'm sure they are."

"I hope so. Do you remember the number?"

He shakes his head. "It's in my cell. My cell is dead."

Right. So is hers. They both had their phones with them on Tuesday, but not chargers. Earlier, Dale tried to get new ones at an electronics store a few blocks away, but it was closed. The sign on the window said it will reopen tomorrow.

Looks like that check-in call to Jerry will have to wait.

Whatever Mack was expecting, this wasn't it.

Numb, he stares at the two uniformed NYPD officers in his living room, trying to absorb what they're telling him.

"I'm so sorry, Mr. MacKenna," the older female cop, who's done all the talking, tells him. "But can you please take a look?"

The other cop, probably a rookie, really just a kid, stands there looking shell-shocked. Mack imagines that he's thinking he didn't sign up for this: thousands of dead New Yorkers, families to notify . . .

He looks down at the little plastic-wrapped packet in his hand.

In it, supposedly, is Carrie's wedding band.

He described it just hours ago at the registry, when he was asked to write down what she might have been wearing. Black suit, size ten. Black shoes, also size ten. He guessed those sizes by checking similar clothes and shoes in her closet. White blouse. Gold watch, gold wedding band, inscribed with her initials—along with his. It also contains their wedding date—the date they eloped because she didn't want a big family wedding, because she didn't like families.

Ah, the irony.

A family is what we were trying to have!

How many times did he scream those words at her? Silently . . . or maybe not. Not on that last morning, for sure.

"Mr. MacKenna," the female cop says gently, "if you want to see if that is your wife's ring . . ."

"Sorry."

"No, no, take your time."

He doesn't want to take his time. He wants to get this over with. His hands shake as he fumbles with the packaging, but no one moves to help him. It's as if this is a sacred relic, or perhaps just a sacred moment, a moment—a burden—that belongs to him alone.

The packaging falls away.

The gold band is in surprisingly good condition.

He clears his throat. "I was expecting . . ."

No. He doesn't want to voice what he'd been expecting.

He checks the inscription inside the ring, nods.

"It's hers, then?" the cop asks.

"Yes." His voice sounds hoarse to his own ears.

"I'm sorry." That comes from the younger cop, who shifts his weight and stares at the floor.

"Mack . . ."

Allison.

He'd forgotten she was here.

He looks over to see her standing a few feet away, giving him space—or maybe giving herself space.

"Are you okay?" she asks. "Do you need to sit down? Do you want a glass of water?"

Water . . . no. He doesn't want water. He wants . . .

What does he want?

He turns to the female cop. "Can I ask a question?"

"Of course."

"Do you know where . . . how . . . it was found? I mean, my wife wasn't . . . she wasn't . . ."

Attached to it.

The female cop shifts her weight. "The ring was one of the first things found down at the scene—picked up on the street Tuesday afternoon by a bystander. Earlier today, we matched the engraved initials against your wife's name on the list of missing Cantor Fitzgerald employees over at the Pierre."

"That was fast."

"We know how hard it is for the families, waiting . . . not knowing."

He nods. "It is hard. But now I know."

"I didn't mean—" She looks flustered. "I'm sorry, I know that this is hard, too—harder, I'm sure—than not knowing."

Is it?

Mack looks down again at Carrie's ring.

What is he supposed to do with this? Bury it in the

family plot in New Jersey, next to his mother who hated Carrie?

I just told Allison about that, he realizes.

Not only that . . . he'd told her how he'd been feeling about Carrie, too.

What must she think of him? What kind of man talks that way about his dead wife?

When he unburdened himself, he was nearly delirious with exhaustion—and yes, guilt. And now . . .

He's nearly buckling beneath the added weight of regret.

He regrets telling Allison how he felt about Carrie, he regrets the way he felt about Carrie, regrets that their journey had to end the way it did.

We were never going to make it all the way together, he acknowledges sadly, *but still . . .*

If I had just waited . . .

Why the hell didn't I wait?

His throat tightens.

"Mr. MacKenna?"

Dazed, he looks up and sees, through the blur of tears, that the female cop is holding out a clipboard.

"We need you to sign . . ."

"Oh. Okay." He automatically scribbles his signature in the general area she indicates.

"Thank you. Is there anything—"

"I'm sorry, I just . . . need a minute." Mack turns and blindly races for the bedroom.

In the end, it hadn't been satisfying at all.

That's the disturbing part.

Jamie can't stop thinking about the young punk—the one who had called Mo a towel head, the one Jamie had followed for several blocks before the street was deserted enough to make a move.

Even though he deserved to be punished, deserved to die . . .

Even though his blood flowed red and warm and sticky, just like the others' . . .

The whole thing had just felt wrong, from the moment Jamie jumped the kid from behind and dragged him into an alley.

He didn't even realize he was being punished; thought it was a mugging.

Feeling the blade at his neck, he said, "Take what you want!" The belligerent tone Jamie had heard in the store had completely evaporated. Now his voice was high-pitched; he was pleading, like a terrified little boy.

Jamie didn't like that at all. Terrified little boys . . .

They're a reminder of Jerry.

"Please don't hurt me. Take my wallet. Please. Just don't hurt me . . ."

But Jamie had no choice. It was too late to back out by that time; the only thing to do was get it over with.

It was so rushed—just one quick slash across the kid's throat, not even time to watch him die there on the concrete. It would have been much too risky to linger.

But it wasn't even worth it.

I needed the connection. I needed to take my time. I needed to make someone suffer more. I needed someone else. I needed . . .

I need . . .

Allison.

Not just yet . . . but soon. And I know where to find her when I'm ready.

* * *

With Mack behind closed doors in the bedroom, presumably trying to pull himself together, Allison looks at the two police officers.

"Can I ask you something about the ring?"

"What about it?"

Allison hesitates, not sure how to phrase the question that's on her mind without getting into gory detail.

"It was found by itself, right? Not with . . . anything . . . um, attached?"

In other words, Carrie's disembodied finger wasn't still in it.

The female officer glances at her partner, who shrugs as if to say, *You're doing fine, go ahead, keep talking.*

In return, she gives him a look that says, *Thanks a lot,* before turning back to Allison. "It was just the ring."

"Could it have slipped off her hand, maybe, while she was trying to escape the building or something?" Allison suggests. "I mean, otherwise, shouldn't there be . . . more than just the ring?"

"The, uh . . . the nature of the scene is that . . ." The cop shakes her head. "They aren't necessarily finding intact human remains."

Intellectually, Allison had already been aware of that fact. But now, hearing it spoken aloud—and after seeing Carrie's wedding ring—

Why did I have to ask?

She glances toward the bedroom, making sure Mack hasn't reappeared and overheard. This is hard enough for him.

"The thing is, there are a lot of people who just . . . vanished into the air." The cop shakes her head. "I'm sorry to put it that way, but . . . that's what we're seeing. Or should I say *not* seeing."

"I understand. I'm sorry I asked. I just thought there might be a way . . ."

Both cops shake their heads grimly, and the female gestures at the closed bedroom door. "He's lucky to have something, even if it's just one of his wife's belongings. At least it'll give him some kind of closure. A lot of families aren't going to have anything at all."

Anything, Allison suspects, but false hope.

"Do you want to knock and see if he's coming out?" the male cop asks, looking at his watch. "We should probably get back over there."

Allison wonders where *there* is. The Armory? The Pierre? Ground zero?

So many sites around the city wear the shroud of mourning tonight.

"Go ahead and ask him," the female cop tells her partner, gesturing at the door.

With obvious reluctance, he walks over, knocks. "Mr. MacKenna?"

For a moment, there's silence.

"Yeah," Mack says from behind the door.

"Do you . . . can we . . . I mean, if you're all right, we'll go ahead and leave so that you can . . ."

Clearly, he's not all right, but Mack replies, "Yeah. Yeah, go ahead. Allison, you too. I'm not . . . I . . . I just need some time."

"All right. I'll be right across the hall if you need anything."

No reply to that. She didn't really expect one.

As she parts ways with the police officers in the hallway, she remembers Kristina for the first time since their arrival at Mack's door.

She had been certain their visit had something to do

with the murder; for a split second, had even wondered if they were coming to arrest Mack.

Now, the notion seems utterly ludicrous.

Back in her own apartment, Allison fixes a cup of hot tea, hoping it will calm her nerves. Clasping the mug in her icy hands, she sits in the living room staring into space.

She can't stop thinking about Mack.

Not just about Carrie's wedding ring. That was disturbing enough, but . . .

She keeps going back to what he said right before the police showed up.

A lot of people didn't like her . . . and in the end, I was one of them.

She really wishes he hadn't told her that.

She bets he wishes the same thing.

Chapter Twelve

Mack is huddled on the end of the couch brooding, as Carrie so often did, when the ringing telephone startles him. He snaps out of his daze, looks around, spots the receiver on the coffee table, and instinctively grabs it and presses the talk button before realizing he doesn't want to speak to anyone.

Swiftly hanging up without saying hello, he tosses the phone aside and wills it to be silent.

A few seconds later, it starts ringing again, as he'd known it would.

Just get it. You can't avoid the rest of the world forever.

But chances are the caller will have to be told about Carrie, and he's not ready to talk about it yet.

When will you ever be ready for that?

The phone rings, rings, rings again . . .

It could be Allison, who already knows about Carrie, and knows Mack's home. If he doesn't pick up, she might show up at his door again, and he isn't ready for that, either. Not yet.

Anyway, the incessant ringing has him on edge; he might as well just get it over with and speak to whoever it is. Shakily, he gets up to answer it.

"Hello?"

"Mack! There you are!" Lynn's voice greets him. "I just tried to call you and—"

"I know, sorry, there was . . . something wrong with the phone."

"Really? I've been trying to call you all afternoon, and I left you a bunch of messages. Where have you been?"

He clears his throat, tries to speak, clears his throat again.

"Mack? What's going on?"

"I had to bring Carrie's DNA samples to the Armory to register her as a missing person . . ."

"Oh God. Was it a nightmare?"

"Yes," he says simply.

"I would have gone with you. Why did you go alone? I could have—"

"No, it's okay."

"But—"

"Lynn, listen to me, it's over."

"*What?* What do you mean 'over'?"

"It's over. They found her. They found Carrie."

There's a long pause. "Is she . . . ?"

"Yeah."

"She's . . . ?"

"Gone."

Hearing the rush of air from Lynn's lungs on the other end of the line, Mack feels his knees suddenly turn to liquid beneath him. How can it be harder to deliver the news than it was to receive it?

Mack sinks onto a chair, gripping the phone painfully hard against his ear.

"Are you okay?" His sister's voice sounds choked.

"Yeah. I'm okay."

"I'll come. I can be there in—"

"No," he says sharply. "Not tonight."

"Why not?"

"Because I really need to be alone."

Alone. Isn't that what you've wanted all along?

It certainly was on Tuesday morning, wasn't it?

You thought that being alone was better than being with Carrie; better than bringing the child you want so badly into an unhappy marriage.

Now what do you think?

"Lynn, I have to go," Mack says, and hangs up the phone without waiting for her reply.

He buries his head in his hands, his entire body trembling.

The phone starts to ring again.

He ignores it.

It rings again.

Again, he ignores it, jumping up and striding toward the door.

I've got to get the hell out of here, he tells himself, *right now, before I lose it.*

Lose it?

Really? What more does he have to lose?

Just my mind, Mack thinks grimly, stepping out into the hallway without a clue where he's going.

Rocky sits back and scowls at the screen of his desktop computer, having reached another cyber dead end.

Where are you, Jerry?

Who *are you?*

How the hell am I supposed to find you when I don't know your last name—or even your first, for that matter?

Is it just Jerry?

Or is that short for Jerome? Jeremiah?

For all Rocky knows, it's spelled with a G—Gerry? Short for Gerald? Gerardo?

He hasn't a clue.

Hoping to locate the guy on a prior, he just wasted an enormous amount of time searching arrest records back to 1997, the year the database was created, for every crime under the sun, petty to major.

No luck. The few perps whose first names and ages made them potential contenders were quickly ruled out when Rocky either looked at their mug shots—not even close to the description of the handyman—or discovered that they're currently serving time, or dead.

But he could be looking in the wrong direction entirely.

Jerry might be innocent; there might be some other connection between the two victims.

Like Dale Reiss . . . who has yet to turn up, according to Brandewyne, who's been trying to find the guy, along with Kristina Haines's ex-boyfriend.

The first responders and people who worked in those towers aren't the only New Yorkers who have gone missing. What about the tens of thousands, perhaps hundreds of thousands, whose lives here imploded in the aftermath?

Rocky keeps reminding himself that in the grand scheme of things, his own problems are minuscule, and yet . . .

I can't catch a freaking break with this case.

His greatest fear is that the killer will strike again, and soon. In a case like this, the cooling-off period tends to get shorter and shorter with every murder.

Earlier, Rocky went to the press in an effort to get the

word out to potential victims that a killer is on the loose in the city, and doors and windows should be securely locked at all times.

Ordinarily, the local tabloids and television reporters would be all over a sensational story like that; so far, he hasn't seen a scrap of coverage. The city is in a state of emergency; every second of airtime and every square inch of newsprint is devoted to the crisis.

Ordinarily, at this stage in a double murder investigation, Rocky would have set up round-the-clock surveillance at the apartment buildings where both victims lived.

The perp often returns to the scene of the crime. Fifteen years ago, Rocky was working the famous Preppie Murder case in Central Park as the clean-cut killer, Robert Chambers, famously watched the investigation with a crowd of bystanders. Happens all the time. That's why the NYPD closely monitors a crime scene in the hours and days that follow, snapping photographs of crowds who inevitably show up to gawk from behind the yellow tape and blue police barricades.

But in these chaotic New York days, ghoulish onlookers are drawn to a far more catastrophic scene, along with the beleaguered officers who keep tabs on them while keeping them at bay.

Whoever killed Kristina Haines could have pitched a pup tent on the stoop of her building and the squad might have missed it entirely.

Manpower is shorter than ever, and frankly, right now, most of the homicide guys have concerns a lot more pressing—and a lot closer to home—than the Nightwatcher case.

Marianne Apostolos's neighbors proved much more accessible than Kristina Haines's fellow tenants—but what good did that do in the end? Marianne had just moved into the building; hardly anyone Rocky and Brandewyne interviewed had ever seen or even heard of her, and no one could shed much light on her movements in the hours leading up to her murder.

All the neighbors knew Jerry the handyman, but not his last name, or where he lives.

A few of them mentioned that there had been a recent rash of petty burglaries in the building—stolen costume jewelry, women's clothing, small change. Rocky attempted to touch base with the officers who had investigated those thefts and was told that one was down at the pile, and the other was among the missing.

Meanwhile, he keeps going back to the long hair in Marianne's hand and the skin scrapings under her nails. DNA could lead him to the killer . . .

But—like the police force itself—the forensic lab is currently otherwise occupied. When Rocky tried to get them to put a rush on his results, his telephoned request was greeted with incredulous silence on the other end of the line.

Right. On the heels of mass murder, there are perhaps millions of people waiting for test results on remains coming up from ground zero. Who the hell is Rocky to request a rush job?

So it seems there's nothing to do but wait—for the things that are out of his own hands, anyway. Which is just about everything.

Again, he thinks of the killer returning to the scene of the crime.

He's exhausted, and the last thing he feels like doing is settling in on a stakeout with Brandewyne instead of Murph for company.

But then, he's pretty sure the last thing his fellow

cops felt like doing on Tuesday was running into a burning skyscraper.

Yeah. His own problems are minuscule.

So get moving.

Jaw set, Rocky pushes back his chair.

Where is Jamie?

Jerry doesn't like being alone at night. It's not something he's had much experience with. He didn't often find himself in this situation before Jamie came back into his life and Mama left.

She didn't really go out much.

She didn't have any friends that he knew of. She liked to keep to herself, because you can't trust anyone in this world. That was what she always said, anyway.

She didn't like Emily.

Well, she didn't like anyone, but it really bothered Jerry that she didn't like Emily, because Emily was never anything but kind to Mama.

That isn't true of most people.

Mama is fat and unattractive. That isn't Jerry being mean. That's a fact.

But there are lots of fat and unattractive people who aren't ugly on the inside.

Mama isn't one of them.

On days when Mama used to go with Jerry to get something to eat at the soup kitchen, Emily would try to talk to her, and she would just grunt in return.

Emily didn't seem to mind. She was always cheerful, with a big smile on her face. The opposite of Mama. Maybe that's why Jerry likes her so much.

He misses Emily. After he started working for her husband and moved to Hell's Kitchen, he stopped seeing her because he doesn't go to the soup kitchen where she volunteers.

Sometimes, he asks Mr. Reiss to say hello to Emily for him, but he wishes he could say it in person. One time, he asked Mr. Reiss if he could visit Emily at their apartment, but Mr. Reiss said he didn't think that would be a good idea.

Jerry wishes he knew how to get back to the old neighborhood so that he could go see her at the soup kitchen.

Maybe Jamie will be able to tell him. Jamie knows everything.

Sometimes that makes Jerry feel like he doesn't know anything at all.

He wanders around the apartment, wishing he could leave or that Jamie would come back. It's hard to stay here for so long with nothing to do.

Coming to a stop in front of Mama's closed bedroom door, he looks at it. Then he leans toward it, sniffs, and makes a face.

It smells really bad in there.

What if there are bugs and rats?

Rats wouldn't fit through the crack under the door, but bugs would. What if they get out of Mama's room and crawl over Jerry while he's sleeping?

He shudders at the thought of that and reaches for the doorknob.

Whatever you do, Jerry, don't open that door. Ever. *Got it?*

Jerry pulls his hand back, remembering his promise to Jamie.

But Jamie would never have to know. Jamie isn't here.

All Jerry has to do is open the door, clean up the garbage in Mama's room—there has to be garbage, because Mr. Reiss said garbage makes things smell bad—and then close the door again.

What if Jamie comes back while he's in there, though?

What if Jamie gets mad the way Mama used to?

What if Jamie goes away, too, and Jerry is left all alone forever?

He shakes his head and walks away from the door, away from temptation.

"I'll be good, Jamie. See? See how good I am?"

But of course Jamie can't see, because Jamie isn't here. And Jamie can't hear him, either, yet Jerry keeps talking.

"Come back, Jamie. I don't like to be alone at night."

Suddenly remembering the way he used to hear Mama in her room sometimes, talking to no one, Jerry shuts his mouth abruptly.

A lot of people said Mama was crazy because sometimes she talked to herself, or to people who weren't really there.

Mean kids—kids from the old neighborhood who called Jerry a retard—called her crazy.

Maybe she *was* crazy.

But Jerry isn't a retard. And he isn't crazy, either.

"Okay, then stop talking to yours—" Breaking off with a gasp, he claps a hand over his mouth. He's talking to himself about talking to himself.

But there's a difference between the way he talks to himself and the way Mama talked to . . . well, whoever it was that she thought she was talking to.

He *knows* he's the only one here right now.

"Jerry?"

Startled, he exclaims, "Jamie! When did you get back?"

"Just now. Sorry, I didn't mean to scare you."

"It's all right. I'm so glad you're back, Jamie. I didn't know where you were, and I don't like to be alone."

"I know you don't. But sometimes I have to go. You know I always come back, right?"

"I know. And Jamie, I listened to you. I didn't go out while you were gone, and I didn't open that door."

"Good, Jerry. That's good."

Jerry smiles.

Things are so much better whenever Jamie is here.

The buzzing of the intercom by the door startles Allison just as she's slipping the chef's knife back under her pillow.

Her nerves were already on edge; the unexpected blast of noise causes her to lose her grip on the knife, and it clatters to the hardwood floor.

For a moment she just stands frozen, staring at the blade that landed just inches from her bare feet.

See? This was a bad idea.

She'd initially taken the knife out to put it back into the kitchen drawer. But in a moment of weakness, paranoia had gotten the best of her, and she had decided to keep it there. At least until the locks are changed.

Now, she picks up the knife and tosses it onto the comforter. She'll figure it out later.

Heading into the living room to answer the intercom, she wonders who it can possibly be. As she told herself earlier, over at Mack's apartment, killers don't ring doorbells, so she's probably safe.

But it's not like she's prone to drop-in company.

She presses the button and leans warily toward the intercom, irrationally envisioning something jumping out at her through the speaker. "Yes?"

"Um, hi. I'm looking for James MacKenna," a female voice says.

Allison relaxes just a bit. "This is the wrong apartment. He's across the hall in—"

"No, I know, but he's not answering, and . . . I'm sorry. I just thought maybe . . ."

"Are you . . . a friend?" Allison asks, not sure what to do.

"I'm his sister."

That's right—he did mention he had a sister. Does she know about Carrie? Is that why she's here? Is Mack expecting her? If so, why isn't he answering the door?

A new wave of worry washes over Allison.

"Do you think . . . could you let me in?" Mack's sister asks. "He's, um, been through a lot and I'm worried that he's in his apartment but not answering the buzzer."

That seems likely to Allison.

But is it wise to let a stranger into the building?

It's a woman—and Mack does have a sister—but still . . .

"I'll be right down," she says into the intercom, deciding it might be wiser to talk to the visitor in a public place.

Tossing and turning in the dark on the futon in her sister's guest room, Emily welcomes the sound of jangling keys and footsteps in the living room.

She sits up and swings her legs over the side of the bed.

"Where are you going?" Dale's voice doesn't sound the least bit groggy; he, too, has been restlessly awake.

They've both been silent, though. They did all their talking before they turned out the lights about an hour ago with just a perfunctory peck good night.

Dale finally grudgingly agreed that they can't stay

here much longer. If they're unable to immediately find a "suitable" furnished place to rent in the city, they'll stay in a hotel until something turns up.

"I hear Jacky," Emily tells him. "I'm going to go let her know we'll be out of here after the weekend."

"Do you have to tell her tonight? Can't it wait until morning?"

"I can't sleep anyway. I might as well get up and go talk to her now."

She pads barefoot across the room, pulling on a robe her sister lent her. Jacky is about five inches taller; Emily has to hold it up to keep the hem from dragging. The borrowed pajamas she's wearing are rolled up at the ankles and wrists, making her feel like she did when she and Jacky were little girls playing dress-up with their mother's castoffs.

She closes the guest bedroom door behind her and finds her sister in the kitchen, reading the note Emily left for her earlier.

"Hi," Emily says, and Jacky turns around.

"Hey. You left me a hot dinner? That's so sweet."

"Well, you know, that's me—so sweet."

Her sister grins. "What are you doing still awake, sweetness? It's late."

"Can't sleep. How was work?"

"Long, hard day, but it just got better. You have no idea how nice it is to come home to a house that smells like home cooking. That hasn't happened around here in . . . um, *ever*." Jacky grabs a potholder, opens the oven, and removes a foil-wrapped plate.

"Have you and Frank ever even used that stove?"

"What, are you kidding? Nope."

"You never did like to cook."

"And you always did. Mom's dream daughter."

"Well, you were Dad's dream son-he-never-had. Good at sports, and you even grew up to be a doctor . . ."

"With the boy name and everything. I always wished you and I could trade places."

"Why? Girls with boy names were always a lot cooler than girls with dead spinster poet names," Emily says dryly.

Accidentally conceived when her parents were students at Amherst College, she had, of course, been named after Emily Dickinson. Jacky came along five years later, in the height of the political Camelot era, and was named for the Kennedys—the president *and* the first lady.

Raised in a decidedly functional family despite the shotgun wedding beginning, Emily always assumed she'd grow up to have children of her own one day. Dale—whose family was decidedly dysfunctional—had no such plans.

Twenty years ago, forced to choose, Emily decided she loved Dale more than she loved the idea of motherhood. She rarely regrets the choice to remain childless, having channeled her need to nurture into her marriage, her church, and her charity work.

"I'm really glad you're here, Em. You'd think we lived hundreds of miles apart for as often as we see each other." Jacky lifts the foil from the dish. "Wow—what is this?"

"Mom's stroganoff."

"Seriously? I haven't had this in years." Jacky grabs some silverware, sits at the table, and digs in. "This is great. Thanks, Em. I bet Frank loved it."

"I think he thought it was too rich." Emily sits across from her. "But he did like the salad I made, with pears and candied pecans."

"Where did you get all this food?"

"Dale and I went out to look for cell phone chargers and stopped at the supermarket on the way back."

"Did you find the chargers?"

"No, we're going to check back again tomorrow. There's a call I really need to make."

"You can use my phone, Em," Jacky says around a mouthful. "You know that's no big deal. Even if it's long distance . . ."

"No, I know—and thank you—but the number is stored in my cell."

"Call directory assistance and get it."

"I can't . . . I don't even know the guy's last name."

Jacky lifts an eyebrow. "Really? Do I smell a scandal?"

"No, you definitely do not. He's just . . . he works for Dale."

"So why isn't Dale calling him?"

"Because I'm the one who worries about him."

"Why are you worried?"

"He's . . . you know, not all there."

"What's wrong with him? Is he mentally ill?"

"Brain damaged, from a head injury when he was about twelve or thirteen, I think. He and his mother used to visit the soup kitchen down in Brooklyn."

"You're still volunteering down there?" At Emily's nod, her sister says, "Someday you're going to go straight to heaven, you know that?"

"Well, let's hope that someday is a long way off, because I'm not in any hurry," she says with a wry smile.

"So tell me about your latest charity case."

"His name is Jerry. I haven't seen him since he moved to Manhattan after he started working for Dale."

"What does he do for him?"

"He's a handyman. You'd think that would be a problem, with his disability—when I asked Dale to hire him, I wasn't thinking he'd actually be able to do much, but . . ."

"A mercy hiring. I'm sure Dale loved that idea."

Emily shrugs. "He was humoring me. But it turns out Jerry works really hard, and he's surprisingly good with his hands."

"Not so surprising, really—his capabilities and limitations would just depend on which part of his brain was injured. What happened to him? Was it an accident?"

"Nothing like that. It was a really sad story. As far as I'm concerned, it's a blessing he lost a chunk of his memory, because he has no idea what happened to him and I hope he never will. It's funny—he would talk about things that happened a long time ago, when he was young, but not anything that happened leading up to the injury. Do you think that'll ever come back?"

"His short-term memory? A lot of times it does, but it would depend on whether or not the loss was due to the physical brain trauma. Amnesia is a tricky thing. Anyway, if he doesn't know how he got hurt, Em, how did *you* find out?"

"Diana, the director at the soup kitchen, told me about it and it broke my heart. Jerry was just a kid when it happened, poor thing . . ."

"When *what* happened?"

"His twin sister attacked him, smashed his head in with a cast-iron skillet."

Chapter Thirteen

Looking up at the dark building looming over Hudson Street, Brandewyne exhales a puff of smoke and comments, "This place still looks deserted."

"Maybe not," Rocky tells her, noting that light spills from the fourth floor windows where Allison Taylor lives. "Let's go."

She stubs out her cigarette as he opens the door with the key they duplicated from the set they found in Kristina Haines's purse—under the circumstances, the only way they could ensure that they'd be able to come and go freely at the crime scene.

They take the stairs up, pausing on every floor to walk swiftly up and down the hallway, searching for signs of life, knocking on doors in the hope of finding another tenant home. No one answers, though, and they hear not a sound, see not a bit of light filtering from beneath the closed doors, smell not a hint of cigarette smoke or food cooking.

Not until they reach the fourth floor, anyway. A faint but distinctly savory, homey smell wafts in the air.

Rocky sniffs. "Smell that?"

"Smell what?"

"Your nostrils must be shot from all that smoke, Brandewyne. Not good for a detective to have only four

senses, you know that? You should quit. I don't understand why you don't."

"Yeah, and you should lose weight. I don't understand why—"

"All right, enough."

"What do you smell?"

"Someone made dinner tonight." Rocky's mouth
waters slightly; he hasn't eaten since the bowl of diner
chili that gave him agita hours ago.

When he called Ange from the car on the way over
here, she said she'd made stuffed pork chops—his
favorite—and was keeping a plate warm for him.

"It's going to dry out," he told her. "Better put it into
the fridge. I don't know when I'll get home again, but I
doubt it'll be anytime soon."

After he hung up, Brandewyne, whose husband recently left her with two teenaged kids to support, asked
if Ange gets frustrated by his long hours.

"Nah. She understands."

"You're a lucky guy, Manzillo."

"Don't I know it."

No matter what happens on the job, he's going to
eventually go home to his wife. That's what keeps him
going, even on days—nights—like this.

"Where do you want to go first?" Brandewyne asks
now, looking from James MacKenna's closed door to
Allison Taylor's.

"Here. She's the one whose lights were on."

He goes over to Allison's door and presses an ear
against it, listening for movement or the hum of a television on the other side. He can't hear a thing, of course.
No paper-thin walls or doors in this old building; the
apartments are surprisingly well-insulated here. Yet

another reason whoever attacked Kristina Haines got away with murder.

So far, anyway.

Rocky knocks on the door.

There's no answer.

He knocks again.

No answer again.

He clears his throat. "Ms. Taylor? Are you in there?"

She doesn't reply. Maybe she's sleeping.

He and Brandewyne exchange a glance and a shrug. He knocks louder, calls louder, "Ms. Taylor? It's Detectives Manzillo and Brandewyne."

Nothing.

There's no answer to his knock on MacKenna's door across the hall, either.

"What do you think?" Brandewyne's tone is hushed.

"Let's go upstairs. We've got to see if Taylor's keys are there like she said."

They return to the stairwell and take the steps up to the fifth floor two at a time. Rocky unlocks Kristina Haines's door, then both he and Brandewyne pull latex gloves from their pockets and put them on.

They duck beneath the yellow crime scene tape stretched across the doorway.

"I'll take the kitchen, you take the living room," Rocky tells Brandewyne.

He searches every possible nook for the spare set of keys, conscious of the three words scribbled on the whiteboard hanging beside the fridge.

Anything is possible.

"They aren't there," Brandewyne announces from the doorway. "I'm going to check the bedroom."

He nods, slamming a drawer shut and opening another. He should have gotten over here to look earlier.

A thought plays at the edge of Rocky's consciousness, but he doesn't want to let it in.

No. Don't go down that road. Not yet.

He finishes the kitchen as Brandewyne comes out of the bedroom. "Nothing there, or in the bathroom. Maybe she kept them someplace else."

"Like where?"

"Her desk at work?"

"She didn't even have a regular job with a desk of her own; she was a temp. And anyway, you keep your neighbor's keys close at hand. That's why you have them in the first place."

"I know. Maybe we missed them. I'll go check the living room again." She disappears.

She's not going to find them. Rocky knows it in his gut. They didn't miss the keys because they're not here. Not anymore.

There's a strong possibility that whoever killed Kristina took Allison's keys . . . then did—or is doing right now—to Allison what he did to Kristina.

I've got to find this guy. There's got to be a way around the red tape.

Rocky reaches into his pocket and dials the phone number of the only person he knows can make something happen . . . now.

Huddled into his jacket, Mack walks past Washington Square Park, remembering the day he met Carrie. It was right over there, on the path near the stone arch.

He was walking through the park heading south, on his way to meet a couple of guys for happy hour; she was coming north—walking home from work, she later told him. They bumped into each other, quite literally.

Kismet. Isn't that the way lovers always meet in movies?

It was an unseasonably warm March night. Mack had found out a few days earlier that his mother had six months to live.

He was between girlfriends. Carrie wasn't conventionally pretty, but there was something about her . . .

So he asked her out. That was his style.

It wasn't hers to say yes, she later told him over drinks at McSorley's. That's where he took her on their first date, not yet aware that Carrie isn't—wasn't—a McSorley's kind of woman. He was certainly a McSorley's kind of guy back then. Which is why it was even more surprising that she said yes to a second date.

"There was something about you that made me want to let you in. That made me want to know you," she told Mack.

"My sparkling wit? My dashing good looks? What was it?"

He'll never forget her answer to that question. It caught him off guard.

"You just felt safe."

At the time, he thought it was an odd thing to say. He didn't know yet about Carrie's past. She told him only after they'd dated for a few weeks. The truth didn't come easily, he knew. Maybe she sensed that he was getting frustrated by her issues, the ones that kept getting in the way of having a normal relationship.

She didn't want to go to a basketball game with him because she didn't like big crowds; she didn't want to drink more than one drink because she didn't like to lose control; she didn't want to sit where she couldn't see the door because she liked to have an escape route . . .

Even now, though, looking back, he remembers thinking that not all of those idiosyncrasies seemed directly tied to what happened in her past. But then, what did he know?

What does he know now, for that matter? He kept trying to convince himself that her awful mood swings were simply due to the infertility drugs, but on Monday night, as he was sitting alone out on the stoop, he admitted to himself that she'd always been that way. It wasn't just the drugs. It was her personality: mercurial, reclusive, difficult.

He couldn't continue to blame it all on the drugs, telling himself she'd make an about-face when it was all behind her. He couldn't even continue to blame it on her past. After all these months of kicking himself for not having told his mother where Carrie came from, because it might have made a difference, he acknowledged that cutting her extra slack because of it might not have been the healthiest thing to do. It wasn't for him.

Back when Carrie first told him, bizarre and unexpected as the revelation was, he found it to be a relief. It explained so much about her—though not everything.

He was, of course, incredulous, thinking it had to be a joke.

The witness protection program? Seriously?

But of course she was dead serious. Carrie wasn't the kind of woman who kidded around—another trait he'd grown to resent over the years. He came from a family of mischievous imps who enjoyed their practical jokes almost as much as they enjoyed socializing and drinking beer—and that included his mother.

Carrie's family, due to circumstances alone, couldn't

have been more opposite. He never did get all the details about what led up to their extraordinary vanishing act. She didn't know—or so she said.

It had all unfolded when she was young, she said, too young to remember much other than being a little girl living with her parents in a city—she didn't know which city, she said, or even which part of the country.

"Didn't your parents ever fill you in?" Mack asked. "Later, I mean."

She shrugged. "No."

"You mean they refused to tell you?"

"I mean, I never asked. What did it matter? All I knew is that I had a normal life, and then one day, I didn't."

Carrie didn't know what had happened, exactly, to land her family in that position, but it involved her father. She told Mack she didn't know whether he was involved in criminal activity himself, or had simply been in the wrong place at the wrong time, perhaps witnessed something he shouldn't have.

Mack had a hard time buying that she didn't know—maybe even on some subconscious level—whether her father was a good guy, or . . . well, a wiseguy.

Carrie claimed it didn't matter to her. He had a hard time buying that, too.

She said that she loved her father until the day he died, and forgave him for the way things had turned out. That, Mack believed.

"We never lived a normal life," she told Mack. "Even after we were settled into our new life, we had to pick up and move again, without any warning."

"Why?"

"They were getting too close, I guess. That happened

a few times. It was hard on my mother. My parents fought all the time. But they couldn't separate."

"Why not?"

"I'm not sure. I just know they always talked about how they were stuck with each other. I guess a separation would have meant one of them would have to leave and never see me again. So they stayed together."

It made as much sense, Mack supposed, as any of the rest of it did. Her parents had chosen to put their love for their child before their own marital needs.

And Mack had chosen, on Tuesday morning, to put a child who doesn't yet exist—a child who may never exist—before his own marriage.

When he told Carrie it was over, he didn't give her the option to change her mind about having a baby. He didn't want that.

He simply wanted out. He'd had enough. He didn't want to live in isolation anymore with a woman who needed only him, and needed him desperately.

People don't change. That was what he told her—not that she'd offered to change. But he said it anyway; told her that she couldn't change who she was any more than he could change what he wanted out of life.

She didn't argue, didn't cry, didn't even speak. She simply left.

He has no way of knowing what was going through her head as she went to work that last morning; no way of knowing whether, had the day unfolded in an ordinary way, she'd have come home that night wanting to talk things out with him, wanting a second chance.

But even now, he knows it would have been futile for her to ask for one. If he had to do it all again, he would make the same decision.

Maybe he'd already made it, subconsciously, even

before she told him on Monday evening that she couldn't go forward with the infertility treatments.

That was why he'd come home late from work. Not because he'd stopped for a beer with Ben, as he'd told Carrie. Ben hadn't gone for drinks after work in years, not socially, anyway. Unless he had a business engagement to attend he was always too eager to get right home to Randi and Lexi.

That night, like countless others, Mack had stuck around the office playing computer solitaire long after his work was finished and everyone else had gone home. Unlike his colleagues, he wasn't eager to be reunited with his spouse at the end of a long, hard day. He dreaded it.

Well, you'll never have to deal with that again, will you? It's over.

Cloaked in guilt, he walks on, thinking about Carrie, and about loss. Not about his own, because it was a loss he'd already accepted, a loss he'd chosen.

But Carrie—her loss that morning was monumental. She'd gone to her grave knowing he was going to leave.

You can't blame yourself for her death. You didn't kill her.

No, but maybe, if he hadn't told her their marriage was over, she'd have somehow found a way out of that building. Maybe she'd have felt she had something to fight for, something to live for.

Tears stream unchecked down Mack's cheeks as he walks uptown, past the barricades, past the policemen and soldiers, past other pedestrians. No one gives him a second glance; tonight, the bruised city is filled with publicly crying people. He's just one more stricken face in the crowd; just another New Yorker whose life lies in ruins tonight.

* * *

Vic's phone rings the moment his head hits the too-puffy—*why the hell are they always so puffy?*—hotel pillow.

As usual, he answers it immediately, sitting up and swinging his legs over the side of the bed, instantly prepared to bolt.

But this call isn't about the terrorists he's been tracking; it's Rocky's voice that greets him.

"What's up?" Vic asks, lying down again, phone pressed to his ear, welcoming a call from a friend. New York is his hometown, but it's never felt so foreign. He thinks longingly of Kitty, and home, but it's going to be a long, long time before he's back there.

It could be worse, though. Much worse.

Every time he remembers that last conversation with O'Neill—remembers how John said, "My business is always a pleasure," remembers all the years, all the laughs they shared—Vic is seized by a renewed urgency to nail the bastards who murdered his friend.

Ah. If only it were that simple.

"I need help," Rocky tells him. "Official help. Well, unofficial, because I don't have time to jump through hoops right now and you guys are all about protocol, I know."

You guys. Vic sighs inwardly. *Us,* and *them.*

"What's going on?"

He listens carefully as Rocky fills him in on the case he's working, concluding with "And this is where you come in."

"Where? You lost me."

"Brandewyne and I are overwhelmed here, Vic, and most of the squad is working the terrorist attack . . ."

Yeah, Vic thinks, *who isn't?*

"Okay, so what do you need from me? I mean, I'll help you if I can, but you know—"

"Yeah, yeah, I know. First things first—we've got to find this guy Jerry."

So now "you guys" have melded into "we."

If things weren't so grim, Vic might have to grin at that.

"I'm headed over to one of the other buildings Dale Reiss owned to see if I can track down Reiss somehow," Rocky tells him, "but I know you've got access to computers that can find anything—and anyone—faster than I can ask a question."

Vic hesitates. Rocky is right. But—

"Can you see if you can find this guy?"

"Reiss or Jerry?"

"Both. And the other thing I need," Rocky continues without missing a beat, "is a rush on the DNA results."

"That, I can't do," Vic says promptly. "Not now, of all times, Rock."

"If it weren't now, of all times, I wouldn't have to ask."

"Listen, I'll do what I can with the computer records. I'll make some calls and see what I can turn up. At least that'll be a starting point for you."

"Thanks, Vic. I owe you one."

Vic snorts. "You owe me a lot more than one, pal. But don't worry—I've been keeping count for years."

"I'll bet you have." Rocky's tone is light, but when he exhales, Vic can hear the weight of the world in his barely audible sigh.

"Listen, I'm on it."

"Thanks, Vic. I mean that."

"You're welcome, Rock. What are friends for?"

* * *

Just off West Broadway, the only open bar in the immediate neighborhood is jammed with people looking for a reprieve. There are no open tables or bar stools, so Allison and Lynn MacKenna have spent the last hour leaning against the back wall and talking, sipping Amstel Light from cold brown bottles.

When Allison first went downstairs to meet Mack's sister—an attractive woman with a long brown ponytail and Mack's light green eyes—at the front door of the building, she fully intended to send her on her way without giving her any information. She had no idea how much Lynn knew, and she didn't want to be the one to deliver the bad news.

But she took one look at the woman's tearstained face and realized she must already have heard about Carrie.

She was right; Lynn said Mack had told her over the phone earlier.

"I got my ex-husband over to watch the kids, jumped into my car, and drove into the city," she said, adding that she'd been forced to leave her car uptown.

"How did you get down past Union Square without a local address?" Allison asked.

"I just showed them my Jersey license and said I was going to help my brother whose wife worked at Cantor Fitzgerald. They let me go."

"I'm surprised."

"Why? Do I look like a terrorist to you?"

Allison didn't respond to that; didn't tell her that looks can be deceiving.

Lynn was a frazzled wreck by the time she'd walked down to her brother's apartment, only to find him gone.

"I'm sure he's all right," Allison told her with a confidence she didn't feel. "I was with him when he got

the news, and he held up pretty well under the circumstances."

"You were with him? Are you a friend of his, then?"

Unsure how to answer that, Allison nodded.

"Really? I mean—don't take this the wrong way, but
I didn't think my brother had many friends anymore.
He and Carrie—well, they kept to themselves. I didn't
really think they were hanging out with the neighbors."

"They weren't," Allison said hastily. "I just got to
know him the past few days with . . . everything going
on." She's definitely not going to mention the murder
investigation, which, in light of the MacKennas' family
tragedy, seems almost insignificant.

"All I did was check in on him a few times, and put up
some missing persons posters and . . . I made chicken
soup," she adds lamely.

"That's so sweet of you. Thank you. I've been so
worried, I kept thinking of him here, all alone—I'm
glad he wasn't. It wasn't easy for me to get to him, and
. . . well, I couldn't really tell if he wanted me here. We
used to be close—he used to have all kinds of friends,
and we have a big extended family, too—but Carrie
kind of alienated everyone. Oh—I don't mean to speak
ill of the dead," she added, and crossed herself. "I'm
sorry."

Remembering yet again what Mack had shared about
his own feelings for his wife, Allison told her, "That's
okay. I don't—didn't—really know your sister-in-law
at all."

"I'm sure that was her choice, not yours. Listen, do
you want to go get a drink? I don't want to drive all the
way back to Jersey until I've seen my brother, and my
nerves are shot. I could use a beer."

Allison opened her mouth to invite Lynn up to her place, but thought better of it, remembering that Kristina Haines might very well have invited her own murderer to cross the threshold.

It wasn't that she thought the woman was a cold-blooded killer—but really, how did she even know Lynn was who she said she was?

Are you serious? Look at her. She looks just like her brother!

All right, so maybe she was, quite obviously, related to Mack.

Still . . . how much did Allison really know about him? What if they were a pair of killer siblings and this was all just an elaborate setup concocted by the two of them to lure her into a trap?

You're crazy, she told herself.

But better crazy—and perhaps overly cautious—than dead, right?

"I passed a bar that was open a few blocks away," Lynn went on. "We can go there. I mean, I can go alone, but I'd rather have company. Will you come?"

"Sure," Allison said impulsively, and here they are.

She's glad she came, even though she's certainly not dressed to be out—though in her old jeans and T-shirt, she seems to fit right in with this crowd. The cash she had in her pocket, left over from the grocery store, was enough to buy a round of Amstels, and Lynn bought another.

Allison never realized that ice-cold beer from a tall bottle could taste quite this good. For the first time in days, she feels herself relaxing, relieved of the burden of suspecting that Mack is a potential killer. It's obvious, from Lynn's account of their parents and childhood, that they were raised in a close-knit family, the kind of family Allison herself secretly longed to have. Not that she'd admit that to Lynn. She has, however, found herself opening up far more than she typically does when she meets someone new.

Mack's sister is so easy to talk to, easy to listen to, that Allison keeps forgetting about all the disturbing things that have happened. Somehow, despite the dark circumstances of their meeting, the conversation meanders along from food to fashion to music to Lynn's children. She has three—two boys and a girl—and tells Allison that she wishes they could see more of their uncle.

"When he's around the kids, he just lights up, and so do they," she says, tearing at the label on the neck of her brown bottle. "But he only sees them on birthdays and holidays—and sometimes, not even then. I keep telling the kids that it's not him—you know, that he's just too busy to see them more often—but I don't really believe that myself. If your wife doesn't want to be a part of things, come alone, you know? Don't turn your back on your family. It's like he's always making excuses for her, protecting her. I don't get it." Lynn shrugs. "Do you?"

"I don't really even know him well enough to get it," Allison tells her, knowing better than to say a word about what Mack confided in her about the state of his marriage.

"Well, I guess it doesn't matter anymore, does it?" Lynn shakes her head. "I can't believe she's dead, can you?"

Lynn has a habit of throwing the conversation back into Allison's court with every comment, making her feel as though she matters when really, she doesn't. She just met Lynn, and she barely knew Carrie, and Mack . . .

Poor Mack. What is he going to do now?

Allison thinks about dead Carrie . . . and dead Kristina . . .

Suddenly, she feels a little light-headed—and dangerously emotional. Maybe it's the beer, or her own exhaustion, but she has to get out of here. Right now. Before she starts crying. Or talking.

"I think I should go," she tells Lynn, looking around for a place to set down her half-full beer. It's her second—or maybe her third.

"Don't you want to finish that?"

"No, I can't. I really need to get home. Do you want to come, or . . . ?"

"Hang on. Let me see if Mack's there yet." Lynn pulls a cell phone from her pocket, dials, and holds it to her ear. After a minute, she shakes her head and hangs up. "He's still not home. I'll stay here until I reach him."

"Are you sure you don't mind if I leave, then?"

What else can Lynn say but "Um, no. Go ahead."

Allison realizes she probably expects an invitation back to Allison's apartment, and she's tempted to extend one. But really, that wouldn't be a good idea. Not because she fears for her safety, but because in this frame of mind, having company isn't a good idea.

Out in the cool night air, she immediately feels better. Not well enough to turn back, but at least her head feels clearer.

As she walks toward home, she tells herself that she did the right thing.

But when she turns onto her block and sees her building looming, she isn't so sure. It would be a lot easier to walk into that empty apartment with company than it will be alone.

Well, get a grip. You are alone, and that's how you wanted it, remember?

She walks closer, glad that at least she left the lights on when she went downstairs to meet Lynn. She even locked the door behind her.

Now, taking her keys from her pocket, she realizes, belatedly, that she never heard back from Detective Manzillo about whether he'd found her spare key in Kristina's possession.

It's all she can do to make herself unlock the door and walk into the building.

Strength is your strength.

She rides the elevator up to the fourth floor.

Strength is your strength.

She considers knocking on Mack's door to see if he's there, but Lynn just called him from the bar less than fifteen minutes ago. Either he's still out, or he doesn't want to talk to anyone.

Just leave him alone, Allison tells herself, and goes past his door to her own.

Strength is your strength.

Unlocking it, she steps inside.

As always, everything appears to be just as she left it.

See? You're home, safe and sound. You can relax now.

She locks the door behind her, still feeling a little woozy from the beer. She isn't used to drinking much, but Lynn ordered more beers without asking her if she wanted another.

Wait—should she have locked herself in before she checked to make sure no one is here, lying in wait for her? Isn't she supposed to do that part first?

She turns back to unlock the door, then stops. That's

not a good idea, is it? What if she walks away and then forgets to lock it again?

Just do a quick check. I'm sure it's fine.

She looks into the kitchen. Not a thing out of place, and really, not a single spot where someone could be hiding. In the living room, as she checks behind the curtains, she wonders what she would possibly do if someone jumped out at her.

You'd be helpless, wouldn't you? So a lot of good this searching does.

With the building empty and the windows closed up tightly, no one would even hear her scream if something happened.

You should have grabbed a knife when you were in the kitchen, like you did before.

Her heart begins to pound. She peeks into the narrow space between the couch arm and the wall, and the shadowy corner near the armoire. So far, so good.

As she walks toward the bedroom, her gaze falls on the answering machine, sitting on the end table beside her art books. The message light is flashing.

She presses play.

"Ms. Taylor, this is Detective Manzillo. Give me a call as soon as you can. We checked Kristina Haines's apartment for your keys, and they aren't there. Be careful, and like I said . . . call me as soon as possible. I need to speak to you about . . . a new development in this case."

Rattled by the news that her keys have apparently gone missing, Allison instinctively reaches for one of the granite bookends on the table. It's so heavy she can barely lift it with one hand, heavy enough to be a weapon.

All she has to do is check the bedroom and the bathroom. Then she can put down the bookend and breathe easily as she returns the detective's phone call.

Crossing into the bedroom, she glances around and is caught off guard by the unmade bed. She never—

Oh, that's right, she'd been just about to—

Suddenly, she remembers: she was standing here with the chef's knife when the buzzer rang earlier. She tossed it onto the bed and went to answer it.

Allison takes a step closer to the bed, her eyes searching for the knife.

It isn't there.

But that can't be right.

She left it there, it *has* to be there . . .

Dear God, where is the knife?

Someone moved it.

Someone took it.

She has to get out of here, before—

Out of the corner of her eye, Allison sees a figure looming.

Chapter Fourteen

A rush of sound startles Jerry awake. He opens his eyes to darkness.

It takes a few seconds for him to figure out where he is: home.

He can tell by the faint stink that hangs in the air.

He turns on a lamp, recognizes both the familiar living room and the sounds that woke him: sirens and another fighter plane flying over the city. He doesn't like the sound of the fighter planes any more than he likes the sirens. The planes remind him of what happened downtown, when the bad guys knocked down the towers.

Jerry wonders how anyone is supposed to punish them for what they did, when they're already dead. They *wanted* to be dead. Jerry heard that on TV.

He thinks about Kristina, and he thinks about Marianne.

They probably didn't want to be dead, but they both did bad things. Not as bad as flying airplanes into buildings, but bad. Jamie says it doesn't matter whether you hurt one person or thousands of people. You still have to be punished.

Jerry stretches and yawns, wondering what time it

is. The last thing he remembers is sitting on the couch, waiting for Jamie.

It feels late. Jamie isn't back yet, though.

Outside, the plane's buzzing has died away, but sirens are still wailing in the night. No, he doesn't like that sound. He never has. For as long as he can remember, whenever he hears sirens, or sees an ambulance rushing past with the red lights spinning, he gets a bad feeling inside.

Jamie said that's because of what happened to him years ago, when Mama hurt his head. Sometimes, Jerry wonders why no one ever punished Mama for what she did to him. Maybe someone should. Maybe Jamie should.

But Jamie keeps telling Jerry not to worry about Mama because she's gone, so he tries not to.

Jerry gets up and walks around the apartment, around and around. He walks past Mama's closed bedroom door a few times, and then he comes back and stops there.

He has to do something about the smell.

He doesn't like bugs. Bugs scare him. If bugs come out of Mama's room because it's dirty . . .

No. That can't happen.

Jerry won't let it happen. He won't. He just won't.

Fretting, he walks away from the door, wondering what to do.

Jamie doesn't want him to do anything, but Jamie doesn't understand about not liking bugs, being afraid of bugs. Jamie isn't afraid of anything.

Well, I am. I can't help it. I was mostly afraid of Mama, but she's gone. Now I'm just afraid of bugs. If bugs were gone, I wouldn't have anything to be afraid of. Every day, I could just be happy.

Jerry would be even happier if Jamie would let him go out of the house.

Maybe tomorrow. Maybe Mr. Reiss will call, and Jamie will say it's okay to go back to work, instead of being stuck here alone with the smell and the bugs and no cake.

Then everything would be back to normal.

Jerry walks back over to the door and checks to make sure there are no bugs crawling out from underneath it.

There aren't.

Still, he should check.

Shouldn't he?

He reaches for the knob.

He turns it.

The door is locked.

But Jerry has a key.

He likes keys.

He goes over to the drawer where he keeps them, and he opens it and takes out his big key ring. He jingles it a little, because he likes the sound the keys make when they bump against each other. If you only have a few keys, they don't make much sound. But if you have lots of keys, like Jerry does, they make a nice, loud sound.

It takes him a few seconds to find the right key—the key to Mama's bedroom door.

There it is.

He holds it for a long time, looking at it and wondering what to do. He doesn't want to disobey Jamie. But Jamie doesn't understand what it's like to be stuck here, alone and afraid of what might crawl out from under the bedroom door. In fact, this whole thing is Jamie's fault. Jamie told Jerry not to leave, and then disappeared. That's not fair. Thinking about it makes Jerry mad.

Frowning, he marches over to the door and fits the key into the lock.

Jamie will never have to know.

Jerry turns the key, and the door unlocks.

He turns the knob, pulls on it, and the door opens.

The smell is overpowering, and he wants to close the door, but he can't, because he has to clean up.

He opens the door wider and the light from the living room falls across the floor and the bed, and he realizes that Jamie is a liar.

Mama isn't gone. She's right here.

Jerry can see her lying there under the bedspread, with her long brown hair spread out around her head . . . so much hair that it covers the whole pillowcase.

"Mama?" Jerry whispers.

She doesn't move, doesn't answer.

"Mama?"

He steps closer, close enough to see that it isn't her hair covering the pillowcase. It's a dark brown stain. And her face . . .

Jerry opens his mouth and screams.

"Finally—a lucky break," Rocky announces, and pulls up at the curb in front of an Italian deli where he's been a regular for years.

"What are you talking about?" Brandewyne asks.

"Murph and I have been coming here for years. It's about time this place opened again. It's been closed since Tuesday."

"Just like everything else. I thought you meant a break in the case."

"Hey, I'll take what I can get. Coming in?"

"Nah." Brandewyne is already climbing out of the car, but she's lighting a cigarette.

"Want anything?"

"Pack of Newports."

"I meant food."

"Eggplant parm hero, and don't forget the Newports. Here—" She pulls a twenty out of her pocket.

"It's on me."

"You hate cigarettes. You don't have to support my habit."

"It's okay. This time. You can owe me one."

"What's yours?"

"My what?"

"Your habit?"

"Food, Brandewyne, but I need to lose weight, remember?"

"Besides food."

"Whiskey."

"I'll buy you one, Manzillo. Johnnie Walker Blue, if we solve this case."

"I won't hold my breath for that."

"For me to buy you expensive whiskey, or for us to solve the case?"

"Either one."

Rocky leaves her on the sidewalk with her cigarette, a faint grin playing at his mouth. She's not Murph, but she's growing on him.

Inside, he's pleased to see his friend Richie D— short for Di Bernarducci—behind the counter, a clean white apron over his Yankees pinstripe jersey. He likes to break Rocky's chops about the Red Sox the second Rocky walks in the door, but today, he greets him with a warm handshake.

"Hey, Detective Manzillo, it's good to see you. I been worried about you. Where's Detective Murphy?"

"On the pile. His brother's missing."

"Jesus. Everybody's got somebody missing." Richie's triple chins jiggle as he shakes his head. "My nephew Vince, he's with the PAPD, but he was off duty when it hit. He's pretty broken up about it, though."

"I'm sure he is." Rocky heard that the Port Authority Police Department is missing at least three dozen officers.

Every time it hits him again—the staggering crisis in this city, his city—he's stunned all over again.

He's always pretty good at compartmentalization; you have to be, if you're going to do what he does. But on this day, tragedy seeps into every corner of his world, blurring boundaries, permeating every line of thought, every conversational thread.

"I didn't know if the bridges or tunnels were even open the last few days, so I didn't bother trying to get in here till now," Richie tells him.

"Where do you live, Jersey?"

"Nah, out on the Island."

Rocky is about to lighten the mood by teasing that Richie's probably the only Yankees fan living out there in Mets territory, but then he sees the somber expression on Richie's face.

"There are a bunch of firemen missing from my town, and a bunch of brokers, too. Guys—women, too. They got up in the morning and went to work and they're never coming back. Who would have thought this could happen?"

Rocky remembers talking about the Island—Long Island—with great disdain when he was younger, twenty-five, thirty years ago. Some of his old friends were picking up and moving away from the Bronx, moving out to the Island or up to Westchester. They wanted to settle down and raise their families where it was safe, they said.

Rocky thought they were a bunch of pansies and told them so. He informed them that they could try all they wanted to shield themselves from the bad stuff, but the bad stuff would find them if that was their fate.

"I hate to break it to you," he said, "but the bad stuff can still walk right through your fancy front door if it wants to."

Yeah, the bad stuff will get you, no matter what, if your number is up. Rocky truly believed that. Still does. Happens all the time.

He thinks of Kristina and Marianne, probably convinced they were safe in their own apartments, and of all those people who died because they went to work on a Tuesday morning.

Jesus. If he were a different kind of guy—the kind who lets things bother him—he'd be so depressed right now he'd want to crawl into bed and stay there for a year.

But that's not me. I gotta do something. Whatever I can.

He'll leave the terrorist hunting up to Vic, but he's going to find this Nightwatcher son of a bitch and put him away for a good long time.

"I need an eggplant parm hero for my friend out there," he tells Richie, "and what've you got for me?"

"Whatever you want. You're my first customer since I reopened. Where the hell is everybody?"

"Give 'em time, Richie. They'll come back. People are rattled."

"You been down on the pile?" Richie asks, turning away to pour Rocky an extra large cup of coffee without asking.

"I was, but then I got pulled off for a case."

"You mean a homicide?" Richie shakes his head. "You gotta be kidding me."

Rocky shrugs. "Life goes on."

"You mean death goes on."

Rocky accepts the coffee and takes out his wallet.

"Put that away. It's on me," Richie tells him. "Sandwiches, too. What'll it be, besides the eggplant?"

Rocky thinks of the stuffed pork chop dinner Ange has waiting back at home. God only knows when he'll be able to eat it.

"Thanks, Richie. I'll take a Sicilian."

"You got it. Extra cappy, right?"

"You bet."

Rocky's phone rings as he's sipping his coffee and watching Richie layer a nice thick pile of thin-sliced capicola on an open hero roll.

He steps away from the counter to answer it. "Yeah, Manzillo here."

"I got something for you," Vic tells him. "Ready?"

"Yeah, yeah, just gimme a sec." Rocky sets his coffee on the counter. His notebook is out in the car. He grabs a pen that's sitting by the cash register and a napkin to write on. "What'cha got?"

"Dale Reiss. He and his wife are staying with the wife's sister in Jersey City."

"You sure? How do you know?" Stupid question, but Rocky can't help asking it.

"I know, okay? The sister's name is Jacky McCann. I'll give you the number."

Rocky jots it down. "Got anything on Jerry yet?"

"Not yet. I'll get back to you when I do."

"Thanks, Vic. I—"

"Owe me. Yeah. I know."

Rocky can't resist busting his chops. "I was gonna say I gotta go—my sandwich is ready. I'm down at Di Bernarducci's on Broome."

"Smart ass."

"You know it."

"Good luck, Rock."

A few minutes later, Rocky steps out onto the street with the sandwiches, two coffees, a pack of Newports, his cell phone, and the napkin with the phone number scribbled on it.

Brandewyne is lounging near the car, smoking.

"You want to help me out here?" he calls. "I kinda got my hands full, and we need to get moving. We just got a break."

"You mean besides the deli being open?" She stubs out her cigarette and reaches for the two coffees.

He fills her in quickly and takes a bite of the sandwich—extra cappy *and* extra roasted red peppers, just the way he likes it—before brushing the crumbs from his hands and dialing the number Vic gave him, glad things are finally starting to look up.

Mack takes a long last drag on his cigarette as he rounds the corner onto his block, sucking the smoke deeply into his lungs. He holds it there as he tosses the butt onto the sidewalk and stops walking to grind it out with his heel.

Damn, that's good. Too good.

Having chain-smoked his way through a good portion of the pack he bought at the newsstand up by the park, he was planning to throw away the rest.

But why? Why not just take up the habit again? He only quit for Carrie. Exhaling tobacco into the damp night air, he's struck by the dismal irony that she might very well have died of smoke inhalation—and that might have been the most merciful way to go, given the alternatives.

But maybe she was blown up in the initial explosion, or maybe she was burned alive before the fumes could smother her. Maybe she was one of the people who made the agonizing choice to jump from the tower. Maybe she crawled outside to a ledge, desperate for air, and fell. Or maybe she clung to life in that torture chamber until the collapse crushed her body.

Walking on toward his building, Mack reaches into his pocket and takes out his keys. Carrie's gold wedding band dangles from the keychain; he fastened it there for safekeeping, uncertain what else to do with it for now.

It wouldn't feel right to wear it around his neck on a chain, as his father wore his mother's at first. Last month, the nursing home staff suggested that Lynn take it back, lest Dad lose it or have it stolen while he's in the throes of dementia.

Picturing his once-robust father trickling drool and wasting away in a wheelchair, Mack wonders if there's any merciful way to exit this world.

If there is, he sure as hell hasn't seen it.

He trudges up the steps and is about to unlock the front door when it's thrown open in front of him. Something—someone, a female someone, seemingly running for her life—barrels into him full force.

Mack teeters, almost falling backward off the stoop.

"Mack! Oh God, call 911! Hurry!"

The last time Emily was awakened by a ringing phone in the middle of the night, it was the emergency room calling to say that her father-in-law had been in a fatal

accident. Mowed down by a bus as he exited his favorite cocktail lounge, old Morty Reiss was feeling no
pain and probably never knew what hit him. But for a
long time after that wee-hour call, Emily's heart started
pounding whenever the phone rang, at any time of day.

Now it's past midnight, and the phone isn't even her
own. It's her sister's, and Emily's first thought is that
something must have happened to one of their parents
down in Boca.

The phone rings twice and then stops. Either the
caller hung up, or Jacky answered in the next room.

Dale, sleeping beside her on the futon, doesn't stir as
Emily slips out of bed and leaves the room. In the hall,
lit by the dim bulb of a nightlight low on the wall, she
finds her sister just leaving her own room, talking on
the phone in a hushed voice.

"Hang on," Jacky tells the caller, "my sister is right
here." She passes the phone to Emily.

"For me? Who is it?"

Jacky just shakes her head, wearing a cryptic expression.

"Hello?" Emily walks with the phone toward the
living room. Jacky follows and turns on a light.

"Mrs. Reiss, this is Detective Rocco Manzillo with
the NYPD. I'm trying to reach your husband."

"Is . . . is everything all right?" Emily asks, but of
course it isn't. The NYPD doesn't call in the middle of
the night if everything is all right.

"I'm investigating a pair of murders over the past
couple of days . . ."

Murders . . . Dale?

Confused, her thoughts whirling with impossibili-
ties, Emily sinks onto the nearest chair.

"Both murders took place in two different buildings owned by your husband."

"You're not thinking . . ." Emily shakes her head rapidly.

Of course not. No one could possibly think Dale killed anyone.

"I'm trying to locate a handyman who works in both buildings. I have a tenant—a witness—who placed him at the scene of the first murder, and we need to question him."

Jerry wouldn't hurt a fly is her first thought.

But then she considers that he was the victim of a brutal crime years ago. She's watched enough episodes of *Dateline* and *20/20* to know that violent offenders are initially often victims themselves.

"Mrs. Reiss?" Detective Manzillo prods, "I need his last name, and an address, and I also need—"

"I wish I could tell you," she cuts in, "but I don't know either of those things, and I'm positive my husband doesn't, either, because I asked him about it just tonight."

"Tonight? Why is that?" he asks sharply.

"Just because I was worried about Jerry, and I thought we should call to make sure he's okay. He's . . . mentally impaired. I'm not sure if you know that."

"I did. How well do you know him, Mrs. Reiss?"

"Not very well." Her head is spinning. "I volunteer for the soup kitchen in his old neighborhood, down in Brooklyn. He moved to Manhattan a few years ago, but—"

"Hold on, back up. Where in Brooklyn? Tell me the old address."

"I don't have the address. But maybe someone who works at the soup kitchen can—"

"Names," the detective cuts in brusquely. "I need names, Mrs. Reiss. Someone I can talk to."

"Diana Wade," she tells him. "She's the director of the soup kitchen. She's been there longer than I have."

"Do you have a phone number for her?"

"I have it in my cell phone, but it's dead, and I can't charge it until I get a charger. I'm sure I have it written down someplace back at my apartment, but . . ."

"Diana Wade," he murmurs, and she can tell he's taking notes. "W-A-D-E, right? Is she married? Or would she be listed under her own name?"

"She's never been married. She lives alone."

"Where?"

"Someplace off Gramercy Park, I think. I'm not—"

"I'll find her. I also need your husband's cooperation in accessing the video surveillance footage of the public hallways. Can you please put him on the phone?"

"Hang on a minute." Emily lowers the phone and hurries past Jacky, heading for the guest room.

"Wait, what's going on?" Her sister trails her. "Is something wrong?"

"Yes," Emily says simply, and goes in to wake Dale.

"What's going on? What's wrong?" Mack keeps asking, but Allison can't catch her breath to explain.

She still can't believe what just happened. If she hadn't noticed the flashing light and paused to check her messages before walking into the bedroom; if she hadn't picked up that bookend . . .

She looks over her shoulder into the dark vestibule of the building, expecting to see someone coming after her. Tugging Mack's arm, she pulls him down the steps with her, away from the door.

"Allison, what—"

"Just call 911," she repeats, dragging him along the sidewalk. Still panting from three flights of stairs, she darts a glance up at her fourth floor windows. "Please. And we have to get away from here, it's not safe. "

Mack reaches into the pocket of his blue jacket, pulls out his cell phone.

She nods and stops walking, pressing a hand against her sternum as her heart seems to smash rhythmically against it, trying to escape.

"Are you okay?"

"Yeah. I'm okay. I was just . . ."

Scared. She was scared. Terrified. Still is.

But even now, she can't bring herself to say it aloud.

"Someone was in my apartment. Please call the police."

"I am, I'm calling, just tell me quickly first, what happened?"

"I came home, and he was there. I saw him before he could—I threw something heavy at him—I think I hurt him, because I heard him go down, but . . . I don't know, I just ran."

"Did you get a look at him?"

"No. I just ran," she says again.

Mack nods and for the second time since they met, she watches him punch three numbers into his telephone keypad: 911.

Diana Wade is remarkably good-natured for someone who was awakened fifteen minutes ago by a phone call from the NYPD in the dead of night. She greets Rocky and Brandewyne at the door wearing a housecoat and a warm smile, but her dogs—a toy poodle and two Chihuahuas—aren't nearly as welcoming.

"Oh, hush, everyone," she tells them above mad barking. "Come in, Detectives."

Rocky steps into the busiest apartment he's ever seen. It's packed with furniture, and every flat surface is covered with stacks of mail, magazines, books—thrillers, mostly—along with evidence of myriad hobbies and relics of devout Irish Catholicism.

She moves a stack of newspapers from a sofa and gestures for them to sit.

They do, wanting to relax her, though they're pressed for time. They're meeting Dale Reiss in about a half hour downtown.

"Would you like some tea?" Diana Wade asks with a trace of brogue. "I can turn on the kettle and it will be ready in a flash."

Brandewyne shakes her head. "No, thank you." What she wants, Rocky knows, is a cigarette. He can tell by the way she's holding a pen between her index and middle fingers.

"We just have a few questions for you, Ms. Wade," Rocky tells her, "and then we'll let you go back to sleep. Again, I'm sorry we had to wake you up."

"Oh, it's no trouble. What can I do for you?" Diana sits on a chair across from the sofa. The canine crew settles at her feet, three sets of puppy dog eyes warily fixed on the visitors. Their mistress looks to be in her early sixties and barely tops five feet, but more than likely surpasses two hundred pounds.

For all her warmth, she's got a no-nonsense aura about her, courtesy of her past occupations as a nanny and schoolteacher, and now running a soup kitchen in one of the roughest neighborhoods in Brooklyn.

"Emily Reiss said that we should speak to you about a man we're trying to find," Rocky tells her as Brandewyne opens a notebook and switches the pen's position, ready to write with it.

"So you said on the phone. Who is the man?"

"His name is Jerry—I don't know his last name—but he and his mother used to live in the neighborhood."

"Jerry Thompson?"

Rocky looks at Brandewyne and shrugs. "He would be in his early to mid twenties, stocky build . . ."

"Mentally handicapped," Brandewyne puts in.

"That's Jerry Thompson."

Thompson—it *would* have to be a relatively common last name, wouldn't it? Why couldn't it be something like Di Bernarducci?

"Poor thing was sharp as a tack before his injury, you know," Diana is saying, and Rocky snaps back to attention.

"Injury. What happened to him?" Brandewyne scribbles something in her tablet.

"His twin sister bashed his head in with a cast-iron skillet, that's what happened."

Rocky's eyes widen. Brandewyne's head jerks up and she meets his startled gaze with raised eyebrows.

"When was this?" he asks Diana Wade.

"Maybe five, ten years ago—yes, ten," she amends with a firm nod. "At least. Time goes by so quickly, doesn't it?"

Brandewyne agrees that it does.

Thoughts whirling, Rocky asks, "What happened, exactly, with the sister?"

"There was always something off about her, that one. Lights were on but nobody was home, if you know what I mean. I always kept a close eye on her when she was around because she gave me such a bad feeling. Some people are just . . . evil. That girl was one of them." Diana shudders and crosses herself.

"Do you remember her name?" Rocky asks.

"Oh, sure. I never forget a thing."

"What was it?"

"It was Jamie."

"Jamie," he echoes, and Brandewyne writes it down. "And do you know where we can find her, by any chance?"

"Oh, she's at Pinelawn out in Farmingdale."

"Pinelawn?" he echoes incredulously, certain he must have heard wrong.

"Yes. We took up a collection for the cremation and mausoleum because her mother couldn't afford to bury her, and—"

"Wait, what are you talking about?" Brandewyne cuts in.

Simultaneously, Rocky asks, "Bury who?"

They can only stare, dumbfounded, as Diana Wade pulls the rug out from under them with a matter-of-fact "Jerry's sister, Jamie. She was killed just a few days after she attacked her brother."

Crouched on the floor beside his mother's bed in a fetal position, Jerry rocks back and forth, terrified.

A few minutes ago, all he wanted was for Jamie to come back.

Now, he's terrified of what will happen when Jamie returns.

Jamie does bad things. Jerry knew that before, but . . .

"I only do bad things to people who deserve it, Jerry. You know that, right?"

That's what Jamie said.

But Jamie is a liar. Jerry didn't know that. Not until now.

Jamie said Mama left, but she didn't. She's right here. She was right here all along . . .

Dead.

Jerry knew she was dead the second he laid eyes on her, lying there in her bed on stained sheets, her skin dark and rotting away.

Jamie must have known it, too. Maybe Jamie is even the one who did this.

Maybe that's why Jerry wasn't supposed to come in here. Jamie was protecting him again.

I should have listened. I shouldn't have come in here.

Now I'm trapped in this apartment with Mama's dead body, because Jamie said not to leave. This time, I have to listen, because if I don't, Jamie will be even madder at me.

I have to get out of here so that Jamie won't know that I saw.

But he doesn't want to stand up, because he can't bear to look at her again. He didn't see any bugs the first time, but what if he does now? What if they're crawling on her? What if they crawl on Jerry?

I have to get out of here.

On his hands and knees, his heart pounding like crazy, he begins inching his way to the door.

Good.

Almost there.

Just a few more . . .

A voice stops him in his tracks.

"What are you doing, Jerry?"

It's Jamie. Jamie is back.

Dialing Rocky again, Vic wonders how clean the hotel room coffeemaker is. The way things are going, there's no way he's getting any sleep tonight. He only had a couple of hours to spare to begin with. Might as well start in again with the caffeine.

As Rocky's phone rings, Vic opens the lid of the four-cup Krups machine sitting on the bathroom vanity and peeks inside. A grungy film of something is growing on the plastic. Ugh. He won't be drinking any coffee that was brewed in there, that's for damned sure.

"Yeah, Manzillo here."

"Rocky, I found him."

"Jerry? Where?"

Coffee forgotten, Vic strides over to his open laptop and the e-mail he received a few minutes ago from a willing tech analyst back in Quantico. "He lives in the West Thirties, in a subsidized building."

"Do you have the address?"

"I do, and I'll give it to you, but do you want to know the rest first?"

"Is it about his sister trying to kill him when he was a kid?"

"You know. And—"

"And then something happened to her right after that, and she died, too. Only a thirteen-year-old doesn't usually drop dead of natural causes. Got any info on what happened to her?"

"Looks like she was mugged during a robbery. They found her in an alley, throat was slit."

"And there's no way the kid, Jerry, did it."

Vic consults the e-mailed report again.

"Not unless he came out of his coma and escaped the hospital without anyone seeing him, then went back and slipped back into the coma again right afterward. He was out of it for weeks," he tells Rocky. "He's lucky to be alive."

"Then who killed the sister? That was no random mugging."

Vic had been thinking the same thing.

"What's the mother's story?" Rocky asks.

"Her name's Lenore Thompson. Single welfare mother, forty years old."

"Drugs? Violence?"

"Who the hell knows? History of mental illness. But she doesn't have a record. Never been arrested."

"What about the kids' father?"

"Name on the birth certificate is Samuel Shields. He was just a kid himself, grew up in the projects, a couple of years younger than Lenore. Samuel's father was a paranoid schizophrenic who tried to kill the kid and wound up in a mental ward. Still there."

"Nice."

"Yeah. Long story short, Samuel gets Lenore pregnant with twins when she's sixteen—"

"Sixteen? And he was a couple of years younger?"

"Ah, May-December romance," Vic says dourly. "Lenore drops out of school to have the kids, he drops out of the picture altogether, far as I can tell—he's a convicted felon, violent character, has a nice, long rap sheet and spent years in and out of juvy before he graduated to jail, then the state pen here and, most recently, out in Ohio."

"Nice," Rocky says again. "Just another happily-ever-after tale of the inner city, huh? Okay, give me a 10–20 on that address. We've got reasonable cause to head over there to find our boy Jerry."

"You're not alone, are you?"

"Nah, I've got Detective Brandewyne here with me." The lady cop Rocky wasn't crazy about, Vic remembers. The smoker who isn't seasoned—not exactly the best quality in a sidekick when you're dealing with a serial killer.

"Want to come along for the ride?" Rocky offers.

Vic is only a couple of blocks away, but he's supposed to be sleeping.

"I know, I know, you can't," Rocky says before he can reply. "Protocol, and all that. Forget I even—"

"I'll meet you there."

What the hell are you doing? Vic wonders as he gives Rocky the address, then hangs up and straps on his gun.

He thinks of his dead friend John, and he thinks of Rocky.

Extraordinary times call for extraordinary measures.

I'm just doing what I can—what I have to—do to help a friend in need.

Sitting in the backseat of a parked squad car with Mack beside her and a uniformed officer at the wheel, Allison shudders, looking up at the brick building.

She can't stop thinking about what could have happened to her up there in her apartment; can't stop wondering what's going to happen to her now.

"What if I killed him?" she asks Mack in a low voice, not moving her gaze from the building, watching for the pair of cops who went in earlier, guns drawn, to emerge.

"I hate to say it, but I hope that you did."

Taken aback, she turns to look at him.

"Sorry," he says, "but if he's the one who killed Kristina—and if he was planning to do the same thing to you—then I hope you got him good."

"But would they charge me with murder, do you think? If he's dead, I mean."

"It was self-defense."

"I know, but . . ." The thought of being responsible for the death of a human being, under any circumstances, is sickening.

"Don't worry, Allison. It'll be okay."

She nods and looks away, feeling as though she's lived a lifetime's worth of trauma with this man in the space of a few days.

How, she wondered, can he have endured so much and still manage to hold it together, when she herself feels like she's going to break down and cry?

Even knowing that his marriage was troubled, that he had his share of doubts . . .

Even now that she's met his sister and gained more insight into who Mack is—and *was*, where he comes from . . .

Strength, quite clearly, is his strength.

Again, she turns to look up at the building. She should feel safe, sitting here in the police car with an armed driver at the wheel. She doesn't.

She won't until they come out with *him* in handcuffs—or on a stretcher.

Whoever *he* is.

When she closes her eyes and pictures the figure she saw in her bedroom, she's frustrated by how little detail there is. She barely caught a glimpse out of the corner of her eye before she reacted, and she never looked back after he went down.

It could have been Jerry, she told the police who questioned her quickly before going inside. But it could just easily have been someone else.

At the squawk of a radio in the front seat, her eyes snap open. The officer at the wheel is listening and responding to whatever is being said, but it's a conversation made up largely of numeric code, and Allison hasn't a clue what's going on. She looks at Mack, who shrugs.

Finally concluding the conversation with a brisk "10–4," the officer turns to Allison and Mack.

"What's going on?" she asks.

"They're up there in your apartment, ma'am. But it's empty—whoever was there is gone."

Standing in front of the bathroom mirror, Jamie vigorously rubs in cold cream to remove the makeup, trying to ignore the excruciating pain brought by the slightest movement.

Stupid, stupid. You're so damned stupid.

You should have known it was too easy, strolling right into Allison Taylor's apartment with her spare key.

Jamie arrived on Hudson Street just in time to see her out on the sidewalk with a strange woman, walking toward the opposite corner. That was initially disappointing. But then, she'd have to come back sooner or later, right? And her absence provided the perfect opportunity to properly set the stage.

The first stop was the manager's office to disable the surveillance cameras and remove the tapes that had just been recorded—including the one that showed Jamie unlocking the front door and walking down the hall to the building manager's office. Then it was on to a couple of other apartments on the way upstairs, where Jamie rummaged through the vacant tenants' belongings for just the right touches.

It's always been thrilling to peek into strangers' drawers and closets. But tonight, there was even greater pleasure in touching, and taking, and imagining the role those stolen items would play in what was to come.

Some silky lingerie for Allison, just in case she didn't have any of her own . . . and some candles to set the mood . . .

Just like with the others. That was how it should be. Yes, that was the only way Jamie could recapture that feeling, the exquisite rush of power.

True, this was different in some ways. Allison hadn't given Jerry the brush-off as Kristina and Marianne had . . . but she'd done something a lot worse. She'd seen him the night Kristina was killed. She was a witness. She had to apologize to Jerry, and then she had to die. Just like the others.

Too late, Jamie realized that there would be no music. That was a stupid mistake. It wouldn't be the same without the music.

"Jamie? Please, Jamie. Please talk to me," Jerry begs.

That's *the stupidest thing you ever did. Trusting Jerry.*

"Shut up!" Jamie barks at him.

"What are you doing?"

"I'm taking off makeup and trying to think."

Jamie tosses another makeup-smudged cotton ball into the trash can, then runs the water until it's steaming.

"Jamie," Jerry says, "please . . . Talk to me."

Jamie grabs a washcloth and starts scrubbing. The water is hot, painfully hot, but Jamie welcomes the pain. This pain.

Jamie did not welcome the pain inflicted by Allison when she threw that boulder of a bookend with all her might.

It wasn't supposed to happen that way. She wasn't supposed to be armed. She wasn't supposed to hurt Jamie; Jamie was supposed to hurt her.

But it was Jamie who went down, hard, in an explosion of blinding agony, utterly immobilized.

By the time I realized what had hit me, she was gone.
Jamie's first instinct was to chase her down. But she had too great a head start.

I never would have caught her in time. The only thing for me to do was get away from there as fast as I could.

Wincing in pain, Jamie went out the window, clambering down the fire escape and limping away through the back alleys to the adjacent block.

The route home was the same but this time there was no satisfaction in it; this mission was unaccomplished.

For now.

But I'll be back. I don't care how long it takes, or how far or fast Allison Taylor runs. Sooner or later, I'll find her.

Jamie turns off the tap and reaches for a towel.

Finally, the makeup is gone, the face in the mirror wiped cleaner than it's been in a long, long time.

"I'm sorry, Jamie," Jerry is saying. "I didn't mean . . ."

"I know, Jerry. I know. But I told you never to open Mama's bedroom door."

"I know you did. I'm sorry."

Jamie sighs, staring into the mirror, hating what has to be done.

"It's too late for sorry, Jerry."

"But, Jamie—"

"Shut up!" Jamie reaches for the doorknob, opens the bathroom door.

There's no way around it. Jerry is going to have to be punished. Jamie has no choice.

Rocky and Brandewyne are a half block away from the address Vic provided when Rocky's cell phone rings.

"It's probably Dale Reiss," Brandewyne comments as he reaches for it, "wondering where the hell we are."

"We're not even late yet." Rocky picks up the phone. "Yeah, Manzillo here."

"Rock, it's Tommy."

The station house desk sergeant. "What's up?" Rocky asks him.

"You still on your way to Hudson Street? Because we had a 10–66 at that address."

A 10–66—a prowler.

"What's going on, Tommy?"

"Female tenant walked in on someone in her apartment. She hit him and ran. I've got a couple of uniforms over there now, but by the time they got up there, the guy was gone. Looks like he went out a window. May have gotten in that way, too."

Or with a key, Rocky thinks grimly. "What's the woman's name?" he asks, anticipating the answer.

Sure enough, Tommy replies, "Allison Taylor."

"Is she okay?"

"Just shaken up."

Rocky asks a few more rapid-fire questions and learns that it all happened about forty-five minutes ago—long enough for Jerry, if it was Jerry, to have gotten back up here. Allison didn't get a good look at the intruder, Tommy says. The officers on the scene called for backup and are in the process of canvassing the building and neighborhood for the suspect, but so far, there's no sign of him.

Rocky looks at the unmarked cars parked in front of Jerry Thompson's apartment building. He can see a tall figure lurking in the shadows near the door. Vic.

"We'll be down there as soon as we can," he tells Tommy. "Tell everyone to sit tight in the meantime. We've got a lead we're checking out."

* * *

"But I'm sorry, Jamie," Jerry says again, panic welling up inside him as he backs across the living room, shielding his face with his forearms. "I am. Please stop saying it's too late."

"You knew it was wrong to open that bedroom door, but you did it anyway. You're just like the others. You have to be punished."

"No!" Jerry cowers. "Please, Jamie! I'm—"

"Shut up! I said it's too late!"

Jerry clamps his mouth shut. For a moment, the only sound is sirens wailing outside, in the distance. Jerry hates that sound. It never ends anymore. Sirens, always sirens.

Then Jamie says, "It's *my* turn to say *I'm* sorry, Jerry, okay? And for me, it's not too late. It's too early."

"Wh-what?"

"I'm sorry for what I'm going to do to you. I really am. And I want you to know that. I only wanted to protect you. If you had just listened to me . . ."

"I did listen, Jamie. I listened!"

"No! You didn't! You never do! They never do! They never listen to me! Your mother didn't, and your sister didn't, and now you . . ."

Jerry's blood goes cold.

That voice . . . it's changed, become guttural, low, masculine-sounding . . . that doesn't sound like Jamie's voice.

"Who are you?" Jerry asks, terrified. "You're not Jamie!"

"Yes, I am. You know I am."

Jerry frowns, confused. He does know that, but . . .

He backs across the room, hugging himself, afraid of Jamie.

He's been stuck here, in this apartment, for so long. Too long. He wants to leave. But Jamie won't let him. Jamie said he has to be punished. That scares him.

He turns to look longingly out the window.

"You know," Jamie says, "they say you're a retard, but they're wrong. You're actually smarter than you look, aren't you?"

"I'm smart," Jerry tells him defiantly. "I am! Emily says so."

"Does she? That's nice. But I didn't say you were smart. I said you were smarter than you look. If you were *smart*, you wouldn't even be here, would you? You would have figured it all out a long time ago. But that's why you needed me, Jerry. That's why I came back here to find you, and help you. Because for all these years, I've been worried about you."

Jerry shakes his head, again glancing out the window, remembering all those people who jumped out of the towers. He wonders what would happen to him if he jumped. Would he survive?

Probably not. The sidewalk is hard. He leans forward to look down at it, and notices something.

"Policemen are here," he tells Jamie.

"What are you talking about?"

"There are policemen. Right there in front of the building. See?"

Jamie curses.

"You shouldn't say that word," Jerry admonishes. "Mama says it's bad."

"Your mother is dead, Jerry. Do you still not get it?"

"I forgot." Jerry's lip quivers.

"You forget everything! Come on! Let's go."

"Go where?"

"We have to get out of here."

A moment ago, that was all Jerry wanted—to get out of here.

But not with Jamie. Jamie is scaring him.

"Let's go, Jerry! Move!"

"You said not to leave the apartment! See? I don't forget everything. You said something bad would happen if I leave!"

"Well, now I'm telling you something bad will happen if you don't, so come on!"

Jerry shakes his head. This is wrong. This is bad. Jamie is bad. Jamie lied. Jamie . . .

Isn't acting at all like Jamie.

Jamie is acting like someone else, sounding and looking like someone else, and Jerry is afraid.

He rushes toward Mama's bedroom. The door is still open. He slams it behind him, locks it, and leans on it, panting, as Jamie screams at him.

"What the hell are you doing? Are you crazy? They're going to get you, don't you understand that? You're going to be in trouble. *We're* going to be in trouble, Jerry!"

Turning the corner onto Hudson Street, Emily is startled to spot the flashing red dome lights of several squad cars parked down the block. Both she and Dale instinctively slow their steps.

"They're in front of our building, aren't they?" she asks her husband, who nods. "I thought we were just meeting those two detectives here."

"So did I. You'd think with everything going on in this city, they wouldn't be able to spare all this manpower for something like this."

"Something like this?" she echoes incredulously. "It's a murder. *Two* murders."

"I didn't mean it like that. I just can't handle all this, Em. Getting dragged out of bed in the middle of the night, having to come down here . . . Come on, let's just get it over with."

Emily glances at her watch as they pick up their pace again. They're late.

They'd borrowed Jacky's car to drive into the city after being assured by Detective Manzillo that the bridges and tunnels were open. Unfortunately, they discovered that didn't include the Holland Tunnel from Jersey City into lower Manhattan, so after being turned away there, they had to drive up to Weehawken to go through the Lincoln Tunnel and head back south—only to be stopped at another barricade, this time at Union Square.

"We're meeting two detectives downtown on police business," Dale told the national guardsmen who came over to the car. But the soldiers refused to make an exception to the rules without the proper credentials, and they refused to contact Detectives Manzillo and Brandewyne for verification.

"No vehicles past this point without prior clearance," Dale and Emily were told firmly.

They had no choice but to park the car and cover the remaining distance on foot. Even the subways and buses weren't running beyond that point.

Walking those eerily empty blocks in the middle of the night was unsettling enough. Now, seeing the cluster of emergency vehicles that are apparently waiting for them, Emily feels as though she's stepped into someone else's life, or onto the set of a movie about refugees in a dystopian, futuristic New York.

There are several cops standing out on the sidewalk, along with a couple who appear to be in their twenties or thirties. The woman, a striking blonde, spots Emily and Dale before anyone else does, and points them out to one of the police officers.

"What's going on?" Emily asks Dale, realizing this has to be more than a simple meeting.

"I have no idea, but those two are tenants."

"You mean that couple?"

"They're not a couple, they live across the hall from each other." He raises his voice to address a cop who's striding in their direction. "Officer, is there a problem in the building?"

"You're the owner, correct?"

"Yes, Dale Reiss, and this is my wife, Emily. We're supposed to be meeting Detectives Manzillo and Brandewyne. Are they here?"

The cop ignores the question. "I need you both to come with me. We have a potentially armed and dangerous suspect in the area."

Armed and dangerous? Emily thinks about Jerry.

Surely they can't be talking about him. Whatever his faults are, she knows in her heart that Jerry isn't dangerous. She'd bet her life on that.

"Open up," Rocky calls, banging on the door to the apartment. "This is the NYPD. We need to talk to you."

No response.

He turns to look at Brandewyne beside him, and then over at Vic, covering them from an alcove a few feet away. Vic nods slightly, as if to say, *Keep talking.*

"Jerry? Mrs. Thompson?" Rocky calls. "You need to open this door right now. We've got the building surrounded."

Not exactly true. There aren't enough guys down-stairs to entirely seal the perimeter. Rocky can only hope Jerry didn't slip out and down one of the stair-wells before they got up here. If he's still inside the apartment, the only way out now is past Rocky, Brandewyne, and Vic—and that's not going to happen.

He reaches out to knock again, but Brandewyne grabs his arm and gestures at the knob. He sees that it's turning, and his hand goes immediately to his gun.

The door swings open and there stands Jerry Thomp-son, tears running down his fat face.

"Help me," he blubbers. "Please."

You always have to do what the police tell you to do. That's the law.

Mama taught Jerry that years ago. That's why he came out of the bedroom and opened the door when they told him to.

He wasn't surprised to find that Jamie was gone. Well, not Jamie. Whoever had been pretending to be Jamie. It wasn't really her. Jerry knows that now.

"Jerry, you need to tell us exactly what happened," the lady policeman tells him, after making him sit down on the couch and answer questions about what his name is and where he lives.

"Okay," Jerry says, and he explains everything to her and to the other policeman and to the other man, the one in the suit. He tells them all about Jamie, and about Mama, and about Kristina and Marianne, and it feels good to finally say it all.

But when he's finished, the police officer—the bald one with the big stomach, the one who seems like he's the boss of the lady—says, "Jerry, you and I both know that's not exactly how it happened."

Jerry blinks. "It isn't?"

"No. First of all, we know that Jamie died ten years ago, after she hurt you, hurt your head—"

"No," he interrupts, "that's wrong. Mama's the one who hurt me."

"Who told you that?" the lady policeman asks.

"Jamie did. Because I didn't remember what happened. Mama always told me I fell down . . ."

"You didn't fall down, Jerry," the man with the big stomach says.

"Jamie hit you in the head," the lady says. "Jamie hurt you. And then she died. Do you know that Jamie died?"

Jerry shakes his head. "I thought she did, because that's what Mama told me, but Mama lied. Jamie really didn't die. She just stayed away because she was afraid of Mama, and then she came back to take care of me. She said Mama moved away, but . . ."

Jerry casts a worried look over his shoulder at the bedroom door. More police officers are in there, taking pictures.

"Jerry," the boss policeman says, "look at me. Focus on me."

Jerry does, because you have to do what the policemen tell you. Police ladies, too.

"Your sister died ten years ago. And your mother— she's dead, too. She didn't move away. Someone killed her. Who did it?"

"Maybe Jamie did."

"Jamie . . . is . . . dead. Who killed your mother, Jerry?"

The policeman and lady are so mad at him. Jerry is afraid. He looks over at the window, again wondering what would happen if he jumped out.

"Jerry, who killed your mother?" the man asks again.

"I don't know!"

"*You* did. You killed her."

"I did?" Bewildered, Jerry shakes his head. "But I don't—"

"Jerry, think about it. Maybe you're just forgetting."

Jerry thinks about it. He thinks hard.

"Look, we found the fingers in a box under the bed in there."

"What fingers?"

"And we found your wig in the bathroom, and it matches a hair we found on one of your victims, and we found your dress, and—"

"But I don't have a wig and a dress—"

"—your makeup . . ."

The makeup!

"I don't wear makeup. Jamie does. That's Jamie's," Jerry adds helpfully, because he really is thinking hard.

The cops ignore him, though, just go on talking.

"You killed your mother," the policeman says, "and you killed those two women downtown at the buildings where you work."

"And tonight," the police lady says, "you went back down to Hudson Street and you tried to hurt Allison Taylor, didn't you?"

"No!" Jerry is sobbing now. "No!"

"You don't remember?"

"No!" He's so tired, and so sad, and scared, and confused . . .

He doesn't remember doing any of the things they're telling him he did. But . . .

Remember, Jerry? She told you she wanted to go live far, far away from here. Across the ocean. Remember?

Jerry doesn't have a good memory sometimes, because he hurt his head. That's what Jamie told him. Maybe he forgot what he did to Allison and Marianne and Kristina just like he forgot that Mama told him she had moved away.

"We know what happened, Jerry. You do, too."

"I don't remember! Maybe Jamie does! Ask Jamie!" Jerry looks wildly around the apartment, hoping to see his sister. But she's gone.

"Jamie isn't there," the policeman says, "because Jamie only exists up here." He taps his head. "Do you understand, Jerry?"

Jerry can only cry. He doesn't understand anything at all.

Back in her own apartment, Allison sits in the living room with Emily Reiss, Mack, and his sister, Lynn, who showed up right after the Reisses did. All four of them are under the watchful eye of a young police officer named Timothy Green, who was assigned to keep them safe until the intruder is apprehended.

Every so often, his radio blasts with staticky voices speaking in numbered codes.

A few times, Allison was able to piece together what they were talking about related to the ongoing search of the neighborhood, along with several unsuccessful attempts to get a canine unit over here.

"I'm sure the dogs are all involved in the search and rescue down at ground zero," Emily commented at one point, obviously unaware of what happened to Mack's wife. He didn't bring it up, and of course Allison didn't, either.

For the most part, the three of them have sat in silence. Dale Reiss is downstairs with the police. They were supposed to be going over the building's surveillance footage, but someone apparently tampered with it, and there was nothing to work with. Nothing at all.

"I just wish I'd gotten a good look at him before I ran."

Seeing the others look abruptly over at her, Allison realizes she spoke out loud. "Sorry. I was talking to myself, I thought. I just keep going over what happened, trying to figure out if I could possibly have seen anything and not remembered."

"Amnesia is a tricky thing," Emily says, and it sounds as if she, too, is talking more to herself than to the others.

"It's not really amnesia, though," Allison tells her. "I just—"

"Oh, I know. I'm sorry. I was just remembering something my sister said to me earlier, when we were talking about Jerry's head injury."

"Head injury?" Allison echoes.

"Is that why he is the way he is, then?" Mack asks. "You know—slow?"

Emily nods. "His own sister—his twin—attacked him about ten years ago. He almost died. That's why . . ."

"Why what?" Allison prods when she trails off.

Emily shakes her head. "I know they think he's the one who killed those women, and tried to hurt you, too, but . . . I know Jerry. I just can't imagine him hurting a fly."

Those words strike a chord with Allison.

She herself had said the same thing to Kristina about Jerry just a few days ago.

What if Kristina decided to trust him because of what Allison said, and it led to her death?

But that would mean Jerry really was the one who killed her.

Why is Allison having such a hard time imagining

that, believing that? She didn't even get a look at the intruder in her bedroom earlier, and yet, she can't seem to wrap her head around the idea that it could have been Jerry.

It just didn't *feel* like Jerry, that's why. Crazy as it sounds, it didn't feel like Jerry's energy.

I'm going to mention that to Detective Manzillo, she decides, *when I see him. It probably won't make sense to him—it doesn't even make sense to me—but I'm going to say it anyway.*

Just in case there's something to it.

Rotting corpse of a mother in the bedroom—distraught son claiming his dead sister killed her—a couple of severed fingers in a box under the bed—and a wig and women's clothes in a heap on the bathroom floor.

"It doesn't get more cliché than this, does it?" Rocky asks Vic as a couple of uniforms escort a sobbing Jerry Thompson out of the apartment in handcuffs. "Split personality. Just like the movie *Psycho*."

Vic shakes his head, remembering Calvin Granger, back in Chicago. "Something doesn't feel right here."

"Jesus, Vic, you're kidding, right? *Something* about this doesn't feel right? Is there anything about this that *does* feel right?"

"No, no, that's not what I mean." He rubs his chin, walking around the bedroom, holding a handkerchief over his nose to block out the stench of death.

His guess is that the mother was stabbed to death at least a week ago, maybe two.

"I can't believe no one reported this stink," Brande-wyne mutters from behind her hand.

"I can't believe you can smell it with all those ciga-rettes you smoke," Rocky says.

"Are you kidding? *This?*"

"Yeah. I'm kidding, Brandewyne. This is hard to miss."

"But it's pretty contained," Vic points out. The bedroom doesn't share a wall with any other apartment on the floor, and the apartment on the floor directly above is unoccupied. And the officer who just canvassed the building reported that the tenants below live in such squalor that it's no wonder they didn't pick up on anything.

The smell of death is unmistakable, though, for those who are in law enforcement. Once you've caught a whiff of it, you never forget it. You recognize it instantly.

It's wafting in the air now downtown, laced with smoke and burning rubber.

Vic pushes the thought from his head. *Compartmentalize.*

There's a Bible on the nightstand.

Seeing that a page is marked, Vic holds the handkerchief over his nose with his left hand and reaches out with his latex-gloved right to open the Bible.

Before he can read through the passages on that page, he notices that something is written on the piece of paper Lenore Thompson was using as a bookmark.

It isn't a piece of paper at all, he realizes, flipping it over.

It's a photograph, showing a sullen-looking adolescent girl and a grinning boy Vic recognizes as Jerry, posing in front of a bedraggled-looking sofa with a smiling man who looks to be about thirty and bears a strong resemblance to Jerry.

Is he the twins' father?

As he turns to alert Rocky, Vic's phone rings. He answers it immediately.

After listening for a moment, he says, "I'll be right there." He hangs up and turns to Rocky. "I have to go."

"I sure as hell hope that's a break in your case now that I've got my Nightwatcher, Vic. I'd offer to help, but I think you guys are probably fine on your own."

"Take a look at this, Rock." Vic hurriedly hands him the photograph. "Just make sure, okay? Be absolutely certain Jerry is your guy, because—"

"What, am I an idiot? He's my guy. Or gal. We have his sick trophies to prove it, and I guarantee you that when they check that strand of hair down at the lab, it's going to come back synthetic, and a perfect match for that wig, just like I said to our pal Jerry before. Or Jamie. Or whatever the hell he/she/it calls itself."

Vic doesn't have time to linger, and he doesn't bother to respond.

This is, after all, Rocky's case, not his. Maybe under other circumstances—less extraordinary circumstances—

But not now.

Rocky has his job to do, and I have mine.

By the time Vic leaves the room a second later, he's got terrorists on his mind again.

The night drags on into the wee hours.

Both Allison and Emily have dozed off sitting up on the couch, and even Officer Green is starting to look drowsy, but not Mack. He's wide awake, as he always seems to be, regardless of the hour or his level of physical and emotional exhaustion.

Watching his sister, sitting in the armchair across from his, cover a deep yawn, he says quietly, "I bet they'd let you go home if you want. There's really no reason for you to stay. You should be there when the kids wake up."

She's shaking her head before he finishes speaking. "I'm not leaving you tonight."

He checks his watch. "It's morning."

"I'm not leaving you this morning," she returns smoothly.

"Well, you should."

"What, are you kidding? With everything that's going on here?" She waves a hand around the room.

He looks from the two sleeping women to the lone cop who's standing in the window, staring out into the darkness as if waiting for something to happen.

"You're right," he tells Lynn dryly, "there's a hell of a lot going on here."

"You know what I mean."

"I do. And I appreciate it, but I'll be fine if you go. Really."

"I know you'll be fine, but . . . you shouldn't be alone. You need family right now, whether you realize it or not. You lost your wife, Mack."

"I feel like I lost Carrie a long time ago. Maybe I never had her in the first place. Maybe I just married her because I was terrified of losing Mom, and I needed someone . . . Maybe I never even loved her. Jesus, I hate myself for saying that, for sounding that way, but it's true."

"Don't hate yourself. I've said the same kinds of things about Dan, and I've probably actually meant them, but even now, if something happened to him, I'd be devastated."

Devastated.

Is Mack devastated?

He threads his fingers into his hair. "I don't even know what I'm feeling right now. It's complicated."

He glances at the other two women, ensuring that they're both asleep. Not that Allison hasn't already been privy to his deep, dark secrets, but still . . .

This is a private conversation he needs to have with his sister alone. She's the only family he has left. The only family he hasn't entirely cut off, anyway, besides his father, who is so far gone most of the time he doesn't even know his own name, let alone his son's.

Mack takes a deep breath. It's time to get the truth out there. The whole truth. Even though the truth makes him look and feel like a coldhearted bastard.

Where to begin?

At the end, he decides. That's the part that's bothering him more than anything. The way it ended.

"On Tuesday morning, before Carrie left for work, I told her I wanted a divorce."

His sister's eyes widen. She says nothing.

"We were trying to start a family," Mack goes on. "At least, I thought we were. But Carrie changed her mind about that. And I changed my mind about her."

"Did you mean it?" Lynn asks. "About wanting a divorce? Or were you just saying it in a moment of anger?"

Mack swallows hard. *Nothing but the truth.*

"I meant it," he confesses.

Lynn gets up and walks over to him.

Officer Green turns as if snapping out of a reverie, glances at them both, and goes back to staring out the window.

Kneeling beside Mack's chair, Lynn takes his hands. The gesture unleashes a torrent of emotion that rushes into Mack's throat, rendering him mute.

"I can't imagine how you must feel," she whispers

sadly. "I'm so sorry. But don't blame yourself for any-thing. You were being honest with her. She didn't de-serve anything less."

Mack tries to speak, but can't.

"You didn't kill her, Mack. You didn't do anything wrong. The two of you weren't supposed to be together. Anyone could see that. But even when you were a little boy, you were drawn to stray dogs, and underdogs, and wounded souls. You always wanted to save animals, people."

"I couldn't save her," he says hoarsely.

"No one could. Thousands of people died on Tuesday morning, and no one could save any of them."

Mack nods. Intellectually, he knows that.

Emotionally—that's another story.

"In time, you'll forgive yourself," Lynn says. "I promise."

"I hope you're right."

She smiles and pats his arm. "I am. And this is the wrong time to be telling you this, I know, but someday, you're going to find the right woman, Mack, and you're going to have that family you deserve."

For some reason, he finds himself glancing at Allison—and then, quickly, guiltily, away.

Jerry's back aches and his head aches and his legs ache, and he can't take it. Can't take sitting on this hard chair in this small room at the police station, can't take these two people, Detective Manzillo and Detective Brandewyne, talking to him, yelling at him, in his face.

"Please," he begs yet again, "please stop!"

"Just tell us the truth, and we'll stop!" the woman shouts back at him.

"Easy, Brandewyne." Detective Manzillo leans in close to Jerry. "I know you're tired, kid, aren't you?"

"Yes."

"I know you just want this to be over with, don't you?"

"Yes."

"And I know you never meant to hurt anyone, did you?"

"No."

"Your mother—she was terrible to you, wasn't she? She hurt you. That's what Jamie says, right?"

Jerry nods. So they do finally believe him about Jamie. All this time, they've been telling Jerry that Jamie is dead, and Jerry keeps telling them they're wrong.

"And those two girls—Kristina and Marianne—they weren't nice to you, either, were they?"

"No." Jerry shakes his head fast.

"I bet that made you feel bad, didn't it?"

"Yes."

"And mad."

"Yes."

"I understand, Jerry. We both understand, don't we, Detective Brandewyne?" He looks at her, and she nods.

"It's okay, Jerry," she says. "They were mean to you, weren't they?"

"Yes."

"You didn't deserve that, did you? You've never been mean to anyone, have you?"

"No," Jerry sobs. "No. I'm never mean."

"When you hurt those women and your mother, you weren't trying to be mean, were you?" Detective Manzillo asks. "I bet you didn't even realize what you were doing—what you had done. Maybe you forgot all about it, because you wanted to block it out, because it was terrible, wasn't it, Jerry?"

He nods. It was. It was terrible, what happened to them. But . . .

He remembers the phone calls.

"They said they were sorry," Jerry tells the detectives. "They said they loved me."

"Who did?"

"Kristina, and Marianne. They told me."

He thinks about how surprised he was when Jamie said that Kristina wanted to talk to him that night. Surprised, and happy. And then sad when he had to say good-bye. "Jamie said Kristina had to die anyway. She had to be punished."

"Because she hurt you, Jerry. Is that right?"

"Yes."

"She hurt you, and so Jamie hurt her."

"Yes. Jamie did. But I didn't."

"Jerry, you did," the lady, Detective Brandewyne, says. "Jamie is a part of you, isn't she? You don't want to let her go, and she's a part of you. Isn't she? You love her, no matter what she's done, don't you?"

"Yes. I love Jamie. Please—can we stop talking? Please . . . I need to go."

"We're going to sit here all night," Detective Brandewyne says, "and then we're going to sit here all day, and we're going to sit here for a week or a month if we have to."

"No, please . . . I have to get up. I can't sit here anymore."

"You can get up, Jerry—we can get you out of this room—just as soon as you tell us what we need to know. But this isn't going to be over until you do that. Do you understand?"

Jerry nods miserably.

"Okay. Good." Detective Manzillo reaches out and

holds Jerry's hand. It feels good, having someone hold his hand. Jerry's fingers are so cold, and the detective's fingers are big and warm.

"So tell me, Jerry," he says softly. "You'll feel better. You need to get it out. That's the hardest part. After you say it, this will all be over, and we'll get you some help, and some food."

Food. Jerry's hungry. Really hungry, he realizes.

"What kind of food will you get me?"

"What do you want? We'll get you anything you want."

"I want cake."

Detective Manzillo nods. "We can do that. We can get you some cake. But not until you tell us what we need to know."

"What do I have to say?"

"Just say the truth. Say that you killed your mother, and you killed Kristina Haines, and you killed Marianne Apostolos."

"But—"

"Say it, Jerry. Tell us what you did."

"I—"

"We're not going anywhere, and we're not having any cake, until you tell us that you killed your mother, and you killed Kristina Haines, and you killed Marianne Apostolos," Detective Brandewyne says.

"You can do it now, or you can do it tomorrow, or the next day," Detective Manzillo says, "but sooner or later, you're going to tell us. Why don't you make it easier on everyone and do it now?"

"What did you do, Jerry? Just say it!" Detective Brandewyne's face is so close to his that he can smell her cigarette breath. "Tell us. Say that you killed your mother, and Kristina Haines, and Marianne Apostolos. Say it!"

"What did you do to your mother, Jerry?" Detective Manzillo asks. "What did you do? It's okay. It's okay. Just tell us."

"I killed her," Jerry says wearily, tears running down his face. "I killed my mother."

"And Kristina Haines, and Marianne Apostolos? What did you do to them? Say it. You'll feel better. This will be over."

"I killed Kristina Haines, and I killed Marianne Apostolos. Please," he begs. "Please . . . Can I have cake now?"

Standing in the corridor outside the interrogation room, Rocky pulls out his phone and dials a familiar number.

The line goes right into voice mail.

"Vic," he says triumphantly, "thanks for everything. He confessed. It's over."

He hangs up and goes back inside to tell Brandewyne they're going out for a drink when the paperwork is finished.

Johnnie Walker Blue. And he's buying.

He walks west, and then north. Eventually, he'll get on the subway and head up to the Bronx. It's the safest way off the island of Manhattan right now. There must be police checkpoints at all the bridges and tunnels.

Not because of him, of course. Because of all that's going on. He doubts anyone will be looking for him, under the circumstances—but just in case.

Anyway, he's always liked to walk.

Even when he was a boy, when things got bad at home, he would take off walking, sometimes all the way across the Brooklyn Bridge into Manhattan.

Walking gives you time to think.

Not like running. Running is different.

He's never really liked to run. But sometimes, you have to.

Sometimes, he feels like he's been running all his life.

Running from his crazy father, running from the law, running from his own stupid mistakes . . .

Face it. You've made a lot of mistakes. That's why you always have to run away.

Or simply turn your back and walk away, like you did when Lenore got pregnant.

He tried to make it right, once, when he got out of prison ten years ago after spending the better part of his twenties behind bars for a violent felony. It was Christmastime and he was lonely and nostalgic, wishing for something he'd never had. He started to wonder if maybe Lenore had been telling the truth when she said he was the father. He'd never believed her at the time, and God knew she was as crazy as everyone else in his life, but what if . . . ?

He found Lenore and called her and asked if he could see her and the kids for Christmas.

She let him.

"I'm not telling the kids who you are, though," Lenore said on the phone, before he went over there. "They don't know anything about you. You'll just be my friend Sam."

Fine, he said. He'd just be her friend Sam. That was all he and Lenore had ever been anyway—friends. Oh hell, not even that.

She was older, and easy, when he met her. Like most boys his age, he had one thing on his mind. When she said she was pregnant, he didn't believe the baby was his—and even if it was, he didn't want any part of it. Especially after he found out she was expecting twins—even though he knew twins ran in his family. His own father was a twin.

He was batshit crazy, too. Tried to kill his own kid.

They say mental illness runs in families, too. Just like twins.

He never wanted to believe that, either, though.

Anyway, when he saw those kids, there was no doubt in his mind that they were his. The boy, Jerry, looked just like him. Acted like him, too. He was a real hellion, back then, before the injury changed him. He bonded with his mother's "friend Sam" right away, almost as if he somehow sensed the connection.

The girl—Jamie—she was different. Quiet. Cold. Looked different, too—she had long auburn hair with bangs and big black eyes, the spitting image of Lenore the last time he saw her as a teenager.

Jamie spent a lot of time watching him, looking from him to Jerry, and it gave him the creeps. He got the idea that she, too, knew what was up. Knew he was her daddy.

He sure as hell didn't want Lenore back in his life. She was mean, and bitter, and crazy, and she looked like shit. But he wanted them. His daughter, his son . . . especially his son.

He figured there was no way Lenore was going to let him have even just one kid. He thought about taking him—taking both of them, even, because they were twins. They should probably be together.

But if he got caught, he'd go back to prison, and he'd had enough of that. Had enough of running, too.

He remembered what the counselor back at the prison had told him when she was coaching him on how to live an honest life on the outside. So after they'd taken a few pictures, and finished eating the chicken and rice Lenore had fixed for them in a big cast-iron skillet, while the kids were washing the dishes, he asked Lenore if he could speak to her privately, in the bedroom.

She lit up. Yeah, she was thinking she was going to get some, he realized. Not a chance of that.

He closed the door behind them, turned to her, and saw that she was starting to undress.

"Wait, no," he said. "I need to talk to you."

"About what?"

"The kids. I want to be a part of their lives."

She appeared to think about it. Then she shrugged. "Sure. I'll take you back. We'll give it a shot. I always loved you—you know that, don't you?"

"No. You don't get it. Not *you*. *Them*. I want to be a part of *their* lives. Not yours."

"What the hell are you talking about?"

"I don't want you, Lenore. Okay? I never did."

"You son of a bitch! Get the hell out of here and don't you dare ever come back!"

"Those are my kids. I have a right to—"

"Don't talk to me about rights. You're a convicted felon. You abandoned me when I was pregnant and you denied they were yours."

"Because you were a whore who slept with every—"

She cut him off with a slap across the face.

Enraged, he grabbed her. "You don't ever do that to me, you bitch!" he screamed. "You show me respect, do you hear me?"

Jerry came running and pounced on him, beating at him with his fists.

And then Jamie came, too, screeching "Nooooo!"

She had the cast-iron skillet in her hand.

He thought she was coming after him, but she went straight for her brother.

It happened so quickly. She swung at Jerry with the skillet and he went down, his head split open.

"What the hell did you do?" Lenore screamed.

"He's our father! Jerry was trying to hurt him and he's our father!" Jamie shrieked back.

"No, he isn't. He's a dirt bag and I want him out of here!" Crying hysterically, Lenore was already dialing 911.

Torn, he looked at Jerry, bleeding and unconscious on the floor. He knew he had to go before the cops showed up. He was on probation. He'd just served ten years. No one would ever believe that he wasn't the one who'd bashed in the kid's head. Like father, like son, they would say.

"No, Daddy, don't go!" Jamie clutched at his arm. "Please!"

He shook her off and ran. Ran, as always.

He didn't realize she'd chased him until he was out on the street, tearing off down the block. He heard someone screaming his name, turned back, and there she was.

"Wait! I'm coming with you."

"You can't do that."

"Please!"

"No! You stay here and help your brother!"

"I hate him." The look in her eyes—it was lethal. It scared the hell out of him.

She'd been wanting to do that, Sam realized, for a long time. She'd been wanting to hurt Jerry. Or maybe just hurt someone, anyone—just for the hell of it.

He knew, because he recognized the look. He'd seen it in his father's eyes, and he'd seen it in the mirror. The same dark urge had festered inside him for as long as he could remember. But he fought it, because he didn't want to be like his father.

Hearing sirens, he abruptly turned his back on Jamie and started running again. He never looked back.

Maybe he knew she was following him. Maybe he didn't.

Whenever he remembers that night, he's never really sure.

What he does know is that later—much later, maybe the next night—he walked out of a bar, and there she was. Waiting for him. She got in his face, telling him that she needed him, that she wanted to come with him, that she wanted him to take care of her—on and on like that.

She looked and sounded like her mother. In his inebriated confusion, he thought she *was* her mother.

She just wouldn't let up. Kept talking to him, making accusations and demands, louder and more shrill until he couldn't take it anymore.

He had a blade in his pocket for protection, as always. He'd never used it, though. Never used anything but his fists. Not until that night.

The next thing he knew, she was dead at his feet with her throat slit, those cold eyes of hers seemingly fixed on his face.

She wasn't Lenore.

She was Jamie. His own daughter.

He'd killed her—killed a part of himself, really— and the strange thing was, his first thought was that it had felt good. For so long, he'd been wondering what it felt like to take a life. Now he knew.

And he wanted to do it again.

He left her there, on the street.

He started running, and he didn't look back. He ran away from his dead daughter, and his injured son. He ran away from New York. Hitchhiked out through Jersey, through Pennsylvania. On the Ohio turnpike, a lady trucker picked him up. They drove for a while, until the trucker said something that pissed him off, and he swore he could hear Jamie's voice in his head, telling him to do something about it.

He tried, when they pulled over at the next truck stop. He pulled a knife on the trucker, tried to use it. Bad idea. Turned out she was a black belt. He regained consciousness to find himself back in police custody.

They never connected him to Lenore, or Jamie, or Jerry . . .

But they sure as hell connected him to his rap sheet.

It was back to prison for him, for years.

And through all those years, Jamie talked to him inside his head.

He gradually came to understand that when he killed her, her spirit left her body and entered his own. Her being melded with his. She was a part of him now, and he was a part of her. Eventually, he let go of Sam and became Jamie.

He didn't tell anyone about that, though. They would never understand. They would have thought he was crazy, just like his old man. Like father, like son. He probably would have been sent to the psych ward.

All he wanted was to get the hell out of prison; to go find the rest of his family, and make things right.

Finally, this summer, he was free. Free to leave. Free to embrace Jamie on the outside, just as he had within. He had always thought she looked like her mother, but when he put on a woman's clothes, and the right wig, and looked into the mirror . . . he saw Jamie. It was like she was alive again. A part of him.

She told him what to do about Lenore. She deserved to be punished, Jamie said, for the way she had treated him.

It felt good, so good, to kill Lenore. When it was over, he waited for Jerry to come home. Jamie wanted him to kill Jerry, too.

But when Jerry walked in the door, another voice started speaking inside his head, drowning out Jamie's. It was his own voice.

He's your son. Look at him. Don't do to him what your father wanted to do to you!

"Who are you?" Jerry asked, frightened, bewildered. He was childlike—but there was no hint of the scrappy kid he'd once been.

He'd been robbed of that. Robbed of so many things.

"I'm . . . your sister. Jamie." The words escaped him before he could think them through, but when he saw Jerry's face light up, he knew it was for the best.

"I thought you were dead!"

"Well, I'm not. I went away, but now I'm back, and I'm going to take care of you."

And that's what I did. It's what I tried to do, until it all went wrong.

Having arrived at a northbound subway entrance, he decides that it's time to stop walking.

He turns to look back over his shoulder.

From this vantage, he can't see the gaping hole in the skyline, or the smoke rising from the ruins a few miles south. From here, he can see only intact buildings, glittering against the starry night sky.

Time to get out of here; time to go far, far away again. At least for a while.

But don't worry, he tells New York City . . . and Jerry . . . and Allison.

I'll be back. You can count on that.

"Allison. Allison . . ."

She opens her eyes to see Mack. "What . . . ? Where . . . ?"

Dazed, she looks around and sees that she's in her own living room. Faint light falls through the window; it's dawn.

Emily Reiss is dozing on the couch beside her, and Mack's sister, Lynn, is in the corner of the room, having a hushed telephone conversation. There's no sign of Officer Green, but she can hear the crackle of a police radio in the next room.

"Allison, there's good news," Mack tells her. "Detective Manzillo just called. They got him."

"Got who?"

"Jerry. The handyman. He did it. He's under arrest. It's over."

"Jerry?" she echoes, stunned. "But . . . are you sure?"

"He confessed."

"Are you sure?" she asks again, because it can't be right.

"Positive."

Wow. So she was wrong.

She had been so sure Jerry was harmless . . .

Guess I'm not a very good judge of character after all.

"Are you okay?" Mack asks.

"Yes," she says. "Are you?"

He nods.

She reaches out and squeezes his hand. He squeezes it back.

"Thanks," he says. "Again. For helping me."

"You're welcome. I'm usually around. Whatever you need. Right across the hall."

He smiles—faintly, but it's a start. "That's good to know."

Keep reading for

an excerpt from

SLEEPWALKER,

the chilling follow-up to

NIGHTWATCHER

from Wendy Corsi Staub

Sunday, September 11, 2011
Glenhaven Park
Westchester County, New York

Her husband has suffered from insomnia all his life, but tonight, Allison MacKenna is the one who can't sleep.

Lying on her side of the king-sized bed in their master bedroom, she listens to the quiet rhythm of her own breathing, the summery chatter of crickets and night birds beyond the window screen, and the faint hum of the television in the living room downstairs.

Mack is down there, stretched out on the couch. When she stuck her head in about an hour ago to tell him she was going to bed, he was watching *Animal House* on cable.

"What happened to the Jets game?" she asked.

"They were down fourteen at the half so I turned the channel. Want to watch the movie? It's just starting."

"Seen it," she said dryly. As in, *Who hasn't?*

"Yeah? Is it any good?" he returned, just as dryly.

"As a former fraternity boy, you'll love it, I'm sure." She hesitated, wondering if she should tell him.

Might as well: "And you might want to revisit that Jets game."

"Really? Why's that?"

"They're in the middle of a historic comeback. I just read about it online. You should watch."

"I'm not in the mood. The Giants are my team, not the Jets."

Determined to make light of it, she said, "Um, excuse me, aren't you the man who asked my OB-GYN to pre-schedule a C-section last winter because you were worried I might go into labor while the Jets were playing?"

"That was for the AFC Championship!"

She just shook her head and bent to kiss him in the spot where his dark hair, cut almost buzz-short, has begun the inevitable retreat from his forehead.

When she met Mack, he was in his mid-thirties and looked a decade younger, her own age. Now he owns his forty-four years, with a sprinkling of gray at his temples and wrinkles that frond the corners of his green eyes. His is the rare Irish complexion that tans, rather than burns, thanks to a rumored splash of Mediterranean blood somewhere in his genetic pool. But this summer, his skin has been white as January, and the pallor adds to the overall aura of world-weariness.

Tonight, neither of them was willing to discuss why Mack, a die-hard sports fan, preferred an old movie he'd seen a hundred times to an exciting football game on opening day of the NFL season—which also happens to coincide with the milestone tenth anniversary of the September 11 attacks.

The networks and most of the cable channels have provided a barrage of special programming all weekend. You couldn't escape it, not even with football.

Allison had seen her husband abruptly switch off the Giants game this afternoon right before the kickoff, as the National Anthem played and an enormous flag was unfurled on the field by people who had lost loved ones ten years ago today.

It's been a long day. It might be a long night, too.

She opens her eyes abruptly, hearing a car slowing on the street out front. Reflected headlights arc across the ceiling of the master bedroom, filtering in through the sheer curtains. Moments later, the engine turns off, car doors slam, faint voices and laughter float up to the screened windows: the neighbors returning from their weekend house in Vermont.

Every Friday without fail, the Lewises drive away from the four-thousand-square-foot Colonial next door that has a home gym over the three-car garage, salt-water swimming pool, and sunken patio with a massive outdoor stone fireplace, hot tub, and wet bar. Allison, who takes in their mail and feeds Marnie, the world's most lovable black cat, while they're gone, is well aware that the inside of their house is as spectacular as the outside.

She always assumed that their country home must be pretty grand for them to leave all that behind every weekend, particularly since Bob Lewis spends a few nights every week away on business travel as it is.

But then a few months ago, when she and Phyllis were having a neighborly chat, Phyllis mentioned that it's an old lakeside home that's been in Bob's family for a hundred years.

Allison pictured a rambling waterfront mansion. "It sounds beautiful."

"Well, I don't know about *beautiful*," Phyllis told

her with a laugh. "It's just a farmhouse, with claw-foot bathtubs instead of showers, holes in the screens, bats in the attic . . ."

"Really?"

"Really. And it's in the middle of nowhere. That's why we love it. It's completely relaxing. Living around here—it's more and more like a pressure cooker. Sometimes you just need to get away from it all. You know?"

Yeah. Allison knows.

Every Fourth of July, the MacKennas spend a week at the Jersey Shore, staying with Mack's divorced sister Lynn and her three kids at their Salt Breeze Pointe beach house.

This year, Mack drove down with the family for the holiday weekend. Early Tuesday morning, he hastily packed his bag to go—no, to *flee*—back to the city, claiming something had come up at the office.

Not necessarily a far-fetched excuse.

Last January, the same week Allison had given birth to their third child (on a Wednesday, and not by scheduled C-section), Mack was promoted to vice president of television advertising sales. Now he works longer hours than ever before. Even when he's physically present with Allison and the kids, he's often attached—reluctantly, even grudgingly, but nevertheless inseparably—to his BlackBerry.

"I can't believe I've become one of those men," he told her once in bed, belatedly contrite after he'd rolled over—and off her—to intercept a buzzing message.

She knew which men he was talking about. And she, in turn, seems to have become one of *those* women: the well-off suburban housewives whose husbands ride commuter trains in shirtsleeves and ties at dawn and dusk, caught up in city business, squeezing in fleet-

ing family time on weekends and holidays and vaca-
tions . . .

If then.

So, no, his having to rush back to the city at dawn
on July 5 wasn't necessarily a far-fetched excuse. But it
was, Allison was certain—given the circumstances—
an excuse.

After a whirlwind courtship, his sister Lynn had recently remarried Daryl, a widower with three daughters. Like dozens of other people in Middleton, the
town where he and Lynn live, Daryl had lost his spouse
on September 11.

"He and Mack have so much in common," Lynn had
told Allison the first morning they all arrived at the
beach house. "I'm so glad they'll finally get to spend
some time together. I was hoping they'd have gotten to
know each other better by now, but Mack has been so
busy lately . . ."

He *was* busy. Too busy, apparently, to stick around
the beach house with a man who understood what it
was like to have lost his wife in the twin towers.

There were other things, though, that Daryl couldn't
possibly understand. Things Mack didn't want to talk
about, ever—not even with Allison.

At his insistence, she and the kids stayed at the beach
with Lynn and Daryl and their newly blended family
while Mack went home to work. She tried to make the
best of it, but it wasn't the same.

She wondered then—and continues to wonder now—
if anything ever will be the same again.

Earlier, before heading up the stairs, Allison had
rested a hand on Mack's shoulder. "Don't stay up too
late, okay?"

"I'm off tomorrow, remember?"

Yes. She remembered. He'd dropped the news of his impromptu mini stay-cation when he came home from work late Friday night.

"Guess what? I'm taking some vacation days."

She lit up. "Really? When?"

"Now."

"*Now?*"

"This coming week. Monday, Tuesday, maybe Wednesday, too."

"Maybe you should wait," she suggested, "so that we can actually plan something. Our anniversary's coming up next month. You can take time off then instead, and we can get away for a few days. Phyllis is always talking about how beautiful Vermont is at that time of—"

"Things will be too busy at the office by then," he cut in. "It's quiet now, and I want to get the sunroom painted while the weather is still nice enough to keep the windows open. I checked and it's finally going to be dry and sunny for a few days."

That was true, she knew—she, too, had checked the forecast. Last week had been a washout, and she was hoping to get the kids outside a bit in the days ahead.

But Mack's true motive, she suspects, is a bit more complicated than perfect painting weather.

Just as grieving families and images of burning sky-scrapers are the last thing Mack wanted to see on TV today, the streets of Manhattan are the last place he wants to be tomorrow, invaded as they are by a barrage of curiosity seekers, survivors, reporters, and camera crews, makeshift memorials and the ubiquitous protesters—not to mention all that extra security due to the latest terror threat.

Allison doesn't blame her husband for avoiding reminders. For him, September 11 wasn't just a horrific day of historic infamy; it marked a devastating personal loss. Nearly three thousand New Yorkers died in the attacks.

Mack's first wife was among them.

When it happened, he and Carrie were Allison's across-the-hall neighbors. Their paths occasionally crossed hers in the elevator or laundry room or on the front stoop of the Hudson Street building, but she rarely gave them a second thought until tragedy struck.

In the immediate aftermath of the attacks, when she found out Carrie was missing at the World Trade Center, Allison reached out to Mack. Their friendship didn't blossom into romance for over a year, and yet . . .

The guilt is always there.

Especially on this milestone night.

Allison tosses and turns in bed, wrestling the reminder that her own happily-ever-after was born in tragedy; that she wouldn't be where she is now if Carrie hadn't talked Mack into moving from Washington Heights to Hudson Street, so much closer to her job as an executive assistant at Cantor Fitzgerald; if Carrie hadn't been killed ten years ago today.

Yes, in the most literal sense, she wouldn't be where she is now—the money Mack received from various relief funds and insurance policies after Carrie's death paid for this house, as well as college investment funds for their children.

Yes, there are daily stresses, but it's a good life she's living. Too good to be true, she sometimes thinks even now: three healthy children, a comfortable suburban home, a BMW and a Lexus SUV in the driveway, the luxury of being a stay-at-home mom . . .

The knowledge that Carrie wasn't able to conceive the child Mack longed for is just one more reason for

Allison to feel sorry for her—for what she lost, and Allison gained.

But it's not as though I don't deserve happiness. I'm thirty-four years old. And my life was certainly no picnic before Mack came along.

Her father walked out on her childhood when she was nine and never looked back; her mother died of an overdose before she graduated high school. She put herself through the Art Institute of Pittsburgh, moved alone to New York with a degree in fashion, and worked her ass off to establish her career at *7th Avenue* magazine.

On September 11, the attack on the World Trade Center turned her life upside down, but what happened the next day almost destroyed it.

Kristina Haines, the young woman who lived upstairs from her, was brutally murdered by Jerry Thompson, the building's handyman.

Allison was the sole witness who could place him at the scene of the crime. By the time he was apprehended, he had killed two more people—and Allison had narrowly escaped becoming another of his victims.

Whenever she remembers that incident, how a figure lurched at her from the shadows of her own bedroom . . .

You don't just put something like that behind you.

And so, on this night of bitter memories, Jerry Thompson is part of the reason she's having trouble sleeping.

It was ten years ago tonight that he crept into Kristina's open bedroom window.

Ten years ago that he stabbed her to death in her own bed, callously robbing the burning, devastated city of one more innocent life.

He's been in prison ever since.

Allison's testimony at his trial was the final nail in the coffin—that was how the prosecuting attorney put it, a phrase that was oft-quoted in the press.

"I just hope it wasn't my own," she recalls telling Mack afterward.

"Your own what?" he asked, and she knew he was feigning confusion.

"Coffin."

"Don't be ridiculous."

But it *wasn't* ridiculous.

She remembers feeling Jerry's eyes on her as she told the court that he had been at the murder scene that night. Describing how she'd seen him coming out of a stairwell and slipping into the alleyway, she wondered what would happen if the defense won the case and Jerry somehow wound up back out on the street.

Would he come after her?

Would he do to her what he had done to the others?

Sometimes—like tonight—Allison still thinks about that.

It isn't likely. He's serving a life sentence. But still . . .

Things happen. Parole hearings. Prison breaks.

What if . . . ?

No. Stop thinking that way. Close your eyes and go to sleep. The kids will be up early, as usual.

She closes her eyes, but she can't stop imagining what it would be like to open them and find Jerry Thompson standing over her with a knife, like her friend Kristina did.

K.I.S.S. and Teal: Avon Books and the Ovarian Cancer National Alliance Urge Women to Know the Important Signs and Symptoms

September is National Ovarian Cancer Awareness month, and Avon Books is joining forces with the Ovarian Cancer National Alliance to urge women to start talking, and help us spread the **K.I.S.S. and Teal** message: **K**now the **I**mportant **S**igns and **S**ymptoms.

Ovarian cancer was long thought to be a silent killer, but now we know it isn't silent at all. The Ovarian Cancer National Alliance works to spread a life-affirming message that this disease doesn't have to be fatal if we all take the time to learn the symptoms.

The **K.I.S.S. and Teal** program urges women to help promote awareness among friends and family members. Avon authors are actively taking part in this mission, creating public service announcements and speaking with readers and media across the country to break the silence. Please log on to *www.kissandteal.com* to hear what they have to share, and to learn how you can further help the cause and donate.

You can lend your support to the Ovarian Cancer National Alliance by making a donation at:
www.ovariancancer.org/donate.
Your donation benefits all the women in our lives.

**Break the Silence:
The following authors are taking
part in the K.I.S.S. and Teal
campaign, in support of the**

Ovarian Cancer National Alliance:

THE UGLY DUCHESS
Eloisa James

NIGHTWATCHER
Wendy Corsi Staub

THE LOOK OF LOVE
Mary Jane Clark

A LADY BY MIDNIGHT
Tessa Dare

THE WAY TO A DUKE'S HEART
Caroline Linden

CHOSEN
Sable Grace

SINS OF A VIRGIN
Anna Randol

For more information, log on to: **www.kissandteal.com**

A V O N

An imprint of HarperCollins*Publishers*

www.ovariancancer.org

This September,
the Ovarian
Cancer National
Alliance and Avon
Books urge you to
K.I.S.S. and Teal:

Know the
Important
Signs and
Symptoms

Ovarian cancer is the deadliest gynecologic cancer and a leading cause of cancer deaths for women.

There is no early detection test, but women with the disease have the following symptoms:

- **Bloating**
- **Pelvic and abdominal pain**
- **Difficulty eating or feeling full quickly**
- **Urinary symptoms (urgency or frequency)**

Learn the symptoms and tell other women about them!

Teal is the color of ovarian cancer awareness—help us K.I.S.S. and Teal today!

Log on to **www.kissandteal.com** to learn more about the symptoms and risk factors associated with ovarian cancer, and donate to support women with the disease.

The Ovarian Cancer National Alliance is the foremost advocate for women with ovarian cancer in the United States.

Learn more at www.ovariancancer.org